Child's Love

BROKEN PROMISES

FRANCES
HANSON

Suite 300 - 990 Fort St
Victoria, BC, V8V 3K2
Canada

www.friesenpress.com

Copyright © 2018 by Frances Hanson
First Edition — 2018

All rights reserved.

A special thanks to Francis Riley for artistic 'Celtic Cross' created for the logo.

No part of this publication may be reproduced in any form, or by any means, electronic or mechanical, including photocopying, recording, or any information browsing, storage, or retrieval system, without permission in writing from FriesenPress.

ISBN
978-1-5255-3956-5 (Hardcover)
978-1-5255-3957-2 (Paperback)
978-1-5255-3958-9 (eBook)

1. FICTION, FAMILY LIFE

Distributed to the trade by The Ingram Book Company

Acknowledgments

To all my family, friends, and foe for bringing out the best to make this book possible.

> "If you appreciate, you have joy. If you have joy, you have happiness. If you have joy, happiness, and love you have everything."
>
> By: Frances Hanson

Chapter 1
Calgary, Spring of 1969

Discovering a lost child, Liv, in the luggage compartment of a cross-country charter bus changed the lives of two families at two ends of the country. She was a missing girl from Montreal, Quebec, found in Calgary, Alberta.

Gayle and Peter Patterson had been sweethearts since university. Gayle was a social worker and Peter was a lawyer in Calgary. They had an amazing life with so much to give. Unfortunately, it looked like the giving would never happen with a child. Late in their marriage it was discovered that having their own children would never happen.

At an early age, Peter had come down with the mumps and it had left him with little to no sperm count. To add salt to the wound of this news, Gayle had suffered endometriosis, a condition so severe that it had required a complete hysterectomy. Ten years had passed since then, but the longing to have children was a constant ache in both of their hearts.

Exploring the possibilities of adopting had its challenges in the 1970s. Being over forty years of age had limited the couple options further for having the family of their dreams. Birth mothers were seeking parents around the age of thirty.

Fostering had possibilities, but Gayle and Peter were concerned that they would become attached to a child that was likely go back to its family once the environment or situation was corrected and ideal. Getting attached would be heartbreaking and there were no guarantees of being permitted to stay in the child's life.

Options were disappearing, and miracles were not falling from the heavens regardless of thousands of prayers. Gayle and Peter loved each other and had each other's backs and each other's hearts. They were hard-working, loving, and stable – an ideal couple. How could this happen? Years in university and the time to develop their careers, pay off their loans, and obtain a beautiful home had taken them to their thirties. Then, the years of trying to have children and learning they were unable while adjusting at every turn was time off the clock.

One day, Gayle's expertise was sought after a child was found in the luggage compartment of a long-distance bus line. In the meeting, she viewed a folder with minimal information. The picture showed a tiny girl suspected to be the age of six. The only information to be had was that her name was Liv. No one knew where she had come from or how she'd ended up on the bus. The only way for Gayle to give advice was to meet the child, who had been placed in foster care. The foster parents were an exceptional couple in their thirties, Sandy and Nick, who gave their time and love to all the children that came into their lives.

Gayle set up an appointment with Sandy to chat about Liv and on the drive to the five-acre farm, she prepared the necessary questions. She needed to know where Liv had come from. What care was needed beyond the basics of life? What exactly was the social system really looking at and taking on? But with the heart of a mother, she had personal questions that would never get satisfactory answers. How could a mother lose a child found in such a deplorable condition? What had this child endured and survived to arrive in Calgary in the luggage compartment of a bus?

As Gayle got out of the car and walked up the steps to the beautiful veranda, she saw Sandy standing behind the screen door.

Sandy opened the door. "Morning."

"Morning. How are you?" Gayle said, looking around to see if the child was in view.

"Good. Liv is in the living room sitting on the window bench. She is quiet, speaks very little, and holds her knees most of the time," Sandy shared.

"I see." Gayle moved into the kitchen. "We can talk first and then I'd like to meet Liv."

"Sure." Sandy had the coffee made, and she poured two cups and sat at the table.

After a half an hour, all the basic questions had been asked and nothing new had been discovered to find the right direction for Liv. During this time, Gayle had been keeping an ear open for any sounds coming from the living room window. Nothing. Silence.

On Gayle entering the living room, her heart skipped a beat. The picture of Liv had shown a little girl who was so filthy dirty that her hair was light-brown and matted. The color of her eyes was not visible as they had been closed and Liv's head was down. The girl sitting on the window bench was a pretty little child with long, blond, wavy hair. She was in a dress with her knees folded up under its skirting. Her arms were white and slender, but her head was still bent down.

Gayle approached her. "Hi Liv. My name is Gayle."

The girl did not move. A minute passed with Gayle waiting and hoping to get to know this little girl. All of Gayle's training had her prepared for such situations. Her heart strings pulled with intensity. It was something she was not prepared for –to battle with her mind and the ache in her heart.

Finally, she asked. "May I call you Liv?"

"Yes." Then Liv paused. "Can I call you Gay?"

Gayle was surprised to get a response – surprised to hear a tiny voice hardly audible. "Yes, of course you can call me Gay." She waited … for what? Then she proceeded. "May I ask you a few questions Liv?"

Liv nodded.

"Liv … what is your last name?"

"Riley. I am named the Life of Riley. I like to be called Liv."

The mind of a social worker could not comprehend how someone could call their child "Life of Riley." She suspected it was a choice made from stupidity. "How old are you Liv?" Liv kept her chin on her knees and spoke in a muffled whisper. "I am eight years old."

It was hard to believe considering how tiny and petite Liv appeared. Surprised Liv was answering questions with cognition, Gayle decided to ask direct questions. "Where did you come from, Liv?"

Liv did not hesitate. "Montreal."

Montreal? So many questions. How had Liv survived on the bus all the way across Canada? What had precipitated her need to leave ... leave from home? Did she go to school?

"Liv. Did you go to school?"

"Yes." The child was fidgeting with the fringe of her dress. Then she simply stated in a quiet voice, "I don't want to go back."

Gayle could not promise anything and though she wanted to reassure Liv it would not happen, she was powerless to do so. "Liv. I will do my very best to make sure that does not happen." Knowing that a child had left home to journey across Canada with no missing child reported made it easier to make this promise. Gayle continued. "Why don't you want to go back?"

Liv was visibly shaking. "I killed a man. I didn't mean to."

Gayle's mind was rapidly asking the five W's. "Can you tell me what happened?"

The silence was a space of quiet. Liv was resting with her chin on her knees. After a few minutes she looked up square in Gayle's eyes. The child's eyes were the most beautiful blue – as vibrant as sapphires. Gayle hadn't expected to see so much life and energy in them and it filled her mind with hope for this lost child. This child was a fighter!

Liv answered. "My mother's boyfriend came up the stairs. I was alone in the house. He was a pervert. I got scared. I kicked him hard in the pants." She rubbed her nose and sniffled softly. "He fell down the stairs and never got up."

Gayle responded, "That doesn't mean he died."

"It sure does. My mother said I killed him." Liv was crying softly. "I don't want to go to jail. Please."

Gayle asked, knowing the answer. "Is that why you ran away?"

Liv clammed up. "I don't want to talk about it."

Gayle nodded, letting time pass and thinking. "I need to ask you about your mother, father, family, and then I will ask no more questions for today."

Liv nodded. "My mother is Ruby; my father is Chuck; they don't live together. I have one brother and two sisters. I was their mother till …" She started to softly cry. "Please. I don't want to talk anymore."

Gayle thought that they'd made progress. "Liv. Would you mind if I come by and visit you again in a few days?"

Liv was direct. "You want to know what I want?" She stopped her fidgeting. "I want to go to school. I want to have a normal life. I want a mother … like you." Her eyes were red from crying. "I really don't want to go to jail."

Gayle nodded, and tears came to her. What was coming over her? No one had ever referred to her as a mother. She was taken by surprise and too shocked to give a reply. Her tongue wanted to stay stuck to the roof of her mouth. Finally, she managed to say, "I look forward to our visits." Then she thought and said, "Is there anything you need that I can bring you?"

In a barely audible voice, Liv stated, "Sandy and Nick are nice. I don't need anything." Then she looked right at Gayle. "I need a home and I need a mother who will love me."

Gayle was speechless, and her hand reached toward Liv. Liv touched the tips of her fingers and gave a soft smile.

Gayle gathered herself left in a daze, startled, bewildered, and intrigued by this child named Liv.

***

Back at the office, Gayle needed to immediately put her objective views of the interview down on paper. She didn't want to lose her insights on and perceptions of the child, Liv.

Her report began with the physical overview, and then the child's stance of withdrawal. Yet, Liv had been interactive and had expressed goals and wishes. The conversation had end abruptly when it came to Gayle trying to get details of her family. Liv had said she was their "mother" till the incident? So many questions that needed answers. Like a dog with a bone, Gayle wanted to know what had happened to Liv. How could she be so withdrawn and yet so expressive? Time ... would it tell?

Gayle's assistant had new information about the child. The mother, Ruby, hadn't reported her daughter missing for several days. A man named Chuck was claiming to be the father, though not legally. An investigation was being conducted with the police and social services. There was nothing further currently.

After writing her report and recommending Liv attend school, Gayle closed her eyes. The subjective part of the interview had her thoughts in a whirl. Liv wanted a mother like *herself*. The girl knew what she wanted, but Gayle wasn't sure what she wanted. The topic of being a mother had been a closed subject for so long. Yet, here she was daydreaming about it – being a mother to a troubled child. What would the future be? For the child? For Peter and Gayle? Could all the love they had benefit a child in need of so much love? It felt like jumping the gun … who said they could be candidates to foster or adopt Liv?

Gayle and Peter seldom brought work home or discussed their cases in any detail. Their professional lives stayed at the office and their personal lives were devoted to each other. Would exploring the possibility of giving this girl a home be the beginning of something good or downright awful? Would the prospect of fostering this little girl, Liv, be something that would destroy their peaceful life?

Chapter 2
Montreal, Summer 1960

Ruby's sisters put on a shower. She was a teenager a month away from giving birth. The kid needed a few things if she was going to bring the baby in the world. The fleece covering a thin sponge on the bottom of a dresser drawer would do nicely for a baby's bed.

Chuck, the father, wanted to marry Ruby and be a family, but Ruby was too busy flirting with the boys. Already pregnant was a sure shot to have sex. Can't get someone pregnant who was already pregnant. Chuck's family was aware of Ruby's reputation and was against the marriage – Catholic or not, Irish or not. Ruby's appetite went from older boys to men in uniform. Chuck was handsome but not a real man in her eyes.

Ruby was the baby of the family. Ruby's mother, June, was busy running a boarding house, cleaning homes, and working as a VON nurse at a convalescent home. The girls; Jewels, the oldest and Emerald took care of Ruby. Diamond, their brother, was out of the house and married. June was a hardworking, good woman, and doted on her children. Her husband was not on the scene. No one ever asked what had happened to him, and June was on her own raising her children. She believed they were as precious as the most valuable gems in life. Thus, Jewels, Diamond, Emerald, and Ruby ... and their last name was Mines.

The shower was a chance for Ruby and her two sisters to get together. There were gifts of a few baby sleepers, flannel blankets, bibs, cloth diapers, rubber pants, a rattle, a teething ring, and two baby bottles – all with a new diaper bag. Ruby was set and ready for the baby. Her mother had tried to talk her daughter into putting the baby up for adoption, but Ruby was enjoying the attention. The news of her pregnancy had spiced up her life. Everyone was worried about her, the baby, and what she was going to do.

Ruby was not a disciplined person. Life was about fun. How hard was it to have a kid? Welfare was easy and getting a free cheque had made her decision. If she had kids, Ruby had money to live. No work and have fun. Ruby was keeping the kid. She secured a small flat in Verdun off Wellington St. Ruby was now on Welfare with not a care in the world.

The shower had come to an end. Jewels was married and needed to get home to make dinner for her husband, Jerry. Emerald was engaged to Edward and had dinner plans with him. Ruby had packed up the diaper bag and was about to leave when suddenly a gush of warm fluid ran down her legs. Looking down, she saw a pool of blood.

The screaming and shrieking at the sight of the blood could have paralysed every person in a ten-block radius. Emerald called a taxi to get Ruby to the hospital. Jewels grabbed towels from the bathroom, trying to do something. Ruby sat on a kitchen chair waiting ... not saying anything.

The taxi arrived but the driver was reluctant to take a bleeding-out woman in his vehicle. Still, the good man took Ruby to the hospital.

"It's a girl," the doctor announced. "What will you call her?"

Ruby blurted out, "The Life of Riley. Liv for short. Her father may not marry me, but she will have his last name."

Liv was born on a humid August summer day. Both mother and baby needed blood transfusions. Only three pounds and purple … the baby's survival prospects were poor.

But Liv survived and was able to go home a week before Christmas. Her weight had more than doubled and she was healthy considering that she was a preemie and blue at birth. Liv had an amazing will to live. The nurses were pleased with their efforts and loved the smiling baby, Liv. Upon her discharge these women felt a pang of fear and regret, suspecting her environment and mother could amount to no good. What kind of life would Liv have? "Liv is a fighter, a scrapper, a survivor," they said to each other. "She'll be o.k."

Ruby was excited upon bringing her baby home. Christmas being around the corner brought a great amount of attention. Ruby couldn't have asked for a better reason to live her own soap opera life. As long as the baby was cute, smiling, and made her look like a good mother, life was good. Liv was a pawn – a meal ticket in Ruby's game of life.

***

Ruby had her plan to show off her baby, but she discovered that it took work and sleepless nights to pull it off.

One week and she was ready to give up. But she couldn't do that because she wouldn't get the free money, wouldn't get the attention either. Being an unmarried mother, she found that many frowned in her presence. Ruby didn't care what other people thought though, only about what she wanted.

Years of manipulating her sisters had taught Ruby how to get what she wanted – it always worked. When she was growing up her sisters did their best to help their mother, but it was arduous. Getting Ruby ready for school, washing or dressing her, or getting her to eat was almost impossible unless the girls gave in to her demands. Mother thought Ruby was adorable and a good girl and would never believe her sweet girl to be so calculating – so manipulating.

In June's eyes, her children were the most beautiful and intelligent any woman could want. Jewels, the eldest, was tall and with blond hair and blue eyes. Jewels had finished school and was working as a waitress. Diamond had married a year ago and moved to Toronto, Ontario. There was not much news from him. Emerald was only two years older than Ruby and was primarily responsible for her. Emerald had light-brown hair and hazel eyes and was slender but not all that tall. Ruby, on the other hand, was a beauty with auburn hair and hazel eyes.

Ruby cashed in on her looks, her finesse, and now her calculating skills of manipulation. Who needed school or work to have fun?

Christmas was here, and Ruby realized the baby did not have a crib, stroller, or playpen. In truth, she couldn't stand holding or touching her child. She never called her Liv, but only referred to her as "the baby."

Ruby did not have a phone or a car. She planned to visit Chuck and his parents on a surprise visit on Christmas day. Buses were not every five minutes as usual. Winter was cold and wet, but this day was not as severe as some days. The baby did not have a bunting bag to keep warm. An old sweater would do.

***

The 60-bus took Ruby and baby to the intersection of Wellington St. and Charon St. Ruby only had to walk a block towards Favard St. to reach her destination. It was 10:00 a.m. Standing at the doorway and catching her breath from the exertion gave Ruby the pause to push forward with her plan. She rang the bell and shuffled her cold feet, waiting.

Chuck answered the door. His tongue was nailed to the top of his mouth – nothing came out.

Ruby broke the silence. "You haven't met your baby yet. I thought you would like to meet her."

Just then, Chuck's father Joseph came to the door to see who'd rung. His eyes glared at Ruby and he noticed the baby. "You are not welcome here." He tried to move his son out of the way to close the door, but Chuck was paralysed.

Ruby would not be deterred. "We came all this way and we are very cold standing outside. Can we come in to warm up for a few minutes?"

Chuck looked at his dad with pleading eyes.

Joseph ran his fingers through his hair and backed out of the way. "I suppose."

Maggie, Chuck's mother, called, "Who's at the door?"

No one responded.

Ruby entered the living room.

Maggie whispered, "Oh."

Ruby noticed the lit Christmas tree and gifts that had been unwrapped. She smiled and announced, "I'd like you to meet your grandbaby."

No one moved or made a peep. Ruby unwrapped Liv from the sweater and opened it like a Christmas package. A precious gift - Liv was smiling and cooing with delight. Chuck's siblings departed to their rooms. Chuck sat with his hands folded on his lap, head down, with an eye on his parent's scornful watch.

Maggie watched her husband, not looking at the baby. Maggie was riddled with rheumatoid arthritis and had suffered deformed hands and feet since her childbearing years. Even if she wanted to hold the baby, it would have been difficult and likely unsafe.

Joseph was not a man without a heart. He had thought it would be best to ignore the pregnancy and maybe the problem would stay away. He then could overlook his son's indiscretion. Now what was to happen? Did Ruby want marriage? What did she want? Joseph's inner voice blurted out. "What is it you want from us?"

Ruby, batting her hazel-green eyes simply said, "I wanted you to meet your grandbaby. Her name is Liv. Thought it would be a nice Christmas gift."

Chuck noticed Ruby's hands were red and cold. "Would you like a coffee or hot chocolate to warm up?"

Joseph and Maggie glared at Chuck but said nothing. *Warm her up and send her on her way*, was their thought.

Ruby put Liv on the sofa and was acting like the perfect mother, touching the baby's hands and cooing at her with smiles. The baby was delighted and so sweet. Everyone else in the room was paralysed with mixed feelings. Chuck placed the coffee on the end table and looked at the baby, seeking answers. *Does this child look anything like … me?* His heart was moved by the giggling, sweet child and he asked if he could pick her up.

His parents nearly fainted. Touching the child was as good as acceptance.

Chuck picked Liv up and cradled her in his right arm. Liv could not keep her eyes off of her daddy. She was baby talking as if she'd found her long-lost friend. Chuck couldn't help smiling. Liv was adorable and sweet – everything a father would want in a child.

Chuck's parents watched and realized the connection. Ruby did not miss the magic of the child/parent love. At that moment, Ruby was almost prepared to hand the baby over and say, she was Chuck's … but then she thought better of it. She wouldn't get the free money without the child.

Chuck decided to talk. "I am working for the rail. I can spare a bit to help. What does Liv need?"

Joseph interjected in a gruff voice. "We are not rich people. I am a welder repairing and building bridges. Maggie is at home and doing her best with our six children. Don't expect much, you understand?"

Ruby was an expert at ignoring what people said, and she continued with her plan. She was clever enough to not start by saying, *I don't have …*. "Liv does not have a crib, stroller, high chair, or play pen, as all I get is a little from Welfare."

Joseph, Maggie, and Chuck looked from one to the other. Maggie observed. "She doesn't even have proper winter clothing, a bunting bag, hat or mittens." She was surprised to see the baby had booties with no socks."

Ruby was smiling, which appeared odd. She was thrilled that she'd made her point that the baby was without basic needs. Her plan had been executed perfectly! She gave the Riley's her address and explained she did not have a phone.

No one made promises, but everyone knew if Ruby did not get help from them, she would surely show up again. The only relief from the unexpected visit was no request for marriage.

Once Ruby had left to catch the bus home, the house was silent. Joseph's only comment was, "I wish you had kept your pants zipped up."

***

Ruby was in a flurry of excitement. A used crib, stroller, play pen, and highchair arrived in the new year. She had been expecting everything new, but this would do. Then came clothes, Pablum, and baby formula to the door. There was no note or anything for Ruby. Oh well, at least she didn't have to spend a dime on the kid. Her money could be spent on her fun. The only problem she had now was putting up with the kid.

Ruby's plan went well for a few years, till …

Chapter 3
Calgary, Spring 1969

Gayle had arrived home and was preparing her husband's favorite dinner; seafood linguini, garlic toast, and homemade Caesar salad. Two glasses of Chardonnay had been poured and were awaiting the spirit of interaction. Peter had been running late with court all day and emergency late-day meetings from panicky clients. The juggling of other people's lives had him wanting to relax, hit the hot tub, and read a mindless book. Gayle was usually busy with her files and research. As he drove into the garage, he felt peace at last.

Entering the kitchen, Peter became aware of the dinner setting and knew something was up. He wondered if he had been neglecting Gayle with his time. Was its time to consider booking a vacation? Putting down his rain coat and brief case, he turned his eyes to seeking Gayle. When he walked into the living room, he saw Gayle was sitting with her legs curled up and looking nowhere … in a dream world. What was she concerned with? … Peter could not think of anything. When preoccupied with work, he had often overlooked their life and sometimes Gayle's needs. Was this one of those moments?

Gayle looked up, smiled, and walked towards her husband. "Just hold me, darling."

Peter embraced his wife, waiting to discover what was on her mind. Soon he would learn what was on her heart.

Gayle snuggled with her head on Peter's shoulder. "You know how we don't bring our work home with us?"

Peter nodded. "Yes."

Gayle then led her husband to the dining table and handed him a glass of wine –smiling with a secret. She served out their salad. "I'd like to discuss something that happened at work today."

Peter wanted to stay in a relaxed mode, and yet his mind was racing. Did this have anything to do with what was on the news – the stowaway child?

Gayle began. "There is this little girl who was found in the cargo compartment of a bus." She paused to weigh her words. "Her name is Liv, and I am on the case." Tears began to stream down her cheeks.

Peter was concerned for Gayle's wellbeing and for what was going on with her. He stretched his hand across the table to show he was listening.

Gayle continued. "The girl said she wanted a mother like me." For some unknown reason she found she was sobbing. "I know I am not supposed to get emotionally involved with my cases. But, I had never been called 'a mother' before. The prospect of being a mother had long since been lost. Now, I am revisiting the possibility of helping this girl. Not just professionally, but personally."

Peter wanted to try and say something, but his brain went into malfunction, and he sat with his mouth open with nothing to utter.

Gayle had had a few hours to absorb her thoughts on the matter and process her proposal. "I'd like us to foster this little girl and hopefully adopt."

O.k. so it was out and said. Gayle remained quiet knowing this was a lot for her husband to take in.

Not knowing how to respond, Peter held his napkin for something to do. "Do you know why she ran away?"

Gayle nodded. "She believes she killed a man." She shared Liv's story with Peter.

Peter considered the information and asked, "She's not a danger to herself or to others, is she?"

Gayle burst out laughing. "One would think. But, no." She fidgeted with her fork and salad. "Liv is withdrawn and I'm not sure why. Though she is highly cognitive and smart, I sense she is a fighter and a survivor. I can't help but feel amazed how well she expresses herself and I'm in awe of what she might have endured."

Peter nodded. He respected his wife's assessment of the girl. Frowning and calculating the odds, he worried about putting a damper on his wife's dreams. There was the social system, the legal ramifications, the holistic needs of the child, and the physical and emotional price to consider in taking this on. Honestly, it scared Peter. This could be a disaster waiting to happen. Peter was a risk taker on most accounts, but his love for Gayle was greater than his love for himself. He feared the pain his wife might experience if he entertained this dream. That was a concern that could tear him apart.

He decided to be straight forward. "I am worried about what would happen if this did not go well for you – for us." He looked down. "I don't want to deprive you of any joy, any happiness, any chance of being a mother and me a father, but at what price?" Looking at Gayle with gentle eyes, he said, "I won't be able to bear it if I agree and then you are hurt."

Gayle nodded. She loved her husband and respected his wisdom and insights. His heart was gold and pure – he was a man with principle. If her husband could not agree, she would try to understand. Maybe his heart had been hurt just as badly as hers with the prospects of not having a family.

Peter took a mouthful of his dinner and put the napkin down. "Why don't you try to qualify to foster? Should that work out we can assess the prospects together with the child in our home."

Gayle jumped out of her chair and straddled her husband with a smile as big as a rainbow. "Peter Patterson, you are the best man I've ever known."

Kissing him with tears running down her face, Gayle knew she would qualify, and the child would reside with them. The question was how hard the journey would be to become a family. How would Liv adjust and what would her emotional needs be, to be healthy? Gayle was willing to take the risk of her heart and to venture the possibility of being a mother to a child in great need.

***

Gayle made a few more visits to Sandy and Nick's home. Liv was interactive and talked about her siblings freely, though not about her parents. She was tight-lipped talking about any grandparents, aunts, uncles, or cousins too.

The new school indicated that Liv had moments of difficulty focusing. When she was engaged in her subjects, though, she did well – in fact excelled. It was perplexing.

Liv asked if Gayle was going to be her mother, but Gayle was not at liberty to disclose the channels in progress or their possible outcomes. Nothing was definite currently.

***

Qualifying to be a foster parent went quickly. This was not surprising since Gayle was a top-notch social worker. The trouble had been when her supervisors got wind of her requesting to foster a child who was her own case. This was considered a conflict of interest and initially denied. With much persuasion, Gayle was able to present the hope of understanding the girl's intricate needs by having Liv in her home for care and observation. The director was no fool and suspected that Gayle had crossed an emotional line by becoming subjective instead of objective in the "Liv case." However, the best person with the greatest experience and know-how was Gayle.

Permission was granted with the understanding that reports and requests go directly to the director. Gayle was not given permission to authorize anything with the Liv girl on her own and she was given strict instructions to remember that she was simply a foster parent. Hopefully, her strong knowledge base and expert understanding of a child's needs would be an advantage to the child and to social services. The director knew the arrangements were a little twisted, but he needed to set out the guidelines. Should this fall into his lap and shed a bad light he wanted his position made clear.

Gayle realized she had only day-to-day care and control. All requests for counselors, special-needs programs, and extra-circular activities would go through the director. Gayle was willing to jump through the hoops just like all foster parents. In this respect, she had no special privileges.

Today was Friday and Gayle wanted to bring Liv home. The director consented to Monday, giving Gayle the weekend to set up and prepare for the child.

***

Peter arrived home early on Friday. Knowing that the foster care application had been approved, his times with Gayle alone would be far and few between. Plans for a weekend getaway had him packing their things in hopes of surprising Gayle. At that moment, Gayle snuck up behind Peter, hugging his back. "What are you doing?" she asked with a smile. "I hope I don't have you so scared that you're packing to go?"

Peter smiled back. "No, my beautiful wife. I thought this would be our only chance to have one-on-one time together before our life changes."

Gayle was now in the full embrace of her husband. "You are so sweet," she said. She paused. "I was hoping to go shopping and set up a bedroom for Liv."

Peter, who thought on his feet, suggested. "We can go by a furniture place, order anything you like, have it shipped on Monday. Then, we can head out for Banff for a nice two-night getaway. How does this sound?"

Gayle agreed and realized she would need to take an extra few days off for the new addition to their life. Shopping for Liv's personal clothes could wait.

The weekend getaway proved to be everything they needed. Talking about being a family – foster family – was exciting to both Peter and Gayle. They talked about being united as parents and promised to talk out all their concerns throughout this process. The excitement in the air was inspiring to their hearts. Neither talked about adoption. Both knew this subject was premature and too far down the road to be a topic at this time. Talking about the joy of blessing a child by sharing their love, gave Peter and Gayle much hope.

***

Monday arrived, and Gayle and Peter took the day off. Liv was to be brought to their home. The doorbell rang, and their hearts leapt with excitement. Liv was in her Sunday best; an Easter outfit Gayle had given her over the holidays. She had gloves, a little purse, and a white hat over her blond curls. Her sapphire eyes sought Gayle's.

Then Peter stepped forward. "Hi, I'm Peter."

Liv looked straight up at him, and then at Gayle. "He's a man," she said. "I said I needed a mother, not a father."

Gayle and Peter stood at the door with their mouths open …

The social worker asked, "May we come in?"

Chapter 4
Montreal, Summer 1962

Liv's first and second birthdays had passed without celebrations. Affection came from her father by way of monthly visits, which usually had passage by way of money when Ruby was in desperate need. Chuck did his best to give his parents the luxury of being grandparents, but his siblings would have nothing to do with Liv and vanished into thin air.

However, during the summer months, Chuck was permitted long stretches of access if they did not infringe on Ruby's plans. In fact, getting rid of the kid and being free as a bird to do as she wished had its benefits.

Chuck wanted to keep Liv to the very end of the summer and to have a birthday party for her. Ruby enjoyed making conditions by saying, "If you want Liv then you can buy her new bed and clothes since she is growing fast." Chuck was supporting his parents by helping to provide for their large family, and he could not dish out the money for such expensive requests. He longed to provide for his daughter, but he simply did not have the money.

Liv loved staying in Terrebonne Heights and watching the country house be built throughout the summer. All her daddy's aunties and uncles had lots with small cabins for the summer. It never occurred to her that these wonderful people who embraced her were her great-aunts and great-uncles. Then, there was her daddy's grandpa – called "Pa" by everyone.

Around the campfire, stories of Pa were spellbinding. He'd had a small convenience store during the Second World War. Times were hard and families in the area had difficulties putting food on the table. Pa's sweetheart had died young and he was a single father to six children, the twins being the youngest at the age of twelve. But Pa could not refuse anyone asking for credit. He believed that people were honest and good for their word. The only problem was that by the time the Second World War was over, so was the store. Pa refused to use credit himself and no longer had merchandise.

Now Pa was an elderly widower and the community took it upon itself to provide care packages every day in appreciation. On Christmas he usually received a pair of overalls, shoes, and a new pipe and tobacco. Liv loved Pa with all her heart and he loved her. She came to love the smell of pipe tobacco – it reminded her of Pa. Terrebonne Heights was a beautiful place, with a loving family that seldom bickered or fought. People spoke kindly to each other with few or no demands. Life was peaceful!

During the day, Chuck would always find Liv playing under the willow tree beside the house. At night, he would find her fast asleep under the low branches of the pine tree, nestled in the soft moss in front of the house. Every morning you would find Chuck fast asleep on the grass beside the pine tree, making sure Liv was safe.

Liv knew who loved her and who didn't. It was time to return to the city, to the woman who never acknowledged her, touched her, or hugged her, and for sure never kissed her.

***

Back home, if that's what one could call occupying space as though one was a piece of furniture, Liv was back in the old routine. Stay quiet, stay out of the way, ask for nothing. Existence was equal to be a stamp on a post card. You got glanced at and discarded. Liv lived for her visits with her dad and more so for the summers with her family who loved her. Days were long, and time was eternity.

Bedtime was right after the slop or burnt offerings of an evening meal. Liv would lie in bed and hear the children playing in their yards and dogs barking, while there was still bright daylight. Mother would have men over chatting and giggling about who knows what.

Then all Hell broke loose that one late September night …

***

Liv was awakened in the silent, pitch-black dark of the night with someone tugging at her panties and touching her down below. The horror had her in tears that someone was touching her, and she sensed that this was not right. She found the courage to say. "What are you doing?"

The man called "Bick" said, "I'm changing your diaper."

Liv screamed, "I don't wear diapers."

The boogie man persisted.

Liv was getting upset and simply said. "Stop!"

Her demand was ignored. Now enraged, she chomped on the man's arm with her sharp baby teeth. She clenched with all her might and her jaw remained locked on the man's flesh.

Bick screeched in terror and agony.

Ruby came running into her room, switching on the light. To her horror, she saw blood squirting from her lover's arm and blood all over Liv's mouth. The vile creature of a man was screaming "She's a vampire, She's a vampire."

Ruby came to her senses and demanded an answer "What the hell are you doing in her room?"

Bick replied, "I was trying to change her diaper."

"You idiot, she doesn't wear diapers." Upon seeing the panties dangling from the child's ankles, Ruby realized what the jerk had been doing and put her hands on her hips. "You, lowlife asshole. I'm not enough of a woman for you? You have to take her to bed, for your sexual needs?!" Ruby dragged Bick by the hair of the head and pounded him with her fists, yelling and calling the jerk every bad word Liv had ever heard.

Liv thought at first that her mother was appalled at what had happened to her but soon realized that Mother did not care about her. She was angry because the boogie man wasn't giving *her* attention.

Suddenly there was pounding on the door. "This is the police. Open up."

Ruby hollered. "What the hell for?"

"There has been a call complaining of disturbance of the peace, ma'am. Open up, we need to ask you a few questions."

Ruby was an excellent actress and had tears running down her face. "This man punched me in the face and I was fighting back in my defense."

Constable Kane recognized Bick as a fireman in the district. The glares between the men were challenges equal to a showdown. Kane was no fool and noticed Bick's bleeding arm. "I suppose she did that too," he said, pointing to Bick's injury.

Bick, not quick on the draw, said with dismay. "No, her daughter bit me and wouldn't let go. Bloodthirsty..." Then he shut up, realizing he had some explaining to do.

Kane wanted to know what child. "Where's the girl?" He was expecting a teenager at least.

Liv was hiding when her mother went looking for her. She came out barefoot in her nightgown with the blood all over her mouth.

Kane could not believe it was this little girl not more than three years old. His inner voice asked, *what would have caused a little girl to want to bite your arm off?* Not waiting for the answer, he announced, "I'm getting social services here right now." His gut told him something was seriously wrong and that these clowns were not being completely truthful.

Ruby always worried about the free money. "Please don't do that, I don't want them to take my daughter away, please."

Her tears were so sincere Kane wasn't sure who he should be protecting. He told Bick, "Get out of here and don't ever come back." Did he protect a man's career and give the woman what she wanted? Somehow the child was involved, and Kane felt it was she he should have protected. He realized he might be making a grave mistake and shook his head. "I still think I should have social services come to visit you."

Ruby pleaded. "Please don't do that. I don't want to lose my daughter. I won't let anything like this ever happen again. I promise."

Kane nodded. "I'll be checking up. I can promise you that. Good night." He turned and left.

Ruby turned to Liv. "Go wash your face and brush your teeth. Don't you ever bite anyone ever again. Do you understand me? I'll take a piece of your hide next time. Got it?"

Liv did what she was told. Even the police couldn't help her.

***

The following spring came, and Liv had a baby brother; "Flick My Bick."

Chapter 5
Calgary, Summer 1969 -1971

Two years had passed since Liv had stood at Gayle and Peter's door, announced she wanted a mother, not a father, and had her foster parents stupefied. Instantly, Gayle had understood Liv had a problem with the male gender. Hurdle one had begun before Liv even entered their home. Fear struck the hopeful couple that their challenges had just begun.

That day, Peter discreetly vanished into the master bedroom. The first few weeks had him walking on eggshells. He stayed at the office later than normal hoping the child would pass the day without the fear of his presence.

Gayle had a glow, a presence of joy not seen before. Yet, there was a sadness when she looked into her husband's eyes. Peter wanted to fulfill his wife's dream of having a child and possibly having their family. But what family? He felt ostracised from being a participant. This could not go on. The current arrangement was not working.

On Saturday morning Gayle had slept with a contentment as never before … she had slept in. Peter quietly went to the front door to collect the weekend paper. Entering the kitchen, he saw Liv sitting in the breakfast nook and looking out the window. He wasn't sure if he should quietly go into the living room and read his paper or try to approach her. With nothing to lose and everything to gain by trying, he decided to say, "Good morning."

Liv looked up. "Good morning."

Peter started to understand what Gayle was trying to convey when she said the girl was beyond her years. Her intellect was far more advanced than the average eight-year-old going on nine.

Before Peter could engage Liv in a conversation, the girl asked, "Do you like cartoons?"

Peter couldn't remember the last time he sat down on a rainy day, much like this morning, and watched cartoons. "Sure."

Together they went into the living room and turned the television on, flipping channels till *Bugs Bunny* came on. Then *the Road Runner*. Every time the Road Runner said "Beep Beep" Liv would giggle. Peter found himself chuckling as well.

Wrapped in her housecoat, Gayle entered and asked, "What are you guys doing?"

Liv looked up from the overstuffed chair. "We are watching cartoons, right, Pete?"

Peter stretched out on the sofa and bearing a huge grin, said, "Yup. Like two kids in a pea pod."

Gayle smiled – pleased to see the family together. Liv was trying, and this brought hope. "I'll make us some thick French toast. How does that sound?"

Both nodded their approval with smiles.

That morning changed everything for Peter and Gayle. There was hope. It seemed that Liv understood and wanted to have a family. Peter was included for the most part.

Gayle was Liv's anchor when she was struggling or having nightmares. The professional social worker and the mother inside became one. Gayle had no trouble marrying her common-sense training and her heart of a mother to reach Liv. In awe of Gayle's care and love for Liv, Peter would watch as the girls talked, colored, painted pictures, sang songs, and played Barbies for most of their weekends. This interaction time allowed Gayle to reach and understand this sweet child. Liv was flourishing ... yet, still withdrawn and quiet at times.

Liv wanted to be an inquisitive observer journeying through life. Gayle found every avenue from counselling to extra-circular activities to get the child to be a participant. Counselling was a must, though Liv was not fond of going or talking. The fun activities took coaxing though they were usually rewarding.

Two years of loving persuasion had made Liv a reasonably happy child. There still remained mysterious unknowns, though. There were many questions unanswered that clouded the child's affect. Both Peter and Gayle debated whether they should dig up all they could to help understand Liv. Or, should they let the water that had passed under the bridge be gone? What was in the best interest of the child?

Peter had consulted with a Detective Warnock to see what he could find. This led to having contact with a Detective Ducharm in Quebec. Both were waiting to hear from Peter with a decision to pursue further information. Peter needed to share what he had done with Gayle and seek her thoughts on the matter. The costs were astronomical. Gayle had hinted towards adoption as a birthday gift to Liv who was now ten and soon to be eleven in August. It would be the gift of truly accepting Liv. They had once agreed that the topic of adoption would not be feasible unless the child truly felt that both Gayle and Peter were her parents. Gayle was called Mom, Peter was Pete, but in all other aspects the three had become a family. Could Peter accept his title of Pete and not Dad?

Peter wanted to be Liv's dad with all his heart and he was, on most accounts. The nagging unknowns of what may have happened to Liv to create her hesitancy towards males scraped his soul like a fork to a plate. The wedge was subtle but present when it came to affection. Peter did get occasional hugs and pecks on the check, but no snuggling or sitting close.

Its tickled Peter's heart when he thought of Liv as a prim and proper little lady. She never yelled, demanded, or acted out in any way. Come to think of it, was Liv making sure she was perfect to have a family? It seemed crazy thinking about it. But, with all the child had or must have lived through, should there have been some form of venting? Peter realized he was preparing himself for the worst. Once faced with her past, would Liv erupt as though a volcano full of anguish and anger? Would he be a target? Peter knew he needed answers – more so to help Liv as his heart was now entangled with love for this little girl … of his.

After much discussion with Gayle, expressing his concerns and pouring his heart out, further investigation was needed regardless of costs.

***

A month had passed when Detective Warnock visited Peter at his office. The report showed Liv's family. Her mother was Ruby Mines. A brother, Flick My Bick, was eight-years-old this past March. A sister, Kandy Kane, was now five-years-old. Another sister, Sugar Kane, was three and a half years of age. Maggie and Joseph Riley, Liv's grandparents, were both heartbroken the day Liv disappeared.

Detective Ducharm's report indicated Ruby, the mother, had been investigated upon Liv's disappearance. She had not seemed distressed, in fact, she seemed relieved the girl was gone. Liv's father, Chuck, had sought legal counsel once he was informed the child was in Calgary and in the care of social services.

The report showed Chuck helping and providing for his family, which consisted of his parents and five other siblings. Joseph, Chuck's father, had recently died in an accident. He'd been a welder working on a bridge. It seemed there were no safety measures and no insurance. These factors had left Chuck as the only breadwinner in the family.

Chapter 6
Montreal, Summer 1971

Ruby was a single mother who could be heard constantly screaming at her children from the detective's car. The detective observed and took photos of various men in uniforms who would visit together, as though waiting their turn for her time.

Detective Ducharm decided to make a visit to see what Ruby had to share. One Wednesday morning, Ruby was ushering her son and daughter off to school on their own. He seized the moment to introduce himself and ask a few questions about Liv.

Ruby was impressed with Detective Ducharm's credentials. She batted her lashes and invited him in for a coffee.

Suspecting the woman's intentions, he proceeded with caution. He was at Ruby's door strictly on business ... not *her* kind of business. Detective Ducharm decided to sip his coffee while thinking of his best question. "So, what can you tell me about your daughter, Liv?"

Ruby weighed the question with her arms crossed and waving a lit cigarette. "Am I under investigation?"

Ducharm, who was quick to defuse a problem in order get answers, said, "It just seems odd for a little girl to disappear into thin air and you don't seem concerned." He had to suppress his urge to ask the question of how a mother could not bother to report the incident.

Ruby, not sure if they were playing a game of the minds, decided to put on the charm. Batting her lashes and flashing her perfect teeth with a pearly smile, she said, "Not really, I honestly thought the kid ran away. Never thought she would not come home. I understand she is living in Calgary and is cared for in the system."

Ducharm could not contain himself. "So, you did nothing." He waited for a reply. "Did you look or ask around?"

Ruby sat down with her shapely bottom wiggling in her chair, watching to see if her body language would get a reaction. Nothing. The detective wouldn't even look her way. Boring man. Ruby was getting agitated. This was no fun. "I did what any normal mother would do. I asked around. No one had seen the kid … I mean Liv. She's fine. That's all that matters."

Ducharm recognized the frustration in Ruby's eyes and went for the kill. "So, what do you think would cause a child like Liv to sudden get up and go and never come back?" He stared at her eye-to-eye without letup.

Ruby put out her cigarette and decided to play the victim. "The kid was evil, you know. She bit the arm of my son's father, Bick. She was more trouble than she was worth. Just as well she's gone."

Ducharm was clever and played along. "Mon Dieu [My God], what happened?"

Getting the attention, she was seeking, Ruby blurted out, "She attacked my boyfriend at the time." Then, remembering there was a report from Constable Kane, she said, "Constable Kane showed up in the middle of the night on a 'disturbing the peace' call. Bick's arm was in shreds and Liv's mouth and teeth was full of blood. In fact, Bick was so upset he was yelling – 'She's a vampire, She's a vampire.'"

Ducharm was familiar with Constable Kane. They had worked together on several cases in the past. Bick sounded familiar, but he couldn't place him. Ducharm suspected he had obtained enough information for now. Seeing Ruby fidget was a clue she was having second thoughts about sharing any further. Ducharm stood up. "Well, I thank you for your time, miss."

Ruby couldn't resist a man with authority. "Come by anytime," she said, dressing her face with a flirtatious smile.

Ducharm sat in his car profusely sweating. He had been divorced for five years and being distracted with work did not entertain much of a social life. He would go to the casino for the cheap meals, slots, and a game or two of poker with a beer or two. But Ducharm's true getaway was the race track. A social life with people did not exist.

This woman stirred his manly emotions into a raging fire. This woman – dangerous, manipulative. Ducharm was not charmed, or enchanted. The testosterone in him wanted him to dance with this woman, but his logical mind was aware of the dangers. Back at the office Ducharm would get in touch with Kane and get his take on the incident. But, first he had to get home and take a cold shower.

***

Refreshed, Ducharm was back in his car on his way to the office. He couldn't help but think that just an hour before his brain had felt like it had freezer burn. Enjoying the spring weather and breathing normally had a calming, peaceful effect. However, going over various points on the Liv case had Ducharm frowning. Usually sharp and on his game, he did not often miss anything. This morning he was a little off his game. Something about the biting issue ... the name Bick ... and Kane on the incident wasn't adding up.

Finally, at the office, Ducharm pulled out the file. Of course, Liv Riley had a father; Chuck Riley. The siblings had different fathers. A boy, Flick My Bick. Oh yeah! Guess who the father had been. A girl, Kandy Kane. *Oh NO! This cannot be.* His buddy – his peer had gotten tangled up with this woman. *Why didn't I see it?* The baby girl, Sugar Kane. Of course, Kane was involved up to his nuts.

Ducharm knew something happened to Liv on that mysterious night. What exactly it was, no one was saying. Kane had been the officer at the scene. How could he get involved to the point of having two children with this witch of a woman? Ducharm suspected...no, he knew the answer. For his own hormones had played havoc with his logic over the same woman.

Ducharm knew he had to talk with Kane. He needed time to think things through. His only interest was what had happened to Liv that night. Ducharm was not going back to talk with Ruby anytime soon. He'd likely get into trouble and never get the answers he was seeking.

***

Ducharm decided to show up to talk with Kane. Calling him or giving him a heads up would give Kane time to be prepared and smooth. Ducharm assessed situations best under the element of surprise. Natural behavior had no time to rehearse. He was not looking forward to putting his buddy; his peer, in his professional squeeze. But, if that's what it took to get straight answers, so be it. Durcham would have no choice but to put Kane in a trap. Watching a man squirm out of a lie was one thing. Watching a man squirm because of the truth was quite another.

Kane was on his phone when Ducharm waited outside his office. Both nodded and Kane opened the door. "What brings you by? I'm about to leave and have lunch with my daughter near her college." Kane got off the phone with Ruby, who was worried about Ducharm snooping around.

Ducharm got right to the point. "I'm looking for some answers regarding the girl, Liv." He sat down to make himself comfortable, a gesture to indicate he wasn't leaving anytime soon.

Kane decided to have a seat. He knew he wasn't getting out of this meeting without a few blow-off answers. "Like I said, I'm on my way out," he announced.

"Like I said, I'm interested in the child, Liv." Ducharm shook his head. "Doesn't anyone give a damn? A kid takes off to Calgary by cargo bus and no one blinks an eye."

Kane leaned back. "So, what's on your mind?" He delivered the question with sarcasm.

"Spoke with the mother, Ruby, who said there was an incident a number of years back. You were dispatched to the house."

"Yeah, for disturbing the peace. Was a domestic issue. Case closed."

"Not so fast. Ruby mentioned the child, Liv bit the arm of a guy, Bick. Sounds familiar though I can't place him. What do you think went on?"

Kane started shifting in his chair thinking out his best options. He realized Ducharm had already checked out the report on the incident and the child wasn't mentioned and neither was the bite or Bick. Kane was nervous and on the hook. He'd had this on his mind for so long and wanted to confide in his friend. "That night Ruby was crying, upset, and she didn't want to lose her child." Head down, hand scratching his chin, he was thinking. "I believed her at the time. Then Bick, a fireman, one of us…I thought fine. I told Bick to go and never come back. Thought I saved a man's job and helped a woman keep her child." Now he was standing, eyes red and mouth with a faint quiver. "I know now that the woman doesn't care about her kids. Bick did something, I'm certain of it. And now the girl is gone. What happened that night I can't say for sure. But, nothing good …"

Ducharm stayed quiet, letting his friend come clean.

Kane continued. "The thing is I know the girl's in Calgary and in foster care for the past two years. Been keeping track. The way I figure it, she's better off where she is. I never told Ruby what I knew and thought it was best."

Ducharm couldn't argue with that. Social services in Montreal and Calgary seem to agree, letting the case rest.

He wasn't sure it was his business about Kane's personal involvement or that he knew about Liv. But then his indignation got the best of him and he said, "Shame, really …." He looked at the man. "Liv has a brother, Flick Bick, imagine that. Also, two sisters, Kandy and Sugar Kane. What about that?"

Kane's breath escaped his mouth. It was all found out and known. His hands were on the desk, his face pale green.

Ducharm was good enough to hand Kane a lifeline. "Hey, none of my business. Let's keep this to ourselves. Hope you're a good father to your kids. We'll stay in touch. I'll let you know how things are with Liv."

Kane realized Ducharm knew where Liv had been all this time. "Who you are working for anyway?"

"Liv's foster parents." Ducharm stepped out of Kane's office. "Take care. Hope Ruby's good to you, buddy."

Kane collapsed and thought he was going to faint.

***

After Joseph had fallen to his death working as a welder on a bridge, Maggie Riley had been taking care of the children as best she could with her arthritis condition. Chuck worked for the rail during the week and got a job bar tending on the weekends to help make ends meet.

Ducharm came by to ask questions. He learned that losing their granddaughter had been unbearable for the Riley's. The family had learned that Liv made it to Calgary and that there were no prospects of her returning anytime soon. Maggie talked about their monthly visits and how summers together had created bonds as though the child was theirs. As far as they were concerned, Ruby, the mother, was the wicked witch of the East.

Ever since Liv had gone missing, Ruby did not make contact; no calls to make visits, no calls for money or purchases. This was disturbing. Maggie couldn't figure how a mother did not try to find her daughter, to seek help from them to find the child, or to see if they knew anything. It was so strange to Joseph and Maggie. The way they looked at the situation, either Ruby had something to hide or blatantly didn't care.

On that horrible day, Chuck had called Ruby to try to get access to have some time with Liv. That is when Ruby simply said, "She isn't here."

Chuck couldn't comprehend how an eight-year-old was simply not there. "What do you mean she isn't there? Where is she?"

Ruby was smoking a cigarette and taking a puff. "She just isn't. O.k. she ran away a few days ago. I don't know where she went. She'll show up, I guess."

Chuck's mind was rattling as though in a cage of scattered marbles. "What the hell do you mean ... you guess?" But he got nowhere with Ruby and wondered if she was lying and trying to stop him from having visits. "Fine, I guess I'll have to make some calls."

"Suit yourself," said Ruby and hung up.

***

Chuck had a bewildered look on his face when his mother asked when Liv would be coming. He said, "Liv is missing. Left home and has not returned. ... A few days ago." He frowned.

Maggie blinked. "That doesn't make sense. What are you going to do?"

"I'm going to go and ask questions, find out what happened, and go from there." He marched out the door.

Hours had passed before Chuck came home, and Maggie had informed Joseph of what she knew. They were sitting at the kitchen table with heavy hearts. "What did you find out?"

Chuck reported, "The short story is that Liv managed to sneak on a bus heading west. I don't know anything else. I spoke to the bus company and it stopped in Winnipeg." His eyes were red. "I don't want to walk out of the family and quit helping as I have been, but I have to find my little girl. I just have to."

Maggie and Joseph handed Chuck all the money they had. "Here son, bring her back home. Hopefully, it will all turn out all right. Just call us when you can. We need to know you are o.k. and what's happening."

Chuck nodded. He packed a bag and was gone.

***

Chuck made it to Winnipeg where the trail had come to an end. After a month he was out of money and got a job as a milkman. With no handyman skills, his options were limited. The job started at 4:00 a.m. and by noon he was done for the day. This gave Chuck the afternoons and weekends to look for his daughter. After two years and being no closer to the truth, Chuck was missing his family and a lonely man. His parents kept him up on what they knew, which was little.

Chuck got the call that his father, Joseph, was dead. He was needed home. Back in Montreal, Chuck was able to secure his old job with the rail and found a job bar tending on the weekends. Chuck was now the only bread winner and he had to help Maggie with the large family; three girls and two other boys.

Four years had passed since Liv left Montreal and it had been two years since the death of Joseph. But still, Chuck was no closer to having enough money to fight legally to get Liv back to Montreal or into his care.

Over the course of these years Detective Ducharm had visited the Riley family several times. He updated them that Liv had been adopted. Chuck had been getting closer to securing legal counsel so that he had half a chance to father his lost girl, Liv. But his money had taken a hit with the expenses of Joseph's funeral and burial. And then there was Maggie with her health issues, who often needed nurses or homecare, and this killed any chance to save. There was no money. There was no hope. Chuck realized he lost any chance of being Liv's father. Liv was now adopted. Hope? Gone!

Chapter 7
Calgary, Summer 1971

Calgary Family Court was preparing to close for the summer and Gayle and her colleagues jump-started the process to completion. Detectives Warnock and Ducharm's reports showed Liv's previous life and the current situation. She had a mother who hadn't reported her eight-year-old daughter missing. Her father was taking no legal action with no explanation. There was a full report on Liv's life from the beginning to the present and it showed that Liv had been abandoned. There was also a report from Liv's child psychologist on her progress over the past two years. And there were various recommendations for Gayle and Peter Patterson to be granted the right to transition from foster parents to adoptive parents.

Peter had been able to get a hearing to ask for an hour of the judge's time to present their case, but Judge McTyre wanted time to look at the case over the summer. Peter and Gayle were close to tears. Peter had his mouth open and Gayle was biting her lower lip. Theirs hearts could not survive two months of waiting for an answer.

Peter's colleague asked if he could approach the bench. "Your Honor, this child was found in the cargo area of a bus."

The judge said, "I'm aware of the publicity around the matter of this case two years ago." Taking his glasses off and putting his hands down, he made a sudden declaration. "I don't want this case to get into the ears of the public. I am going to make my decision after an hour recess. I hope this suit you and your clients."

Peter and Gayle could not relax and decided to go for a walk around downtown. They went through the Eaton's store, up the escalator to the walkovers to Devonian Gardens. Devonian Gardens held a special place in their hearts. It was where Peter had proposed to Gayle and they had accepted a new life together. It was where their dreams had begun years ago. Would it also be the place where their dreams to be a family would begin?

Together, they held hands and sat on a bench not saying a word. All they could do was hope and pray. It had been thousands of prayers to date. Would this be the one prayer that got answered in their favor? Their nerves did not permit any thinking or any feeling. They were numb and chilled with fear for the worst.

Peter and Gayle smiled at each other, not having to say anything. They had each other and the hopes of more ... their family.

Peter smiled and squeezing Gayle's hand, he said, "This is where all my dreams come true... I got to marry you. Right?" They smiled and got up to walk back to the court house, hand in hand.

The hour had passed. "Order in the court," announced the bailiff. "Please rise, Honorable Judge McTyre presiding."

All eyes were on the judge as he sat at the bench saying, "Please have a seat."

All in attendance sat. Gayle and Peter on the plaintive side of the courtroom. The air was stifling.

Judge McTyre spoke. "Let me say that I am aware Gayle Patterson is a social worker and has performed miracles to aid the child in question, Liv, onto a road toward well-being. Also, noted is that Gayle Patterson is one of the foster parents wishing to adopt the child, Liv." He paused for a full minute to read something from the file. "Peter Patterson, the other foster parent who is seeking adoption in this case, is a lawyer." He paused again.

Gayle and Peter were fearing their positions would be held against them. They could hardly breathe. "The adoption of Liv – Life of Riley has been granted to the plaintive, Peter Patterson and Gayle Patterson." The gavel hammered…and Peter and Gayle's hearts jumped out of their chests with the greatest excitement of their lives.

Their lawyer suggested they get the child's name changed as soon as possible. Leaving the court house had Gayle and Peter whole and complete, legally, members of the long-dreamed, long-wished for family. They found themselves embracing each other and kissing. Their love had endured so much and persevered … their emotions were higher than the visible sky … and now were sealed with their kiss.

***

The summer was full of fun and adventure for the Patterson family. Peter and Gayle took Liv to Disneyland and took advantage of local events and weekend getaways that spurred the desire to create solid memories. On Liv's eleventh birthday, she was with friends from school, and she had ballet, soccer, and girl scouts. That weekend Peter and Gayle spent hours creating a play that concluded with a story about them, their hearts, their love for each other, and their love for their little girl, Liv, and they presented a scroll showing they were now a family.

Liv was so shocked and pleased. "Does that mean you adopted me?"

Peter and Gayle both nodded with huge smiles. The squeal of delight from Liv was everything the new parents could have hoped for. They were a solid family with so much love for each other.

Quiet and deep in thought Liv asked. "What will my name be?"

Peter and Gayle answered in unison. "Liv Patterson, of course."

"Yes, a normal name, a normal life, a wonderful mother, and an incredible father. I love you both more than you could ever imagine."

Peter and Gayle stood smiling together with tears in their eyes. Prayers get answered. Dreams had come true for Peter and Gayle … especially for their little girl. Liv ran and hugged her parents. Hugs are hugs but this one sealed the deal.

***

Liv was thriving and growing into a beautiful young lady. Where did the time go? Peter and Gayle were now planning her sixteenth birthday party. The gala event was more like a coming out. Liv knew her parents had been known to go over the top to please her. This gala event was overwhelming and disturbing for her. She had no trouble with Peter and had called him Dad ever since that incredible day five years ago. But, this coming out thing was not something Liv wanted. If it meant inviting both her girlfriends and guys to this grand party, putting her on display … to … be charmed by a boy…? To date? To what?

Liv had never cared for guys who came across as charmers. Why, she wasn't sure. But, she'd never had the tolerance or patience for fake smiles, fake words, and for sure for those who tried to touch her. Anyone who was persistently assertive and didn't get the message would learn in short order to get lost. Liv did like calm, quiet, self-assured guys who knew themselves but didn't have anything to prove. She loved to learn if they were intelligent and if they had goals. Then and only then was she prepared to have them as friends and only friends.

***

Peter was in Toronto for a seminar and he took a side trip to Montreal to touch base with Detective Ducharm. Peter was willing to pay for Ducharm's time for any information or updates. A time to meet was set the Friday afternoon before Peter headed home to Calgary.

Chapter 8
Montreal, Fall 1976

The men exchanged pleasantries and got right down to business. Ducharm started. "I believe we have found the reason Liv took off and left home. I don't think you'll like what I have to tell you."

"I'm listening," Peter said, getting settled with one foot over his knee.

Ducharm began. "Days after sending the report and faxing it to Warnock, I received a call from the father."

Peter's eyebrows raised but he said nothing.

"He was looking for his daughter, which had led him to Winnipeg. The lead ended there. He was sending money home and saving for legal costs in hopes of finding Liv and getting custody, so he couldn't afford a detective. He wanted to know what my interest had been in the case. I informed him the police had found it odd that a mother loses a child and no report was filed. I found the case of interest." Ducharm shuffled his papers. "I did not think it wise to disclose who I was working for, and I left the father to his own research."

Peter could only say, "I appreciate that."

"Visiting the grandparents, Maggie and Joseph Riley, was easy and they opened up by asking a lot of questions in hopes of learning anything." Pausing and thinking, Ducharm continued. "They are heartbroken about their lost granddaughter. There's nothing more of interest about them. The mother, on the other hand, is a unique, self-purposing kind of person. Everything has a means to an end as long as it ends with her." Thinking of her Ducharm congratulated himself for avoiding her like the plague. "However, through her I was able to begin getting bits of information that led me to this report." He handed Peter a folder.

"In a nutshell, there was an incident that happened when Liv was three years old. A domestic disturbance brought a peer of mine to the household, Constable Kane." Ducharm looked at his copy of the file. "What Kane surmised out of the situation was that the woman, Ruby, was upset with her lover, Bick, a fireman. There had been hollering, hitting, and kicking going on. The usual domestic stuff. However, Kane noticed the man's arm bleeding and asked about it." Pausing to think of the words in the report, he said. "Bick, in his excitement over the situation, informed Kane that the child had bitten him and wouldn't let go, and there was a nasty tear through his skin and muscle tissues. So, Kane wanted to see the child, thinking it must have been an older child, more like a teenager." Looking at Peter, he continued. "It turned out to be three-year old Liv. Kane then said he was bringing in social services. That's when the mother got upset and said she would do anything to not lose her child."

Proceeding further, Ducharm said. "Kane made a decision and told Bick to leave and never come back. He thought he had saved a man's career as a fireman and the woman got her wish. Later, he realized he may have done the child an injustice."

Peter leaned forward. "To say the least."

"It gets better. It took all these years for Kane to slowly share his concerns about Liv. When he had seen Liv at the time of the incident she had blood all over her mouth and teeth. Bick kept calling her a vampire." Ducharm took a sip of coffee. "Ruby finally informed Kane that the loser had said he was trying to change her diaper, but Liv wasn't in diapers. Her panties were dangling from her ankles. The pervert had been feeling up the girl and she'd told him to stop. He wouldn't, and she bit him and got scared and her jaw locked and would not let go. The bite was bad, but the tear was worse."

Peter was not prepared for such details. In all his legal matters with corrupt people, he had never defended a pedophile. Peter's little girl had experienced so much at such an early age. It was unthinkable, unimaginable, beyond comprehension.

Ducharm asked, "You want me to continue? The short version or the long?"

Peter knew he couldn't read the report. He wanted the short version but feared he'd miss the fine points and said, "The long version."

"As you know there is a child by the name "Flick My Bick," who came to be. The father has never had contact or for that matter knows. As you know from previous reports there are two girls named Kandy and Sugar." Ducharm decided to leave out the last name, "Kane." "What you might not know is that Ruby, the mother, isn't much of a mother. She has her kids as she puts it and collects Welfare. Her life consists of her fun at night with her men in uniform." Ducharm stood to stretch. "Liv took it upon herself to take care of her siblings. She loved them very much, apparently."

Peter spurted out, "Well something must have happened for her to leave and travel so far."

Ducharm smiled. He liked working with intelligent clients. "I'm getting there." Walking around the desk, he said, "Ruby never changed her ways and continued with her liaisons, a woman of the night except homebased. She informed Liv that she was never to bite anyone ever again and threatened her. Then another incident happened one spring afternoon. Ruby's current boyfriend had arranged for her to have her hair done. He told her he would take care of the children. Instead, he sent them off to a babysitter, except for Liv, the oldest. When Liv arrived home from school the place was quiet – no one around, or so she thought. The boyfriend, I believe he was named Johnny Pepper, came up the stairs. Liv thought her family was coming home and opened the door. Before Johnny could enter she kicked the man's house of jewels and sent him head over heels down the stairs. The neighbor called the police and Johnny was unconscious and off to the hospital.

"Ruby wanted to know why Liv had done such a terrible thing to such a generous man. Liv told her he played with 'her lady parts in the night' and remembering she was not allowed to bite anyone, she had been helpless to do anything about it. So, when Johnny showed up, Liv knew what he was up to and let him have it. As she told her mother, 'No one told me I couldn't kick anyone.' The only problem was, Ruby guilted her daughter for this and led her to believe she had killed a man. Which wasn't true."

Peter was sick to his stomach with anguish and grief. "Please tell me there is no more."

Ducharm stated, "Liv believed she was in trouble…that the police were after her because she killed a man, so she ran for her life."

"She was only eight years old," Peter said sadly. "and that's how she ended up in the luggage compartment of the bus."

Ducharm had a bit more information. "I have had the odd time to chat with her brother, Flick, who knew Liv was going to Calgary. He said Liv had told him she would send for all of them when she could. He is now fourteen, has a paper route, shovels snow and mows lawns to get the money for him and his sisters to be together with Liv – in Calgary of course." After pausing for a moment, he said, "You remember the guy, Johnny Pepper? Well Ruby was pregnant at the time and had a little boy name Salt.

Peter stood up. "I think I need some air."

Ducharm had another report. "I have some information about the father."

Peter had heard enough and stood to leave. "I can't listen to anymore. Unless the father is a threat I'll take the report and look it over later."

Ducharm remembered, "Oh there's a report on Ruby's family. But, nothing of concern." Seeing Peter's look of despair, he stood up and shook the man's hand. "You have a safe flight home."

Peter nodded. "I'll have a check in the mail."

Peter left and walked a few miles to clear his head. He got turned around and forgot where he'd left his car, so he hailed a taxi and gave the driver the detective's address. Upon arrival, he found his rental car and headed for the airport. All Peter could think about was ... if this had been himself in Liv's situation ... surely, he too would have ended up in the luggage compartment of a bus as a stowaway. "How can some people live with themselves?"

Peter decided to stop asking questions that would never get answered. His heart was broken for his little girl running away from this place ... at least he had a home to run to.

Peter sat on the plane drained of emotion. His thoughts brought him to Liv. Now he understood her more than ever. He was in complete respect and awe for her strength and courage. It was a miracle to be so blessed as to parent this beautiful child.

The stewardess asked, "Do you need anything?" and handed him a Kleenex. To Peter's surprise, tears were running down his face.

Chapter 9
Calgary, Fall 1976

Peter landed in Calgary after 10:00 p.m., picked up his car from the ParkNJet, and headed home. The girls were up and chatting around the fire. They often had girl time in their pajamas. Liv insightfully noticed her father looked pale, if not ill. The concerned look on Gayle's face prompted her to discreetly depart for the night and leave her parents alone.

After a warm embrace Gayle and Peter headed to the kitchen, and Gayle started the kettle. In a joking manner, Peter said, "I think I need a bottle of good whisky."

Gayle knew her husband. "How was the seminar?"

"The seminar was fine." He took a sip of cognac on the rocks. "I took a detour to Montreal to chat with Detective Ducharm."

Gayle hadn't heard that name in years. Thinking that once they adopted Liv they had all the information they needed, she asked, "What made you do that?"

"Years ago, I worked out an arrangement with the detectives that the files were technically closed. However, I told them that should they come across anything of interest I would be happy to reimburse them for their efforts."

Closing his eyes and not so sure he wanted to have the rest of this conversation, he said, "Got a call from Ducharm and thought I'd follow up."

Peter was fit as a fiddle, just a little stressed out. Gayle knew how to prod the man she loved. With a smile she said, "The trip was exhausting or there was too much in one trip." Her hand reached out for her husband. "It might be too much to talk about this late in the night and after a long trip."

Peter smiled. Gayle was giving him an out for the moment. He loved how she pressured him and knew when to let go. "How about I give you the two-minute condensed version and then we can discuss it at length another time?"

Gayle appreciated her husband's discernment though she was aching to know the key points. She at with her cup of tea, ready to listen.

Peter said in a whisper, not wanting Liv to hear her truth. "I know why Liv left Montreal and ended up on that bus."

Gayle gasped. "Do tell."

Peter reflected on the courageous aspects of the story and couldn't help smiling. "Our little girl was abused first by molestation at the age of three. In fact, she bit the arm of her offender to shreds." His eyes flickered with glee. "Imagine that. The courage to object and to defend herself ... at three years of age." He shook his head.

Gayle was wide eyed and frozen. Processing the situation, she realized her husband had edited the scenario for her benefit. "Go on." Sipping her tea. Thinking when the story concluded she would need something stronger.

Peter continued. "Over the years, Liv was like the mother to her siblings, taking care of them." He sipped his spirit. "The last incident had Liv kick a man in his valuables sending him tumbling down a flight of stairs."

Watching Gayle's reaction, he continued. "The man was knocked unconscious and sent to the hospital."

Gayle could not fathom the reason the child would run away. "There's more, I'm guessing."

"Liv's mother lied and told her she had killed the man." His skin was going pale again.

Gayle's mind was in high gear and she reminded herself to just listen.

"Well, Liv thought the police would be after her. So, that's why she ran.

Gayle burst out laughing, seeing a visual of the incident. "She kicked the pedophile in his treasure box and sent him onto his head. She was only eight years old."

Peter smiled. "I know. Isn't that amazing!"

Gayle said she wanted to see the report, but Peter informed her that the details were so painful that he did not want her to be reading it alone. They would go over everything together … just not tonight.

Peter felt better. Arm in arm, he and Gayle went upstairs to their room to retire. Though their thoughts were bewildered, their hearts were filled with joy. They were so proud of their daughter Liv.

***

The weekend weather report promised sunny days with cooler evenings. Liv had retired to her room initially. Then, her heart had wanted to know what was going on with her father, though she was not usually prone to eavesdropping.

She stayed in the shadows in the unlit hallway. The whispers were hard to hear. Liv realized her parent's conversation was about her, about her past life with a family she hardly remembered. She slumped to the floor and knew that what her parents were talking about was her truth. She had been abused and had defended herself on multiple occasions. The bite maybe, the kick in the scrotum for sure. Her mother told her she'd killed a man and she'd run for her life. It was coming back to her.

Liv wondered if she'd suppressed those memories because she loved her life in the present. Her siblings were a faint memory. But, yes there was Flick, Kandy, and baby Sugar.

Liv settled into bed but woke frequently with images of her siblings and the last conversation ... a promise ... that somehow, she would send for Flick and the girls, so they could be together. The baby had been a baby then ... how old were they now? Flick fourteen. Kandy maybe ten or eleven. Sugar eight for sure ... Liv had been gone for eight years. How could one forget such a promise? Her father and her grandparents...what must they think and how come they never come for her? Aunty Jewels, who took her in for three years, must have been worried. *How could I have blocked all these people out of my mind? But I can't go back now. I can't hurt my parents, who love me and adopted me.*

Dad said last night that my mother lied to me that I killed a man ... oh yes, he fell down the stairs. So, he survived ...I'm glad but in a way it's too bad. Can't go back and deal with the stupidity of my so-called mother. You can't fix stupid. How could I get my siblings to Calgary? What would Gayle and Peter think? Would they be supportive? Would they even understand?

The night was long as her body turned with the turns of her mind.

Liv came down the stairs around 10:00 in the morning. Usually she got up with her parents and planned activities for the day or weekend. Her parents were sitting in the breakfast nook debating whether to wake her up or not. It was most unusual for Liv to sleep in as she was always eager for their adventures.

Gayle and Peter took one look at Liv and became concerned. She looked ill.

Gayle asked, "Sweetheart, are you feeling all right?

"I'm fine, Mom."

Peter stated. "You don't look fine." He sipped his coffee. "You sleep well?"

Liv helped herself to a cup of coffee and sat in the breakfast nook not sure how to answer. "I had dreamed all night. Tossed and turned on every thought."

Peter and Gayle gave each other a look. Peter asked, "What were you dreaming about?"

Liv knew she could tell her parents anything in the whole world. But, pride made her hesitate. She was embarrassed that she had purposefully listened to their conversation. She had only hoped to know why her father had come home looking so bad.

She decided to come clean. "Last night I was worried about Dad. You looked so bad after your trip to Toronto." She hesitated. "I longed to know what happened and why you looked so stressed."

Gayle and Peter knew ...

"I overheard you talking about my past life." Her head was down, and her hands were on her coffee cup. "How did you come to learn about my past?" It was said in a whisper and without malice.

They stared into an abyss of oblivion. They had been going to ask Liv what she had heard. Now their minds were trying to answer her last question. How had they come to learn about her past?

Peter unglued his tongue and began. "Before the adoption, we wanted to make sure you had been abandoned." His lips were dry, and he went to get a glass of water. "We had two detectives scouting for information. One in Calgary and one in Montreal." He sat back down and hugged Gayle.

Gayle said, "We knew so little – just that your biological mother didn't file a missing persons report." Peter was about to say something when Gayle put her hand on his lap. She continued. "This information was presented to the Judge during the adoption process. We were granted the adoption, granted being parents of you, our little girl."

All three had tears in their eyes.

Peter sat forward with elbows on the table and fists closed together. "The file was closed with both detectives after the adoption. However, we had an agreement that should any information arise that might be worthy of our attention, we wanted to know." Looking at Liv with a smile and then back at Gayle, he said, "Just after my trip to Toronto for the seminar, I went to Montreal. Detective Ducharm had told me he had a few files with more information that I, we, could view."

Liv said nothing with tears coming down her face. "You are ashamed of my past."

Peter and Gayle jumped into protective mode. "Not at all. We are in awe for your strength!" Gayle said.

"Your courage was amazing. You were so young. We love you so much," Peter added.

Liv stood up and faced her parents. They stood up. "I love you more than you could ever know. I don't want my past to hurt you now or ever." All three hugged and held on tight.

Liv poured more coffee for the three of them. "I want to see the files, the reports." The request was delivered with a flat affect.

Peter and Gayle were not prepared to share the details. They hadn't looked at the report themselves to appreciate the magnitude of what Liv was asking.

Liv suggested that she go shopping with her girlfriends and to dinner and a movie. Peter and Gayle were relieved. This would give them the hours needed to go over the reports and files. "We have a VISA card in your name with $1,000.00 on it. We were going to give it to you on your sixteenth birthday. Today is a good day to give it to you."

Liv was not a spoilt girl. She smiled shyly. "I will never need that much money. You are great parents and have provided more than I ever needed." She took the card. "I will be respectful and take care. I promise." Before going to her room, she said, "All I ask is that you give me the whole truth and nothing but the truth. I expect you to edit the gory stuff. But, I want the plain truth. Is that reasonable?"

Peter wanted to ask what her dreams had been about but decided Liv would reveal them as they discussed the horrific details on Sunday. "We can spend Sunday afternoon sharing the information. Is that reasonable?" he asked with a gentle, loving smile.

Liv smiled back. "Reasonable."

Liv was out of the house by 1:00 p.m. Peter and Gayle were in for an afternoon and evening of hell. To Gayle as a social worker this was the case of her life; the little girl who came into their lives, the gift that permitted her to be a mother. To Peter it was the case of his life that allowed them to be a family. Because of Liv … they were living their dream as parents. Their hearts were beating as the clock was ticking.

***

Saturday afternoon was arduous for Peter and Gayle. The evening was treacherous and long. Sunday morning permitted a few hours of exhausted sleep. Noon arrived with a well-planned outline and presentation of Liv's past life and events without the reports and files present. They simply could not let Liv see for herself the details … details of horrors no person should have experienced.

Sunday afternoon Liv came down to the family room around 1:30. It had been another night of dreams, unknowns, possibilities, hopes, and disappointments. The violent incidents brushed her mind only lightly. However, the faces of people she loved kept haunting her dreams. Awake most of the night, she only got a few hours of exhausted sleep late in the morning.

Gayle prepared a Sunday brunch in silence, working with her hands as her mind prepared for every question. Her heart ached with every concern on the issues that would be presented. Peter was lost in his thoughts along much the same line of reasoning as Gayle's.

The family took plates with food sitting at the breakfast nook. All were lost in their own's thoughts. Peter decided to begin with the character of Ruby. Her sources of income, her lifestyle, the men of the night, and of course her siblings. Gayle presented her father, grandparents, foster-care history, and Auntie Jewels. Nothing was mentioned about the police involvements, the biting incident, or the kick that landed a man down a set of stairs on his head – for fear Liv would think they were judging her.

Liv thought her emotions would get the best of her. However, her being became paralysed as her past unraveled before her. Just sitting and listening was hypnotic. She felt no real emotion. Then she said, with her head down, "You know I left because I thought I killed a man. I thought you would hate me if you knew I was a murderer."

Peter and Gayle stayed quiet letting Liv talk, even if the pauses were eternity.

"I am glad to know that I didn't kill anyone. I am glad … because I know I won't lose your love … I was always afraid if you found out I killed someone you'd hate me. I kept this in my heart for years." Tears were pouring like a fountain now.

Gayle hugged her daughter. "I'm glad you didn't kill anyone either. But, if you must know … for the first time in my life … I wanted to kill someone … that man that did horrible things to you ... all those men." Now Gayle was crying, vocalizing her thoughts, and knowing they were true and honest. She had learned that she was capable of murder to protect her daughter.

Peter was initially shocked to hear such words from his loving, principled, law abiding wife. Then he smiled. "No, I would have been willing to go to prison to dispose of a man who could do such things to my little girl."

Liv sat stunned, discovering the hearts of her parents. Could love cause someone to defy their own principles and commit murder? Justice is a balancing act. How ironic that the justice scales weigh what is fair to counter-balance what is unfair. Liv smiled. "I'm glad neither of you had to murder someone to protect me." She sat deep in thought.

Gayle and Peter sat quietly too, lost in their own thoughts. Peter finally asked, "What are your dreams about?"

Gayle gave Peter a look that made him think this question was too soon.

Liv looked at her parents knowing she could tell them anything. "I see the faces of people I once loved. My father, my grandparents, my Auntie Jewels. Mostly, I see the faces of my brother and sisters."

Gayle and Peter both nodded.

Liv continued. "You know I made a promise to my siblings?"

Peter knew. Gayle stared.

"I told Flick that once I got to Calgary I would send for them and we would live together." Her heart ached knowing she had lied. "I forgot about the promise. My life has changed. I wouldn't know where to begin to find them and help them, or if I should even try. Would I hurt my life, your lives – hurt their lives, bless all our lives, and now what can I do?"

Peter and Gayle froze. The mother, Ruby, would find out about Liv. She would surely blackmail them. Sending for the children would cause so much trouble and grief. Keeping their life, their little family happy, was paramount. Delving into this prospect would only cause hardship, pain, and grief unmanageable. They suspected that Liv was reaching out in hopes of them helping her with her promise.

Making dreams happen was one thing. Keeping promises another. The reality of the situation was quite another …

Liv changed the subject. "We have my sixteenth birthday party to plan. Let's get the party started."

CHAPTER 10
Montreal, Summer 1976

Chuck never forgot Liv's birthday. His daughter would be sixteen years old today. Eight years had passed, and he had long-ago learned he had failed to secure his rights as Liv's father. He had, however, succeeded in helping his mother raise his siblings after his father's death five years ago. Maggie was a great woman but she still endured pain every day, all day long, with her RA. Raised with integrity and loyalty to family, Chuck tried to juggle his responsibilities and his desire to get Liv back in his care. Money went to his father's funeral and burial. Money went to providing for the siblings. Money went to a court case when Maggie tried to sell the country house in Terrebonne Heights. There was never any money to get Liv home.

The country house had been sold in a private deal. The buyer had promised to pay monthly payments until the full price of $10,000.00 was met over five years. Maggie was required to pay the property taxes until the property went into the buyer's name. The man did not make a single payment, but he lived in the country house for a few years until Chuck had enough and pursued legal action. Chuck had believed the money would help his mother provide for the children, so his money could go to seeking his daughter. The matter had just settled, and the judge had informed the buyer he was required to purchase the property at the current value. The man was outraged. It turned out that he'd had the house raised and had long since put in a basement. The house was completely updated, and he felt the decision was unfair. Nonetheless, Maggie received $50,000.00 and she offered it to Chuck to help get Liv back. But it was too late as Liv had been adopted years ago.

Chuck had seen two of his sisters get married. Martha, pronounced like Marta, settled in Pointe Claire. Scora settled in Kirkland. Declan, Jean, and Jake were in their teens, working and finding their way in life. Chuck was not the father of the house. However, he would be the voice of authority when his mother required her wishes to be enforced. The siblings resented Chuck's interference, but they would comply to avoid disappointing Maggie.

Maggie was now in a convalescent home in NDG. Chuck had some time off and was not needed at the bar till later in the evening. He decided he would go and visit his mother.

Maggie was in an oxygen tent and was covered in a clear plastic casing when he entered her room.

Chuck disturbed the quiet of the room. "Hi Mom. How ya doing?"

Maggie looked at him. "Fine enough. You got a cigarette?"

Chuck blinked. "I can't give you one. You'll blow up."

Maggie demanded. "I don't give a damn. Get me a cigarette."

Chuck simply stood there gasping for air and saying nothing audible.

Maggie ordered, "Fine, get the nurses to get me out of this plastic box."

Chuck went out the room and explained Maggie's request. The nurses arranged to get her into a wheelchair and explained how Chuck could bring her to the gardens. There she could have a smoke.

It was late September, sitting in the gardens. Maggie could hardly hold the lit cigarette with her crippled hands. Yet, she held the damn thing with both hands like a clamp. The ashes fell to the gentle wind. Maggie closed her eyes with each inhale. Imaginary peace, at least for the moment. Chuck did not want to break the silence and sat wondering if Maggie's life would have been different without her RA. He saw a beautiful woman in her sixties and wondered what she might be thinking at this moment.

"You know I was born into a beautiful life. My mother was so loving and smart. She started her own grocery store in a French-speaking community, though she only spoke English. She died just before I married Joseph. Pa, my father, your grandfather, continued the business. Allowed people credit during the Second World War. When the war ended, so did the store. My brothers, your uncles, worked for the post office and were professional boxers. My sisters, your aunties, are incredible women. Pa, your grandfather, died eleven years ago and from that day my life went to hell."

Chuck said nothing, listening and remembering his wonderful grandfather.

Maggie continued. "When I dated your dad, we used to love to skate in the winter. Canoeing and swimming in the summer. Our whole lives ahead. Dreams of raising a family. Believing hard work pays off."

Chuck nodded, realizing Maggie was on Memory Lane.

"Joseph had the most incredible, deep, masculine singing voice with an Irish twang." She dropped the butt on the table. "I could listen to him sing for hours."

All Chuck could do was shake his head remembering the baritone Irish voice.

Maggie needed to vent. "Then we lost our granddaughter, Liv." Staring into space, she continued, shaking her head. "Joseph gone. Now my health is poor." She paused. "The children are mostly grown up." Tears came into her eyes. "You did all you could to help me. I want to say thank you." Maggie's lip was trembling.

Chuck didn't know what to say. He gave his mother a reassuring smile. "I did what a good son would do."

Maggie gave her son a gentle smile. She looked tired. "Bring me back to my room please."

Chuck did as he was told, and he waited till the nurses helped Maggie and settled her back in the oxygen tent – just stood waiting, letting Maggie know he was there.

Maggie's last words to Chuck were, "The older I get, the less I know. Life is a vicious game. It promises dreams but delivers no promises … maybe only hell."

Chuck reached under the tent and held Maggie's hand. This was her last breath. Maggie was gone, vanished from his life in a single moment.

***

Ruby's eldest sister, Jewels, had established a wonderful life for herself and her family. She was married to Jerry and had four children and a lovely home in Chateauguay. Jerry worked as a luggage carrier at the Montreal airport, while Jewels secured head waitress at the Rustic. She was sought after for her exceptional manner and service despite her poor French. The Montreal Alloettes and the Montreal Canadians often had meals and meetings at the Rustic. It was understood the teams would not order unless Jewels was present. The individual team members would tip, and the team managers would also include a generous tip. Wages were minimal and a token in comparison to Jewel's tips. The family was able to prosper because of Jewels and Jerry's commitment to each other, to their children, and to the quality of their life.

Ruby had many conflicts with social services. She believed her problems were related to her daughter, Liv. Often Liv had ended up in foster care and often, was abused. Liv developed a tough exterior and a driven work ethic to avoid trouble or negative consequences. Aunt Jewels continually stepped up to the plate and had taken Liv into her home as her child from age four to seven. There Liv felt safe, secure, and loved. Uncle Jerry looked like Dean Martin. Liv always liked the end of Dean Martin's show when he'd get on the phone and promise his wife he would be home after just one drink. The brandy glass was as large as a fish bowl. Uncle Jerry had a similar sense of humor. He always fulfilled his promises and the ones to himself as well. When it looked like Uncle Jerry compromised, he ended up on top. Aunty Jewels loved him and knew he was clever.

When Liv was seven, Ruby managed to prove her home was clean, safe, and habitable. She had worked hard to do it, as the extra money per child made a difference for her fun money. Jewels suspected the motive but had no choice to return Liv back to her mother. Ruby had a plan for Liv babysit her younger siblings so Ruby could do as she pleased outside the home. Jewels had little faith that Liv would be safe, and she knew trouble was around the corner. There was nothing she could do to circumvent Liv's return, though, as Ruby had proven herself in the meantime.

It had been eight years since Liv disappeared. Initially, Jewels believed the child had been abducted that spring day so long ago. Later, she'd learned Liv had made it to Calgary and had since been adopted. The heart of a mother ached for the loss of her niece. The unknown created a crater-size hole that would never permit closure. Hope was long gone as the years went on. Jewels never accused Ruby of being involved in Liv's disappearance. But in her heart, she knew Ruby was responsible somehow, some way. Their relationship became strained.

Ruby became defensive and accused Jewels of wanting to take Liv from her. What disturbed Jewels was the lack of care for the child while Liv was in Ruby's home. Now, there was no emotion, only derogatory statements about an innocent child, gone and lost forever.

Over the years, Ruby and her other sister, Emerald – Aunty Em had been as close as two friends could be. When Ruby would say, Liv "seduced" her man or men, Emerald believed it to be true. They talked out their interpretation of all the trouble Liv had caused. Liv being gone was just as well. Jewels found this kind of talk and these conclusions and thinking abnormal. She never understood how a child could be guilty of her own abuse when it had been handed out in the course of Ruby's care. Jewels heart ached when she thought of Liv.

The sisters would get together with all their children on festive holidays. Aunty Em found great pleasure in teasing the children. She'd tell them one story, watch them be engaged and gullible, and then prove how stupid they really were. Jewels couldn't stand the games. Finally, she would only visit without her children, because she felt such games were abusive. Ruby and Em thought it all entertainment and training for life.

***

Fourteen years old, Flick had had to grow up fast. Ruby was supposed to have stopped having men in the house, but Flick was no fool. The sounds coming from the shed told him his mother was up to her old tricks. Liv had been gone for eight years. Everyone initially believed she had been abducted or had died. Flick, being the man of the house, knew different. Every breath of his life was getting money for him and his younger sisters to get the hell out of Montreal and head for Calgary. Kandy and Sugar were eleven and eight now. Liv had left when she was eight. The time to go was soon. Since he'd been twelve, he'd had a paper route. He mowed grass for two summers and shovelled snow the past winter. Twice Ruby had found his stash of money, which then vanished. Flick caught on and hid his money in various places. Should Ruby find one stash, as least the remaining money was intact. Flick was aware that Liv knew their address, but he realized she couldn't write for fear of their mother discovering they'd had contact.

If Calgary was as big as Montreal, he had no chance of finding Liv. Flick was biding his time, getting older, and finishing school in hopes of securing work that would sustain them all. This life was no life at all. Anything would be better than this deplorable home in which they currently resided.

In Flick's mind … his mother was not a mother. In Flick's heart … his sister was his only mother. Flick could not stand the sounds coming from the shed. It was midnight and the air was fresh with a cool, crisp bite. He found himself needing to go for a stroll and as he was walking past a bar, he heard a scream and saw a man dragging a girl by the head of her hair.

He approached. "Leave the girl alone."

The girl, who was a waitress at the bar, gave Flick a filthy look; she was over eighteen and legal. The beast laughed and said, "Yeah, what you going to do about it?" He punched Flick in the face, and then turned and dragged the girl back inside the bar.

Flick shook off the sting of the punch, entered the bar, and tapped the beast on the shoulder.

The beast gave the kid a glance and said, "What do you want? Mind your own business." He picked up the girl over his shoulders and headed towards the door.

Flick could not stand back and watch the treatment of this girl without doing something. He picked up a beer bottle on a nearby table and cracked it hard on the back of the man's head. The beast stopped and fell flat on his face. The girl managed to find her feet and ran out of the bar.

Two police officers were eating dinner on their own time. They came up to Flick and asked, "You want to lay charges?"

Flick was confused. He shook his head.

The officers informed Flick, "He hit you first."

Flick was baffled and said, "No. I think he will suffer a nasty headache as it is." He walked out into the night air.

As he was walking home, the same officers drove up to Flick and rolled down their window. "We need to talk."

Flick was finishing his cigarette and he tossed it on the ground. "About what?" They had witnessed everything.

The police looked from one to the other. "The man is dead. That changes things." They said they were sorry.

***

Flick spent two years in juvenile detention; a boy's home. There he finished his high school and was awarded an apprentice opportunity to become a plumber.

Chapter 11
Calgary, 1976 – 1980

"Happy birthday, sweetheart," Gayle said while embracing her daughter.

"Happy birthday, darling." Peter added.

The three walked down the elaborate spiral staircase of the Palace Hotel in Calgary. Family and friends took pictures.

Gayle had wanted Liv to walk down the spiral staircase alone, but Liv said she would walk down only with both her parents. It was a compromise that became a cherished moment.

The gala was newsworthy, though it did not make the papers. Gayle and Peter were private people. Never wanting to draw attention to themselves, they donated thousands anonymously instead of giving gifts. However, this gala declared how proud they were of their daughter. Family and friends knew the unique circumstances of the creation of their family. Gayle and Peter believed in making your dreams come true, even if the odds were against you. They inspired all and were caught up in the fairy tale.

The night was filled with magic. Liv's loving parents secretly hoped there would be a Prince Charming. Liv detested the concept. Liv had dreams of becoming a nurse. Deep down, she wanted to be a doctor, but she was reluctant and lacked belief in her ability. Peter and Gayle believed differently. They believed Liv could do anything, be anything, just do it!

The next few years, Liv focused on keeping her grades up with an impressive 4.0 GPA. She qualified for scholarships. Peter and Gayle were too proud and wanted to pay for all of Liv's post-secondary education. Secretly they were impressed that Liv could have received her education strictly on her discipline and hard work.

Liv's graduation ceremony was long and boring on all accounts. To Gayle and Peter, it was exceptional. They were so proud that Liv had graduated with the highest honors and distinction.

Liv was invited to grad parties and declined. She wanted to celebrate with her parents. Peter planned a great week away with an Alaska Cruise returning to Vancouver. Rewards always included the whole family. Gayle and Peter embraced these developments and changes. Their hearts claimed a different feel … their daughter was leaving home soon, pursuing her own life. The house would feel empty with Liv away … gone.

Liv decided to go to Lethbridge Community College and go through general studies. Many of these courses would give credit to any program she would finally decide upon. Liv's decision was also based on something personal. She was aware that Peter and Gayle were getting on in years and she wanted to be no more than a few hours away. She was far enough away to stay focused and near enough to be within reach.

Peter and Gayle had wanted Liv to go to Toronto or B.C. University, but they were secretly pleased that she decided to go to Lethbridge. It was only a few hours' drive away, and they could visit. Liv would be away but not far away.

***

Liv had a shoebox unit on the campus. The walls were paper, and the noise was distracting. The parties were on going all night most weekends. How did anyone function on lack of sleep or focus on their studies in all the chaos? Ear plugs became a valuable investment.

The first year came and went and Liv received highest honors for the general studies diploma. She moved into an apartment near the university. She needed her space to stay focused. She liked making friends who were pursuing their goals and seeing their dreams become a reality.

Liv decided her grades were good in chemistry and biology … and thought she'd go for becoming a doctor. Gayle and Peter were pleased. Liv was accepted at the University of Lethbridge to obtain her Bachelor of Science, which she completed in two years. While waiting to be accepted at the University of Alberta, Liv continued working toward her masters. Wanting to have hands on experience and interaction with patients, she was looking for work. Gayle and Peter wanted Liv to concentrate on her studies. Over the years Liv came home to Calgary for every holiday and school break.

Christmas break before Liv would start working on her masters, she asked her parents if she could bring a friend home for the holidays. Gayle was pleased it was a male fellow student. That was how Peter and Gayle had met years ago – at university. Life had slowed down drastically for the aging couple. Both had retired and focused on travel at every opportunity. But they were always home for Liv on holidays and school breaks.

***

University life was task orientated. This suited Liv as she was disciplined, hardworking, and determined to excel with her assignments and papers. Often, she could be found in the library doing research or at home on her computer doing her papers.

One day when the fridge was empty, and she needed nutrition, Liv was forced to venture out to the grocery store. Shopping was a chore, not a leisure activity. Charging through the aisles, she sought the basics. Juice, milk, coffee, fruit, vegetables, dressing, rice, single portions of meat for stir-fry, whole-grain bread, and Tylenol. She had turned a corner when another patron crashed in to her cart. She looked up about to say, *you need to look where you are going.* But then she recognised a fellow student wearing a sheepish grin…who said, "Glad to bump into you. How are you?"

Liv did not consider the interaction a social event or occasion. "Fine, must go, things to do, time is of the essence."

Ignoring the excuses, the young man announced, "I'm Gideon and you are?"

Liv, trying to move around the collision site, ignored the introduction. "Excuse me."

Gideon said, "I'll excuse you if quit ignoring me."

Liv went around him. She had all her items except the Tylenol – the one thing she needed now more than ever. This headache would not go away. Finally, at her destination with a bottle of pain relief in hand, she realized Gideon was standing behind her. Looking up, displeased and shaking her head, she thought, *another headache that just won't go away.*

Gideon, perceptive and not moving, shyly whispered, "I'm not trying to be a headache." He touched Liv's arm.

Liv looked down, not sure what to think about the touch. There were no further words. They both just looked at each other, each trying to figure the other out.

Liv quietly asked, "What can I do for you?"

"Have a coffee or pop with me. I can't afford to impress you with a dinner or a date."

Liv was about to decline when Gideon sent her world into orbit. "I have never approached a woman, asked to talk, or anything. I don't know the social norms, or even know what to say … You are the most attractive girl I have ever seen. Please forgive me if I'm being too forward. I just know that if I don't try … I'll never see you again. My heart won't survive the loss. Please!"

Liv stared with her mouth gaping open. "I don't know what to say." She flushed.

"Please say yes," he said with pleading eyes that shone with admiration.

"Yes." Liv then darted to the checkout.

Her mind scrambled and got lost in confused thoughts. Who was this man who said such things? *Oh, how I hate a charmer. He's charming but in a quiet, polite, kind way. He spoke from his heart and exposed his vulnerabilities. What have I done? I don't have time for a relationship. What on earth was I thinking to say yes?*

Gideon caught up with Liv out in the parking lot. "Let's take a breather and go over to the Duke of Wellington Pub. Just a coffee to chat. You don't like me after that, fine." Seeing Liv's hesitation, he paused. "Listen I won't even ask for your phone number or address. I'll leave it up to you if you want to continue to get to know me. Honest. I promise, even if I see the love of my life walk away and it kills me. O.k?"

The Duke of Wellington had trivia questions on various television screens. Gideon started whispering the answers. Liv found it intriguing how smart he was and asked, "You like Trivial Pursuit?"

Gideon's smiling eyes twinkled. His sharp mind and his inner voice spoke out. "Only if it means getting to know you better."

Liv was awestruck. Good answer.

The next two years had evolved around her studies, his studies, and their time together. Not once did Liv permit Gideon into her personal life, disclosing very little. She mentioned her amazing parents, their great love for each other and for her, and how blessed she was to have a great family. She never said she was adopted or talked about her earlier life as a child.

This earlier life often had her depressed and disappointed in herself for not fulfilling her promise to seek out her siblings to be together. She labelled herself as selfish or a coward. In truth, Liv was afraid of hurting her parents.

And she was afraid of Ruby, her reactions, and the consequences of her involvement. Her siblings deserved better but how could she help? Liv did not have a nickel of her own. Getting a career, seeking her independence, building her resources would enable her to pursue her siblings. And as her siblings matured to an independent age, it would give Liv the power and courage to do something. But, that was a long away from today.

For Gideon, the moment he laid eyes on Liv, he wanted a life with her forever – whatever it took. Gideon never questioned the degree to which Liv was able to show affection. He knew Liv's heart to be sweet and kind and her mind to be sharp and clever. Being straight and honest was the only avenue of communication between them. Neither knew how to be mean or unkind. Both did not tolerate head games. The couple embraced their relationship and valued it more greatly than all treasures. Physical intimacy was not explored. Liv seemed to have a guide-line. Sensing this reluctance would be overcome with only her parents' approval, Gideon adored Liv for her old-fashioned values.

Assignments had long since been completed, papers were finished and marked, and exams were over. Christmas was in the air. Gideon and Liv were busy packing to spend the holidays in Calgary with her parents.

When they climbed into Liv's car and headed out on the road, the air was crisp and full of wonderment for Liv. She wondered what Gideon would think of her parents, or of her afterwards, since she knew her parents would share anecdotes of her childhood. What would her parents think of Gideon? He looked like a Grizzly Adams who had a spirit with nature – more rugged than refined. Many of their weekend getaways had been hiking in the mountains in Waterton Park, Huddo's in Writing on the Stone provincial park, or bridge jumping in the canals near Raymond.

Gideon was lost in his own thoughts and wondering what Liv's parents would think of him. He knew they were financially comfortable people who enjoyed the finer things in life. He thought they might be concerned that he would not do well for their little girl. But he was determined to not let his negative thoughts dominate the opportunity. He promised himself to "be himself," and hoped that it was enough to not lose the love of his life.

Calgary approached, and Liv was navigating through the holiday traffic with intensity when Gideon whispered, "I love you Liv."

Liv remained focused. Not sure she'd heard right and not sure what to say, she gave a glance to him.

Gideon whispered, "I love you with all of my heart, most beautiful woman who has graced my heart."

Liv heard and couldn't think. "You are going to make me have an accident." She was smiling.

They parked at a Mac's store. Liv needed to breath. Her heart was responding. She knew she loved Gideon more that her heart had ever felt. To Liv it was the most romantic way to hear Gideon's declaration. It wasn't after a romantic movie, or a shared moment of weakness, or a public display of affection. It had been said with heartfelt truth in a quiet moment. Gideon always surprised her, and this was no exception. She took off her seatbelt, reached out, and hugged him with all her being. Her heart burst and her tears flowed with the sincerity of her love. "I love you too." She paused and smiled. "No, I love you more."

***

They were walking up the steps of her parent's home, when the door flew open. Gayle and Peter had been watching out the window and waiting for their daughter to come home. It was the event of the year for this loving, wonderful couple. And the excitement in their hearts to meet the man in Liv's life was a Guinness World Record. They had always wondered if Liv would ever open her heart to know and have love in her life. It was a gift they wanted for their precious daughter, though something they could not simply purchase. To Peter and Gayle, it was a miracle and they only hoped Gideon was everything their girl would ever dream in her life.

"Come in. Please, come in." Gayle said, hugging her daughter and then Gideon.

Peter just smiled. "Hi, I'm Peter." He took Gideon's hand to shake it, and then gave him a one-armed hug. Peter then had his chance to hug his daughter. Both her parents had tears in their eyes.

Liv broke the ice, smiling and teasing her parents. "Look at you guys, tears in your eyes, getting soft in your old age."

Milly, the live-in maid, asked, "May I take your luggage to your room?"

Liv and Gideon gasped. Liv stated, "I'd like my old room. I hope it's o.k. for Gideon to have the guest room?"

Gayle and Peter nodded, not sure if their daughter was being respectful in their home or if the young couple were, in fact, not that intimate. Milly took their bags to the respective rooms and turned down the beds. There were towels and robes at the end of their beds and candies on the pillows.

Gayle and Peter had finger foods on the kitchen island. "Are you hungry?"

Liv and Gideon shook their heads no.

Peter had thought they would relax in the living room, but Liv went to the breakfast nook and asked for coffee. Gideon followed her and sat opposite. He didn't want to make her uncomfortable or come across as possessive.

Gayle brought out the wine. Milly returned from her chores and served up the glasses.

Peter wasn't sure where to begin with chatting and everyone remained quiet. "We made reservations at the Owl's Nest for us tonight," he said.

Knowing it was the most expensive restaurant in the city, Liv protested. "That's too much, Dad. We're not accustomed to such fine dining."

Gayle, seeing the positive, announced. "Then it will be an experience." She smiled at the "kids," not letting them say no. "You will enjoy it very much, Gideon."

Gideon was charmed and smiled.

Gayle, who found her voice, got right into her skills of discovery and asked, "So, how did you guys meet?"

Liv and Gideon instantly smiled. Both spent an hour sharing their individual versions of the event. Peter and Gayle loved hearing their thoughts and feelings and enjoyed hearing how their relationship had been growing. It was clear that Gideon was a gentleman with a rough exterior, but a gentleman none the less. They appreciated how his eyes glowed so gently with admiration and obvious love for their daughter.

The snacks came to the table and the wine glasses got refilled. The chatter was engaging, and time escaped them all until Peter looked at his watch. "We better get a move on. We'll be late or worse, miss out on our reservation."

The night was filled with shared stories of Liv as a little girl. The affectionate renditions of events had Liv laughing and smiling. Gideon embraced the stories as though his heart would not hear anything less. Peter and Gayle were enchanted with the couple – their hearts so filled with the love in the air. Liv showed small gestures of affection towards Gideon. Nothing escaped Gayle's and Peter's vision. They were seeing a side of Liv that had them believing their little girl had blossomed into a beautiful woman.

That night, Gayle and Peter chatted into all hours of the night in their bedchamber, reflecting on the day Liv had arrived at their door. The challenges, the fears, the joys had all been worth the heartaches and had brought them their family. The rewards were great. Gayle had thoughts of grandchildren running away with her. Peter laughed, knowing his wife. "Honey, I have a feeling these two are the professional sort."

The comment hit Gayle. "Oh no, you're right. I hope they don't make the same mistake we did and wait too long."

Peter hugged his wife. "Have faith. They'll find their way."

Gayle knew her husband. She smiled. "I have a feeling you're asking me to mind my own business."

Peter grinned. Their exciting day was evaporating, and fatigue had taken them into the night. Tomorrow was another day. There was a week of bliss to be had with their daughter and her companion. What more could they want? They planned on making every day count, every moment last. This would be the best Christmas ever!

Chapter 12
Montreal, 1980

Another five years had passed for Chuck. His parents had gone to their deaths. His siblings had disowned him as a loser. Life had dealt him a bad hand. The hell in his heart didn't hold a candle to the loss of his daughter, Liv. Loneliness was a comfort that did not cause chaos. The paralysis of his toxic life had Chuck in a hamster cage treading his wheel to nowhere. Dreams and ambitions no longer existed. There was only the comfort of the rotation of the sun and moon, the rotation of the seasons. These brought the only forms of absolutes. Life, people, justice, were unpredictable and had hardened his heart against ever believing in the concept of "good."

Bartending permitted Chuck an avenue of provision, survival, and existence. His life had no graces of the love, fun, or adventure that people chatted about as options. People were afforded abundance, some, or none. Chuck was afforded none of the things that gave life quality. He was fully aware, but fully did not care.

Chuck had become a man with little to say, little to share – the perfect bar-person to confide in, who never gave his opinion or judgements. He just listened and smiled. The bar scene with its brawls had Chuck wandering in the back finding something else to do. He made it a point to never notice anything, to never get involved, should chaos evolve in the establishment.

Christmas Eve was a hard time for many. A kid sat on a stool at the bar with his head down. Didn't seem to care what was going on around him. Didn't have anything to say –lost in his mind. So young with the world on his shoulders. Chuck decided the kid looked *too* young. "Can I see your I.D., young man?"

Flick pulled out his wallet. "A beer please."

Chuck kept looking at the license. The kid was nineteen. The name "Flick" rang a bell, but he couldn't place it. Chuck needed to know who this kid was. "What brings you to this place, in the middle of a blizzard, on a freezing cold night?"

Flick looked up and thought … *How's it your business?* He held his tongue. "My shitty life."

Chuck was in a strange mood and said, "If there was a shit storm my life would be in it." He laughed at the thought because ironically it was true. "How bad could it be? Your life has just begun."

Flick needed a friend. "No one would believe me. No point telling ya. My life IS the shit storm."

The place was empty. Chuck had nothing better to do. "Try me."

Flick was in a strange mood as well. "Don't say I didn't warn you. O.k.?" He took a sip of his beer.

Flick was out of juvenile detention and doing all he could to help his sisters. Absent from the family home for a few years, he'd come home to find the girls, Kandy and Sugar, loose and fancy free, much like their mother. Night school as a plumber had Flick on the go day and night. Conversations with Ruby and the girls had him throwing his hands up. He felt exasperated for the lack of action or a plan to give these girls a shake. Maybe Liv had gotten it right in the first place when she'd left for Calgary. Flick could only hope that she was living a better life. This dead-end life for Flick, for Kandy, for Sugar, had no solutions, no hope. It boiled Flick's blood hearing Kandy and some guy in the shed. He wanted the best for himself, for his brothers, and his sisters, and he had his heart in a rage of frustration. There seemed no hope for change. Looking at the man behind the bar, he thought *Why should he care?* Then he shrugged, *What the hell?*

"I have a sister, Liv ..." he began.

Chuck's eyes tripled in size. His heart raced. His mouth felt glued shut. Brain turning back in time, he decided to just listen. Chuck was all ears and wanted to know everything.

An hour passed with Flick pouring out his heart. He didn't care what the bartender thought as Chuck was a stranger. No one could help him or make a difference. He had nothing to lose venting and giving the details. Abruptly he got up and said, "Thanks, appreciated your ear. You saved me a counselling session. Thanks again." He slapped a twenty on the counter and started to walk out.

Chuck was lost in his own thoughts, startled with what had transpired. This kid was Liv's half-brother and was just as tortured about the loss of his sister. His brain was absorbing the information and didn't register the kid was exiting the door. "Stop, wait!" he shouted, running around the counter and approaching Flick. "What if I told you that I am Chuck Riley and Liv is my daughter?"

Flick fell back on the door. "What did you say?"

"I'm her father. Liv's father. I'm Chuck. Please! We need to talk more. I need to tell you some things as well." Walking back inside, he hoped Flick was following.

Flick couldn't feel his legs. He thought he'd need a keg of ale just to absorb what he had heard, but he found his way back to the stool. "You got the coffee on?"

Chuck smiled, first time in a decade. "Sure thing."

***

The most unusual friendship was developing. Both had a deep love for the same person. One for his daughter. One for his sister.

Chuck could not believe the environment Flick and his siblings were living in. On the other hand, he was aware of the woman, Ruby, who had ensnared his heart and manipulated him, his parents, and everyone around her. He remembered how Ruby had treated Liv with little regard and he had always suspected that Liv was a means to an end for her. Welfare – A meal ticket. His own child, Liv, being called "Life of Riley" was bizarre to say the least. Now he'd met Flick, called "Flick My Bick." What the hell was Ruby thinking? Ruby's kids were a joke to her and she made their lives a joke as well. Chuck learned that there were two girls; Kandy and Sugar Kane. You've got to be kidding. Now there was a the youngest called Salt N. Pepper. Ruby would think the kids' names were creative. It was simply cruel.

Flick talked and talked like it meant his life. It did. He couldn't believe his good fortune in finding someone who cared as much about Liv as he did. Flick tried to remember Chuck in his early years and nothing came to mind, but it didn't matter now. Chuck seemed a broken man who had sprung to life as though given a life line.

Chuck confirmed many things about Ruby and shared what he knew about Liv. He disclosed how he'd learned Liv had been adopted, and how he had tried to get the money to fight legally to have his daughter back, so he could be her father. He explained how he'd failed.

Flick felt bad – he knew how easy it was to destroy one's life. There were so many scavengers, liars, thieves, and opportunists in the world. The crap in his mother's life had taught him enough about shit people. Trust was not in Flick's vocabulary. But he was intrigued with this man, Chuck. He admired the man's heart.

Their conversations over the next few months were a morass of revelations. Appreciating that they had so much in common, they began to develop a father/son relationship. Finding Liv became their constant goal. The plan for the two of them to head to Calgary was the first of many thoughts. It was best that the siblings remained in Montreal until after they found answers to their questions, hopefully found Liv, and decided upon possibilities afterwards.

Maybe, just maybe, things were turning around.

Chapter 13
Calgary, Christmas 1980

Christmas in Calgary was amazing. Peter and Gayle were beside themselves with joy. Liv and Gideon thought they were in a kid's paradise. The week was therapeutic and needed. Being welcomed with so much love and getting spoilt beyond reason had Liv and Gideon in a whirlwind.

Gifts of bedding, linens, winter attire were too much for Gideon and Liv. They tried to decline the generosity, but their objections were rejected and shushed. Gift certificates for Safeway, The Bay, and a dozen restaurants were over the top.

The two couples spent quality time together. Many times, the guys would take off and share a beer. This was the time during which Gideon had shared his career goals with Peter and asked him for Liv's hand in marriage. Peter was worried that Liv was not fully aware of Gideon's intentions and that the plan might backfire.

The girls would take off and shop till they dropped as Gayle explored her daughter's heart about Gideon. Liv confided in her mother and freely answered her questions.

Knowing Liv was a private person, Gideon asked Peter if they could stay home on New Year's Eve. He was more confident since he had Peter's blessing to pop the question. His budget for the ring was $1,500 and he was surprised when Peter wanted to go shopping with him to select the ring. Taking it as approval, he went shopping with him. Peter kept this secret from Gayle and was excited that both girls would be surprised. While shopping, Gideon was uncertain about what kind of ring Liv would like. The jeweler asked questions about Liv; her personality, her style, and he showed incredible wedding and engagement sets. Gideon could not afford what his eyes seemed glued to. Peter picked up the set that Gideon's eyes kept seeking.

Gideon did not want to disappoint his father-in-law to be, but he was a practical man. Pointing to the ones in Peter's hand, he said, "Problem is, we are students on a student's budget. It seems I can only afford a simple engagement ring with a simple wedding band."

Peter smiled and said. "Yes, I understand. I'll pay for the engagement ring and you pay for the wedding band. Then, Liv can have this extraordinary set. The one she deserves and would love."

Gideon had his misgivings. But as with the Christmas gifts, he had a hard time refusing Peter's kind offer.

That night the girls were dressing up, doing their hair and their make-up, having fun and giggling all afternoon. The boys were relaxing in the living room and talking quietly.

Gideon was standing in front of the mirror over the mantel, fidgeting with his tie. Peter found himself observing this down-to-earth man struggling with his attire. He rose and asked if Gideon would like a drink. When he returned, he noticed Gideon in quite a tangle with his tie. He placed the drinks on the mantel and offered, "Can I help you with this?"

Gideon, feeling awkward, surrendered. Peter showed him how to place the short end of the tie to the right and twist in various motions of over and under three times to create a perfect knot.

Peter turns Gideon around and placed the tie in position, and then Gideon took over with great effort. Peter broke the silence and asked, "Will you be living apart while you both finish your education?"

Gideon frowned. He was concentrating on the twists and turns of the tie. "I leave such decisions up to Liv. I want to work on her timetable."

Peter chose his next question carefully. "With you about to propose for the purpose of marriage…you both being students, would it not be wise to pool your resources and move into one place?"

Gideon wasn't sure how much information he wanted to share, but he realized Peter deserved an honest answer. "I love your daughter with all my heart. I would never put Liv in an awkward situation that would make her question my integrity or intent." He noticed that Peter looked perplexed. "I guess what I'm saying is that we have not become intimate. My respect for your daughter and our relationship has me not pushing the issue."

Peter approached and assisted Gideon with the final touch to make the perfect knot. "I believe it might be time for you to broach the subject. You guys are going to tie the knot."

Smiling at the irony of the moment, both found themselves laughing. They picked up their cognac and retired to their leather chairs. Peter felt comfortable saying, "Liv is doing her masters in the new year. Still has a few years to complete her education and get her doctorate."

Gideon acknowledged the comment by nodding.

"How do Liv's goals fit with your plans?"

Gideon, relaxed and feeling comfortable, answered, "Both Liv and I will be completing our education at the University of Lethbridge for the time being. Liv has applied to U of A and is waiting to hear if she'll be accepted to become a doctor."

Inquisitive, Peter asked, "Will that work with your plans?"

Gideon nodded. "I only have two years left to finish my engineering degree. Should be able to accomplish that with Liv's goals.

Peter ascertained that Gideon was completely devoted to his daughter – virtuous to a fault. He understood and appreciated how his little girl had come to adore Gideon. Peter was getting to know the core of this special man, Gideon and felt he was a worthy man to marry his special little girl, Liv.

The topic of children came up in Peter's heart. "Can we expect to hear the patter of little feet running around anytime soon?" He smiled with mischief.

Gideon found himself smiling as well. "One hurdle at a time. I don't think Liv is prepared anytime soon. It has been in our conversations, to answer your question. Yes, but after establishing a home location and career first."

Peter concluded he liked this practical man.

Milly insisted on preparing a wonderful sit-down dinner of roasted duck, roasted potatoes, yams, mixed vegetables, Yorkshire pudding, and salad with cheesecake for dessert. There were also tons of leftover Christmas baking for any gap in anyone's appetite as well as more finger foods for the New Year's celebration.

They all retired to the living room with New York on the T.V. bringing in the New Year at 10:00 p.m. Calgary time. The girls were giddy with wine and the spirit of the night. The boys had smiles knowing they had a secret.

At eleven, Peter gave Gideon a nudge and whispered, "This might be a good time to pop the question. The girls won't see it coming." He grinned with mischief.

Gideon stood by the fireplace. "I would like to make a toast." Everyone raised their glasses and waited. Then Gideon asked Liv to join him. Liv stood, confused as to what Gideon had in mind. She thought he might give thanks for all her parents had done to make the holidays so special.

Gideon began. "I'd like to say this has been the most amazing Christmas. Amazing because of the people. Peter and Gayle, you are so kind and too generous. Thank you for everything. Soon, I hope to thank you for something more precious that has my whole life full of love."

Liv stood baffled ... from the wine?

Gayle had a feeling ...

Peter had a knowing ...

Down on one knee Gideon said, "Liv, my heart came alive the day we met. You are my best friend, my hopes, my dreams, my life … I can only hope that you will accept my offer of love … I am asking you as a humble man to be my wife forever."

Liv had not seen this coming. Her hands trembled as her mind realized the most incredible moment had just happened. A full minute passed, and all were waiting – hoping and waiting. Liv was not normally a crier. Yet, tears escaped and came down her cheeks. In a whisper, she said, "Oh, my goodness. Yes." Smiling and trembling, she hugged Gideon and kissed that man, who had stolen her heart. The moment was sealed with a kiss – sealed in the hearts of these four-special people.

Gayle and Peter sat together holding hands and smiling. Peter declared, "To think we didn't even need the mistletoe to witness this kiss!"

***

Peter was afraid they would be meddling in the lives of their daughter and soon to be son-in-law when they purchased a condo in Lethbridge. They paid cash and handed the keys to Gideon. The young couple could move in the middle of January. They were shocked and dismayed, but they obeyed and moved in together. Opening the door of the condo, they found the home fully furnished and complete with dishes, appliances, pictures, fixtures, and cupboards complete with food. All Gideon could say was, "I think they forgot to fill the closets with clothes." Liv couldn't help chuckle.

During the next two years, Liv shared that she had been adopted, loved and nurtured by her parents. And she'd explained her life prior to arriving in Calgary. Gideon was amused at how resilient his sweetheart had been. It explained so much; Liv's hesitancy, cautiousness, and painfully long wait before she would trust.

Peter and Gayle occasionally shared with Gideon about the little girl of then-eight; her strength, her courage, her love for them. Gideon realized Liv was long past being so vulnerable and had grown into a woman of incredible substance…all because of these two incredible people, Peter and Gayle.

Gideon and Liv graduated; Peter with his engineering degree and Liv with her Master of Science. The moment was special. Peter and Gayle came to Lethbridge to witness the occasion and participate in the celebrations of the day. However, Gideon and Liv had a secret that day … Liv had just found out they were expecting. At dinner at the Keg, the news was shared with Peter and Gayle.

***

Back home in Calgary, Gayle and Peter could not have been more pleasantly surprised. So many thoughts crossed their minds. Marriage would have been preferred before the baby. However, their concern about having a grandchild or children had been answered.

Wedding plans were quickly arranged – July, the next month. A Friday wedding at the Lodge in Lethbridge could be accommodated with ease. Liv and Gideon had long since learned to let her parents do as they pleased simply because they would with no stopping them. Sudden arrangements in Calgary were next to impossible with such short notice.

Gayle hired a wedding planner, who pulled off miracles with every request. Gayle did not understand the word no when it came to her daughter's wedding. No expense was spared or even blinked at. For Peter and Gayle, this was the event of the century and the pinnacle of their dreams fulfilled.

Gideon was worried about seeking employment. Liv was concerned with her goals and decided not to pursue being a doctor. Their family was the most important consideration. Peter and Gayle were busy with the wedding. They expressed their wishes for Gideon and Liv to come to Calgary and set up a home. The sale of the condo would make a nice down payment to secure a nice property and they promised to co-sign the remainder of the mortgage.

Gideon and Liv were in a daze with the flurry of activity of the wedding and with seeking employment. Considering Peter's and Gayle's offer to move to Calgary had them feeling constant stress and concern. Most people might feel their life was being handed to them on a platter. Gideon, worried about work, moving, and Liv's well being, not to mention the wedding, was overwhelmed.

The month passed in no time and the wedding was about to happen.

That Friday morning of the wedding, Gideon accepted an incredible offer with an engineering company in Calgary and agreed to start at the end of August. Liv was offered an opportunity at the University of Alberta and declined.

The wedding had three hundred guests and was celebrated with every opulence and elegance. Liv and Gideon felt a sense of accomplishment with their education. However, their wedding proved to be the pinnacle moment that meant everything that could possibly be achieved in their lifetime. Their love was pure and true. Their love was growing … a bundle of love … made by the two of them … sharing the moment with them … inside Liv.

Peter and Gayle could not have been prouder. As private people, they took the couple aside and handed them an envelope from Gayle. It held tickets for a honeymoon on a two-week Caribbean cruise all expenses paid and a check for $5,000.00. The flight was departing in the morning. Gideon was glad that his employment start date was the end of August. Then Peter handed them an envelope. It was the deed to a 4,000 square-foot home two blocks away from Gayle and Peter's home, paid in full.

Gideon and Liv gasped in shock. "You have gone too far. Honestly, this is too generous. You can't expect us to accept," Liv announced.

Gideon said, "I agree.

Peter and Gayle were excited and full of glee. "Please don't burst our bubble. You are our family. We don't want to miss out loving our grandchild, maybe even our grandchildren. Please," Gayle pleaded.

Peter added. "We're not getting any younger. We're giving you your inheritance as you need it." He smiled. "These are trying times for you. We can help. Besides, we're a bit selfish. We love you guys and want you close. We want to be a part of your family, sharing the memories. We have all the time in the world since we retired." He lost his words in his emotions.

Gayle finished. "You will make us complete, fulfilling our dreams of being loved and giving love till our dying days." A single tear escaped down her face, which showed a sweet smile.

Gayle and Peter held each other, waiting and hoping their daughter and new son understood their hearts.

Liv said, "We can't thank you enough."

Gideon nodded. "A thousand thank-yous will never do. But, we thank you with all our hearts."

The newlyweds went on their honeymoon and Peter and Gayle arranged their move to Calgary while they were away.

Upon the young couple's arrival at the Calgary airport two weeks later, Gayle and Peter were waiting to greet Liv and Gideon. "Hey, what are you guys doing here?" Liv said with a huge smile and so pleased to see her parents. She hugged them. Gideon, too, embraced them with affection.

Peter spoke up. "Well, we moved you while you were away. We thought you might want to know you are going home to Calgary."

Gideon was quiet and politely not pleased. He simply said, "Thank you for all your hard work. We can take it from here."

Liv blinked and realized her husband's words had a finality to them. Gideon meant more than just getting home.

Chapter 14
Montreal, 1981

Chuck and Flick became tight with a common goal. Finding Liv had been a pang of distress that needed relief. Having lost the detective's business card years ago, Chuck went on a search for him that took a half year. Finally, a meeting was set for Chuck and Flick to go to Ducharm's office. Ducharm never refused potential information – potential business.

Lingering in the waiting room had Chuck fidgeting, Flick had his head down with a frown. Both were deep in their own thoughts and hopes when Ducharm greeted them and motioned for them to enter his office. They sat down in the two obvious chairs and waited for Ducharm to take his seat behind the desk.

Ducharm blurted out, "What can I do you for?"

Chuck began. "As you know, I'm Chuck Riley. This is Flick, Liv's brother." With his mouth feeling pasty and dry, he continued, "We have been looking for Liv all these years. I spoke with Constable Kane, who let it out that you were hired by Liv's foster parents – now adoptive parents, years ago."

Ducharm said nothing.

Flick wanted to get right to business. "These people who hired you are no longer your clients. We want to hire you to locate Liv. She is an adult now and can make her own decisions whether she wants to meet with us, or not."

Chuck then moved in. "We know that Liv is in Calgary. She was adopted. We want to know if she would be inclined to have contact with me or her brother Flick – both or none."

Flick interjected. "We are willing to spend money to find out instead of going on a wild goose chase and getting nowhere in Calgary."

Chuck concluded, "Are you interested? Will you help us? You are the man with the most information."

Ducharm was leaning back on his chair and twirling his pen. "I might be opening a can of worms that no one wants open." He stared at the pen, thinking. "But then it wouldn't hurt to get paid to find out. I take this on, there are no guarantees. I only promise to put out feelers and get back to ya."

Flick was no fool. "What you are saying is that your actions will be dependent on your previous clients. If they don't want our involvement then you are going to brush us off, and get paid to do it?"

Ducharm smiled. "I like you kid, you're sharp." Still grinning, he said, "I'll tell you what, I'll do my best to present the situation as though it was in their best interest."

Chuck stood up. "Can't ask more than that. Thank you."

Ducharm needed the money for his gambling problem. "That'll be $5,000.00 down plus expenses."

Flick laughed. "We'll give you $1,000 down for your one phone call." Dishing out the money, he said, "Contingent on you proving to us that *we* are 'the clients,' – paying clients. Also, on whether the information is satisfactory and well researched and disclosed in a timely and appropriate fashion. Only then may we want to continue with your services. You treat us on a 'need to know basis,' we put you on a 'pay as you go,' got it?" He stared at the detective, eyeball to eyeball.

Ducharm got red in the face. He didn't like being told how things were going to go. He liked being in charge… but he was too desperate for the cash, so he simply nodded.

Ducharm hollered out. "How did you know Liv is in Calgary?"

Chuck wanted to say, *that's for me to know and for you to find out.*

Flick grinned and hollered back. "I knew all along. My sister Liv planned to go to Calgary and was going to send for us when she could, but that didn't happen. It doesn't mean I don't want to know my sister."

Chuck and Flick walked out of the office without looking back, but Flick hollered back. "Expect to hear from you within twenty-four hours. That's when the cash flow stops."

***

Ducharm racked his brain and realized he could play both sides and get paid handsomely. Pulling out the old file and looking everything over, he made his plan. It was seven at night when he dialed the Pattersons' number.

Peter answered the phone. "Hello."

The line opened up. "Ducharm here. Is this Peter Patterson?"

Peter had dosed off in his reading chair and was trying to wake. "To what do I owe the pleasure of your call?" Peter – the gentleman always.

Ducharm stated his business. "I have new information. You interested?"

Peter thought it over. "Not really."

Ducharm needed to throw a carrot. "Well, Liv's brother, Flick, knew all along that Liv was going to Calgary. He is in hot pursuit, trying to find her. I have no interest in paving the way for him since you were my clients first."

Peter sharply asked, "So, he's your client?" Then he realized Ducharm was hinting about getting paid – bribe money. "What's it going to cost me?"

Ducharm was pleased that his plan was working out as he'd thought. "I believe derailing the kid is worth my time for $5,000." He waited for Peter to think it over and said, "By the way, how is the girl?"

Peter, still thinking, said, "She's a beautiful woman, engaged, graduated with a degree, doing well." There were clicking sounds in the background. Peter was checking the bank accounts. "We'll wire you the money. We have an understanding?"

Ducharm was pleased. "We have an understanding." The line went dead.

***

The next day Ducharm contacted Chuck, as he was not too sure about the kid. He set up a meeting and indicated he had a load of information.

Back in the office, everyone settled in their chairs and Chuck and Bick waited.

Ducharm stood up and pulled up his pants. "I talked with the father." He grunted. "As we thought, he wasn't inclined to help." He stared at his clients. "His position is the same."

Flick was on the ball. "What the hell are we doing here?"

Making a snorting sound, Ducharm barked, "Hold your horses. I found out that Liv is engaged and has graduated with a degree."

Flick was quick with his thoughts. "It only matters if you know where." He glared at the man he did not trust.

Ducharm realized he had been slacking off. "Wouldn't give that information." Thinking quick on his feet, he grinned and said, "I have a plan. Interested?"

Flick sharply stated. "Let's hear the plan, then we'll let you know if we're on board."

Ducharm needed some water. "Well these people are upper crust, but not necessarily high society. I found the engagement announcement in the Calgary paper." Ducharm had not found any bills with Liv's name and he suspected the parents paid all the bills. He also hadn't found Liv as a student anywhere in Calgary or Edmonton. However, he did find Visa transactions in Lethbridge, though he wasn't going to disclose this information at this time.

Chuck was about to say something when Ducharm put up his hand. Ducharm had realized he would have to disclose the name of the man who had married Liv. "His name is Gideon Harley."

Chuck nodded. "Now what?"

Flick had no more patience for this detective. "Well, we paid for this information and we are settled."

Ducharm said, "That was for opening up the case. I expect another $1,000."

Chuck had been afraid of that, but Flick was done. "That was worth five bucks." He dug a five out of his pocket and said, "Don't spend it all in one place."

Chuck wanted to know more. "Did you do a check on Liv? School, bills?"

Ducharm said, "Yeah, her parents pay all the bills. All I know is that Liv is not in school in Calgary or Edmonton. She could be either east or west is my guess."

Chuck continued. "What about Gideon Harley?"

Ducharm grinned. "Didn't get paid to check him out. Sorry." He was pressing for more money.

Flick was in a foul mood. "I know you're getting paid to divert our intentions. You take us for fools? Think again." Seething and spitting out his last words, he said, "The way I see it we paid enough. Not interested in being strung along."

Chuck was desperate. "Listen, you got anything solid I'd be interested, o.k.? Anything that will get us closer to finding Liv would be appreciated."

That's all Ducharm had to hear. Months passed and then Ducharm noticed an announcement in the Calgary paper – the wedding of Liv Patterson and Gideon Harley. Time to make a few phone calls.

Chapter 15
Calgary, 1982

Their Caribbean Honeymoon had Liv and Gideon feeling relaxed and refreshed. They spent every waking minute together enjoying the sun, food, and adventures. After two weeks, though, the newlyweds were eager to get home, pack, move, and set up. Gideon made it clear that Liv was not going to lift a finger. Liv made it clear that she would pack everything up carefully but would compromise by not lifting anything heavy. She would arrange for movers and cleaners.

Gideon was looking forward to his new job with a prominent engineering company in Calgary. Starting at a junior level was expected, but the pay was respectable. With no mortgage, Gideon believed he could provide for his family with reasonable comfort, and even add the odd luxury. Both decided that Liv would not pursue a career at this time. Liv was not one to waste time and thought the time off would afford her the luxury of getting her PhD, although she hadn't mentioned this possibility to Gideon and held the hope secretly. It was a discussion for another time.

Since the day of the wedding they had been given the gift of a paid-off home, the couple wanted to see the premises. Landing in Calgary, they thought they would find a hotel and stop by to see Peter and Gayle to view their new home the next day.

Prior to preparing for landing in Calgary, Gideon had put off the subject of Liv's parents and their generosity. Liv brought her chair forward and buckled up, and Gideon leaned over and whispered, "Honey, we need to talk about something before we land."

Liv looked up and waited for the something.

Gideon continued now that he had his wife's attention. "It's about your parents. We need to say something about their generosity." His mouth was feeling dry and the words were coming out painfully. "All I'm saying is that we need to make decisions as a couple working together."

Liv whispered, "You know my parents mean well. They love us very much. No need to worry, dear."

Gideon wasn't so sure. "It's not that I don't appreciate all that they've done."

Liv tapped her husband's elbow. "I understand. You want to be the provider." She grinned.

Gideon realized he was not getting his point across. "I just want us to have a say in making decisions that affect our lives. That's all." He smiled back. Somehow, he found himself constantly surrendering to Peter and Gayle's treasures of their hearts.

The plane had landed. The hustle and bustle to the luggage carousel, picking up Liv's car, getting a hotel, getting dinner, and settling in for the night had been the couple's plan. Liv was tired, and Gideon was anxious to see the end of the day.

Upon entering the carousel area designated for luggage pick up, they discovered Peter and Gayle.

Smiling Liv said, "Hey, what are you doing here?" She was pleased to see her parents and she hugged and kissed them on the cheeks. Gideon embraced them with affection.

When Peter announced, "Well, we moved you while you were away. We thought you might want to know you are going home to Calgary," Gideon had mixed feelings. One was appreciation, as always. One was anguish that they had made decisions without consulting them. Liv knew her man and could see the emotional conflict in his manner.

When Gideon put their luggage on a cart with full swings and slams, and simply said, "Thank you for all your hard work. We can take it from here," he had seen Liv blink. He suspected they might have their first fight and he would be in the dog house. If there wasn't a dog house, he might find himself in need of one.

Liv, the peacemaker, said, "Can we follow you, meet you at the new house?"

Gayle was quiet and perceptive and knew they had gone too far. Peter sensed something wrong but believed that they had done everything with great thought, hard work, and immense love, so what could be wrong? He concluded the couple must be tired. Gayle did not share her husband's view and knew something had changed ... and not necessarily for the better.

Gayle and Peter drove to the Bonavista area and stopped in front of a classy older house. Liv and Gideon parked behind the stopped vehicle. Gayle remained in their car while Peter got out, came up to their window, and handed the keys to the house to Gideon.

Knowing her parents, Liv thought this was odd. It had seemed likely that they would come with them to the door and walk them through the house. Especially since the house was a gift. In fact, the front door of the house was draped with a huge red bow and ribbon.

Peter simply said, "Enjoy your new home. Gayle sends her blessings." He walked back to his car and drove away.

Gideon was relieved and looking forward to getting settled down, going for dinner, and finding their bed. He used the key to unlock the door, and Liv entered the home first, searching for the light switch. A grand foyer with a chandelier welcomed them to their new home. It was breathtaking and beautiful. The house had been upgraded, fresh and new. There were refinished hardwood floors throughout the main floor. A sitting room was on the right, formal dining room on the left and a curved staircase led to the second floor with an archway leading to a hallway. The hallway to the right had a bathroom and laundry area. To the left was a butler's pantry and an entrance to the garage. Farther down the hallway was the massive kitchen, eating area, and family room. The home was well organized.

Upstairs to the right was a guest room with an ensuite and a large room with French doors, ideal for an office, which included a two-piece bathroom. On the left were two bedrooms with a shared Jack and Jill bathroom. The landing could accommodate a sitting area. Directly in front, facing the stairs, were huge, ten-foot French doors. These doors were inviting and went to the master bedroom. The master bedroom had a sleeping area, a sitting area, two huge walk-in closets, and a master bathroom with a double vanity, jetted tub, shower, and throne. The upstairs was fully carpeted in a light champagne color. There were brass fixtures throughout – the latest style for the '80s.

Back downstairs and off the family room were triple sliding doors and double sliders off the eating area. There was a single door off the kitchen. The tour took a half hour and it was made in silence. Views of the yard showed it was beautifully landscaped with a rock waterfall, covered pool, and hot tub. There was a covered patio from the balcony off the master bedroom, and it was furnished with patio set and loungers.

The early evening sun was setting slowly, letting the night become present. Fatigue had the couple decline exploring the basement at that moment.

Nothing had prepared them for the grandeur or stature of such a magnificent home. Both Gideon and Liv felt immensely privileged and a little guilty that so much had been given to them with so much love. Gideon felt guilty for his feelings and for what he'd said at the airport. Both knew Liv's parents would have wanted to show off their gift to them. Gideon's comment had made her parents step back. Liv and Gideon's hearts were bursting from the extravagance that was before them. Their minds were conflicted. All their furniture, pictures, lamps, beds, linens, kitchen, bathrooms, drawers and closets were set up and in place.

A dinger from the double ovens rang. A note on the kitchen island told them dinner was ready. "Milly made lasagna, garlic toast, salad in the fridge." Red wine with a corkscrew and two glasses awaited them. The eating area table was set for two. There was a huge gift basket on the fireplace and a card with congratulations welcoming them home. The wine remained unopened as Liv wasn't drinking alcohol because of her pregnancy.

Gideon hugged and held his wife with tears running down his face. Liv was quiet and felt so many emotions that her mind and tongue could not coordinate a coherent thought. They sat down, held hands, said grace for the first time, and then had a quiet dinner, deep in thought.

Gideon had a smile on his face and Liv looked perplexed. Then he said with an amused laugh, "I have a feeling that even the phone is hooked up."

Liv nodded and laughed. "I bet you're right." They finished their dinner and Liv asked, "You don't mind if I give them a call?"

Gideon knew she was talking about Peter and Gayle. He went to the phone in the kitchen, picked up the receiver, and heard it was alive, before placing it back on the cradle. "What do you say we go over to your parents and thank them?"

Liv smiled and said, "Why don't we call them? They're dying to come over. I think we should show our appreciation."

Gideon agreed.

When the phone rang, Gayle picked it up on the first ring. Her "Hello" was said with a smile.

Liv simply said, "We'd like you to come over. It would be so nice if you could."

Gayle didn't wait for a second, or for a second invitation. "We'll be right over." She hung up.

Five minutes later the doorbell chimed, and Gayle burst in with all the excitement of a school girl. Peter stepped in cautiously and quiet.

Liv and Gideon welcomed them both with gleeful smiles, hugging them with tears. Gayle went off to show Liv all the surprises she'd missed; the basement with the family room, bar, and entertainment area complete with pool table, pinball machine, and dart board.

Peter stayed at the door.

Gideon said, "Let's have a drink and talk."

Peter showed the way and stood before a set of doors to a mini bar in the sitting room. He opened it up and poured two glasses with cognac and ice he got from the mini fridge. Gideon gasped with surprise. Peter found himself smiling.

The men sat in leather chairs with their spirits. Peter broke the ice. "You know we only wanted to make you and Liv very happy?"

Gideon nodded, trying to find the right words that would make his painful comment at the airport palatable. "We never doubted your love. Never misunderstood your kindness and generosity." Pausing to capture his thoughts, he tried to find a way to express them without hurting Peter. "I have a small problem," he began.

Peter listened, acknowledging. "Go on."

"I want to be the man Liv expects and deserves." Realizing he sounded jealous of the bond Peter and Liv shared, he said, cringing at the thought, "I know I'm coming across as jealous, but I want to provide as a husband and father. I want us, Liv and myself, to make decisions as a family." He sipped his cognac. "We need to work things out as a team. That means building our lives, our dreams, our hopes while working out our challenges."

Peter waited while the words settled in the air. "Gayle thinks there will be problems if we don't back down. Problem is, we're so excited for you kids, excited about our grandchild, and only want the best for you." He paused. "Is that so much to ask?"

Gideon was a caring man. He saw Peter reduced to a few words short of pleading and he wanted to reassure him without making promises that might fail. "No. It's not too much to ask. We want you a part of our lives and the lives of our children – now and forever."

Peter got a faint smile, knowing the conditions were coming.

Gideon said in a gentle voice, "I need to be the head of our home. Liv needs to know I am a man she can count on just as much as her father. I need the space and time to prove myself to her for the sake of us and our growing family."

Peter's lawyer mind came into action. "So, where is the compromising line here?"

Gideon liked how Peter thought and found it easy to finish what was on his mind. "You and Gayle have a one hundred percent right to be a part of our family. To love Liv without question, to love me with questions." He smiled. "To love our child or our children with all your hearts." Pouring out another shot in their glasses, he continued, "Proving your love does not mean opening up your wallet at every turn. You're perceptive and seem to know our needs. I need to learn these skills, to step up to the plate, and find a way to satisfy the needs of our family."

Gideon needed to make this simple. "Just ask us before splurging. Find out what we have in mind. Let us make decisions. My fear is that you have spoilt us. I don't want our children spoilt to the point of no return."

Peter smiled. "So, I can spoil you, our daughter, and your children with love."

Gideon confirmed. "Yes, now and always."

"I'm o.k. with this proposal. I don't think Gayle will be too pleased. In fact, I'm glad. Thought we were heading for the poor house at the rate we were going," Peter announced with a smile.

Gideon laughed. "Hope you don't mind me saying, glad to hear it."

The men shook hands – the deal was as good as done. A compromise had been made. The parameters set. Both men discovered – they each had great respect for the other.

The girls came to join them in the sitting room. Gayle asked, "What are you boys talking about?" Liv already knew by the look on the faces of the two men she loved.

Gideon answered, "I'd like to make a toast to say thank you for all your kindness, your generosity, and most of all your love." His tears flowed without Gideon realizing how much he appreciated all that had been done for them. His nerves had him rattled as he tried to rein in his emotions.

He feared hurting the ones he loved while trying to get a grip on the situation. But he knew Peter would understand the need for him to be the man of the house. Though he wasn't sure how Gayle would feel about the conversation that had just taken place. Little did Gideon realize it was Gayle who had asked Peter to slow down and let the "kids" discover their life.

***

Gayle and Peter arrived home exhausted from the visit. Their hearts were united, their minds divided. Peter wasn't sure giving their dream home up had been such a good idea. They had spent years on the project getting it perfect as their retirement home.

Before Peter had retired as a lawyer he was involved in a property case with the banks. The property had been owned by a grow-op and the place had been destroyed. The bank was ready to let the house go for next to nothing. Peter liked the layout and had discussed the place and the possibilities, with Gayle. They'd secured the home for a song and dance and had spent extensive time and money making it extraordinary over the course of years. The place looked like a mansion. Peter thought it was a palace.

When the kids had informed them of having a child, getting married, and where they would settle, the discussion began. They talked about the option of giving the young couple their old home in hopes of having them come home and be close by. To Peter that would have been the ideal solution.

Gayle sat frowning. Peter asked, "What's on your mind?"

Gayle was afraid to say what she was thinking and hesitated for a moment. "You know I love the new house. It's our dream retirement home." She paused a bit too long for Peter, who was tapping his finger on the table gesturing for her to get on with it. She continued, "I'm worried that the kids would feel awkward about sleeping in our old room. Our old room would be their room. I have a feeling they would decline. That's all."

Peter weighed Gayle's words. "What do you have in mind?"

"As I said, I love the new house, it's beautiful." She was cautious about saying what was on her mind. Peter's tapping started up, and so she said it. "I would be willing to give up our dream home for the kids' happiness. It would be perfect for them."

Peter hadn't thought of the new house as an option. The new house was perfect for them. Though he had means, Peter was not a materialistic man. His only concern had always been the needs of his wife. Gayle's happiness was his happiness. But, in Peter's mind this was a huge sacrifice. It symbolized all their hard work over the years. He said, "I'll have to sleep on it, sweetheart."

Gayle was content with Peter even considering her idea.

The day of the wedding the decision to hand over the keys to the newly renovated home was made with great love. The kids would never know how great their love was for them or to what extent they had sacrificed. Settling into bed with smiles and hearts full, Gayle and Peter fell asleep knowing they had made the right decision. Their family was only two blocks away ... nice and close.

Chapter 16
Montreal, 1982

Ducharm had read a graduation announcement about Liv Patterson receiving her Master of Science. Also, he'd read about the wedding that had taken place between Liv Patterson and Gideon Harley. He didn't know if they were still living in Lethbridge, or if they'd had a change of location.

Time to call the Pattersons.

Gayle answered the phone. "Hello."

"Hello, this is Detective Ducharm. May I speak with Peter?"

"I'm afraid he's not home," Gayle replied. Peter was up with the roosters to get some tee time. "How can I help you, Detective Ducharm, is it?"

Ducharm not sure how to proceed but couldn't back out now. "It has come to my attention that Liv's half-brother has been trying to find her." He waited to hear Gayle's response. Nothing.

"When information arises, I understand that you are interested in knowing," He stated, trying to get a reaction.

Gayle and Peter talked about everything and they had talked about the extorted money extorted from them some time back. Gayle was going to have nothing to do with Ducharm ever again. "Well, Mr. Ducharm. It seems the cash cow has run out. We are not interested in anything you have to say or offer." She thought about Liv and felt guilty. "In fact, you can have the brother phone our number. It's time we had a chat with him. It might be time the two meets."

Ducharm said, "I can arrange that for a fee." He was thinking of the loan sharks nipping at his heels. Over the years his betting had been Ducharm's downfall. He now owed over $50,000.00 and with interest escalating the debt at twenty-five percent, it was snowballing. Ducharm had been roughed up and beaten within an inch of his life. He was a desperate man in need of money. Gambling as a pastime had seemed innocent, but trapped and desperate for money, he was trying now to save his life.

Gayle knew he was calling in hopes of getting some more money. "We are done giving you money. If you can't find it in your heart to forward a call to bring two siblings together, then do us all a favor and don't ever call this number again." She hung up.

Ducharm had not been expecting this reaction. He'd thought they would want no contact with anyone ever associated with Liv's past life. He figured he'd play the hero navigating their troubles and be rewarded. He had thought wrong.

Plan B. Contact Chuck and let him know he had information and a contact number. That should pay the bills. On second thought, there was no mention of Chuck, the biological father, making contact. Ducharm was going to have to contact Flick. Getting a paycheck would require Flick knowing that he had an in, a contact number. He was going to make the kid pay.

***

Several calls had been placed to reach Flick, but all forms of contact had been ignored. Ducharm had no choice but to spur interest with Flick through the father. Chuck was easy to reach at the bar. Working on the clock or working to pass the time, Chuck could be found almost anytime there. Chuck liked to keep busy, working most hours on his own time. The employers didn't mind.

Ducharm placed the call. "Chuck please."

"Chuck here."

"Detective Ducharm here. Have you got a minute?" He tried to sound relaxed

"Yup," was all Chuck offered.

"Seems the adoptive parents don't mind having Liv's brother make contact. I've been trying to reach Flick for weeks with the news." He was expecting excitement to ring through.

Chuck and Flick had decided that the detective was crooked and out to bleed them. They had no intentions of doing business with the bloodthirsty hound. The information about possible contact had Chuck wondering why the sudden change of heart and what cost would be entailed. Flick had instructed Chuck to forward all contact to him and he would set the jerk straight. "You'll have to take that up with Flick," he said.

Exasperated, Ducharm stated, "As I said, I've tried with no success for weeks. Could you let him know I called and the news, please?"

Chuck said with no emotion, "I'll pass it on." As his hands were stocking the front bar, he dropped the phone from where he'd tucked it between his ear and his shoulder. He picked up the phone. "Sorry, I dropped the phone. I'll let Flick know."

Ducharm realized he wasn't getting anywhere slow.

***

Flick was impressed with his kind of dad. Chuck hadn't given the asshole detective any hope of interest. Just like the detective hadn't given them any hope of finding Liv. So many years had passed that time was not a pressing issue. But Ducharm seemed in a sudden rush believing they would always be interested and jump to any tidbit of crap he dished out. Flick was on the ball and Chuck was learning. Months passed, and they waited, knowing Ducharm was the anxious one; the one in need.

Ducharm watched Ruby's house and realized Flick was no longer living in the household. There was no activity of his comings or goings. Ducharm ended up at the bar, acting as though he was surprised to see Chuck. A detective with half of his marbles always knew where he was going.

Chuck didn't buy the surprised act and he was impressed that Flick had Ducharm, figured. "So, what's brought you into this part of town?"

Ducharm looked at the man behind the bar. He saw a broken man with no hope of setting straight things that had gone so wrong decades ago. There was no life in Chuck's eyes. Now that there was hope of finding Liv, it was long gone – no hope, not a spark to indicate that what Ducharm had to offer was life-changing.

Ducharm stated that he had the parents' number and they were expecting Liv's brother to call. Flick was out back having a smoke. He came in and realized Ducharm was at the bar doing his sales pitch. Ten minutes' worth.

Flick was not a patient man. "Why don't you take your bullshit and sell it to someone who cares?" You play both sides. Lie, deceive, connive, with a poker face. You expect us to jump for joy because you have some news." Flick couldn't stand the man. "You pretend to be a trustworthy man and instead you cheat us out of information that has made us bitter about justice." He shook his head. "Then you want us to believe that you're here with good intentions and that you speak truth."

Chuck was working away as though what was happening was a small difference between patrons. But he was all ears. All of sudden Flick's statements rang true. Chuck had had enough and his disdain for the man erupted into a verbal volcano. "I suggest you get your sorry ass out of here before my son kicks the shit out of you."

Losing his cool, Ducharm did something he had never done before in his business life. He slapped down the number and said, "Here's the number. Should it turn out to be true I expect an apology and a thousand dollars for my month's worth of hard work trying to get through to you knuckleheads." Slamming the door in frustration, he walked out.

Chuck, hunched over and cleaning a cooler, looked up at Flick, hesitating to touch the piece of paper. It couldn't be true. What did they have to lose by trying the number? Flick picked the piece of paper up and grinned. "That was cheaper than I thought." They both laughed.

Smiling, Chuck thought, *It DOES matter who has who by the balls.* This father and son had more in common than they realized. Both had had their share of bullshit and vultures. Both didn't trust; Chuck in a withdrawn catatonic way, Flick with fury till the day he would die.

Flick was twenty-one by this time. The girls were in their late teens and had made choices that could not be reversed. Salt was a troubled fifteen-year-old. Ruby would make fun of him and call him a "stupid retard." Salt was slow in the mind and had a raging temper. Not aware of his strength, he would fight back, and he'd hit Ruby till she was unconscious.

Social Services had gotten involved this past year after Salt had assaulted his mother. They wanted to take the girls out of Ruby's home. Kandy was nineteen and Sugar was seventeen. Both were troubled teens sporting attitudes. Their years of being abused had become the norm. The men wanted sex and Kandy had what they wanted. Sugar played along. Kandy protected her little sister with a vengeance. Money on the side allowed the girls to shop for all the girly things they liked. Men paid for the drinks and life wasn't so bad. Ruby tried to get them to pay their share of the household expenses. That was never going to happen. Money went missing when the girls were sleeping, and Ruby was snooping. That was life.

The only information the social workers had was that Salt was not doing well in school. Tests taken without Ruby's knowledge showed that he was to be considered disabled. Ruby's check went up as a result. As far as she was concerned that was a win/win situation.

Constable Kane had an older daughter who would not acknowledge her half-sisters. It was a shame because she could have been a good influence on the girls.

As time went on, Kane continued his involvement and couldn't stay away. There were two more Kane boys. Gunner and Gavin. Kane would not tolerate the clichéd names of the girls, Kandy and Sugar. Gunner was twelve and mentally slow. He was gentle as a lamb and his eyes watched everything. Ruby encouraged Gunner to act stupid, so they would get more money. That was exactly what happened. Ruby's check was increased for Gunner who was also declared disabled. Ruby was pleased with the win/win result. However, the youngest, Gavin, was sharp as a tack and had the same spirit as Liv.

Flick had spent time in a boy's home for killing the man he'd hit – a man who'd been brutalizing a helpless girl. Upon returning home, Flick realized nothing had changed and he left. He had spent most of his life protecting his sisters from the pigs of the night. When the girls went to bed, he would curl up on the floor, guarding their beds. No one would touch his sisters. Flick took over Liv's role and took his job seriously. But since he'd had to go away for a couple of years there was nothing more he could do to protect the girls.

Trouble started when Flick went back to school at nights to become a plumber. One might think that Ruby would be jealous of the attention the girls were getting. As it happened, her boy toys were giving Ruby big money, so they could have their way with Kandy and try with Sugar. They had their way with Kandy – Sugar was untouchable. When the girls figured things out over the course of a year, they demanded the money for themselves or threatened that the Johns would not see any action. The girls were clever. They knew the men's professions and threatened to rat them out. Business was business and the money went to the girls, who informed Ruby she had to work out her own problems.

Salt could not stand the flurry of men visiting. The house was in constant party mode and he was often in a fit of rage and lashed out at his mother. Police were called once again. Salt was taken away and social services got involved. Salt was placed in an all-male youth home. All-males always had Salt in a tight knot. Finally, the head of a department of social services figured out the boy's agitation. They couldn't put him in a girls' youth home. What on earth were they going to do with this boy?

Salt went to Auntie Jewels, who set up living quarters in her basement with a bedroom and bathroom. Meals were with the family and Salt went to school during the week. Salt liked his routine throughout the weekdays. His evenings were peaceful and quiet. On the weekends, though, Salt missed his family, regardless of their dysfunctional ways.

The child left in Ruby's care worth worrying about was Gavin. Flick took it upon himself to spend as much time with his brother as possible. Often, he took him for long walks, ice cream, dollar-flicks, and occasionally the arcade. Gavin loved his big brother and the time they spent together.

As usual, Ruby had a plan. Having kids at her age was getting to be too much. She didn't like them unless they were useful. Gunner brought in $1,000.00 a month for being disabled and there was the usual amount for Gavin. That would take care of the basic household bills. Ruby always had money from her boy toys for food and incidentals. They would be all right. Ruby agreed with social services and had her tubes tied.

Flick found out and thought, *Finally, an end to bringing children into the world – her world of massive dysfunction.*

Chapter 17
Calgary, 1982

Gayle visited Liv throughout the week while Gideon was away at work. Peter would golf with old friends or relax at home. This gave the couples time together in the evenings. On the weekends, Gayle and Peter consulted with Gideon and Liv to make plans. Often, the newly married couple would opt to be alone. Just as often, though, they would do something adventurous with Peter and Gayle. A happy pattern was forming.

Liv was the only one who was starving from the quiet time. She had goals of getting her PhD and it would be costly. This was something she hadn't discussed with Gideon. She knew not to talk about money for further education with her parents. They would provide without a second thought, but Gideon would be offended.

Often, she thought about her siblings and her heart ached for them. She had been a mother to the three of them; Flick, Kandy, and Sugar. Her motherly feelings were coming alive each day as her own child grew within her. Talking with her parents about finding her siblings would be a sensitive subject. As for talking with Gideon about finding her past family, she simply did not know his thoughts on the matter.

Liv wondered if the changes that had taken place in her life had left her feelings idle. She was so used to a hectic routine. Yes, her mother occupied her days in mindless ways, and time with Gideon in the evenings was a luxury, especially since the baby was coming. Time together would be a precious commodity. Time was what Liv had plenty of and she was desperate to make it meaningful and productive.

Liv realized she needed to discuss these matters with Gideon to see if they had the resources to further her education. She needed to find out how Gideon would feel about her seeking out her siblings and again, if they had the budget to accomplish the feat. Liv and Gideon had become pregnant around spring break. Their sweet baby was going to be here soon … the due date was December 25th.

***

Dinner was on the table when Gideon arrived home from work. September had not been as hot as August, though it was warm just the same. Gideon took the plates out to the patio to eat and relax, because the evening was perfect. The smile on his face showed delight.

Liv noticed. "What are you smiling about?" she asked with a grin.

"Your lovely bump is getting bigger. You can't sit right up to the table anymore," he observed with a smile.

Liv decided to broach the topic of further education. "I was wondering…" she began. "with me being home if it might be a good idea for me to go after my PhD? I'll have the time."

Gideon knew Liv still had goals and dreams. He wondered how things would work out with the upcoming changes of them having a baby. "Well, your grades would qualify you, that's for sure. The earliest you could possibly start would be the beginning of the year." He knew where he had to go on the subject. "The only concern I have is the baby will be here. Sleepless nights and focus could be a challenge. I'd worry about your health – you trying to do so much. Me trying to prove myself at work. Knowing I may not be as much help as needed." He plugged his mouth with a bite of dinner.

Liv chewed as she thought. "You have valid points. I may have to put that goal on the back burner for a while." Her thoughts went deep into her other topic and she wasn't sure how to begin.

Gideon, a wise man, was comfortable in quiet times. He finished his dinner, brought the plates back into the house, and filed them in the dishwasher. Liv sat outside and put her gaze in the trees where the birds were settling in for the evening. She was lost in her thoughts.

Gideon prepared a pot of tea and brought it out onto the patio. Liv tried to get up out of the chair, but Gideon noticed that it was a bit of struggle. He said, "It's o.k. I can pour the tea. You relax."

Liv smiled, feeling awkward in how her body was changing. Her mobility did not obey her mind and made her appear clumsy.

Gideon took a sip of tea. "What do you think about the idea of taking a painting course or joining a book club over the next few months till the baby is born?"

Liv appreciated her husband. These ideas had never occurred to her. The options had good possibilities of keeping her occupied till that grand day of their baby's debut to their world.

She smiled. "I like those ideas." She held her tea cup with both hands. "I was thinking about something else actually."

Sipping his tea, Gideon kept eye contact with Liv, letting her know he was attentive.

Liv frowned. "Well, I was thinking about spending time looking for my siblings. I just want some information. Not sure where it would take me – us – but there are so many questions that have never been answered. Mostly, I just want to know they are o.k. I'm not ready to create a larger family structure, that's for sure." She tried to smile.

Gideon knew the heart of his woman. Her desire to find her siblings did not surprise him. That Liv had idle time was an opportunity to explore this possibility. "It sounds like you have explored both the positive and negative possibilities of this venture."

"I hope so. That's why I would like to proceed with caution and decide together on the information, whatever may come."

"How would you go about seeking information?"

Apprehensively, Liv stated, "I thought of talking with my parents. They had detectives years ago that had information and might shed new light on the current situation. I don't know." She was little emotional, which was encouraged by hormones. "I also worry about my parents. How they would feel. I never want to hurt them…ever."

Gideon understood completely. "What do you think the cost would be?" He waited for an answer, but Liv did not have a reply, so he continued. "I was just thinking about the budget and weighing the possibilities of making it happen. I don't want to get into debt trying. That's all."

Liv nodded. "That makes sense." The air was getting on the chilly side and she needed to stretch. While getting up, she said, "I need to think this out a bit more. I'll keep you updated." She gave Gideon a gentle smile.

Gideon smiled back. "Sounds good."

***

Gayle was by, visiting Liv. She liked the idea of the book club and Liv possibly finding a painting class. Then she decided to let her know about the phone call.

Gayle had her cup of coffee and Liv had her cup of tea.

"I have something to share with you." Gayle started.

Liv, in a facetious mood, said, "You're pregnant too?"

"Oh, dear God, no," she laughed. "We received an interesting phone call last night."

Liv listened. "Oh? How interesting?"

Gayle blurted out, "Interestingly enough, it involved you."

Liv led a quiet life and couldn't think of any call that would involve her. "Me, you say?" she said in a teasing tone.

Gayle carried on. "Yes you." Then she paused, selecting her words. "It seems your brother, Flick, has been searching for you from the time he could mow a lawn." This was partly information from the call and partly information from Detective Ducharm's report. She watched her daughter. "It seems Detective Ducharm gave him our number."

Liv was half paralyzed, and half electrified with excitement. "You spoke with Flick?"

Gayle smiled. "Yes. Talkative fellow."

"What did he say?"

Gayle began, "Well it's a long story."

Smiling, Liv interjected immediately. "I have all day."

The ladies loved their "chat dance." Especially if one had more information she would slowly disclose, enjoying the reactions as the words flowed.

"As I said, Flick called. Dad was asleep in his reading chair, so I answered…" The story was being told…

Chapter 18
Montreal, 1982

With the paper and number in hand Flick asked if he could use the bar phone. Chuck didn't think It was a good idea. "Tell you what, I'll call the owners and ask," Chuck decided.

Jocelyn and Serge were good people and appreciated how Chuck kept the business going. He was hard-working and honest to the bone. They had no complaints. He made the call and promised that he would take care of all the charges. "No problem," the owners said. Permission granted.

Flick ran around the counter to get to the phone. Excited, he could barely control his movements, so he dialed in slow precision so as not to make a mistake. "You know this dial thing is a dinosaur. They have push buttons now you know," he teased his dad.

The phone line rang, and they waited. A lady answered. "Hello."

Flick started yammering, "My name is Flick. I have a sister Liv. Do you know her?" Without waiting for a reply, he said, "I need to talk to her." Trying to slow himself down, he stopped on the spot like a car that had hit a tree.

Gayle looked in the TV room and saw Peter was sound asleep. "Ah, yes. We have a daughter, Liv. You are her brother, you say?"

Flick in his nervousness stammered his words. "Yeesss ma'am."

Always a lady, Gayle asked, "How can I help you?"

Flick had been surprised that the number was good. He'd half expected it to be a false lead. "Ah, I would like to talk to her. Is she there?"

From Gayle's social work experience, she had a good ear, and she could hear the man's anxiety – maybe excitement and the earnestness in his voice. The tone expressed care, maybe even love. She informed Flick, "Liv is a full-grown lady and doesn't live here anymore, my dear." Once Gayle had retired and learned she was going to be a grandmother, such expressions would slip into her vocabulary.

Flick realized he was talking to an old lady but could not get off the phone. Afraid that he'd never make contact again, he was squeezing the phone with intensity. "Can you give me her number?" He hardly breathed, waiting for an answer.

Gayle did not answer right away. "I think it best that I let her know you called. I don't want her to go into premature labour. Can I have your number, young man?"

Flick's brain went into overdrive. "She's pregnant? Don't let me get my hands on the bastard."

Gayle chuckled. "Flick, I appreciate you're a good man. Liv is married to a wonderful man. I think the pregnancy is a wanted blessing. You don't have to worry about such things." She was amused and smiling.

Flick unscrambled his mind. "O.k." Then he hollered to someone, "What's the damn number here?"

***

Flick was a frazzled basket case. This was the closest they had ever come to anything positive with hopes of finding Liv. His stomach was rolling, and he hadn't eaten all day. The headache was unbearable.

Chuck had overheard the conversation and got most of the drift. Seeing the kid was a bag of nerves, he handed him a smoked-meat sandwich, water, and a couple of aspirin.

"What, you a mind reader now?" With half a smile, Flick sat the counter downing the pills and chowing down the sandwich as if he had no time to spare. "What now?"

Chuck threw the dish towel over his shoulder. "Wait. What else can we do?"

That's wasn't what Flick wanted to hear. "What if she doesn't call back?"

Chuck was afraid of that. "I guess we'll know our answer. Either she will never get the message, or she has chosen not to call."

Flick was defensive. "The first part I can believe. The second part, no way. I know my sister. She loved us then and loves us now." He shook his head.

Chuck nodded his head. "Don't know, my friend. Don't know any more than you do right now." Then Ducharm came to mind. "What about the detective? I guess we'll have to square with him."

Flick was on his game and grinning. "No way, we pretend we never got through and the number must be a hoax. O.k. we'll pay him. Just going to string the jerk along a bit." He was happy the number was good, but he didn't want to apologize to the detective anytime soon. He got up. "What do I owe ya?"

Chuck had forgotten about the meal. "It's on me," he said, putting money in the till.

"It's Thursday, right?" asked Flick. "This Saturday I want to see how my brother, Salt, is doing. Then I'm going to Old Montreal with Gavin in the afternoon." He marched out. "Have a good weekend."

Chuck shook the towel and nodded. "Yeah, you too."

***

Often referred to as an "Indian summer," this September was blistering hot in Montreal. That Saturday, Flick marched down the street to Aunty Jewel's home to see Salt's place, whistling a cheerful tune. Family was most important and making contact, possible contact, with Liv had Flick's heart singing.

He rang the doorbell and waited a minute.

Salt answered the door. "Sorry, was in the bathroom." He opened the door wider and went back into the suite. Flick entered, looking around.

The place was a studio and nice for one person. A twin bed with big pillows against the wall served as a sofa during the day and a bed in the night. The bathroom was very small, but the windows were big and brought in the daylight. *Nice*, Flick thought.

Not used to having his own place or having company, Salt was a little nervous and didn't know what to do. "Want a glass of water? I have two new glasses." He smiled.

"No. No thank you." Realizing Salt was trying his best, Flick smiled back at him. "So, what's new, little brother?"

Salt shrugged. "School is o.k. The week I don't mind. The weekends are boring." As he realized he was complaining, he blushed. "I shouldn't complain. I do like it quiet. Then, sometimes I don't like the quiet." He frowned, thinking he wasn't making sense. He didn't want to be called a stupid idiot.

Flick knew Salt well and loved him. He was impressed that Salt had a better life with Aunty Jewel's help. How he'd obtained his independence was out the ashes of their mother's horrific life. Good for him. At least one of them had a little luck going his way. "You got any plans this afternoon?"

Salt fidgeting did not answer.

Flick suggested. "You want to go to Old Montreal with Gavin and me?"

Wanting to go, Salt spurted out nervously, "I'm on the bowling team." He shuffled his feet. "Practice is this afternoon." Biting his lower lip, he wished he could get out of the bowling, so he could go with his brothers.

Flick was surprised. "Hey, I didn't know you played. That's great. You have a good time."

Salt nodded. "I have to make lunch and then go."

Flick felt he was being dismissed. "Oh, o.k. I'll visit next weekend. That work for you?"

"Yup." Salt closed the door behind Flick and stood for a half hour till it was time to make his lunch.

***

Leaving Salt's place had Flick smiling. *What do you know? Bowling. Isn't that something. Maybe the social system is not so bad after all.* Well, for a guy like Salt, it was looking pretty good for him. He was pleased to see his little brother having a life.

Flick stopped by the bar to see if there was any news and maybe grab a bite of lunch. Entering the bar, he took his usual seat at the counter. Chuck was on the phone and listening intently, whispering a few words. Then he leaned close to Flick's ear. "I think you have a phone call over there."

Flick stared at Chuck. Was it who he thought it was? Liv?

Chuck smiled. "Hurry up before she hangs up. It's a girl for you."

Flick jumped off his seat and was behind the counter in a second. He picked up the phone. "Yeah?"

It was Liv's voice in a woman's tone. "Hi Flick. How you are doing, buddy?"

Flick's legs buckled, and his tongue got tied up with his scrabbled mind. "Good, good. And you?"

Liv was just as nervous. Her heart was excited to hear Flick's voice, but her mind was wrenched with guilt for not keeping her promise – not getting in touch. "I'm great."

Silence. Neither knew what to say.

Flick stammered a few words. "So, what did Dad and you have to say?"

Liv was confused. Peter hadn't said anything and wasn't visiting. "What do you mean?"

Flick clarified. "Chuck, your dad, handed me the phone when I came in."

Liv gasped. "That was Dad?" Her emotions came alive. "He didn't say who he was. At first you weren't there and then he said you'd just come in. That's all he said. Sorry to sound surprised. Just that, well, my adoptive parents had a report from some detective …"

"Ducharm. Can't believe a word that man says," Flick said with disgust. "Yup." With a smile. "Do you want to talk to him?"

Liv was hesitant. What would she say? Chuck sounded like a quiet man. Her dad was Peter. "If it's o.k. with you, I would like to talk with you. Then, learn about the girls. I don't know if I'm ready to talk to adults right now. Sounds crazy, right?"

Flick understood. "No, doesn't sound crazy at all. I understand."

The siblings chatted for over an hour. Liv gave Flick her number, so they could talk any time they wanted. Both expressed how much they cared. The love came through without the words. As they hung up they both smiled and said to themselves. "This is a great day." It was a new day for new beginnings.

When Flick got off the phone he saw his father, Chuck, smiling. "Good call?"

"Great call. Best day ever."

Chuck was pleased. Just then they both noticed Ducharm had been sitting in a booth within ear shot. How long had he been there?

Ducharm was now smiling. "I think you owe me an apology. I'll be happy to settle for a beer. Thanks."

Chuck handed Ducharm his beer and Ducharm took a sip. Chuck pointed at the beer. "I take it you accept our apology."

Ducharm was in a good mood and flashing a cocky grin. "Yeah, and I'm ready to accept my payment of a thousand dollars right about now."

Chuck asked Flick to mind the bar while he went upstairs to his room to fetch the money. Back in a few minutes, he walked over to Ducharm. "We are square."

Ducharm took the money and opened his empty wallet. "You boys ever need my services you know who to call." He walked out.

Flick had been about to whiplash Ducharm with his thoughts when Chuck had kicked him in the shins and he sat back down. "All I wanted him to know was I would rather rot in a bin of apples with maggots before I'd ask for his help."

Chuck smiled. "He did come through. You did get to talk with Liv. That's more than we ever expected in a hundred years."

Flick nodded. "True. What's the lunch special?"

Chuck handed him a bag with two steamed hotdogs. "I think you're late having the afternoon with Gavin in Old Montreal."

Grabbing the bag, Flick muttered, "Damn, you're right. Thanks." He stumbled off in a hurry and was out the door in a shot.

Shots rang out in the air. Ducharm was beside his car, face up, eyes glazed over looking into space and nowhere. Dead.

***

Gavin was sitting on the door step waiting for Flick. "What took you so long? You're late."

Flick smiled. "Yeah, sorry. A girl called me and ... well, you know ... we got talking."

Gavin might be young, but he was sharp and gave his brother the gears. "Oh, so a girl was more important than me?"

"In this case. Yes." They walked towards the bus stop to get to Old Montreal.

Flick was excited about the call. The day had been so great, and he had to share it with Gavin. "You know we have an older sister named Liv?"

Gavin blinked. "Yeah, Ma talks bad of her. She left us and caused Mom a lot of trouble. That's what I hear anyway."

Flick decided to set the record straight. "Is that so? Let me tell you something. Liv is such a beautiful person. She left because Mom was bad to her. Like Mom is with Kandy and Sugar. Liv left and made a life for herself." He was still hurt that she'd never come for them. But, that was in the past. They were talking and that's all that mattered. Liv was in his life. He wanted them all in his life.

Gavin, listening and hearing his big brother's excitement, asked, "Can I talk to her?"

Flick thought about it. "She called at the bar. You're not old enough to go there. I'll see what I can do. No promises. O.k?"

Gavin wanted promises. Flick never failed with his promises. O.k., sometimes he was late but that was o.k. "O.k. But, you'll try right?"

Flick nodded. "Right."

The boys had a great time. Artists were hanging out on the cobblestone streets and selling their pieces. Jugglers and performers competing for attention were fun as they engaged the audience and made people laugh. It was such a good time. Such a great day. They walked a few blocks to Chinatown and had a bowl of won ton before Flick took Gavin back home.

This day was *the* day to remember. It was the greatest of all!

Chapter 19
Calgary

The day started on a lovely Saturday morning when Liv placed "the call." The call that linked her to her past after sixteen years. To support his wife, Gideon sat at the kitchen table and sipped his coffee. Liv was nervous, fingering the rim of her tea cup and biting her lower lip. Gideon smiled a reassuring grin.

Gideon could tell that the call was awkward at first, but he thought Liv handled her feelings well. He wasn't surprised that she wasn't prepared to contact Chuck just yet. Liv loved and adored her father, Peter. Gideon knew his wife well and could see her heart alive with love as she spoke with her brother. Her mind seemed divided with the thought of talking with Chuck. Understandable.

Liv had been quiet when Flick was sharing the facts about Kandy and Sugar. Her face showed fear, sadness, and heartache. Shaking her head, she covered the mouthpiece of the phone, telling Gideon, "Unbelievable, Ruby never changed."

Liv shared the details of her life and Flick shared that there were more siblings; Salt, Gunner, and Gavin. Liv could not believe she had so many siblings. Before hanging up, she covered the mouthpiece once again. "Don't mind if I give Flick our number?" she asked Gideon.

Gideon smiled and whispered, "That's o.k." It tickled his heart to see his wife filled with excitement, and he was pleased that Liv was bridging the years lost and now found. Secretly he was happy that the contact had been made by Gayle. It helped that Liv's mother was on board and with no hurt feelings. Then again, Gayle was a social worker who understood Maslow's Hierarchy better than anyone. Peter and Gayle provided all they could for their daughter to reach Maslow's best place in life... her "self actualization." Even though Liv had been lavished with acceptance and love, there was a gap that prevented their daughter from being fully whole, fully complete. The gap was coming to peace with the past, coming to peace about promises never fulfilled.

Gayle, a wise woman, knew that all they had invested in their daughter would never bring them regret. She knew that love multiplies and does not divide. With never a jealous bone in her body, Gayle had been concerned about Liv's earlier years with Ruby, her biological mother, manipulating them and causing them grief. Liv, now a woman, and married with her own life was capable of sorting things out for herself. She was a grown woman who knew her heart and possessed a great mind.

It was time to bridge the past to the present and move on to the future. Whatever this might prove to be.

***

CHILD'S LOVE

Liv's heart felt complete. The love of her husband, her parents, her baby snuggled inside of her, and now of her brother had her bursting with joy.

Learning of her sisters broke her heart and she wondered if she had fulfilled her promise, whether things would have been different for them. Discovering that her family from the past had grown, three more boys in her absence, had her mind in a whirl. Two of the boys had disabilities. Apparently one of them, Salt, had his own home, was active in bowling, and had a simple, quality life. Memories flashed of when she had resided with Aunt Jewels. Her heart knew she was loved and cared for. It bothered her that the other boy with disabilities, Gunner, was still at home under Ruby's thumb. Then, according to Flick, the youngest was Gavin, who seemed to be a lot like Liv.

Ruby had been briefly mentioned when Liv and Flick had discussed how the girls had been living. Flick did not hold back his thoughts and how Ruby was responsible, or more like irresponsible. Liv could feel his disdain with regards to this situation. He'd expressed how he had tried with all his heart to protect the girls. He was upset with himself that he was not home, because he was going to night school and getting his education to become a plumber.

Flick hadn't been able to bring himself to tell Liv he had killed a man and spent time in a boys' home – juvenile detention. He was proud that the end of this year he would be a master plumber. Liv was so proud and pleased with Flick's devotion to family and commitment to bettering himself.

Gideon and Liv chatted about the phone call over lunch. Then the phone rang ...

***

Gayle was on the phone, eager to find out how the call had gone. She remembered the anxious loquacious young man, who'd first called her a few days prior asking to speak with Liv. Flick was a little rough around the edges, but one could sense integrity, loyalty to family, intense with his passion to contact Liv. Flick's heart had apparently never weakened over time, if anything it had intensified, his love for his sister Liv was so evident.

"How did the call go?" Gayle asked with her heart in a flutter, smiling.

Liv was smiling. "Oh, you want the details?"

Gayle suggested that Liv and Gideon come over that afternoon for coffee. t

Liv wondered, "How does Dad feel about this?"

"He's always concerned; he loves you of course. He wants to hear what happened. So, do I," said Gayle in a cheerful tone.

Liv explained to Gideon that Peter and Gayle would like them to visit because they wanted to know what had happened. Liv felt it would be good to share what she had learned and find out how her father, Peter, was feeling. Gideon agreed.

"We'll be right over."

***

They met in the afternoon with excitement and hesitation when discussing "the call." Gayle had prepared Peter, explaining the need for their daughter to come to terms with her past. Peter tried to understand, knowing that he and Gayle were getting on in years – they were in their seventies. Gayle knew Liv was set in life with a wonderful man. Their home would bring the couple a lifetime of memories, especially with the little one on the way. Having a big family would complete Liv's life before Gayle and Peter were no longer a part of her future.

It was time for Liv to know her siblings. Regardless of how these people turned out to be, Gayle was confident Liv had all the tools necessary to navigate her thoughts and emotions. She believed Liv would be able to come to terms with whatever she discovered and find peace. Gayle knew Liv was a well-prepared woman. Peter though, was always concerned about the unknowns. Secretly, he was most comfortable being his little girl's hero.

All attention was on Liv as the story unfolded. Peter weighed every word; the consequences and possible results, just like the lawyer he was. Gayle hung onto every word, paying attention to the impact emotionally, holistically, much like the social worker she was. Gideon listened to each little story, considering whether there would be further ideas and ideals his wife would be exploring.

Liv chatted about how Flick had gone to night school to become a plumber and that he would soon be a master plumber. She was thrilled her brother was making something of himself, but she spoke about Kandy and Sugar with great concern and expressed that she would not be interfering with their lives. She felt that she wouldn't know how to help the girls or help them make changes for the better. Gideon said, "It's hard to paint over zebra stripes when you want a horse. Or to remove the spots from a Dalmatian." Chuckles filled the room.

Peter and Gayle were hoping that Liv would let the girls alone as they were walking in the footsteps of their mother. Ruby was trouble on her own, and with the girls it was triple-fold. Nothing good could come of encouraging these girls to become family. Gideon knew the heart of his wife, but he thought much the same as Peter and Gayle. He knew Liv's heart was rooted deeper, hoped greater, loved grander, and fell harder than anyone's he knew. He suspected that if there was a way to better the girls' lives Liv would find that way.

Peter and Gayle had not been aware of the three other brothers. Salt had been born after Liv left Montreal. Since despite his handicaps Salt was living on his own in a suite at Aunty Jewels, and involved with a bowling team, Liv felt o.k. about him. Anyone out of Ruby's home had a chance. Then there was the boy, Gunner, still residing in Ruby's clutches. Liv suspected Ruby was making sure Gunner would never leave home, as she needed the money. The youngest was Gavin. Liv smiled, talking about what she knew about him. She liked what she'd heard about his character. He reminded her of herself. He had spunk and wouldn't put up with Ruby's ways.

Each with his or her own thoughts they kept their ears alert, quiet and listening, wanting to know what Liv was going to do with all this information. Thank goodness Liv was a cautious sort, a planner, with a bit of spontaneity. Would she want to go and visit her siblings in Montreal? Would she try to have them move to Calgary, like she had planned when she was a little girl?

Liv was perceptive and said, "I'm not going to do anything right now. I am going to take care of myself, have our baby, and enjoy the family I have."

Everyone smiled, pleased with what they'd heard.

"I will stay in touch with Flick. I like him and want to get to know him better." Liv lowered her head. "There is one more thing. I have no desire to make contact with Ruby and I'm not sure about Chuck. The things I remember about him were wonderful. I don't understand why he never tried to find me."

Everyone's smile faded.

"I have mixed feelings about talking to him. I do remember some moments very clearly. I know he loved me dearly. I want you to know, Dad… You are the only father that has my heart, but I want to make peace with the man, Chuck. I understand he is a broken man over my disappearance, and I feel I owe him the decency to show him that there are no hard feelings. I want to let him know how you cared for me, loved me, and gave everything so I could be the person I am today. I don't want Chuck to die unfulfilled, having never found me." Her voice got quieter. "But, I don't want to hurt you." She looked at Peter.

Peter wanted to say, *then don't,* but instead, he said, "That will never happen. You do what your heart tells you. You are MY little girl, now and forever." Trying to be a bigger man, he smiled, but the tears did escape his eyes.

Gayle understood her man. Peter couldn't share Liv and wanted never to do so. She said in his defense, "He just loves you so very much, dear."

Gideon suggested going out to dinner at the Calgary Tower. Peter said it was good idea, but he thought reservations were required.

Peter stepped out into the kitchen and called the restaurant to see their possibilities. Then he came back to the living room. "We're set. Everyone ready?"

The evening was enjoyed with chatter about Christmas. The best Christmas gift to be unwrapped would be – the birth of their child on Christmas Day. Of course, Christ too… but, their child and grandchild.

As they enjoyed their evening drinks, a sticky subject was about to fill the air. Peter thought the relaxed environment would give Gayle and him an edge in their favor to accomplish providing the treasures of their heart. "We'd like Gayle and Liv to go shopping for the baby's furniture. It would be our only Christmas gifts for all of you. It would be nice to have everything set up and ready, don't you think?" Gayle believed it was important to start Christmas shopping as early as June. You could get the gifts that mattered, have the best selection, and never be disappointed. September was running late as far as Gayle was concerned.

Liv said nothing and smiled at her mother. Everyone was waiting to hear what Gideon had to say, knowing the conversation had not gone so well the last time.

Gideon knew he was on the hot seat. "I'll tell you what. We have a budget and would like to provide for our child. Gayle and Liv can go shopping. Should Liv's desired set exceed our budget you can provide, within $1,000." Everyone wanted to know the budget because Gideon hadn't disclosed the number to Liv to date. The suspense was beyond all their patience. Then the number was shared and deemed reasonable. The first obstacle to Gayle and Peter's gift giving had been overcome and the spirit of Christmas was still over three months away. Liv knew she was going to be busy the coming weeks. But, she was more excited about this Christmas than any other. It was about her expanding family.

Later Liv and Gideon settled into bed with Gideon hugging and spooning. He loved falling asleep snuggling Liv and feeling the baby.

In the wandering of her dreams, Liv realized that downtime was so important to preparing and planning to be a good mom ... *to be the best, great mom, it's all in the planning. And of course, in the doing. But let's not forget the execution of the plan. What can go wrong, usually does ... be prepared to re-evaluate the plan.* Liv fell asleep from pure exhaustion due to the emotion that had started the day from "the call."

Chapter 20
Montreal, 1982

Every week Flick called Liv from the bar. Chuck was present – he couldn't stay away. His only connection to his daughter, who didn't know him, was through eavesdropping on Flick's calls. Chuck was sad his parents had gone to their deaths, but he was glad that they didn't know his limited connection to Liv. Liv's disappearance had been more than Chuck's parents could manage, their hearts had been broken.

Over the course of the fall, Flick completed his masters in plumbing. The final exam was the first week of December. Flick had ideas about showing up in Calgary and asked Chuck to come with him.

Chuck wanted to see his daughter, but he wasn't sure Liv was ready. He'd sensed she had reservations about him since Flick's first contact. So, he decided it wasn't a good idea and declined Flick's offer.

A Christmas party for a business function was scheduled at the bar. That evening, Chuck was working mostly for the tips. The owners, Jocelyn and Serge, put chains on the back door to prevent people from walking out without paying. As luck would have it, a fire broke out in one of the bathrooms. Chuck tried to get people out. Everything Chuck ever owned; the money he'd saved, pictures of his parents, siblings, aunts, uncles, and of Liv, went up in smoke. The place went down.

The fire department did all they could but found many dead at the back door. Police were talking to the owners and Chuck overheard Serge blame him for the chains on the back door… blame him for the deaths. He also overheard the police say, "It doesn't matter; you are responsible for your establishment." Serge went pale. Jocelyn threw up.

After all his hard work, free hours, and keeping the business in operation, now Serge and Jocelyn were trying to make him the fall guy. Chuck honestly hadn't known about the chains on the back door. The police spoke with him and realized he was a patsy. They told him to not leave town because they might need him to testify.

Chuck stood in a daze watching the smoke and chaos. Flick showed up. "What the hell is going on?"

"The worse hell ever," Chuck said, shaking his head. "Let's get a cup of coffee down the street." He didn't know where else to go.

Flick agreed. It was freezing in the middle of winter, but Chuck hadn't noticed from the heat of the fire. Both walked in silence, deep in their own thoughts. The café was open, and Flick took care of the bill. Chuck realized he didn't have a dime in his pocket. The cash register had been handled by the owners when business was rocking. The tips in the jar had gone down with the flames. Besides, Chuck had been too busy helping people escape with their lives. He hadn't thought about the effect of the situation that would plague his life from now on. It hit him like a brick: *I'm penniless, I'm homeless!*

Chuck couldn't believe his bad luck and trying to muster up his courage, he said, "If it wasn't for shit luck, I'd have no luck at all."

Flick was multitasking, weighing his own thoughts and listening to Chuck.

An hour had passed when Flick brought forward his proposal. "It might be time for a change. Now's as good time as any."

Chuck threw Flick a look that said, *don't go there*.

Flick was impatient. "What have you got to lose? Going to Calgary, the odds are better that you will get to see or get to know Liv." Daring Chuck to say differently, he added, "I have enough money to get us to Calgary by bus, enough to set us up in a simple place. I can get work right away, o.k.? In the new year." He waited to hear what Chuck was thinking and then continued, "We can do this. We won't be alone trying. I believe our luck is turning around."

Chuck, catatonic, said, "I'm not allowed to leave town."

Flick said, "You can tell them you'll stay in touch – get their business card. I would just leave, to hell with them all." He smiled.

Chuck got up after the last sip of his coffee. "I'll be right back." But Flick followed.

Chuck went to find the officer. Now Homicide was on the scene. The crime scene had yellow ribbons all over the place. Officer Kane came out of the rumble. He recognized Flick, took a second look at Chuck, and then approached. "What do you guys have to do with this?"

Flick barked, "Nothing."

Chuck blinked. "I was a bartender here. I was told to not leave town."

Kane writing notes, asked, "What's your name?"

"Chuck Riley. Can I have your business card? I don't know where I'm going to be. I was living on the top floor till …"

Kane knew the name and looked hard at the man. "Sure. Where you going to stay?"

Flick had the answer. "My place."

***

Back at Flick's studio apartment, the two sat at the bistro-style table with two chairs. Flick pulled out a towel and a set of clothes. "We're the same size. You're full of blood and soot. Here. Take a shower."

When Chuck came out of the bathroom, he saw that the single-bed mattress had been pulled to the floor. Flick took the box spring with a blanket and gave Chuck the mattress. Both settled in for the night, awake, lost in their own thoughts.

Morning came. Chuck said, "I'll go with you. I'll get a job right away Sorry, to be a burden, son."

Flick was thrilled. He ran out the door and a half an hour later came back with coffee and donuts. "I talked to my landlord. He's not too happy about the short notice, but I negotiated, and he settled with the apartment being left furnished. Figured he'd get more now with me gone. We can go anytime."

Early Sunday morning, they bused themselves to Ruby's for Flick to see his siblings and say a quick goodbye. Flick had bought a backpack for Chuck with a change of clothes. He carried a duffle bag for himself with his clothes, certificates, and cash.

Chuck wasn't too pleased going near Ruby's place after all these years and hearing the stories. He sat on the steps even though the weather was in the minus. Flick went into the flat and Chuck could hear the kids' excitement upon seeing him, and then the words of, "No, don't go." The young boys were crying and pleading. The girls were not up yet. Cringing, Chuck suspected it had been a late night due to their occupation and lack of direction from Ruby. He hated the thought that she had anything to do with the young girls being street walkers. But the hard fact was; he was not their father.

From the corner of Chuck's eye, he saw someone look through the drapes and peek out the window. He heard Ruby ask, "What's he doing here? How do you know him?"

Flick mumbled something not audible and was out the door within a moment's time.

"Let's go. I have to see Salt. Just remembered." He wanted to say he was sorry for another delay, but he was sorting his emotions and thoughts on the run.

Chuck sensed Flick was preoccupied. Without a dime in his pocket, he found himself on the boy's clock. One more bus ride took them to Salt's at Aunty Jewel's. The boy was not home, and so Flick left a note under the door. "Gone to see Liv. Will be away for a while. Coming back to get you, if you want. Think about it. I have your address. Will contact you." He was about to write, "Don't tell Ruby," when he remembered the boy couldn't read. He'd probably have Auntie Jewels read it for him.

Flick had fire under his heels now, and they were off to the next bus to get them to Berri-du-Montagne. The Voyageur Bus was leaving at 9:00 that night for the border of Ontario. The next bus would be direct to Winnipeg. Then Winnipeg to Calgary. Fifty-eight hours would have them arriving on Wednesday morning if all went well.

They settled in at the back of the bus. Both were tired with the running around and waiting, and they slept when they could with the constant sound and motion of the running bus.

The next morning, Flick and Chuck were in Ontario picking up coffee and muffins to go and making the connecting bus to Winnipeg. This time they sat up front to take in the scenery, in hopes of keeping their minds occupied.

The bus had been on the road for an hour when Flick asked, "What changed your mind about coming?"

Chuck had to think for a minute. "I couldn't think of a thing that was keeping me in Montreal. Couldn't think why I shouldn't go when my whole goal in life had always been providing for my siblings and hoping to find Liv." Shrugging his shoulders, he said, "I had everything to gain by trying. Felt excited about the prospect of going to Calgary and being closer ... maybe even meeting Liv." He smiled. "I have to try. You gave me the chance. In fact, I can't thank you enough."

Flick smiled too and nodded.

Chuck had a few questions on his mind for Flick. "Back at the fire, Constable Kane seemed to know you?"

Flick said, "Yeah. He was the officer involved when Liv bit Ruby's boyfriend's arm. Suppose it was my father, John Bick. Never met him."

Chuck sensed there was more and waited, listening.

Flick knew Chuck was waiting. "Well, Kane would visit Ruby. Kane is Kandy and Sugar's father."

Chuck wanted to puke.

Flick tossed his empty coffee cup on the floor. "Yeah, I know him." He paused and thought ... might as well give Chuck the whole story. "You know my brother Salt has a father named something Pepper. That's why his name is Salt N. Pepper. Cute right? Ruby's clever mind. You know the Ducharm guy?"

Chuck looked at him from the side and nodded. He remembered seeing the man dead outside the bar. Shot in the side of the head. It had happened so fast the man didn't know what hit him, and Chuck guessed it was best.

Flick continued, "He was a real bastard. Pervert. Feeling me up when I was a kid. Well, Gunner and Gavin might be his kids. Ruby tangled Kane into believing he was the father. You see Ducharm had a gambling problem and Ruby couldn't get a cent from the asshole."

Suddenly Chuck understood how this kid had the detective figured. This explained why Flick couldn't stand the guy. Also, he'd known the double agent was in need of money and how to play him. He smiled. "It all makes sense now."

Flick smiled back. "I thought it would."

The journey to Winnipeg felt like it took a week. Getting off the bus, they stretched their achy muscles and stiff bones. The cold air was refreshing. After a few minutes, though, it had them seeking out their next connection to Calgary.

Wednesday morning arrived and so did the guys in Calgary, faced with blistering cold weather as they got off the bus. They stayed in the bus terminal to stretch, get a coffee, and look at a paper to find a rental place.

Chuck had heard about men's hostels and some of the stories had him believing the situation was not safe. For himself with no money, he didn't care. But he had a sense of fatherly protection that had him wanting to find their own place that would be safe. People came and went, ignoring them. They'd lacked a bath and hadn't had a change of clothing in days. They looked like bums from their journey.

Flick found a map of the city and compared the areas advertised for rooms, seeking the cheapest that would put them in a warm place for the time being. He took his change and started making calls. There was a place along the Elbow River about twenty blocks from downtown and not far from the Stampede grounds. The lady he called had a little girl crying in the background and gave him the address. She said she had to meet them and then she would decide. The phone went dead.

With no idea of the bus routes in the city, they decided to walk. According to the map the streets went one way and the avenues another. It didn't seem too difficult.

Walking briskly in the cold air, they arrived within the hour and knocked on the door. A lady introduced herself as Annabelle and explained she was a renter on the main floor.

The owner had retired to Mexico or some hot place. She looked at the two with questions in her eyes.

Flick was quick and said, "This is my father Chuck. I am a master plumber." He showed her his certificates. My father is a bartender. We are hardworking people. We would like to get out of the cold and look at the suite."

Annabelle hollered to a man to keep an eye on the baby, took her jacket, and walked around to the back of the house. Down a few stairs led to a hallway with several doors. She explained the first door was a shared shower stall and the second door was the shared toilet, and she always reminded them to lock the suite door even when using the shower or toilet. At the end of the hall opened a suite with a small, L-shaped kitchen. To the left was a larger room with a twin bed. It looked like a living room with a recliner, desk, and a small TV with rabbit ears. There was a phone jack in the wall near the kitchen. The price was $500.00. Then the lady explained it was $250.00 rent and $250.00 deposit. This was the only suite with a kitchen. They took it on sight.

Annabelle informed them there was a second-hand store not too far that might interest them. Safeway was down two blocks in the same direction. They spent the afternoon picking up two sets of twin-size bedding, towels, a thick piece of foam to make up another bed, a few plates, bowls, cups, glasses, cutlery, a kettle, and a banged-up set of pots and pans. After setting everything up, they headed back to Safeway to get a few groceries. It was after seven in the evening before they sat down on the twin bed to eat dinner. There was no kitchen table, but no one was complaining.

Flick was pleased and said they would have to get a phone hooked up with an answering machine. Much needed when job hunting. Christmas was a week away and the job hunt didn't look too promising. The paper was scant with prospects this time of year. Chuck nodded in agreement. They put the TV on, which had two channels, to catch the news and get a feel for the new city.

One took a shower and then shaved in the kitchen sink. Then the other did the same. After that, they set up the beds and took to sleep faster than one could blink. The journey had been long. Their first day had been endless. Tomorrow would bring them into their new lives. Flick fell asleep remembering he was going to call Liv. Yes, she would have the surprise of her life. Her brother was in town …

***

Flick woke early in the morning eager to get on with the day. He wanted to get pen and paper and put a notice up with a phone number that he was a master plumber looking for work. S he had to get the phone going before anything else. Once the clock struck 9:00 a.m. they were out the door. Chuck tagged along as Flick was at the drug store asking questions and getting paper and pens. The girl asked if they needed resumes as she would be happy to type them up for a small fee. The boys said they would take her up on the offer as soon as they obtained a phone.

Both Flick and Chuck were feeling better about their luck. Walking by a laundromat, they noticed a commotion. The pipes had broken, and the owner was opening the door with water gushing out the sidewalk. On a freezing day, this was disastrous. Flick asked if he could help and explained that he was a master plumber looking for work. The guy showed him into the place and where he thought the problem had surfaced.

Flick told the man he would be back and went to the second-hand store to get a few basic tools that would take care of the issue. Back at the laundromat, he took charge and instructed Chuck on what to do to help. Watching, the owner was so impressed as his problem resolved before his very eyes.

The man was a foreigner and spoke with broken English. He told them his Canadian name was Bob. Then he asked with a smile, "How much I owe you?"

Flick explained he was looking for work and did not have the resources to start up a business and that they, he and his dad, had just arrived yesterday in Calgary.

Bob nodded then smiled. "I am businessman. We clean up water. Then we talk. O.k.?" Bob's wife Lilly was told to take care of the laundromat and Bob walked out, motioning to

Chuck and Flick to follow. They went to a café where Bob talked with a buddy. They all were wet and freezing. The coffee was welcomed. Bob sat down, eyes flickering in thought as if calculating with an abacus before uttering another word. The boys sat quietly waiting, wondering what Bob had on his mind. Just being out of the cold, in a warm place with hot coffee, kept them interested in the moment.

Bob spoke. "I see certificates, Flick."

Flick pulled out an envelope with his credentials for Bob to view.

Bob looked and then stared with a flat expression. "I do business with you. I help you set up. I take thirty percent of profit. I send people to you. We do good you and me." He watched to see their expressions.

Flick wasn't sure if it was a good offer and said, "I'd like to talk it over with my dad and get back to you tomorrow."

Bob smiled. "Tonight. Have lots to do. Go to City with business name. Want it in your name. I take additional 20% for costs to set up business. You pay back setup costs then the 20% stops. Then, we make good money." He wrote his phone number down. "What business name you like?"

Flick had a sense of humor and wasn't serious when he said, "Dirty Deeds Plumbing."

Bob grinned. "I like it. It will be your business. We have a deal?"

Flick looked at Chuck to gauge his thoughts on the proposal.

Chuck whispered, "It seems our luck is turning for the better. What do we have to lose?"

Flick wanted to know when they would get paid. Bob explained how the clients pay in increments. Half up front to get materials to do the job. Then, other twenty-five percent before hook-up and final inspection. Once hooked up, a check for the remainder. Bob explained he would go on jobs with Flick to put in estimates and was certain to get most jobs they went out for. He mentioned he could get the word out with his friends to put in new hot water tanks, new furnaces, and to do furnace cleaning. He wanted to bid on contracts with new businesses and locations such as boutiques, hair salons, nail salons, dentists, chiropractors, etc.

Flick nodded and then said, "I want my dad to follow in your footsteps and learn how you bid. He could save us lots of time and be out their securing work. My father is a quiet man, business focused, and a quick learner. I can do the jobs, sometimes with my dad's help. Do we have a deal?"

Bob nodded then smiled. "Deal." Tapping a pen, he said, "I want to see you in morning. I know I have work for you. I know you need tools, we make purchases. We use old van there." It was a beat-up, old blue van.

Flick said, "If it runs, it will do."

The men got up. "8:00 a.m. here. I have news, o.k?"

Flick walked out with his mind on business. Chuck walked out wondering how the hell this had happened. Walking back home, Flick laughed. "Our luck was changing."

Chuck had to laugh too. "It sure seems that way." Laughing harder, he said, "I don't know a thing about plumbing and you got me a job as well."

Flick was on his game as usual. "Ah, a little bullshit goes a long way." He smiled.

The fact was, Chuck was a quick learner and would prove to be the best man for the bidding jobs.

***

Flick didn't forget anything. He remembered the girl at the drugstore and that he'd promised to hire her for their resumes. They had gotten a phone line hooked up, but resumes were no longer needed. He entered the drugstore and made eye contact with the girl. "So, what do I owe you for two resumes?"

The girl blinked. "Well, I haven't done them up yet."

Flick smiled. "We got jobs right after we left here the other day. I want to pay you anyway. I'm a man of my word."

The girl smiled too. "I am a girl of my word. I only charge for the work I do. You were kind to consider me and it didn't turn out. That's o.k."

Flick wanted to get to know this girl. He had a good feeling that she was honest and hardworking. "I'm Flick. And you are?"

The girl did not think he would be interested in her. She considered herself plain, too quiet, and too busy to be adventurous. This man standing before her had a charisma she had never seen before. He seemed a straight-forward, honest, with a little charm, and busting with energy. "I'm Hannah."

Flick knew he had her interest. "When's a good time to have coffee?"

Hannah shared, "I go jogging tomorrow, every Saturday morning and stop over there for breakfast and coffee. You'll find me around 9:00 a.m." She smiled and went back to work.

Flick was at the café 9:00 a.m. sharp. He forgot about his usual call to Liv at 9:00 a.m. Calgary time.

Chapter 21
Calgary, 1982

Saturday was Liv's favorite day of the week. Talking with Flick each week had been a social outlet with someone who was family, a friend, and close to her age. She loved the chats, jokes, and interaction. Flick had interesting views about life. He once said his family was a beautiful garden that needed maintenance. You had to pull the weeds to keep the garden healthy. The weeds were the people's crap, in other words: bullshit. A little crass, a lot of truth – that seemed to work for Flick.

Nine a.m. came and went. This was the first call ever missed by Flick since the beginning with "the call" last September. Liv was a little worried and decided to call him. She dialled the number and the recording said it was out of order. Wasn't that the number to the bar that Chuck worked at? Strange as it seemed, Liv found herself needing to stay by the phone. She sensed something was not right, but she had no idea what would prevent Flick from calling or why the phone number was not in service.

Liv sipped her tea. Gideon was busy setting up the playpen and jolly jumper in the family room. Christmas was one week away, Saturday, and their baby was due. Liv hadn't been feeling all that well the past two days. Her tummy was hard to the touch and the baby wasn't moving nearly as much. In fact, there'd been no movement at all this morning. She'd tried to eat toast and after one bite thought it would come up. Liv's back had ached all night and she was more uncomfortable throughout the day.

She stood up to see Gideon's progress on the small builds. Suddenly there was warm water running down her legs. Frozen for a moment, she looked down. "Honey, I think my water broke."

Gideon was at her side in a second and looked at the puddle on the hardwood floor. "Yup, I would say it's time to get to the hospital." Smiling, he ran to the garage to pick up the already-packed overnight bag and warm up the car. Then he returned to help Liv walk to the car and held her with his strength. He might as well have carried Liv, as she was only tip-toeing with her belly bulging and losing her balance.

Liv reminded Gideon to make a quick call to her parents to let them know the event of their life was unfolding. Once she was seated in the front with the seat as far back as possible, Gideon ran into the house. He made the call and then ran back to the car and reassured Liv they were ready for this. Driving as though he was a race car driver he was smiling all the way.

Liv hung on for dear life, panting and breathing irregularly as the contractions came with great intensity and then relaxed. A few minutes passed, and the contractions were present each time. The drive to the hospital was only ten minutes, but it felt like an hour as Gideon was in a hurry dodging the light traffic of people heading to the malls to get their Christmas shopping accomplished. The shoppers must have thought Gideon in his car was a maniac.

They made it to the Rocky Mountain Hospital in record time. A porter with a good eye came out with a wheelchair ready to help. Liv was paralysed with contractions and waiting for a reprieve. The porter and Gideon assisted her out of the car and wheeled her to emergency. The nurses were quick to get her to the delivery floor and then a room. Gideon stayed back for the paper work, but he was anxious to get to his wife. His mind thought, *they take any longer and I'm going to miss the birth of our child.* Gideon was finished with admissions when Gayle and Peter came running to his side. Gayle was eager to know everything. "How is she?"

Gideon said. "Just got here – they took her to labour and delivery. I'm trying to find her. She's in labour that's for sure. Don't know anything more."

A porter directed the three of them to the appropriate floor and Gideon was ushered to the delivery suite where Liv was in labour. Peter and Gayle took a seat in the waiting room. Two hours later, Gideon came out and announced, "It's a baby boy. Eight pounds, five ounces. Oh, and his lungs are good." Smiling, he ran back.

Peter and Gayle laughed. They had heard the fierce and powerful cry of a baby a few moments earlier.

Liam Anthony Peter Harley made his debut to the world on December 18th. Mother and baby were doing well. Liv liked acronyms. Liam meant 'Love I am.' Anthony was for Gideon's dad. Peter was for Liv's dad. Gideon was sharp and a little worried the baby's initials would spell L A P H – in other words, laugh.

Mother and baby were sent to the Maternity/Child ward and Liam got settled after his exhausting journey to meet his parents. Peter and Gayle entered the room with tears in their eyes as they shared the joy of being grandparents. Another blessing that had enriched their lives because of the miracle of Liv.

Gideon's family arrived later and shared in the excitement of baby Liam as the new addition to the family. Gideon's dad was touched and pleased the baby would share his name, Anthony.

Baby Liam was scheduled for discharge home by Wednesday the 22nd. A rocking cradle had been set up in the sitting area of the grand master bedroom. The new parents wanted their baby close by.

***

Flick called on Saturday around 2:00 p.m. No answer. After trying numerous times, he chose to not leave a message. He wanted to tell Liv he was in Calgary when he was talking with her, and he wondered if she had tried to get a hold of him. Then he realized the place had burned down and the number would not ring. By Sunday afternoon with no answer, Flick wondered if Liv had gone into labour.

Sunday evening, Flick was having dinner with Chuck and informed him of his missed call – how he'd been busy meeting the girl, Hannah, from the drug store and had forgotten about the Saturday ritual of talking with Liv. They wondered if Liv had the baby and only hoped all was well. It was up to Flick to reach Liv.

Suddenly, a lightning bolt of thought jolted Flick. It was then he realized he'd saved the sacred piece of paper that Ducharm had thrown on the counter. It was Gayle and Peter's number. Of course, he would give them a call.

It was around 8:00 p.m. when Flick called the Pattersons' home. After few rings, Gayle answered, "Hello." Peter had nodded off to sleep after a full dinner and the evening news.

Flick had not talked with Gayle after that initial call and hoped she wouldn't mind his inquiry. "Hello, this is Flick," he said, hesitatingly because he was not sure of the welcome. Somehow, he felt as if they knew that he was close and in Calgary, but of course they did not know. "I missed my call with Liv this Saturday. Was trying to reach her all weekend and hoped she was doing o.k?"

Gayle remembered Flick well. He was often part of the power chats she and her daughter shared. She didn't think Liv would mind divulging personal information to Flick. He was family, her friend, and Liv enjoyed and looked forward to their interactions. "Liv wondered what happened on Saturday. She missed your call."

Flick, feeling guilty, said, "I know. I'm so sorry." He didn't want to say his mind had been on a girl and he'd forgotten to call.

Gayle was quick to let him off the hook. "Liv did call the bar and found it disconnected. We were worried something happened."

Flick, so busy with coming to Calgary, working, setting up a business ... starting to have a personal life ... had completely forgotten about the fire. It seemed like a lifetime ago. "Yes, the place burned down.

Gayle was taken aback. "I hope no one was hurt." Knowing he was employed at the bar, she was thinking about Chuck.

Flick said, "Yes a number of people died."

Gayle, so kind-hearted, reacted. "Oh, no. That's terrible." Her lip trembled. Such news made her nervous. "Can I ask if Chuck was injured?"

Flick reassured Gayle. "He made it out alive. Helped a lot of people to out to safety. Saved a lot of lives. He is doing well. You're nice to ask."

"Well, he is Liv's biological father." She realized she had given the man credence.

Flick didn't know what to say. "Ah, is Liv o.k?" he asked, getting back on track as to why he'd called. "I haven't been able to reach her these past few days."

Gayle was lost in her thoughts of acceptance of Liv's biological father. "Oh yes, there is news. Liv had her baby. It was a boy. Eight pounds, five ounces. His name is Liam."

Flick, being a family man, was thrilled to know he was an uncle. "How are they doing?"

Gayle shared, "They're doing great. Should be home in few days. I'll let her know you called. She'll look forward to hearing from you on Saturday. I'm sure."

Flick asked, "Can I ask what hospital?"

Gayle thought he wanted to send flowers. "Oh yes, Rocky Mountain Hospital." Thinking, *How sweet.*

The call came to a pleasant end.

***

In the confined space, Chuck had overheard the conversation and was busy with his own thoughts. Flick wanted to talk to see if he was being too pushy if he went to the hospital to visit.

Chuck realized what Flick had said. "It might be too much. Liv doesn't know we're in Calgary."

Mischievously, Flick declared, "It would be a fine time for Liv to find out. Don't you think?"

Knowing Flick, it would be fine...after Liv recovered from a heart attack.

Tonight, was too late for a visit. Flick would make time tomorrow. Next day, he arrived at work to find out the day's plan. Bob always had them busy with little time to spare from 8:00 a.m. to 8:00 p.m. This Monday, though, Bob wanted to take Chuck on a few jobs for bidding. Flick had little to do and would be able to find time after lunch.

He went to a floral shop to pick up a nice bouquet of flowers for Liv. A Teddy bear larger than the baby probably was, got tucked under his arm. He made his way to the hospital, then the information desk. Given Liv's room, he took the elevator, stopped at the nurses' station, and introduced himself as family.

Liv was occupied with breastfeeding Liam and absentmindedly listening in on conversations just outside her room at the station. A man's voice said, "My name is Flick. My sister, Liv, just had a baby. May I go in to visit?"

Liv looked up and threw on a receiving blanket to cover the baby and her breast. With her mind racing and wondering what he might look like as a young man, she tried to figure out how Flick could be here. The picture in her mind had been the little boy from years ago. There was no time to prepare herself or her emotions, and she braced herself as she heard footsteps heading towards her door. The steps stopped, paused. Then, a man peeked in with a huge grin.

"Hi Liv," Flick said.

Liv being sharp as well said, "Hi Flick. Nice to see ya."

Flick wondered how she knew, and then quickly realized she'd heard his announcement to the nurses just outside her room. He was so happy to finally see Liv after all the years that had passed. A lifetime ago. He placed the flowers on her nightstand and the Teddy bear on the second chair. Then he stood for what seemed like eternity and just looked, pleased, and smiling, watching mother and baby. Liv was not a child anymore. She was a woman with a child of her own. Incredible! Not wanting to disturb the peaceful bond of mother and child, Flick came up to the bedside and put an arm around Liv, cheek to cheek. Grinning, he stepped back and took a seat. "So, how've you been?" he asked, knowing the questions would come.

"Good. We are both doing well." She smiled. "What brings you here?"

Flick replied, "You, of course."

Liv put the sleeping baby into his bed. "You know what I mean. How did you get here?"

Flick simply said, "By bus."

"I guess I'm going to have to pull teeth out of you. One tooth at a time," she said with a chuckle.

Flick decided to explain how he'd missed her call. He started with the fire and ended with the business opportunity, sharing the whole story including Chuck along the way. He explained how he'd managed to make it a condition of the business agreement that Chuck would be groomed to learn how to bid on jobs.

Liv liked hearing how Flick was looking out for Chuck. It touched her heart that Flick never lost sight of family. Now he was here for her. Her brother, her friend, her family as well. Amazing just thinking about it.

A twinge in her heart reminded Liv that she had not been the one to reach out to her sibling or siblings. It was Flick who had reached out to her. She owed him so much for loyalty, integrity, and devotion for family. He was a better man than she was a woman.

Flick insightfully said, "Don't feel bad. I understand. I wouldn't have come if I thought you'd stopped caring."

Liv had tears mixed with embarrassment, confused motions, and jumbled-up concepts of her mind, her damn hormones, and the love that filled the room because of Flick. She wanted to know how he'd found her at the hospital. Flick explained that he'd called Gayle. "I asked what hospital." Feeling deceitful, he added, "I know she thought I was still in Montreal. Probably thought I asked to send you flowers…but I liked bringing the flowers myself."

Liv touched a petal. "They're beautiful. Thank you. You really are sweet on the inside. Rough around the edges." It was how she remembered Flick and she liked him just the way he was.

Flick was in his own head – a tear escaped down his cheek. "I know it might be too much to ask…" He hesitated for a moment. "Christmas is less than a week away. I would like to visit you if I could. Think it would be easier than you are bundling up the baby to share an hour on that day."

Liv thought about what he said. "Can we touch base about a time? I know Chuck is here with you and I can't stand the thought of him being alone at Christmas." She teared up so easily. Darn hormones. "We'll be having time with my parents. I don't want to hurt my dad, Peter. I guess I want to find a way to share Christmas with both of my dads… just separately this time." Biting her lower lip, she said, "It's all that I can handle at this time. I hope you understand."

Flick nodded and laughed. "Chuck will be surprised to hear that you want to include him. He will be touched. If you said 3:00 a.m. he would be there."

Liv giggled. The visit was over an hour long now and Liv was getting tired. "I need to rest. The baby will wake soon."

"Sure." He got up. "Liv?"

Liv looked up.

Flick shook her heart. "I have never said these words in my whole life. 'I love you very much.'" He gave Liv a long hug and quietly walked out trying to hide his tears.

***

Flick arrived home with his heart bursting and his mind sorting feelings. He started preparing dinner just to occupy his hands with something to do. How could someone's heart feel so good and feel so bad at the same time because of the exact same person?

So, elated to have seen Liv, Flick's heart was bursting with joy. Yet, he felt bad for all the years lost. Had she chosen to forget her family in Montreal? Flick had to stop his mind from questioning Liv's heart. Was he afraid of the answers? Stop! She hadn't turned him away. He was proud that he had never forgotten Liv and had found her. Build on that ... her acceptance. It was a miracle that Liv wanted to include Chuck in their Christmas festivities. She was trying to work out a solution to embrace everyone she loved. Yes, there was hope of being family. To pick up where they'd left off would be difficult. Pick up where they started and build from there, they'd have a chance. Yes, start fresh and let the relationship grow. Flick was taking the weeds out of the family garden so that it might flourish. His mind was coming to terms with his heart.

Dinner was almost ready when Chuck walked in the door smiling. He'd closed a huge contract with a line of nail salons that was popping up in all corners of Calgary.

Dinner was tasty, but the conversation was heart wrenching and thought provoking for Chuck as Flick shared his visit about Liv. Now they just had to wait to see what time was good for Liv and her family to include them in their Christmas holidays.

***

Gideon came by the hospital after work, and Liv shared what had transpired that afternoon. Little did Liv and Gideon realize that Gayle and Peter had been about to enter the room and then stopped. They had overheard Flick's and Chuck's names and so they waited before entering. The problem was that they had become a dilemma that tortured their little girl's heart. She wanted to have time with Flick and she wanted to include Chuck and get to know him a little. But, of course, she didn't want to hurt Gayle and especially Peter. The two stepped back to the elevator and went home to talk.

Gayle realized now that when Flick had asked what hospital, it was about more than delivering flowers. It was to surprise Liv and make contact in person. Was that a bad thing? She couldn't fault him for wanting to.

Peter was sorting his mind and heart, not sure how he felt. They talked to all hours of the night. They only wanted what was best for their little girl and they could still hear Liv's voice expressing her wishes and trying to reason with her divided mind.

Gideon had been listening to Liv's concerns and did not give advice at the time Gayle and Peter were eavesdropping.

Chapter 22
Montreal, 1982

Christmas was around the corner for Ruby and kids. Kane spent Christmas Eve with Ruby's family and always managed to get each child a special gift – something they would never be able to afford. It was Nintendo and games for the boys and spa treatments for the girls. Kane was kind to Flick and Salt and would also get them each something at Christmas. Salt was spending the holidays at Ruby's. Flick was gone. Kane had plans on Christmas Day with his other daughter from another mother.

Noticing he was not around, Kane asked, "So where's Flick?"

The kids stayed quiet. Ruby said, "He came by last week and said something about being gone for a while. Would be back. Story of my life, kids leave. Some stay away, some may come back." She shrugged her shoulders. Too Ruby it was her way of going with the flow. Kid was in his twenties and was going do whatever he wanted. She never mentioned that Chuck had been at the door and was leaving with him. The less said, the less one had to explain.

The girls made meat, cheese, and cracker trays, fruit and vegetable trays, nuts and bolts, chips and pop. There were games and movies for the night. Ruby and the kids were always invited to Aunty Em's on Christmas Day for turkey with all the trimmings. Aunt Jewels would bring trays of Christmas baking and goodies. Gift unwrapping was understood to take place before coming for dinner.

Boxing Day was a quiet day as the boys played with their games. For the girls it was "the day to go finger shopping." The stores were busy with customers and exchanges and had no time to focus on shoplifters. The girls' motto; The busier the store the easier the free pickups.

The holidays done and gone, the boys missed Flick. Life was more quiet than usual. Playing their games, they were less competitive and there were fewer conflicts. Ruby never noticed and hung around watching romantic movies. The days felt like babysitting, the nights were where the action and fun took place. Ruby expected her lovers to be generous at Christmas time. This year Kane had only focused on the kids. The other guys found excuses that they had to be with their families, money was tight, etc. The kids had no allowance to purchase something small for Ruby. Life was the shits. No one cared or thought of her. Flick wasn't here, and he usually made the boys get cheap earrings or bracelets for their mom as wrapped gifts. But there had been nothing this year.

Ruby wasn't going to let the guys have fun tonight unless they showed some gratitude. However, the guys had things figured out – flash a few bucks, and the fun was at full volume. Same routine most nights. What was to change? Nothing.

Kane was at Ruby's door on Boxing Day. "Ya miss me?" Ruby said with a smile. Then she noticed another officer present.

Kane spoke with his official voice. "Here on police business."

Officer Martin stated, "We have your daughters, Kandy and Sugar in the cruiser, on several accounts of theft."

Kane stepped in. "We need to take them down to the station. Kandy is nineteen and will be charged as an adult. Sugar is seventeen and charged as a minor." Pausing while looking at his notebook, he said, "You may want to come down and help them through this ordeal. I told Officer Martin that you're a good mother and would want to be present."

Ruby was so mad about being overlooked, with not a single gift under the tree, that she saw her opportunity to lash out. "The way I see it," she said, looking at Kane, "you are their father. No need for the two of us to be there. I'm sure you will do just fine." She closed the door.

Martin stood staring at the door trying to comprehend what Ruby had announced. "Did I hear right?"

Kane sputtered on the way to the police car, "I'll take care of it." All he could think about was *Some kind of mother.*

Kane returned the girls back a few hours later with a warning. "Smarten up and get your act together. I'm not going to save your sorry asses in the future. Got it?"

Ruby let the girls inside and slammed the door on Kane. Ruby thought, *what does Kane think? I'm going have a welcoming committee?' Serves him right feeling rejected.*

Kane didn't know what he had done wrong. He'd given as much as he could for his kids and explained to Ruby that he was doing everything in his power to help, short of living in a dog house. He remembered Ruby being referred to as the wicked witch of the East. Her potions were unavoidable, her needs were simple – money, lavish gifts. Then, it hit Kane – he hadn't had a gift for Ruby at Christmas. He would pay for that one way or another.

Salt was visiting his siblings over the holidays. He'd received a Christmas card from Flick saying, "Miss you buddy. I now have a job. Hope to see ya in the summer. Merry Christmas, Love Flick." The envelope had no return address and was useless as far as Ruby was concerned. Come the summer, Ruby would play the victim and bleed Flick for whatever she could get. What the hell – he was working.

That night Ruby had three guys over who came with the booze. The girls were in their rooms. Kandy expected a visitor, knowing how the night was going. Sugar allowed being felt up but would scream if anything else happened. Often Kandy would wrap Sugar in a blanket making it clear she was off limits. To Sugar, her mind had been raped, because she was often present when sex was happening. Kandy tried to reason with Sugar about the advantages. Sugar just couldn't bring herself to understand or to want anything to do with these filthy pigs.

Kandy left the room and went out with one of the guys. Ruby was busy in her room with company and Sugar was scared for her life. She hid under the bed and behind the clutter of girl things. Often, she fell asleep on the hard floor.

That night, the police arrested Kandy. The guy had pimped her out on the streets. Kandy was in the slammer. Ruby thought she'd gotten what she deserved because she wasn't smart enough to keep it a home-based affair.

Sugar wished Flick was there. Occasionally, she got to stay over at his place and play Monopoly or cards. Have fun, fall asleep, be safe. That world was over. No one was safe anymore.

Chapter 23
Calgary, 1982

Christmas Eve, Gideon, Liv, and Liam were over at Gayle and Peter's for a light dinner. Milly had prepared a lovely spread of Bailey's Irish Cream of Chicken served over broad noodles, with steamed broccoli and carrots and salad. For dessert there were cheesecakes and squares.

New grandparents, Gayle and Peter, were enchanted with baby Liam. Liam either was being breastfed or sleeping. This allowed the couples to have a relaxing evening and heartfelt discussion.

Liv started by saying, "I had a visitor yesterday at the hospital." She was trying to create the chat dance Gayle and she loved. Somehow the room remained silent. Liv had expected something ... oh, Santa Claus ... anything. But, nothing.

Gideon sensed the silence and said, "Flick has moved to Calgary. Came by to see Liv."

Peter simply said, "Oh."

Gayle said nothing. She just listened to let Liv share what had transpired, giving her room with no judgements, no expectations.

Liv interpreted the silence as disapproval, and worried about their feelings and reactions she found her emotions getting the best of her. "I have mixed emotions. I suspect my hormones are not helping." She tried to smile. Gayle came over and gave her a hug and a smile and Peter sent a reassuring nod and smile.

"We talked for an hour, it was strange, yet familiar at the same time," Liv shared. "In truth, it was wonderful. I have a brother, a friend around my own age, who is family."

Peter and Gayle touched hands, smiling at Liv.

Liv continued. "They're in a little suite not far from downtown. Alone on Christmas Day."

Gideon filled in. "They, being Flick and Chuck. Chuck is Liv's biological ... "

Peter finished the sentence: "Father." Getting up to sit beside Liv he said, "I am your dad, always will be."

Gayle picked up and said, "It is good for you to understand, to know your brother and biological father. It will help you be complete, be the best woman, the best wife, the best mother you can be."

Liv stared. "You support my relationships with these people?"

Peter smiled. "Yes, we do."

Liv thought. "I'd like you to come over in the morning for gift giving and a buffet breakfast."

Gayle said, "We would love to."

Liv nodded. She couldn't finish her thought to say that her brother and father would visit in the afternoon. But all present knew, though no words were spoken about it.

The night ended with packing up the baby in the car and heading home. Yes, it was only two blocks away, but it was icy and fiercely cold.

***

Christmas morning was crisp and nippy in the air. From car to door would chill one's lungs and redden cheeks and noses in a minute. Peter and Gayle arrived with armloads of gifts. From the sitting room window, Gideon pointed to the garage while it was being opened. In the hallway their guests entered with smiles and reddened noses that would have made Rudolph envious.

Baby Liam had an early breakfast and was settled in his pram, which was now set up in the family room. He didn't stir from the familiar sounds of his grandparents as they set gifts under the tree. Liv brought coffee to her parents as they sat by the fire. Milly arrived early in the morning to prepare the buffet. This was a little gesture from Gayle and Peter. Everything was set out and ready for all to partake in.

Gayle and Peter were looking forward to having pictures with Liam on his first Christmas. Liam, only days old, slept and was content to miss all the festivities. Once the morning meal and clean-up had taken place, the couples sat in the family room. Simple gifts were given out and words of appreciation expressed.

Peter and Gideon sat close by each other, whispering. Liv noticed and glanced at Gayle, who was rocking the pram and watching her grandchild sleep. Peter then asked Liv to come sit on the ottoman – A seating that would have Liv facing both her favorite men.

Gideon then said, "Your folks and I have a surprise for you. A very special Christmas gift."

Peter announced, "We have found a way to help you fulfill one of your dreams."

Smiling with mischief. Gideon continued. "We have you registered for your PhD and you start in the new year." He waited to see Liv's reaction.

"How did you do that?" Liv asked. "How am I going to work on my PhD and take care of Liam?" Saddened, she said, "You should have talked to me first."

Liv's parents and Gideon looked from one to the other. Gayle smiled and said, "Darling, your dad and I want an excuse to have time with little Liam. With Milly's help, and Gideon's blessing we are able to make this happen. We were so excited to help you go back to school and achieve your dream." Gayle knew how to reach her daughter's heart. "Only family would take care of Liam. You would have time in the evening to have Liam to yourself with Gideon."

Gideon, Peter, and Gayle had met earlier in the week and had coffee. They'd talked about Flick and that Liv might become consumed with her siblings. Each had misgivings and doubted anything good would come out of Liv having time, the heart, and the desire to pursue her other siblings. But Liv obtaining her PhD required an air-tight plan of support. With help from grandparents taking care of baby Liam and Milly and Gideon on board – the plan would work. Liv would achieve her goals and not be sidetracked with negative influences that could anchor her heart.

Liv was trying to weigh the sudden change of heart with going for her PhD. She did sound shocked at first but then absorbed the possibility of obtaining her goal. Suddenly, she realized the she was going to back to university. This dream was possible. Then she asked how this all came about. The men stayed quiet for a moment each selecting his words and thoughts.

Peter spoke up and said, "Well as you know I promised Gideon that we, Gayle and I, would run expensive ideas though him what with him being the man of his house." He smiled. "Gideon was concerned that on your own the financial burden would be too much, with care for Liam a concern. Well, as a family we could be of support on all levels and make your dreams come true. Merry Christmas, our wonderful daughter."

Liv was so pleased, and she looked at Gideon for approval, finding her man all smiles. "Merry Christmas, sweetheart." Gideon said.

Liv could not believe her good fortune. "This truly is the best Christmas ever. Thank you so much."

Peter and Gayle returned home feeling a sense of accomplishment. Their love, hard work, commitment to their daughter, their family, and grandchild, would all come together. Knowing they had put this into motion was in Liv's best interest. Creating diversions that would help their daughter aspire to Maslow's "Self-Actualization" by way of her education was in the making. Some would consider the actions of Liv's parents' manipulative; other ways would view the plans as love paving the way to a bright future.

***

In mid-afternoon, a taxi arrived in front of the house. Gideon watched from the sitting room window and announced to Liv, "Chuck and Flick are here." The bell chimed, and the door was opened with smiles. Gideon let the men into the house. Making their entry a welcoming one. he said, "Please come in."

Liv said. "Yes, come out of the cold. Can I take your coats?"

Flick entered and embraced his sister, but Chuck stood at the door and waited to slip inside unobtrusively.

Gideon shook Flick's hand and extended his hand to Chuck. "Please, do come in."

Chuck stepped in and followed Gideon's lead through the hallway to the family room. Flick was already in the kitchen area with Liv, who was attending to baby Liam. Liv realized she had been preoccupied when Chuck entered. Gideon took Liam from her and she walked over to Chuck with a sheepish smile. "Hi. So good to see you."

Chuck was looking into his little girl's eyes. Emotions of a life long gone swept through his heart. Lip quivering and tears running down his face, he said, "Good to see you too." Just holding tips of fingers and searching for comfort, lost in thoughts, they were holding the moment both thoughts would never come. Here they were, almost a decade and a half lost, but it now was found. They embraced each other with overwhelming mixed emotions over the lost years and renewed encounter. Chuck had lived for this moment. Liv wanted this moment too as her dreams had assured her of the kind man standing before her. She began to tremble and cry knowing full well her hormones had nothing to do with these emotions. A life taped back together?

Flick and Gideon stood back and watched. Chuck smiled and said, "Life begins today. That's if you will have me as a friend, your biological father?"

Liv smiled. "Of course."

Once everyone was settled by the fire in the family room, the visit became relaxed. Liv remembered stories about her grandparents, great aunts and uncles, the willow tree, the pine tree, and memories of a loving family building the country house. Chuck was amazed she remembered so much. Flick just listened – he'd had no idea of the history shared.

Smiling, Liv recalled the most amazing person of all. "I remember 'Pa,' the kindest man on earth. I recall stories of how he helped people during hard times. But, mostly I remember the smell of his pipe."

Chuck was impressed with Liv's memory of being five and younger. He didn't update her about his parents. He didn't want to taint the wonderful memories now being shared by the only two people who had this history. Chuck would share when Liv was ready to ask the questions.

Flick and Gideon were spectators in a live story-telling afternoon. Baby Liam was stirring, hungry, and needed Mommy in an instant. The men went about their business as Liv went upstairs to breastfeed Liam. Chuck and Flick went outside in a desperate need for a smoke. One to pacify their nerves from the emotional afternoon, and two for the hours' delay without a cigarette since they'd arrived. Gideon checked on the turkey dinner. It was a stuffed turkey ball with both dark and white meat, enough for four adults with vegetables and roasted potatoes. Gideon was thickening the drippings to make a gravy. The boys came back inside and helped set the table.

Baby Liam was changed, satisfied, settled back in the pram. Liv looked refreshed with a touch of lipstick. Dinner was ready, and all were hungry from the draining afternoon. The boys chipped in and cleaned up the table as Gideon stocked the dishwasher. Liv served up beer for the boys and sparkling apple juice for herself for a toast. She raised her wineglass. "To friendship now and always."

Chuck and Flick said, "Aye aye."

Gideon and Liv smiled and said. "Aye."

Today was Christmas Day, with the gift of sharing. No one expressed concerns, expectations, or demands. All thought about the promise of long ago. For Flick and Chuck, it was the beginning of being a family, though Flick thought of their siblings and his heart ached wanting to be with them at this time of year.

Christmas was a time for new beginnings; being a new mother, a good wife, a good sister, a good daughter to two fathers. Not to forget being a good student.

Gideon's family would be visiting on Boxing Day. The holidays were filled with renewed connections, family, love, memories, and new beginnings with Liam, Flick, and Chuck.

***

The new year rang in a flurry of activity as Liv had so little time to prepare and adapt to a new routine. In the middle of January, classes started. Liam was only three weeks old. Early morning had Liv expressing her milk for the day. Gayle arrived at 6:00 a.m. to take the task of caring for Liam. Only Liam was up at 5:00 a.m. Liv was in the shower and Gideon was having toast and coffee before heading to the office. Peter stayed home and enjoyed a quiet morning. Come spring he would be out on the golf course with the early morning risers – and roasters. Around 10:00 a.m. Peter would show up with baked goods and coffee.

Liam became accustomed to the care and routines of all the people who loved him. Time with Mom first thing in the morning. Wake up to Grandma. Later wake up to Grampa. Supper, then play time with Dad. Bath time with Mom. Falling asleep in Mom's arms.

Liv was tired going full tilt with early mornings with Liam and late nights with research and papers. Her folks kept her family together. Her husband was the glue and support that motivated her to keep on and just do it!

Weekends were reserved for family. Rarely did Liv allow her studies to encroach on their family time. Baby was growing fast as the weather was getting warmer. Spring was in the air and baby Liam was exploring his world by crawling about.

***

The new year was beginning as a blast from a cannon. Fireworks from New Year's sparked the energy and had Flick and Chuck on the run from sunrise to sunset. Business was rolling as though they had been established for years. Truth was, Calgary was growing and the demand for the professions could not be satisfied. Buildings in the downtown core were popping up like mushrooms. Prefab bathrooms required installation of fixtures for these high-rises. Flick and Chuck could take on ten floors with three to five bathrooms that had many stalls, in each setup per week. Chuck was exceptional with bidding. Flick was flooded with work eighteen hours a day, six days a week. Chuck often helped Flick. They usually managed to get in dinner and the nightly news before bed.

Flick insisted on having Saturday 9:00 a.m. coffee with Hannah faithfully. He would also spend time with Hannah Saturday night till mid-Sunday morning. Often, they would see an event, walk along Princess Island, or take in a movie. By spring, Hannah informed Flick she was expecting in October. Flick clarified. "We are expecting."

Life was moving fast and furious for Flick. Often, a month would go by before the siblings, Liv and Flick, would get to enjoy a bantering chatter over a cup of coffee. Liv hadn't seen or invited Chuck to visit since Christmas Day. She often felt bad about this, but her schedule had become tight and time was so precious it was sacred. Finding time for everything was as complicated as a Rubik's cube.

One May weekend had Gideon up with the birds and getting Liam dressed in light warm clothes. Antique cars were being presented and Gideon thought it would be a great idea to develop some "guy" time. Liv thought it was a great idea and she decided to have a few hours with Flick and Chuck. They had been planning to go to an Antiques show but they switched gears to have some time with Liv.

They met at Cheese Cake Café and had lunch. Flick shared that he was seeing Hannah and they were expecting. Hannah had a small two-bedroom place that would be o.k. as they started out in life together. Flick had invited Chuck to move in without discussing the matter with Hannah. But Chuck knew better and stated he'd kind of grown to appreciate the little suite they had. It would be perfect for just himself. It was bigger than the room he'd had over the bar in Montreal. He appreciated the little kitchen and the privacy of his own space.

Flick wanted to know if Liv, Gideon, and Liam would like to attend a small wedding in June. Hannah wanted to get married and have pictures taken. Liv was having a break from university in June and she offered to have the occasion in their yard. She would have to talk with Gideon but didn't see it as a problem. Flick thought it would be a good idea and said he would take the matter up with Hannah. Chuck enjoyed the interactions with his children and appreciated how each considered or helped the other. Maybe years apart had made them appreciate what they had today.

Liv invited Flick, Hannah, and Chuck over for a Sunday brunch. Should their partners agree, they could plan and prepare for the little wedding.

Chapter 24
Montreal, 1983

Ruby's household was running the same. Men visiting in the night. Occasional afternoon delights when the kids were at school. Nothing had changed in decades. Kandy was now twenty, Sugar eighteen, and Salt sixteen. The girls had found a letter to Salt from Flick. There was an address and phone number.

The plan began to stash enough money to get to Calgary. They thought they could save enough to manage for about three months. Kandy knew if she stayed in Montreal, her life would turn out much like her mother's. She decided she would like to be loved and have a family and a happy, productive life. Staying in Montreal would not facilitate this simple but currently impossible dream. Kandy shared her thoughts with her sister, Sugar. Sugar understood and agreed that having the picket fence would never happen in their lifetime if they stayed in Montreal. Sugar loved her brothers and mentioned that Salt would want to come with them. Kandy wasn't sure she could afford all the boys but thought she could manage Salt on the journey.

The girls gave a special hug to each of the boys, Gunner and Gavin, without saying goodbye. Gunner did not pay mind. Gavin, on the other hand, picked up on the abnormal. "What's the hug for?"

Sugar said, "We hug you all the time."

Gavin agreed. "Yeah, but something's not right."

Sugar whispered, "Don't tell Mom – we're leaving."

Gavin was quick of mind. "Calgary, right?"

Sugar nodded.

Gavin said, "Take me too."

Sugar wanted to but said, "Mom would Have our hides, call the police."

"No, she won't. Didn't do anything when Liv left, so I have heard," he said sulkily.

Sugar thought. "You keep Gunner company. Be a good boy. Love you so much. You need to be the man of the house. O.k.?"

Gavin nodded. "I will."

Salt was visiting this weekend. Kandy smiled and asked, "You want to go for a ride in my new car?"

Salt was excited, but he answered with a dull tone. "Yes."

Sugar joined them.

Spring was in the air and change was about to happen … At the end of May, Kandy, Sugar, and Salt headed out to Calgary. Kandy purchased an old Dodge Dart for $50.00. They would drive and sleep on the go. It would be cheaper than three bus tickets across Canada. If they stuck together, they would be safer on the journey. A bus ride for three would cut into Kandy's savings and she couldn't afford a plane ride for all three of them. So, the car would do just fine.

Kandy felt bad for Aunty Jewels and put a note on her fridge explaining that they needed to find their own way in life and that Salt was with them. She asked her to not let their mother know and she let Aunty know they loved her very much.

It took a full week to get to Calgary, stopping for gas and washing up in washrooms each morning and living on McDonalds' on the road. Everyone looked haggard and orphaned when they showed up at six o'clock Friday morning at Chuck's door.

Chuck was having a morning coffee when he heard a stampede of feet down the back steps towards the suite. A knock had him open the door to three unfamiliar faces. Kandy introduced herself and her siblings, asking for Flick.

Chuck explained Flick had moved with his girlfriend. He gestured for them to come in quietly as his neighbors were still sleeping. Everyone went into the living room area and sat on the twin bed that doubled as a sofa, sitting quietly and not knowing what to expect next. Chuck wasn't sure what they wanted or expected from him. He had plans to go shopping for a pair of dress pants and a shirt for Flick's wedding the next day and to find a nice wedding gift after he finished work for the day. These kids couldn't stay with him or with Flick for that matter. Both places were too small. Knowing how early it was, Chuck offered to call Flick. He had to get to work himself and was running out of time.

"Morning Flick. Sorry to call so early." Thinking of how he was going to announce the latest news, Chuck said, "Kandy, Sugar, and Salt are here to see you." He listened as

Flick went over the deep end with a dozen questions Chuck could not answer.

"Right." Chuck hung up. "Flick said he'll be right over." He loved his boy's spirit.

Chapter 25
Calgary, 1983

Flick showed up at 6:30 a.m. The siblings were so excited to see each other they were unable to keep the commotion to a dull roar. Neighbors shouted, "Shut up. People are sleeping you know."

The reunion was filled with joy and tears. The kids were tired, dirty, happy, and relieved to have arrived in the embrace of their older brother. Though they'd arrived safe and sound and had been found there was still a sense of loss. Chuck did not have much for food to feed the bunch. Flick suggested taking them out for breakfast to figure out what they were going to do. Chuck said he had to get to work and would catch up with him later in the day.

Flick had wrapped up work late the night before, knowing he would be busy with preparations for his wedding for Saturday. Now, he was elated with his family being in Calgary. There was so much to do for tomorrow and now the need to get the kids settled. Where did one begin?

Flick carried a monster-size cell phone provided by his business partner, Bob. The phone rang and he explained that three of his siblings had arrived unexpectedly and he would not be able to do any work for the day.

Flick listened intently as their food was being served. The kids were quiet and hungry, eating without complaint. They heard Flick say into the phone, "Sounds good. We'll be over in an hour. Yeah, see you then." He hung up.

All eyes were on Flick as the kids wondered where they were all going. Kandy said with a mouthful of food, "What's up?"

The kids thought Flick was important. They had never seen a phone not attached by a cord or to a wall. Salt thought Flick might be friends with Captain Kirk from *Star Trek*. They were all in awe, impressed, with respect that Flick was somebody.

Flick wanted to have this relaxing time with the kids to explain he was getting married tomorrow. Sipping his coffee, he needed to share what was happening the next two days. "I want you to know that I am getting married tomorrow." Everyone was shocked. They'd never heard of a girl in Flick's life. "Her name is Hannah. We're going to have a baby in October."

Kandy observed, "You've been busy." Everyone smiled. Sugar and Salt giggled.

Flick continued. "That was my business partner, or boss, and he has an apartment over his laundromat that is empty." Flick frowned. "I did some plumbing on the place last month. The place looks rough and needs a good cleaning. It's empty and I'm not sure what it's going to take to set you guys up in a day."

He was thinking about his budget to make things happen. Liv had helped a lot to mitigate expenses by having the wedding at her home. He realized he would need to give her a call and let her know there would be three more in attendance. What was he going to do for clothing for his siblings? They looked like orphans.

It wasn't even 8:00 a.m. The kids were finishing up their breakfast and quiet from the long journey.

Flick dialed on his monster phone. "Hi, this is Flick. Sorry to call so early."

Liv reassured Flick she had been up for hours. She teased him, saying, "You already worried about the wedding?"

Flick answered, "No. And yes."

Liv was burping Liam. "Oh."

Flick clarified. "I'm not worried about the wedding. Me or Hannah. But, Kandy, Sugar and Salt arrived in Calgary this morning."

Liv asked. "We're you expecting them?"

Flick. "No, but that's not the point." Trying to soften his anxiety, he said, "I need to get them set up. Get clothes for the wedding, and I needed you to know there will be three more guests."

Liv offered, "Anything I can do?"

Flick had so much on his mind. "I'll let you know. Just on our way to look at a place. Call ya later, k?"

Liv had to go and change Liam. "Sure." The line closed.

Flick took care of the bill and they all walked over to the laundromat to a side door that led to the apartment on the second floor. Bob was waiting for them.

Bob smiled at Flick with his crooked, over-lapped teeth. "I show you. K?"

Everyone followed up the stairs and down the hall. The apartment had a greasy kitchen, filthy walls, and windows without coverings. The floors needed cleaning and there was no furniture. Negotiations were made with Flick about a price on a month to month basis. Flick made it clear the place was to get cleaned right now and by noon or no deal. Bob handed the key to Flick and ran off to get his wife Lilly.

The kids were tired but too excited about the events happening from minute to minute with Flick taking charge. Flick remembered the second-hand shops that had helped Chuck and him last Christmas. He was able to get three twin beds, linens, towels, mixed dishes, utensils, pots and pans, and a toaster. He found dresses for the girls with shoes and dress pants and a shirt for Salt for the wedding. The girls thought the clothes smelled funny. Flick noticed an iron for two-dollars that satisfied their needs. They planned to wash the clothes by hand, dry them, and press them in the morning.

Flick had the kids go with him to Safeway to get a few cleaning products; dish soap, Comet, bar soap, laundry soap, shampoo, toothpaste, milk, bread, margarine, cold cuts, Kraft dinner, cans of tomato soup, crackers, bananas, cheese slices, Shreddies. This should tide them over for a few days. Everyone helped carry bags to the new apartment. The beds were being delivered by 1:00 p.m. Lilly was washing the floors and explained the fridge and stove were as clean as she could get them. Flick nodded, smiled and said, "Thank you."

Surprisingly the apartment had two small bedrooms, a small den room with no closet off the living room, a kitchen, and an eating area. If Salt didn't mind the den as his room, the girls could have their own rooms. Sugar talked with

Flick and asked if they could go back to the second-hand store to get a few sheets to cover the windows. Flick saw how shy Sugar felt about the need for privacy. He hollered to Kandy and Salt. "We'll be right back." Sugar followed him, and they soon returned with drapes. The store clerk was kind and generous to include rods.

The kids were as set as they could be on such short notice. Flick had a list of things he had to get accomplished for the big day. He needed to drive Hannah to the floral shop for her bouquet and to get corsages for the men. And he thought he should get two wrist corsages for the girls and a boutonniere for Salt. Hannah had her wedding dress. Flick needed to be at the men's shop for his tuxedo rental pick up at 3:00 p.m. The wedding was to be a small, simple affair. There was no rehearsal dinner the night before.

Saturday, the justice of the peace would marry the couple at 1:00 p.m. in front of the waterfall in the garden. There were tables of finger foods, quarter sandwiches, mini cakes, and squares to hold appetites over till the sit-down dinner. Milly was paid extra for the catering of the event.

The girls continued cleaning and setting up the beds. They put away items in cupboards and food in the fridge. Then they washed their clothes by hand and hung them to dry in the bathroom. It was Kraft dinner with wieners for dinner. The kids each had a shower and were in bed by 9:00 p.m. The day had been draining from the time they arrived in Calgary and found Flick, to setting up home.

Kandy's last thought for the day was … that she hoped Flick did not forget them … Had he said he would pick them up around noon?

***

Saturday morning started early for Liv. Liam was up at 5:00 a.m. expecting breakfast on demand. He sat in his baby chair while being fed mashed bananas in Pablum. Coffee was always set for 5:00 a.m. and ready for Liv to get a cup of motivation. Liam was getting heavier these days and it took two hands and arms to hold him to breastfeed. Liv was going over her to-do list, for the wedding and for last-minute things not to forget.

There was no time for her to catch a few more minutes of rest. The day had started with no rewind, no pause, no rest, and hopefully with no regret. Liam was playing in his playpen while Liv went over her list and checked the garden. The rental chairs had been set up with beautiful, large, teal bows on each. The gazebo was set up with a table inside for the signing of the marriage certificate, and it was dressed in teal satin and white flowers. A stone sitting bench by the waterfall would be perfect for photos. The stage was set, and the morning sun was ready for the great day.

Liv tried to stay focused on her part of the preparations, but her mind wandered to the three siblings who had suddenly arrived the day before. Sipping her coffee, she wondered how she would feel – how would she respond? The day was Flick's, of course, and Hannah's. To Liv it was a big day for her meeting her two sisters after decades apart. Then to meet Salt, a brother she'd never known.

Liv had thought about Chuck at the wedding and the fact that her parents had never met her biological dad. This day was to be an emotional one for all. Hopefully, the tears would be for joy and the beginnings of new and wonderful things to come.

Gideon came down to the kitchen to get a cup of coffee. He gave his wife a kiss. "Morning sweetheart."

Liv instantly smiled. "Morning darling." She put her cup down. "Mind if I sneak off and take a shower?"

Gideon settled at the table watching Liam. "Not at all. Enjoy."

The phone rang at 7:00 a.m. Gideon answered. "Hello."

It was Gayle. "Gideon. Good morning. Is Liv there?"

"She's in the shower."

With a sigh of relief. "I need to talk with you, Gideon. Peter had chest pains last night. He's in the hospital under observation. We're hoping it wasn't a heart attack."

Gideon was standing in an instant. "Gayle is there anything we can do?"

"I'm not sure we should tell Liv. She might cancel the wedding. I don't want her to get stressed."

Gideon knew his woman. "I would tell Liv so that she can handle anything that might happen. Can I do anything for you?"

Gayle thought. "I wonder if you can take me to the hospital. I hope to take Peter home. I might need help."

"Done. I'm on my way. See you in a half hour. K?" Gideon reassured her.

Liv was towel drying her hair with her housecoat wrapped around her. "Who was that?"

Gideon put his cup in the dishwasher. "It was your mom. She needs my help. Peter had chest pains last night and is in the hospital under observation."

Liv was quiet. "Did he have a heart attack?"

"I think they are trying to rule that out. Gayle is hoping to bring him home this morning. I'm going with her to see if I can help."

Liv smiled. "Thank you, sweetheart. I appreciated you being there for my folks. Call me if you know anything. O.k.?"

He ran off to the bedroom to get dressed. "Will do." Then he ran back and kissed his wife on the cheek.

***

Gideon had picked up Gayle by 8:00 a.m. At 9:00 a.m. the phone rang. It was him.

"Peter is fine and doing well. Labs showed his tropes were low. That is good news. Needs to take ASA 81 mg daily to keep the blood thin and less stress on the heart. Taking him home now. Doctor was in to see Peter with orders. Now he's on a heart-healthy diet. Should be fine."

Liv was relieved. "How's Mom?"

"She's holding up well. I see her eyes are red. She didn't sleep all night. She's a trooper. I think I'll take them to their home to rest for a few hours. They say they would like to come to the wedding even if they need to go home to rest right after."

Liv understood. "O.k. I have to go; the doorbell just rang. See you soon. Love you."

***

Hannah and her mother were at the door with the wedding dress draped over one arm and bags of articles with undergarments, shoes, make up, hot curlers, and hair spray for the grooming preparations. Susy, her sister, was right behind them, the maid of honor. Flick was having Chuck as his best man and would be arriving just before the wedding started. This would give the girls three hours to get ready.

At 11:00 a.m. Milly and her assistant were at the door with trays of food for the afternoon snacks. Also, they had to get the prime rib in the oven for the evening dinner. Much preparation was needed as there were to be thirty guests. Not a lot, but enough to keep two women busy.

Gideon was back at 11:15 a.m. to help Liv with last-minute preparations and with keeping Liam occupied. Gideon had rented a champagne fountain and was setting the pump and glasses that would have the sparkly liquid flow. A chocolate fountain was set up by Milly with trays of fruit and white cake pieces for dipping. Gideon and Liv had gone over the top to make Flick's wedding a special affair.

Liv called Flick to remind him to pick up Chuck and his siblings.

At noon, the bridal party had a light lunch provided by Milly. At 12:15, Hannah's family arrived and went to the yard. Milly's assistant provided refreshments as the guests arrived. Flick arrived with Chuck and his siblings at 12:30 and they sat in the garden with their refreshments.

Liv was busy making sure the bride and maid of honor were set and ready to make their grand entrance for the event. Flick and Chuck were instructed to stay in the sitting room with their refreshments.

At 12:45, Gayle and Peter arrived. They had a garage opener of their own and entered through the hallway. Liv rushed to their sides, hugging her parents. Her eyes sought reassurance that her dad was all right. Gayle smiled, and Peter gave a gentle grin. "I'm o.k., my sweet girl." They walked to the backyard and took their seats.

Liv went to turn on the stereo, to have the music playing. The sound of the music was to let everyone know the wedding was about to begin. Hannah was adorned in a simple, silk, long dress with a two-foot-long train and veil. Her rainbow bouquet of flowers set the tone as Hannah glided down the beautiful staircase and stopped. She waited for her dad to walk her into the garden. Chuck stood at the fountain, waiting with smiles. The justice of the peace began to share anecdotes of the couples' relationship. Liv had done a wonderful job of making the ceremony a personal occasion.

The simple affair ended with, "I now pronounce you husband and wife. You may kiss your bride." Everyone clapped, the birds sang, and hope was in the air for the lovely couple.

Spring had a way of paving the way for changes: Changes for the new couple – married life and expecting a baby. Changes for the siblings – new life with new jobs settling in Calgary. Changes for Peter and Gayle adjusting to new health concerns. Changes for Chuck? Changes for Gideon and Liv with their expanding family.

There were congratulations to the newly married couple. Liv was so pleased to share in their special day. She turned to hug Flick and Hannah, thrilled to see them so happy.

In the flash of an instant all eyes were on the girls. Flick turned to Kandy and Sugar to acquaint his siblings with one another and to meet his new wife and her sister and family. Peter and Gayle watched with smiles. They were so pleased to

Child's Love

see their daughter embraced with a larger part of her family. Now they knew she would never be alone. Salt stood stoic until the girls turned to introduce their brother. He shyly walked towards Liv and allowed her to give him a stiff hug. The girls said, "Ah, for Pete's sake hug her, she's family." Then Salt hugged Liv so hard he didn't seem to know how to let go.

Tears of joy came from all, knowing the wedding was uniting more than just a couple. It was uniting a long-lost family. With the vows of "death do us part" and "for better or for worse," each had his or her own thoughts and interpretations. Liv felt the power of the words applied to the long-lost commitment of seeking out her siblings and she vowed in her heart to never let go again.

Peter and Gayle vowed to help their daughter to keep her family. Gideon felt the vows towards his wife and son, being committed to be the best man he could be for all those he loved.

The day was more than a wedding. It was about family.

For Liv it was about love, about her immediate family, her parents, and now her siblings. She pondered on her failed promise, feeling the bonds so strong and wanting to fulfill her promise of commitment now that a second chance had presented itself ... on this very day!

A child's love filled with broken promises. A woman's heart, a love so strong, a will with ability, to see the promise fulfilled. This was Liv's vow. To stay connected, to help with all she could, to never let go, and to love always and unconditionally. Never to fail again!

Life has a way of challenging such promises ...

Chapter 26
The Reception, 1983

The wedding was beautiful. Flick and Hannah looked in love and radiant. Everyone in attendance shared their joy. The next greatest moment had been when Flick introduced Liv to Kandy, Sugar and Salt. The girls recognized each other after all the years apart. Tears flowed as well as the compliments.

Peter and Gayle sat back and watched the pure joy shared amongst the siblings. The sisters squealed with delight, laughed and cried. Salt was adorable as he met his older sister for the first time. Gayle noticed a sincere quality; a transparency of genuine love. So shy and reserved. The older couple watched and watched Chuck, Liv's biological father. They realized he was in his early fifties. They were in their seventies.

The afternoon was spent visiting in the beautiful yard. Pictures were taken around the waterfall and gazebo. Milly replenished refreshments and snack trays during the afternoon. Gideon, Flick, and Chuck helped set up tables in the kitchen and family room area and temporarily moved the furniture into the garage. The complete back part of the house looked like a restaurant. Milly and her assistant adorned the tables with table settings, linens, and floral arrangements. Little did Flick, and Hannah know that the china used for the wedding would be given to them as their good set of dishware. Liv was clever and knew Flick would not mind the dual purpose. The boys helped bring the chairs inside and set them around the tables.

Peter and Gayle went upstairs to the guest room to relax. There was so much excitement and energy it was overwhelming for the aging couple. Dinner was announced at 6:00 p.m. and they rejoined the party. Flick asked to have Hannah's father say grace. Plates of salad were served. Chuck excused himself from the table and went over to Peter and Gayle. Peter stood and shook the man's hand and they introduced themselves.

With gentleness in his eyes Chuck said, "I want to thank you for doing such a wonderful job taking care of Liv. She is a beautiful woman. Many thanks to both of you." Then he hugged the man. Gayle had tears on seeing Chuck's appreciation. He was a humble man who'd lost his daughter so long ago to these people who obviously loved her deeply. Gayle knew he could have been bitter and resentful towards them. But instead, he showed great humility, kindness, and gratitude. Peter nodded, not knowing what to say. He didn't trust his mouth to speak what was in his heart. In in his younger years, he had been confident and very little had swayed or surprised him. As the years crept up, though, retirement had relaxed Peter into a comfortable routine and simple life. His heart had became so deeply attached to his wife, Gayle, and his daughter, Liv. He could not see himself sharing his father role with another man. Peter had adjusted well when Liv married Gideon – he knew he would always be her father. But with Chuck, Peter had mixed feelings and no desire to share his father role with this man.

Chuck saw Peter struggling with his presence. "I want you to know I respect that you are and always will be Liv's parents; her father and mother. I don't ever want to take that from you. I am grateful for just having the privilege of getting to know Liv. Again, thank you."

Chuck walked outside to have a cigarette. He wanted the best for his daughter, Liv, and knowing her relationships with her parents had left him in a grateful position. Afterwards, he returned to the dinner table where the main course was being served.

There was a toast to the new couple. Clinking glasses encouraged a few kisses. After the dinner, the boys removed the tables and set up the chairs outside. Music played to allow the young to dance. The girls were daring Flick to have a first dance with Hannah. Hannah danced with her new husband, and then her father. The girls teased Chuck and egged him on to have a dance with Hannah.

Peter touched Chuck's elbow and motioned him towards the sitting room, where he began, "I want to say thank you for letting us know how you feel with regards to Liv." Sipping his cognac always paved the way for fuelling his words in manly discussions. "At first, when learning that you here in Calgary, I was protective of Liv. A bit jealous at first. Now, I see how foolish I have been. I see a good man with a good heart. A man who has enough love for his daughter to let go for the sake of her happiness." He wanted to continue to say, *a man young enough to be our son,* but discretion held his tongue in check.

Chuck smiled. He liked the man. "Well, it would be an honor to be of help, like family, anytime you need." He had overheard Liv saying her father had arrived at the wedding straight from the hospital. Offering to help to this wonderful couple would be helping his daughter. Holding his cognac glass, he said, "Mow the grass. Shovel the snow." On the one hand, he was joking. On another hand not – half serious. It would be a tough way to fit into the family, Chuck thought. But he decided he was sincere with the offer.

"We have a husband and wife team that take care of us." Milly's husband did the landscaping and snow removal when needed. Peter liked the humble man, Chuck, and asked. "You play golf or cards?"

"Golf? Can't say I've had the pleasure. Cards, depending on the game." Chuck smiled, giving the man credit for trying to find common ground.

"Poker?"

"Played a couple of times. Good when there's money on the table. Hate to lose my hard- earned dollars, though. You play?"

"I'd like to learn to play. Maybe later with a few trusted friends."

Chuck offered, "I can teach you the basics. Much like Kenny Roger's song. Learn when to hold them, learn when to fold them." Both let out a laugh.

"So, there's some truth to that song, eh?" Peter said with a chuckle. "Especially, when you need to know when to walk away and know when to run." They both laughed. "Why don't you and I get a poker set, get together, and get familiar with the game? Mondays are good. Just not this Monday."

Chuck nodded. He wanted to jokingly say, *winner gets to be the father for the week, but* thought better of it.

Gayle entered and announced, "The girls are having a chocolate fight in the backyard. Might need your help."

The men put their glasses down and followed Gayle to the back of the house. Approaching the sliding doors to the garden, which was beautifully lit with white party lights, it looked like a fancy, three-ring circus. The girls had spread chocolate all over the patio, the furniture, the waterfall, and gazebo. They themselves were covered in chocolate and jumping in the pool. Liv stood holding Liam with her mouth wide open in shock.

Gideon was trying to take command and get the girls out of the pool. But Kandy and Sugar were experts when ignoring adults and carried on as they wanted. It was Flick who took charge and informed the girls, "Get out of the pool as you were told." Coming around, he took his tuxedo off till he was in his briefs. The girls stopped and realized Flick was preparing to get them out of the pool by force. In his underwear if need, be. "You like your hair?" he shouted, taking his socks and shoes off.

"Yeah?" both girls answered.

Flick dove in the pool and had them by the hair of the head. At first the girls squealed and laughed, finding his shenanigans amusing. Once they were losing chunks of hair and being dragged up the steps with their bottoms pounding about, the fun was over. Then they were screaming and cussing at Flick.

Hannah and Liv were horrified seeing Flick in his skivvies and the girls carrying on with no regard to others, the property, or themselves. Peter and Gayle excused themselves and found their way home.

Gideon went to get towels for the brood. By the time he returned, Flick was issuing the orders. "You two ever do something like this again, I'll have a truck load of manure poured all over you." The girls reached for the towels, but Flick was on a roll. "Forget the towels." Grabbing the garden hose, he sprayed them with the freezing water. "Now sit down."

The girls did as they were told, shivering in their new dresses.

"First, you are going to apologize to my wife for ruining her day. Got it?!" His eyes glared with warning. "Then, you are going to apologize to every single person here right now." He was daring to be defied. "Once you have accomplished that, you will go home. Tomorrow, you will be cleaning this whole place up. Polishing every stone, nook, and cranny till Liv and Gideon find their smiles again and declare the place acceptable. Do you understand me?" Hyperventilating with anger, he was struggling to catch his breath. "Now get up and move your sorry asses to the car. I have a honeymoon to get to and you're holding me up."

Once the girls, Salt, and Flick left, the guests remained silent for a full minute. Gradually, the guests departed with well-wishes to Hannah and thanks to Liv and Gideon. Milly and her assistant had the house in running order except for the furniture stored in the garage. The back yard, though, looked awful with the wet chocolate splattered everywhere. It was unsafe to walk out on the patio for now.

While Flick had been giving the girls a piece of his mind, Liv settled baby Liam to bed. It was 11:00 p.m. Flick returned to pick up Hannah after dropping off Salt and the girls. The house was quiet. Gideon hugged Liv and gently kissed her. He guided her arm and arm up the stairs to call it a night.

***

Sunday morning was quiet. Liv had been up with Liam twice in the night and was still asleep. Gideon made coffee and looked out the sliding doors, shaking his head. The chocolate had hardened, and the mess would not permit them to relax or enjoy their yard. He decided to start hosing down the yard. It was nine o'clock before the worst of the mess was washed away. The sliding door opened with Flick and the girls ready for work. Flick ordered. "Get the buckets, bleach, brooms, and start scrubbing." The girls looked upset.

Gideon walked back into the house. Flick followed and helped himself to the coffee. Gideon got out the eggs, bacon, orange juice, and some fruit plates from the wedding. "Would you like some breakfast?"

Flick smiled. "Love to, can I help?"

"Sure." Glancing at the girls working quietly, Gideon asked, "Should I set aside plates for the girls?"

Flick growled. "I'd like to say 'no.' But, they can eat after they're done."

Gideon, busy about the kitchen, nodded.

Liv came down in her housecoat not expecting company. Gideon handed her a cup of coffee and smiled. "Seems Flick is a man of his word."

Liv whispered, "I knew he was. But I didn't expect him to be so diligent on a Sunday morning. Especially, when he should still be on his honeymoon." Seeing the girls hard at work, she smiled.

Liv talked about her fathers. She'd noticed they had some man to man time in the sitting room the night before. Then she remembered Peter had a scare and gone to the hospital. "I'd like to check in on Dad. He wasn't looking good last night."

Gideon remembered and said, "That's a good idea." He dished out the plates. "Have something to eat first."

Liv wasn't sure she had her appetite but humored her loving husband, took a plate, and nibbled enough to scrabble the food. She took a few sips of coffee and headed upstairs to change. Minutes later, she was out the door to jog the two blocks to her folks.

***

The door bell rang at close to 10:00 a.m. Gayle was not expecting anyone this early on a Sunday morning, but she answered. "Good morning sweetheart."

Liv stepped in. "Good morning, Mom. How's Dad?"

After walking into the kitchen, Gayle poured coffees. Both sat in the nook. "He's tired these days. I can hear him in the shower right now."

Sipping her coffee Liv asked, "I mean with Dad's health after going to the hospital."

Gayle nodded. "Yes. We had a scare. The doctors took labs and they're good. Arteries are partly blocked. Somewhat reasonable for his age. But he'll need to watch his diet, exercise and take aspirin."

Liv's science studies helped her understand the anatomy of her dad's situation. But she was not familiar enough to make any further suggestions than had already been advised. "Sounds like Dad needs to take care of himself. Always worried about 'his girls.'"

"True. It's time we took care of him," Gayle agreed.

Both were quiet and thinking about the wedding last night and they smiled, knowing the other one's thoughts. Liv started. "So, what did you think about the wedding yesterday?"

"The wedding was nice." Gayle held back on what had transpired after the event.

"You know what I meant. The shenanigans with the girls."

Gayle nodded. "You are asking what I thought or are you wanting my advice?"

Liv decided. "Both."

"Well, the fiasco was quite a performance. Not appropriate at an outdoor wedding." Gayle paused. "I was impressed that Flick took charge. A little rough I might say, but he took charge. Those girls are loose cannons. They seem to be the result of little or no discipline. Shame really. With few or no guidelines, they don't seem to have respect for themselves or for others."

Liv listened intently. "I fear there is no hope for the girls even if they went to charm school."

Both giggled. "More like boot camp," Gayle added. "I believe Flick is the only person who could get a grip on these two. Which isn't fair to him or Hannah as they are starting their life together and with a little one on the way."

Liv had similar thoughts. She nodded.

Gayle asked, "You're not thinking of getting involved, are you?"

Liv shrugged. "I'd like to help. I just can't see how."

Gayle understood her daughter and knew her heart. "It isn't about the promise you made when you were a child, is it?"

"A little. Feel I owe them something. I have the need to help. I want them to know I care. I just don't know what to do."

Gayle advised her. "I think you spend some time with the girls. Get to know them. I fear that if you hand them all they need, you're just teaching them to come back and take more."

"Throw them a bone and they want the whole cow?"

Gayle laughed. "Something like that. I'm not trying to imply they are bad girls. I sense they are desperate."

Liv and Gayle were on the same trend of thought. Both were thinking of Ruby's influence. Gayle, a wise woman, said nothing but Liv felt comfortable to say, "I suspect the girls' actions and behaviours are a direct result of their upbringing. I suspect they are a little like their mother, Ruby."

Gayle nodded. "You can't dismiss that notion."

Peter entered the kitchen fully dressed, hair wet and groomed. Gayle handed him a cup of coffee.

"Good to see you my girl," he said.

Hugging her dad, Liv jumped right onto topic. "How are you?" "I mean now that you are home after being in the hospital."

Peter looked at Gayle and then realized his girls were worried about him. "I'm fine. Promise to take care and follow the doctor's orders," he said with a reassuring grin. He sat down sipping his coffee.

Liv realized she had to go. Liam would be awake. "You better." Putting her shoes on, she added, "You better take care. You better listen to what the doctors tell you."

Peter had never heard a firm voice from Liv towards him. He was taken aback but understood her love for him. "I promise. I will." Standing at the door with Gayle, he said, "You know I will. I love you and your mother more than I love myself. My sweet wife here had me make the same promise the other day."

Liv ran off with a wave. "Good." She jogged towards home.

The sound of a lawn mower echoed as a backdrop on this early Sunday morning. The sound was coming from the side of the house. Gayle and Peter went down the front steps and found Chuck busy working on their lawn.

Peter blinked, and Gayle gasped. "What do you think you are doing?"

Chuck turned and looked up with a smile. "Followed Liv and decided to get busy. Then I decided to borrow stuff from Gideon. This place needs help. O.k. with you?"

Gayle smiled. Peter frowned and went back in the house.

Hours later, the premises looked amazing. Lawns back and front had been cut, trimmed, and weeded. In the back Gayle came out to talk with Chuck. "Would you like some lunch? Now that the yard is prim and beautiful, we can sit and relax over lunch."

Chuck followed Gayle into the house. "There are face-clothes and towels in the bathroom down the hall. Help yourself. Lunch will be ready in a minute."

Chuck came back to a platter of crabmeat with cream cheese on croissants. There was also fresh fruit and leftover white cake from the wedding, which Liv had brought over. Sparkly fruit punch had been poured into tall glasses and there was a pitcher of ice water. The sun was trying to come out and the noon had a slight breeze. The three enjoyed a nice lunch. Gayle stayed quiet, wanting her husband to initiate a conversation and possibly make a friend. Lord knows the man had been walking around without any male companionship since retirement. O.k. a few rounds of golf with retired peers.

Peter would have stayed quiet but sensed his wife's silence. "So, what did you think about the shenanigans last night?"

Chuck had thought about the incident. "I would have been embarrassed if they were my girls."

Peter smiled. "Shocking when Flick undressed and then dove into the pool. We left. Very embarrassing I would say."

Chuck laughed. "Oh, so you didn't see how he handled the girls?"

Gayle grinned. "No. Not all of it. What happened?"

Chuck sipped his sparkly fruit drink. "It was a sight. Flick pulled the girls out of the pool by the hair of their heads. Screaming of course. Hosed them down with the cold water with the sprinkler. Gave them a piece of his mind.

How they were to apologise to his wife for ruining their day, apologise to every guest. And oh yes, they were going home because he was supposed to be on his honeymoon and they were holding him up. His exact words. I understand they are back at the house and scrubbing the place to perfection as we speak."

Gayle said, "Liv didn't say anything about that. But, she was worried about Peter, I guess."

Peter smiled. "Well, someone has to tame these girls. Out of control. Heathens if you ask me. No offence I hope."

Chuck grinned. "No offence here, not my children."

The afternoon was enjoyed, and a friendship was in the making.

Chapter 27
The adjustments, 1983

Summer passed, and Liv was busy with her thesis. She decided her major was psychology, with a minor in sciences. Opportunities as an instructor in the Justice Department at Calgary University had been offered to Liv for the coming January semester. Lack of time was worse than a tight budget. Finding quality time as a family offered occasional weekends together. Most nights Liv's focus was on Liam, playing, nurturing, reading him to sleep.

Gideon and Liv always took a half hour to sit together in the sitting room talking about their days, their goals, their dreams. This commitment to "their" time strengthened their bond – their love. The strains of their obligations had challenges, but their relationship was solid and afforded support to conquer and accomplish.

The subject of Liv's siblings remained on the back burner. Often, on Friday afternoons, Liv would try to take the girls to lunch, to connect, to get to know them better. She asked about their goals and what they wanted to be but received blank stares. Liv realized they had been surviving on their wits with no direction. Other than Flick fine-tuning their behavior, no further obligations were expected.

The last week of August the girls came up with ideas of who they might want to be. Laughing and thinking herself funny, Kandy said, "I want to be an astronaut."

Sugar noticed Liv's look of dismay. "I just want to be a baby maker – it worked for my mother."

Liv listened and realized she had two extreme personalities; characters that would be a challenge to help with having a focus. It was especially difficult because Sugar tended to follow Kandy. Kandy believed she knew more than most people, though she was not educated. She had no trouble ignoring other peoples' suggestions and enforcing her own perceptions. This gave the illusion Kandy was strong and able, and Sugar found solace and safety in that.

How does one unravel the fabric that has been meshed with dysfunction? How does one create a new pattern to something more functional, more beautiful? Liv spoke with her mother to get ideas. Gayle suggested counseling. It might help the girls see the direction they were heading. No one had ever given Kandy and Sugar the idea of options or possibilities, not to mention the concept of "goals."

Flick visited Liv when he could. Usually it was on Sundays when Chuck would do lawn care for Peter and Gayle. The last visit, Liv wanted to know how she could help the girls.

Flick explained, "I have them cleaning offices at night to cover their living expenses." He hoped he was instilling responsibility and independence. "Problem is, I have a feeling that after work the girls hit the bars and carry on with the lifestyle they're familiar with." Then he asked Liv, "Have they mentioned if they met anyone or are seeing anyone?"

Liv knew the girls did not share much with her. "No."

Flick nodded. "That's what I thought."

Liv looked perplexed. "Why?"

Flick gave a gentle smile. "I get the idea the girls believe you're too fancy for them, that you wouldn't understand or appreciate they are down-to-earth girls."

Liv stayed quiet. She believed *she* was a down-to-earth girl. She decided not to correct what was said and knew they were entitled to their perceptions. If down-to-earth meant lost-with-no-direction, then they were right. Liv was not that kind of down-to-earth girl. Being herself, insightful and tactful, she said, "I would like to be a mentor, a compass, to empower and enlighten them in a course or direction productive to their well-being."

Flick was not used to such talk. He knew it was the voice of education. Who was he to argue with Liv seeing the quality of life she and Gideon were living? "Kudos to you for trying. You might as well be challenging Mount Everest with those two."

Liv knew he was right. Climbing Mount Everest meant great planning and execution to be successful. Then, that was what must happen. "What would the girls think about getting counseling?"

"They would think something was wrong with them. They're not good enough. Take offence. Tell you to shove it," he said, half grinning.

"What do you suggest?" Liv was scrambling for ideas.

Flick knew Liv meant well and admired her for wanting to help. "Well, the girls told me about your 'goals' conversation the other day."

Liv nodded.

Flick was formulating an idea. "Could bring them to a college of their interest and have them sit down with the education counselor."

Not a bad idea. "Have to first find out what the girls' interests are. Any ideas?" Liv asked.

Flick smiled. He had already had a blunt conversation with the girls about man pleasing and baby making and how that wouldn't get them anywhere near the "picket fence" dream life. "Kandy told me she takes care of Sugar, that she is motherly. The easy route would be a nanny. I explained she couldn't even manage herself on a good day." Kandy had not been pleased with his observations. "It seems she would like to become a nurse. I suggested that she become a PCA first to see if she would like that kind of job."

Liv asked, "A personal care aid?"

Flick nodded. "It would take six months and some money. But, it would be doable. She could still clean offices at night for a few hours. This would keep her out of trouble, I hope. It's just finding the cash. Right now, we're trying to save to qualify for a two-bedroom duplex. I have a prospect in North Calgary and the owner is selling both sides. I can only afford one side right now. The other side would allow me to keep on the girls."

Liv was thinking about the girls and how this option would help both of them. They had a caring nature. The side by side duplex would not be a bad idea. Flick would be close by and on them. She wondered how she might be able to help. "Let me talk with Gideon about both girls taking the PCA course. Also, about helping to secure both sides of the duplex. I think these options would help you and the girls. How much time do you need to have an answer about the duplex?"

"It's about the bank not trusting my business being less than a year old. I have enough of a down payment for both. Chuck has secured a ton of work. High rises are going up like mushrooms in the downtown core. Builders can't find enough tradespersons and plumbers, especially master plumbers. So, I am one of a few that are under contract with the primary installation. Also, once the pre-fab bathrooms for the various floors are installed, I'm contracted to install the plumbing fixtures. The contracts for the next two years would have both sides of the duplex paid off with money to spare to live on."

Liv was speechless. "That's impressive."

Flick laughed. "Tell the bank that."

Liv had an idea and asked Flick to come for dinner on Saturday. She wanted to talk with Gideon and her parents about financing the duplex. She trusted Flick, though not so much the girls. She decided to look into the PCA program; the pre-requisites, the when, and the costs. She might be able to finance their education to help get the girls on their feet. This would only happen, though, if Gideon was on board.

***

Gideon arrived home from work. Liv was preparing dinner and keeping an eye on Liam crawling around in the family room. "Hi hon," Gideon said while sorting through the mail and a few bills. Then he kissed her on the cheek.

Liv was quiet and rehearsing her thoughts to be presented to her husband. Gideon knew something was up as his wife seldom failed to kiss him back. Liv looked occupied and distracted and dinner was going to be a serious conversation. He decided to crack open the case. "Anything new happen today?"

Liv looked up, wondering if Gideon was on to her. He was. He just didn't know what about. "Spoke with Flick today," she said. "Trying to figure out how to help the girls. We came up with a few ideas. Would like to run them by you."

Gideon nodded. A chill went up his spine as though he knew he wasn't going to like this meeting of her mind. Somehow, he sensed it would involve his or their participation. Gideon was a frugal man, though kind and generous to her and Liam. He was not a philanthropist by nature.

The plates were set on the table. Liam sat in his high chair while Liv fed him his pureed version of their dinner. Gideon ate quietly waiting to hear what Liv wanted to discuss.

"I have been taking the girls to lunch most Fridays and trying to get to know them." She wiped Liam's mouth before giving him his cup with a sipper. "When I asked them if they had any goals, they looked at me as if I had just landed from Mars."

Gideon held his thoughts for the moment and continued eating.

"It turns out that Flick has had the same conversations with a little better success." Liv shared.

"So, he knows what they want to do?"

Liv nodded. "It seems Kandy wants to be a nurse. I thought that was a good direction. Flick suggested that she become a PCA first to see if she liked this field."

Gideon interrupted. "PCA?"

"Yes, personal care aid."

Getting into the meat of the issue, Gideon asked, "What's it going to take?"

Liv continued, "I'm going to look into the pre-requisites for the course, when, how long, and how much. I believe it would be six months and a few thousand dollars for each girl."

Gideon asked, "Both girls?"

"We're thinking it might be good for both girls. Test the waters in that field."

"Six months and who will support them during their training?" Gideon queried.

"Flick has them cleaning offices for a few hours each night. He would have them continue while going to school. Keep them responsible, occupied, busy, and with a goal." She paused. "He feels it is doable with a little help to finance their education." Waiting to hear a response, she got nothing. "I was hoping to have your blessing to help the girls find their footing in a positive direction."

Gideon stared at his plate as he ate, not wanting to commit to this project of Liv's without thinking it through. "You might want to ask your father to write up an agreement of sorts. Obligations and consequences, should one or both fail. I have a gut feeling if you pay for the course for each of them — hand it out, they will not take it seriously and not bother to complete the program. They haven't lost anything, and you have lost the money you invested in them. The only person disappointed would be you. Hypothetically speaking, of course."

Liv grasped his meaning. "I think that's a good idea. Sort of a contract with an agreement, an understanding." Now she started to eat her dinner while Liam played with his plastic keys.

Gideon took his plate to the dishwasher. "It's more than that. It's the consequences should they not fulfill their obligations. They should have to pay every bit back to you. Just my thoughts on the matter."

Hesitantly, she asked, "You wouldn't be opposed to me or us paying for this part of the girls' education?"

"No, it would be all right with a contract. It's your money you've saved even though it was from your parents," Gideon noted.

Liv had forgotten about the account that had a generous amount in it. "I might mention this to my parents, letting them know how much has not been used. They might be pleased to have the money help the girls with their education. At least I hope so." Liv smiled at the possible solution.

Gideon picked up Liam to play with him. Then he realized Liv had not finished her dinner and was deep in thought. "Is everything all right, my incredibly beautiful wife?"

That got Liv's attention and she smiled. "There is something else. Not certain you have the time right now to hear the rest."

Gideon appreciated his wife's insightfulness; how she respected his with his son. "Is it urgent?"

Liv shook her head. "Not at this moment. But, before the night is through. I have to give Flick an answer about something important in a few days. I'd like your take on this matter as soon as possible."

Gideon smiled. "O.k. Give me one hour with Liam. One hour for me to relax in the hot tub, and then I will devote an hour to you. How does that sound?"

Liv said with a smile, "Perfect. Thank you."

Liv went to the study, worked a bit on her thesis, and later settled Liam to bed. She put the kettle on for tea and watched her husband soak in the hot tub with his eyes closed. She waited in the family room with her own eyes closed rehearsing the next conversation that needed to take place. She must have nodded off to sleep because she found Gideon standing over her with his bathrobe on and a cup of tea in hand. "Darling. I'm here for you," he said with a smile and in a gentle voice. He sensed his wife being burdened with university and worried about her aging parents – Peter's health, her siblings. Still, she took incredible care of Liam and him with so much on her mind. It seemed Liv could barely move from emotional and physical exhaustion. "Sweetheart wake up. Let's have a chat."

Liv pushed herself up onto her elbows to rise. She hadn't realized how tired she was and almost wanted to head to bed, thinking the chat could wait, but knowing it couldn't. "O.k.," she said, finding a smile. "Flick has been doing amazingly well with his new business. Chuck keeps getting contracts, good contracts. Downtown is growing, buildings are going up. Flick is one of several master plumbers selected for the primary stages on several high rises. Not only that, he has contracts when the pre-fab bathrooms are installed to put in the fixtures."

Gideon didn't see a concern with too much work. "Sound incredible to me."

Liv smiled. "It is." She sipped her tea. "Flick found a side by side duplex in the North that would work well for him and Hannah. The girls could be next door and Flick would be able to keep a handle on them."

Gideon was not so quick to agree, knowing there was a glitch. He continued to listen.

"As life would have it, Flick's business is less than a year old – not much financial history. He has a sizable down payment for both sides but can't qualify for the mortgages." She let this last statement take hold of the conversation. "I was wondering if we could co-sign to help Flick and it would help the girls at the same time."

Gideon frowned and stayed quiet. It seemed like an eternity that Liv waited for a response. Finally, it came. "I trust Flick," he said. "The girls are a wild card. They could run off and leave him hanging with the mortgage. I just don't know. This one is going to take a bit of thinking." Gideon sat beside his wife with an arm around her shoulders. "Would your parents help Flick? They might be inclined toward a business venture."

Liv thought about it and wasn't so sure if Peter and Gayle would want to get involved. "I guess it wouldn't hurt to ask."

Gideon stood up and took both Liv's hands to help her up. "It's late, my sweet girl. Let's go to bed."

***

The next day Gayle came over to visit Liv. Being a grandmother was the greatest gift a woman could be granted. In most cases, it was none of the work and all the fun and pleasure. Gayle had the privilege of the help of her maid, Milly, to take care of Liam while Liv was at university. Today Liv had off, and Milly was at the house. When Liam saw Grandma, he wanted her attention. It took a while before the girls got to chat and Liam settled on the floor playing with his toys.

The ladies sat in the family room with their coffees. Liv started the conversation and so badly wanted "the chat dance" with her mother.

"I had coffee with Flick the other day. He shared some information about the girls," Liv started.

Gayle remembered Liv's thoughts about the girls' goals, or the lack thereof. "He knows what they want to do?"

Liv smiled and shared the plan to send the girls to college; the PCA program. "I wanted to talk to you about the account you had for me while I was a student. There's quite a bit of money left that would actually cover the costs."

Gayle nodded. "I can't see why that money couldn't be used to help the girls. Do you think they would complete the course?"

"Gideon asked the same question. He suggested I have Dad write up an agreement of expectations, conditions, and consequences. Again, I think this is a good idea."

Gayle endorsed it. "I agree."

Liv was pleased with her mother's input and that they were of the same mind. Now she was preparing to talk about the duplex business idea. For some reason it was of a greater magnitude and a more complicated topic.

Gayle realized Liv was deep in thought. "You have something else on your mind?"

Liv nodded. "There's more. Flick found a duplex, side by side, that would work well for him, Hannah, and the coming baby. The other side would have the girls nearby so that he could keep an eye on them."

Gayle understood.

Liv shared the complications of Flick qualifying for a mortgage, not to mention two mortgages for both sides of a duplex.

Gayle absorbed what was shared. "It sounds like he might need some help?"

Liv agreed. "I'm afraid more than Gideon and I can offer." She was trying to muster up her question about her parents playing a part or engaging in a business venture to help Flick.

Gayle jumped now to say, "Hold that thought."

Liv blinked thinking to herself. *What thought?* She listened.

"I need to talk with your father. I have an idea that might be the ideal solution. I can't say anything right now. Give me till tomorrow morning and I'll let you know one way or another if what I'm thinking will be a possibility. O.k.?"

What did Liv have to lose by being patient and waiting? "O.k." She smiled, knowing that with her mother's heart and her sharp and clever mind, the outcome would be good.

Liv walked her mother to the door. "Flick is coming to dinner tomorrow."

Child's Love

Gayle knew Liv was hoping to have a plan that would help Flick and the girls. Her incredible daughter had been burdened with a promise – a promise that a little girl could never fulfill. Now she was a woman with the same aching heart, striving to help support her siblings and in some way keep that promise.

Chapter 28
The Plan, 1983

The weekend arrived, and Liv was anxious about Flick coming to dinner. With no specific plan how to help, she was nervous. Gayle had not made contact about her ideas or thoughts about Flick securing the duplex. Ideas were one thing but creating a plan of execution to forge ahead to success was another.

Flick arrived and hung out around the kitchen while Liv and Gideon made tweaks on the dinner preparations. Excited to see his uncle, Liam was all smiles when Flick picked him up and tossed him the air. Flick was not aware that Liam had just had his dinner. He upchucked all over Flick's face with warm vomitus of pureed meat and potatoes. In a dash, Flick was in the bathroom washing off the aftermath.

The phone rang. Gideon answered as Liv was busy cleaning up Liam. "Hello."

"This is Gayle. Would you mind if we came over for dinner as well? We would like to join you. I understand Flick will be there and we would like to talk with him."

Without hesitation Gideon said, "Most certainly. Do come over and join us for dinner. You like salad and Shepard's pie?"

Gayle confirmed, "We do. Be right over."

Ten minutes later, the door to the garage opened and then Peter and Gayle entered the hallway. "Hello everyone," Gayle announced, going towards her grandson. "You're such a cutie."

Liam was all smiles.

Dinner was set, and wine was served in hopes of creating a relaxing environment. It was more so to relax Liv's nerves. She couldn't explain why helping Flick was so important to her. She suspected that it was an avenue that demonstrated her desire to assist her siblings – helping them get a good footing for the future. Or was it to ease her feelings and conscience? Either way, the need was present and had to be addressed.

Peter was quieter than normal. The ladies kept an eye on his demeanor, not certain if it was his health or his mind that was creating the solitary stance. When the salad was finished, and the main course served, Peter cleared his throat. Everyone sat at attention; quiet, waiting, listening.

Tearing his dinner bun apart, Peter started to talk. "Usually I wait to discuss business after dinner, in the sitting room, with a cognac." All eyes focused on the patriarch of the family. "It has been brought to my attention that Flick has an interest in a property in the North, a side by side duplex. His reasons for the purchase are for the sake of family. Admirable."

Flick nodded while chewing the lamb-based Shepard's pie.

Peter continued. "Gayle and I do not usually share what properties we have purchased over the years. We have been fortunate to obtain over a dozen." He wondered how much he should disclose. "On several occasions, we had the privilege of purchasing trashed properties in prosperous locations at a fraction of the cost. However, the costs came later with renovations. After everything was said and done, half of these properties got sold immediately, and half were rented out to executives over the years. During our retirement, we have been blessed with the rewards of our good decisions."

Gayle touched his hand with a smile encouraging him to continue to the finish line.

"My dear wife and myself have a few properties left and have been in the process of liquidating them. We are getting too old to manage the upkeep." Peter smiled at Liv and Gideon.

Liv sat motionless and unable to eat, waiting, and hoping ...

Peter jumped back into the discussion of the duplex. "I understand you are interested in a duplex in the North," he said, looking at Flick.

Flick said, "Yes, I am." He was smart enough to remain quiet till the elder man finished his point.

Peter had a frown and grin at the same time. This was often perplexing to those who did not know him well. The frown was a front that gave the appearance of deep concern. The grin was an indication that he was up to something. Liv caught his facial expression and relaxed with knowing.

Peter was now ready to declare his proposal. "I have a property in this area, which is in demand. It is large and has a mother-in-law suite with two bedrooms, one bathroom, kitchen, dining area, and large living room. The house itself has four bedrooms, two and a half baths, a double garage and a large backyard. It's well kept.

Flick was getting red in the face. "I know I won't be able to afford this property, nor would I qualify." He shook his head, believing this offer only proved he was a struggling man with dreams.

Gayle noticed the look of despair on Flick's face and tugged at Peter's arm to get to the point.

Peter stepped up and asked, "What is the price of the side by side duplex?"

Flick disclosed the amount.

Peter nodded and looked at his wife and Gayle smiled back and nodded. This secret body language, like a dance, could only be shared with years of friendship and understanding.

Gayle got up and said with a gentle laugh, "If you don't tell them, I will."

Peter said. "O.k. We would like to offer you this house with the mother-in-law suite for the same price as the side-by-side duplex. It would have to be approved by Liv as it is her inheritance. You would have to put down the five percent as with any purchase with a bank. However, the interest these days is seventeen to nineteen percent, which is high. We expect five percent. You'd pay the minimum over twenty-five years. Any payments over and above go directly to the principal without penalty. The property will have Liv's and Gideon's names on the title as mortgage lenders. Of course, you, Flick, will be on the title. Legal fees will be taken care of by myself and drawn up by my peers. If this appeals to you, we would like to show you the property."

Flick was speechless for the first time in his life and looked at Liv for direction. Liv nodded with smiles.

Flick, not understanding the legal titles asked, "So when will the place be mine?"

Peter stated, "When the property is fully paid. The title will be transferred to your name only."

Flick then asked Liv, "What do you think?"

Liv smiled. "I think it's a great offer. I think the mother-in-law suite is better than the duplex on several accounts. One is the property itself; the location and the price, not to mention that legal access is better."

Flick asked, "What do you mean legal access is better?"

Liv realized she had too many thoughts she was trying to convey, and she needed to clarify. "I mean, with the duplex, the girls would be tenants and could deny you access because it's legally a separate property. You'd have to give twenty-four hours notice of entry unless in an emergency. Whereas, the mother-in-law suite is a part of your house. Thus, you can enter any part of your home and cannot be denied. Then the girls are simply living with you, yet you all can have your privacy."

Everyone was finished their dinner except for Peter. Flick was up on his feet. "Let's look at this house." What Liv had shared made sense and made for a better arrangement with the girls. He needed to have the power to get Kandy and Sugar on the best possible track in life. Yet, he needed to have his life with his family as well. This could be the solution. He realized he was being given the opportunity to have a quality property at a discounted price with financing in place. Bonavista was pricey for the smallest of homes. Then Flick went over to Liv. "That is, of course, if you agree with Peter and Gayle's offer?"

Liv stood up and hugged her brother. "I agree."

In all of these negotiations, though, Flick realized he had another problem. Salt.

***

Flick arrived home and waited for Hannah to finish her shift at the drug store. He wanted to share what had transpired that evening. Liv had sent him home with a plate of leftovers for Hannah to have a late dinner.

Entering the apartment, Hannah looked exhausted. Flick didn't want to overwhelm her with his excitement and he tried to contain his emotions. His eyes were dancing with eagerness. Hannah thought he was in the mood and was touched by Flick's reaction to her, though she only hoped to have something to eat and relax. Fatigue was the theme of her days with the pregnancy. Pleasing her man was important...just not this moment.

Flick decided to do his best to ease in the information about his day. Seeing how tired Hannah appeared, he took her coat from her and hung it up. She walked into the kitchen and found a plate prepared. The smell was delicious, but the lamb was a strong scent that had her stomach heaving. Flick wanted her to eat something and thought Hannah was turning her nose up.

"It smells wonderful. But, it seems to be getting to me. I think I'll have soup and crackers. It's all that I can handle right now." She is explaining her nausea while holding her distended belly. The baby was due the next month; October.

Flick got busy heating up a can of chicken soup while Hannah sat on the sofa unwinding from her day. Normally work would not be a challenge, but these days with the baby inside it felt like double duty and she would get tired more quickly. Flick was never out of energy, though he tried to understand his wife's condition.

Sitting with Hannah at the table, Flick bit his lower lip and fidgeted, struggling to contain himself to be patient. Their relationship was not about walking on glass. They had promised to do their very best to be honest and patient and to seek understanding. Flick found it difficult at times since Hannah would hold her concerns inside. She would need to be drawn out. Flick, on the other hand, had no trouble saying what was on his mind and found he had to slow down his pace when communicating something important.

When he was all revved up, this was that moment to slow down. It was a conflict within Flick's being that challenged his patience. Hannah, on the other hand, thought he was seeking intimate attention and was avoiding eye contact. She could not refuse those intense blue eyes.

Flick watched as Hannah ate the last spoonful of soup. Time to talk. "Seen a place today that is perfect for us and the girls."

Hannah looked up but said nothing.

"Peter and Gayle have a property that they are willing to sell to us for the same price as the side by side duplex. Except it's a nice house, in a nice area, with a mother-in-law suite."

Hannah was engaged in the conversation. "What good is that when the bank won't approve a mortgage?"

Flick had his mischievous grin of knowing. "That's just it. It's Liv's inheritance and she will be financing it for us. 5% down, 5% interest. 25-year term. Can pay the minimum to as much as we want without penalties. The house is four bedrooms, large backyard. The suite has inside access and a private entrance. It's a two bedroom."

Hannah thought for a minute. "Where is Salt going to live?"

Flick nodded. "I was thinking about that too. I want him downstairs with the girls, but with them working and studying for school, I can't see all three living comfortably. It would be too tight.

"So, he'll be living with us?" Hannah concluded.

"For now." Flick offered. With four rooms he didn't feel there should be a problem, though secretly he knew their privacy and personal life would be in jeopardy. "Can we give it a try? I don't have any other solutions right now. I'm asking you to work with me."

Hannah nodded, too tired to argue. "When can I see the house?"

Flick was thrilled he'd gotten past his worst fear about Salt. At least for the time being. "I can call in the morning and ask. Hopefully, they wouldn't mind in the afternoon."

Hannah smiled and headed to the bathroom and Flick ran ahead to run the bath. He liked sitting on the toilet lid and chatting as Hannah relaxed. He felt connected to the one person who loved him, and he loved so much. He loved feeling the baby kicking his hand when they snuggled off to sleep. It bought him contentment and peace beyond anything he'd ever experienced.

Falling asleep, he thought to himself that moving to Calgary was the best thing he'd ever done. It was also the hardest work he had ever done to keep his family together.' It had all been worth it! Seeing the faces of Gunner and Gavin he fell asleep.

***

Sunday morning began with the sounds of raking leaves. Peter and Gayle smiled knowing Chuck was puttering about and doing the fall cleaning on the property. Around 10:00 a.m. they invited him in to have a coffee break and some breakfast.

Sitting at the table with Gayle and Peter chatting like old friends. Chuck was like the son they never had. He came and went without demands or expectations. While they were eating the phone rang. Gayle was standing at the kitchen counter and answered. "Hello…Just a minute. I'll let you know." She turned to Peter. "Flick would like to see the house today. To show it to Hannah."

Peter nodded. "Would 3:00 p.m. be all right?"

Gayle chatted a minute to Flick and then replied, "Yes. That would be fine. We'll meet you there at 3:00."

Peter realized Chuck had not been made aware of the recent events and he updated him on the goings on with little detail. "We have a house for sale and Flick is interested. Wants Hannah to look at it."

Chuck sipped his coffee. He was pleased for Flick. "I'm glad for him. He's a good kid. I should get back and finish the yard."

Peter asked as Chuck was going out the back door, "What do you think of coming over Tuesday and teaching this old guy a bit of poker? I bought a new set the other day. Think we should break it in?"

Chuck had forgotten about the poker game and he smiled. "Sure thing. How's about 7:00 p.m.?"

Peter grinned. "Perfect."

***

The viewing took place and Hannah loved the home. She agreed the house was big enough for them and their new baby. The mother-in-law suite was small but perfect for the girls. Her only concern was Salt, but she would have to make the best of it. Her husband was trying so hard to help his siblings and make her happy. He was wonderful, and she would try to appreciate, to understand the great strides, accomplishments, and miracles Flick had achieved for all their benefit.

On Monday, the papers would be drawn up and ready for signing on Tuesday. Flick and Hannah were thrilled about their good fortune. They couldn't have planned a better start for their life if they'd tried.

Liv and Gideon were pleased at how things were working out. Liv was sleeping better these days and so much happier. Gideon sensed it was the power of Liv's parents that had helped Flick and their siblings and ultimately enabled Liv to assist Flick, Salt and the girls to be better situated with a great start.

The child in Liv had made a promise long ago – a promise to get her siblings to Calgary so they could live together. Liv had never quite forgotten her promise and guilt had played misery with her heart. With her parents' guidance and help, she had accomplished setting her siblings up in a lovely home and close by.

Salt was indifferent. He missed the bowling team and soft ball team. Emotional connections to people were not his strong suit. He loved his family but did not know how to show affection. Salt's passion was in the things he could accomplish, and he ignored what he could not do. When he had seen the suite for the girls, he would have liked the privacy for himself, but he would not complain. Flick was the man of the house and he would listen to him.

The girls had mixed feelings about the move. They liked the new mother-in-law suite, but they liked being in the apartment above the laundromat more. They had more freedom and enjoyed the night life. Flick would be in their faces now and they knew that was the plan. Then they were told they were taking the PCA course. Kandy was annoyed – it wasn't real nursing and it seemed like a waste of time. But what choice did she have? Sugar had no interest but would go along if Kandy was going to do the program. The girls signed the agreement with regards to their education. Neither was pleased when they discovered they had no wiggle room and would simply have to go to school. They had to achieve the best they could with all their efforts or they would have to pay back every cent to Liv. Just passing was not an option. The bar of expectation had been set and the girls felt the chains of restraint. Instead of seeing the opportunity as an avenue for greater things, for them it was a trap of resentment.

Chapter 29
The twist of Fate, 1983

For one week everything that was planned had been put into place. Then, what had seemed perfect started going wrong. Flick and Hannah moved into the house right away and prepared the baby's room. Hannah was ordered by Flick to stop working and she had no fight left in her to argue. Flick made it clear he was the man of the house and it was his job to provide. Hannah understood the tough exterior was Flick's fight to survive. She knew he took his roles seriously and with conviction, and that it was a great responsibility. The siblings moved in; the girls' downstairs and Salt in his room upstairs.

On September 6th, after Labour Day weekend on Tuesday, the girls started their PCA course. Flick was working around the clock with Chuck at his side. Flick had decided to keep Chuck busy as they didn't need any more contracts for now.

The girls came and went between school and cleaning jobs in the evenings. They would blast their music till the clock struck 11:00 p.m. and then the floors below would become silent.

The environment in the main part of the house was strained. Salt stayed in his room most of the time, staring out the window for something to do. Hannah would have a plate on the counter for him with toast and an egg, juice and coffee in the morning. Lunch was a sandwich and glass of milk for Salt's taking. Then there'd be a plate of dinner and tea for the evening. Hannah always went to her room with no desire to have contact with Salt.

Salt would come out to eat if he could find something and then return to his space. He was lost, confused, bored, and didn't know how to express himself. Inside he was getting wound up like a top. Any setback could be a trigger. He was in a prison of confusion. He could hear the girls coming and going. Flick was gone most of the time and returned home late in the night. Salt sensed that Hannah did not care for him and believed she did not like him. Everyone was occupied with their lives and did not notice the hell Salt was spiraling within.

The next day Hannah wondered where the soiled dishes were. She knocked on Salt's door and entered. Salt was standing in the same clothes he'd been wearing the night before. His bed was untouched, and he was staring out the window. The dishes were stacked on the nightstand.

"You need to get the dishes in the kitchen sink," said Hannah. She believed she was talking to a full-grown adult. "You might want to take a shower or something and change your clothes."

Saying nothing, Salt turned around and stared at Hannah. He waited for her to leave, picked up the dishes, and brought them to the sink. Then he found a change of clothes and entered the bathroom. Aunty Jewels or the girls used to start the shower for him, lay out a towel, point to the soap and shampoo, and he would take it from there.

He was lost as to what he should do. He turned on the shower full blast and pulled the lever. Then he jumped in to find the water scorching hot and screamed. Hannah ran in while Salt was thrashing about in the tub. The towels in the bathroom were only for show, and she ran out to the linen closet to get a towel. Returning, she saw the steam and felt the heat and realized Salt didn't know what to do. She bent over, shut off the water, handed Salt a towel and left the bathroom exasperated that she had to deal with an idiot.

Salt was dressed and in his room within the half hour. Sounds of whimpering could be heard, but Hannah was not going to investigate. She wasn't sure what she would find or how she would handle the situation. Better to let Flick know what had happened and he could take care of Salt.

That afternoon, Hannah discovered the shower curtain shredded and off the hooks. The bathroom floor was soaked with water. Feces were streaked on the toilet and the side of the counter. Hannah could not take much more. She marched over to Salt's door and knocked. No answer. Quietly, she opened the door and found Salt asleep, supine on the bed. His eyes opened quickly, and he glared at her in the doorway. Though he said nothing, his eyes said, *what do you want?*

Hannah wanted Salt to know that his habits were not acceptable. "You need to clean up the bathroom. You left a huge mess. Get in there and clean it up. The crap, poop is disgusting. Don't ever spread poop in my bathroom ever again." She waited for Salt to get up, but he didn't move. In a huff, Hannah marched out of the room in disgust.

Salt got up and went to the bathroom. He looked for something to clean up the mess and found Comet powder with bleach in the lower cabinet. There were no rags or clothes to be had. Noticing the towels on the rack, he took them and began to scrub with some water and cleanser, scouring compulsively to make it perfect. But he didn't know how to get rid of the powder residue, so he kept at the problem for an hour.

Hannah wondered what was taking Salt so long to finish the task. She knocked on the door. Silence. "Can I come in?" she asked. There was no answer.

Hannah opened the door to find every wall and surface caked with Comet and her new towels removed from their showcase place. Salt was standing there with the bleached rags in his hands. He wasn't sure what to say but he hoped Hannah would be pleased with his efforts.

Hannah gasped, enraged. "What do you think you're doing? Look at this mess. It's worse than before. Look at my new towels. They're ruined." Frustrated and angry she yelled, "Are you a stupid idiot?"

Salt's fuse exploded inside, and he erupted into a rage and lunged at Hannah with all his fury. Grabbing hold of her neck, he picked her up and bashed her into the hall wall. Hannah fell to the floor gasping for air. Salt kept kicking her repeatedly, saying nothing. Hannah tried to wrap her arms around her baby to protect her fetus. Salt only saw his mother, Ruby, pregnant as usual. No one was going to call him a stupid idiot. The thought fueled his anger and the beating didn't let up.

Hannah could no longer feel impact of each kick. Her mind and body shut down into a coma state. She was catatonic, paralysed, and in shock. Salt looked down and saw a rag doll covered in blood. He stopped, walked to his room, and shut the door. Knowing he had done wrong, he waited in fear never leaving his room. Standing ... and waiting.

Flick arrived home around 9:00 p.m. and found Hannah unconscious and lying on the hallway floor. He honestly thought they had been broken into. But the place looked in order, so a burglary was not the intent. So, what had happened? Flick called the police explaining how he'd found his wife. In minutes the ambulance arrived. Hannah was barely alive. Blood was gushing between her legs. The police were right behind the paramedics. The story told to 911 had the police believing Flick had battered his wife and was trying to pin the crime on a fictitious person. He was promptly arrested.

Down at the station, Flick was anxious, upset, and worried about his wife. The police believed it was an act they'd seen a hundred times. He was locked into a room with a two-way mirror hollering, "I get a phone call, right?" An officer entered the room and then escorted Flick to a phone and guarded him until the call was accomplished.

It was midnight. "Hey, Liv. I'm in trouble."

Liv listened as Flick explained what he'd come home to and how he'd been arrested. "They think I did it. They believe I beat up my wife."

Liv couldn't understand what had happened to Hannah. Thinking of who was in the house, she said, "The girls wouldn't do something like this?"

Flick then thought of Salt. He hadn't seen him when he'd arrived home and hadn't see him when the ambulance or police arrived. Was he in his room? Flick hoped he was o.k. Then the thought crossed his mind – could Salt have done this to Hannah? He shared these thoughts with Liv. "Can you go over to the house and see if Salt is all right?" he asked desperately. "I know it's late. Please."

Liv wasn't going to put herself in jeopardy and suggested. "I think you need to tell the police about Salt. Ask them to check on him – to go in the house and check all the rooms. If you do that I will enter your place and check on Salt with the police."

Flick thought it wouldn't hurt. "I'm on it. I'll ask the police to give you a call. I don't think they'll let me have a second call."

Liv said she would go over to the house and wait for the police. She hung up.

Gideon was already in bed, half asleep. Liv explained the phone call and Gideon was out of bed and scrambling for a pair of jeans. "No, I'll go over."

Five minutes later, Gideon entered the house. Lights were on as he walked down the hallway and saw a blood bath on the walls and carpet. What had gone on around here? He checked the rooms one by one till he opened Salt's.

There stood Salt waiting and staring at him. There was blood all over his runners.

Gideon calmly asked Salt, "Come out to the kitchen so we can talk. All right buddy?"

Salt hesitated but needed the bathroom. After a few minutes, he came and stood in the kitchen. Gideon had called the police explaining what he'd found.

The police took their sweet time, about twenty minutes, but Gideon was able to get Salt to talk. He stuttered in choppy sentences. Hannah had called him a stupid idiot and then he'd kicked her. He explained that his mother had called him names and he'd hit her too. He was upset and scared because he knew he had done something wrong. The police stood back, observed, and listened. The boy was just under seventeen. Social services would need to be called in. The police called the station explaining they had the wrong guy and maybe they should drive Flick to the hospital to see how his wife was doing.

Just then, Gayle and Peter showed up, and Gideon explained the situation. Gayle went over to Salt and chatted calmly to the young man. The police had already heard the story and their shift was coming to an end. They still had the paperwork to do and time was ticking. Gayle explained she was a social worker, now retired.

Gayle explained to Salt that the police would have to bring him to the station and ask him questions. She promised to help him through all the confusion. Salt trusted Gayle and went in the police cruiser. By the time they arrived at the station, Flick had already gone to the hospital. Gayle and Peter could sit with Salt during his questioning.

When Salt went with the police the girls came up to see what the commotion was about. Gideon explained what had transpired.

The girls stood in shock. Kandy asked, "Where's Flick now?"

"I believe he's on his way to the hospital to see how Hannah is doing." Gideon looked around at the mess. "You guys all right?"

The girls looked around and nodded. "Think we might try to clean up this mess. It looks pretty bad."

Gideon agreed, nodded, and left for home.

As he entered his home he wondered how Gayle and Peter had known and then showed up. He suspected Liv had talked with them. All the same it had worked out to help Salt. He only hoped Hannah and the baby would be all right, but he feared she had lost the child.

***

When Flick arrived at the hospital, Hannah was in the delivery room. Hours passed before any news of her condition was known. Alerted by Liv, Chuck arrived within the hour to support his son.

Flick was a nervous wreck. The police had informed him that it was Salt who had battered his wife. Flick went on about how he felt guilty. Hannah had tried to explain to him that she didn't trust Salt. He should have listened. He hadn't known how to solve her concerns to make everything right. Now, sitting and waiting with regret had him in knots. He worried about his child and hoped that the doctors could pull off a miracle and save both mother and child. It was a night of hell. Was it of his own doing? He was sure his wife would let him know.

Around five in the morning, a doctor came out to the waiting room. "You are Flick?"

Flick stood up. "Yes, I am. How is she?"

The doctor announced, "Hannah made it. Lost a lot of blood. She's resting right now." Pausing and choosing his next words, he said, "The baby didn't make it. I'm sorry."

Flick choked up with tears in his eyes. "Can I see her?"

The doctor nodded. "She's tired. Needs her rest. Needs to get stronger. Try not to keep her too long." Then he walked off.

Flick ran to the nurse's station asking to see Hannah. He was given the room number.

On entering her room, he didn't recognize his wife. She was black and blue, bandaged up, and with lines attached every which way. He called her name. "Hannah?"

Hannah opened her eyes. There was a flicker of recognition and then disappointment. It was a look that said, *what do you want?*

Flick was a strong man with a backbone. Looking at Hannah had him weak in the knees and feeling like a jelly fish. He was drained of emotion at the loss of his child and at seeing his wife's condition, knowing he could have prevented the catastrophe. How he could have, he did not know. He should have for sure, just – how? Hindsight has perfect vision.

The road to recovery would be greater than a few bruises healing. The loss of their expected child and the brutality of the assault were traumatic. Flick hoped that time would heal, and he'd have his wife home safe and sound.

Chuck advised him to get some sleep and drove Flick home. The man was exhausted and felt beaten. When he opened his door, he found the place cleaned. The carpet in the hallway had been scrubbed with bleach and a huge patch was discolored from the surrounding beige. The girls came up to greet Flick and hug him. They felt bad at what had happened. They should have made room for Salt to live with them downstairs. They knew his needs and how to handle his day-to-day care. Looking back, it had been unfair to expect Hannah to know what to do or how to handle Salt.

The girls made breakfast for Flick and themselves in the kitchen. They had coffee and listened to the events of the past night. The girls had news of their own but weren't sure Flick could handle any more. The problem was more severe than they thought. Hannah had lost a child.

Kandy usually spoke on behalf of them both, but Sugar spoke up in a gentle voice. "Flick we need to talk with you. It's important. I know you're so tired. But, what we have to tell needs to be said before Hannah comes home."

Flick had half finished his breakfast, and he took a sip of coffee. "Get it out. Let's have it. What do you have to say?"

Sugar continued. "Both Kandy and I are pregnant." They had been up all night trying to create solutions to their dilemma.

Kandy interjected. "With Hannah losing the baby and us having babies, we thought it would be a major problem."

Flick's brain could not handle much more. He was worried about Hannah and worried about Salt and wondering what was happening with him. Now the girls had lambasted him with being knocked up. "Yeah, I think Hannah would have a problem with that, right about now." Getting up out of his chair, he said, "I would have a problem with you guys pregnant anytime. For God sakes. Can't you keep your legs closed?"

The girls stayed quiet, letting Flick vent. Pacing with a cigarette in his hand, he barked, "I want to know the bastards that did this to you guys." Seldom did he smoke inside but this wasn't the moment to suggest going outside. "What about your schooling? Just figured a way to help you guys and you have to fuck it up." He shook his head.

Kandy said in their defense. "We're still going to finish the schooling. You don't have to worry about that."

Flick sharply responded, "Yeah, Who the hell will hire you when you're both looking like balloons when you're finished?"

They looked from one to the other and said nothing. They honestly hadn't thought things out that far to have an answer.

Flick put the cigarette out. "I've got to go find out what's happening with Salt."

Kandy stated. "You need sleep."

Flick blew up. "I need you guys to give me a fucking break. I lost my child last night. My wife's life is hanging by a thread. She looks at me like this was my fault and won't look me in the eye. I have a brother likely in prison, and two sisters knocked up." Almost screaming, he continued,

"Who the hell can sleep at a time like this? The shit pile keeps getting bigger. Got any more news I need to know?" He walked out.

***

Salt was put in a juvenile detention home for the time being. Social services were not prepared to create solutions for him till the criminal aspects of his case were clear and understood.

Flick felt helpless. The more he tried to keep his family together, the worse things got. He'd done everything he could to help his siblings and it all seemed to be a waste. They didn't appreciate all that he and Liv had done to make their lives better. Flick realised he'd failed Salt. Salt was quiet and the least of his concerns, so he'd thought. Now, it was Salt who was the greatest concern. The man was an eight-year-old child inside. Flick had failed to educate Hannah, to show her, or teach her how to interact with Salt. Everything happened so fast; the move, working around the clock, not enough time, and now the incident. Could he have prevented any of this?

Now his sisters were pregnant, and his wife was not. Flick's whole world had turned upside down. His gut felt inside out. How had everything ended up ass backwards? Finally, home, Flick hit his bed and crashed from pure exhaustion. He thought he would sleep a few hours, but he didn't wake till the next day.

Chapter 30
Readjust Plan, 1983

Sunday morning Flick was up and having coffee when the doorbell rang. Chuck walked in. A few minutes later Liv entered. Ten minutes later Gayle and Peter arrived. Half hour later the girls were in his kitchen with the clan.

Making another pot of coffee, Flick announced, "I hope you guys aren't expecting a family dinner." It was quite the unexpected reunion. Everyone laughed.

The conversation began with Liv asking how Hannah was. Flick shared his concern about the loss of their baby. He'd never seen her look so bad, bruised, and bandaged. It was evident that he was upset. Gayle asked if he'd heard anything about Salt. All that was known was that Salt was being held while his situation was assessed. Flick did not want to press charges. Hannah, on the other hand, might. Flick did not say anything about Salt returning home. Everyone felt that was a bad option and that something else had to happen for Salt. Flick couldn't talk about Salt and Hannah in the same discussion.

The girls were quiet. Liv asked how the course was going. "It's o.k. Not that hard right now," Kandy shared.

Sugar was more precise. "We're learning how to make beds. As if we don't know how." Kandy gave her a nudge and Sugar smiled. "We are there every day, doing our homework, on time for everything." Then Kandy kicked her shin. Sugar was letting everyone know they were complying with the agreement, but Kandy thought she was being sarcastic.

Chuck was quiet and took Flick outside in the back to talk. "How are you doing?" he said, lighting up a cigarette. "I'm a little worried about you."

Flick shrugged. "What do you expect? Nothing is going good right now." He took a puff. "I feel like my whole life is being flushed down the toilet." It wasn't often Flick felt sorry for himself and he reassured Chuck, "I'm a little beaten, but I'm not broken."

Chuck understood. "How are the girls?"

Flick winced. "Now, that's another subject."

Chuck was surprised – he'd thought they were on the road to stability. "Oh, what's up?"

Flick shook his head. "As life would have it, my wife is no longer having a baby, but the girls are both pregnant."

Chuck choked on a puff. "You're kidding?"

"I'm not kidding." Flick put his cigarette out. "I don't know how Hannah's going to handle the news. I'm going to see her this afternoon."

Chuck patted the man on the back. "I'm here for you if you need me. Anytime. Got it?"

Flick appreciated the offer. "Yeah. Thanks."

Chuck asked, "Does Liv know?"

"Not that I know of."

Heading back inside, Chuck said, "You have a lot on your plate these days."

Flick agreed.

Everyone was silent when the guys walked back in the house. You would have thought it was a funeral. Flick looked around and had a great sense of pride. These people were his family. They were there because they cared. Concern was the expression on each face that greeted him.

Overwhelmed with a sense of belonging, he said, "I love you guys. Each one of you. Appreciate how much you care. How you care for me, for our lost baby, Hannah, the girls. Even Salt after what he did. You are all incredible people. I'm so fortunate."

Everyone got up and they had a group hug.

The girls smiled. Flick went over and gave them a special hug. "Thank you for cleaning up the mess."

Sugar laughed. "Aw, it was nothing compared to trying to clean the Comet powder off in the bathroom."

Kandy added. "Yeah, I was done the hallway long before Sugar was finished the bathroom."

Flick didn't know or completely understand what had gone on in the bathroom. The girls had an idea, though, knowing Salt. Flick figured he would get the pieces of the story once he and Hannah had time to talk. He sensed it would be pulling teeth to get her to utter a word. In difficult times, she was reserved and tight lipped.

Chuck, Peter, and Gayle then chatted with Flick to let him know they were there for him. Peter said, "We are all family."

Gayle added, "To help and support each other."

Flick nodded, trying to stay glued together and be a man. "Thank you. I appreciate it. More than you know."

With Liam, Liv and Gideon came up to him and shared their thoughts and that they wanted to be there for Flick.

The company left to go about their days. Flick took a shower and headed out to the hospital.

***

Hannah was sitting in a chair by the window when Flick arrived. Never had he liked this scene in the movies, showing someone frozen and still with life lost, gone, or paralyzed. His mind believed it was not a good sign. His gut knew for certain.

Flick moved forward with his hands in his pockets, realizing he had come with no gifts. Flick was not a man who believed that gifts solved serious problems or transgressions. He believed smart people talked out their problems. Gifts were a tool of manipulation. Yet, here he was wanting to do just that. His guilt for what had happened to Hannah had him wanting to make it better. Not ALL better, just a little bit better. Reflecting now, he realized that gifts were a man's way of trying to show he cared. Women believed you cared if you thought about them. Flick had always believed you could just tell them you cared, but hindsight was telling him that women wanted to be shown. The bottom line – gifts were physical evidence of effort.

Hannah didn't move from her still position, didn't look up to see who'd entered the room, and didn't acknowledge or seem to care that he was there for her. Flick walked out. Hannah sensed his presence from his walk out. She knew her man by the scent of his personal care. Flick never flattered himself with after-shave or cologne. Then and only then did Hannah look up to an empty space. She walked towards the door to see where Flick had gone. He'd vanished. She sat on the edge of the bed wondering if she been too hard on him.

A half hour had passed before Flick returned with flowers behind his back. The doctor was talking with Hannah about discharging her with a care plan and follow up at his office the end of the week. He explained he would like to talk with her about getting counseling to help her through the trauma. Hannah simply listened. The doctor nodded at Flick with a faint smile and left.

Hannah looked up at Flick and then she walked over and fit herself into his embrace, holding him. She held on like she would never let go. A few minutes passed.

"Honey are you allowed to go home?" asked Flick

With tears in her eyes and lips trembling, she said, "Yes." And then she added, "I'm afraid to go home."

Flick hadn't thought about that and realized Hannah had been in a thoughtful trance. "Will it help knowing that Salt is never allowed back in our home?" It occurred to him that it sounded like he had made that decision for her benefit. In fact, it was because Salt was incarcerated, and society was making the decisions as to what would be best.

Hannah looked up, hopeful. "Never?"

"Never," he said with a reassuring smile.

Hannah was wearing an outfit Liv had bought her and brought to the hospital. Liv had instructed the nurses to discard the bloody clothes and Hannah's few personal items were in a bag. She and Flick left the room and went to the nurses' desk before leaving. Hannah's affect was not as grim nor as disturbing as Flick had feared. He decided it might be good to spend the day together, having lunch, walking, talking, and listening. Just being there for each other. They took a hotel for the night, so they could come home when Hannah was ready.

The next day had Hannah wanting to go home to change her clothes. She had the flowers draped across her lap while in the car and one hand holding Flick's for comfort. For reassurance?

They entered their home. Hannah was hesitant about what she would see or feel. The place looked wonderful. Flick's mouth fell open with surprise. Their home had undergone a make-over. Peter and Gayle had pulled a fast one again, only this time with Flick and Hannah.

The home was furnished with Peter and Gayle's old furniture, only five years old, but expensive and in exquisite taste. Drapes, mirrors, vases, and throw rugs had been lavishly placed with care. The hallway carpet had been covered with a wide Italian rug runner that matched the living room and dining room rugs. Hannah went from room to room to see what other changes had taken place.

The baby's crib had been taken down and was in the closet. The nursery was now a simple reading room with a day bed, a small elegant desk with a table lamp, pictures, and a huge fern in the corner.

The guest room was made up with a beautiful, slender, four-poster bed in rich royal blues with gold canopy, bedding and pillows, with two nights stands and gorgeous lamps. There was a gold-framed picture over the headboard and a matching seat bench at the end of the bed. There were no dressers – no room for that matter.

Salt's room was done up as an office with classic bookshelves and a beautiful desk with a leather swivel chair and lamp. There were two wing-back chairs with a floor lamp in the middle. On the wall was a royal-blue and gold metallic map of the world. It was all so tastefully done with a masculine presence. The bedroom closet had a cabinet and upper glass shelves that were stocked with the best of scotch, brandy, and cognac along with appropriate glasses. The lower cabinet hid a mini-fridge that contained ice.

They entered the master bedroom and gasped with the princess-like quality of the cream-satin quilted bedcovering with gold tassels and pillows that defined luxury. The matching drapes had gold accents. The pictures were a Claude Monet-style painting of ladies walking in a garden with umbrellas. The serenity of the room had Hannah's eyes fluttering in shock and excitement.

Flick had heard about the fiasco of Peter and Gayle setting Liv and Gideon up without their knowledge. He remembered their mixed feelings but that he had thought how fortunate they were to have such great parents.

"Who would do such a wonderful thing?" Hannah gasped in her new domain.

Flick didn't realize that Hannah wouldn't know it was Liv's parents. "It was Peter and Gayle." That was for sure. He had seen all these furnishings in their home.

Flick could not argue with the effect the transformation was having on his wife. He was just grateful the house didn't look like a crime scene. The place looked like a swanky hotel. It was paradise to Hannah.

Hannah entered the bathroom, remembering where the incident had occurred. She found it decked out in a paisley gold wallpaper, a gold mirror, a royal-blue shower curtain, and three-piece bath mats and matching towels. A shelf over the toilet held a supply of luxury white towels.

Hannah concluded, "The place doesn't look or feel the same. It's amazing."

The sofa set was white with soft, pastel-colored pillows. Cream and gold area rugs were under rustic white-oak coffee and end tables. The dining set matched the living room furniture. The main area had exquisite drapes in cream and gold. The only thing that had not changed was the whole kitchen. Even the clothes in their closets had been reorganized in their new dresser drawers.

At first it was too fancy for Flick's taste. Then he thought with a smile, *I could get used to this.*

The home was Hannah's haven and Flick's castle.

"What happened to our new furniture? The stuff we bought when we moved in?" Hannah asked.

The girls came up the stairs giggling. "It seems we inherited your old stuff."

"What happened to your stuff?" Flick wondered.

Kandy answered with a laugh, "That old Salvation Army hand-me-down stuff?"

Sugar said, "I think to the garbage bins."

Hannah asked, "You guys had a hand in all of this?"

Both answered, "No. We were busy salvaging your old stuff though."

Looking around in awe, Flick was beside himself. "I was only gone a day?" He was trying to figure out how this could have transpired. Realising the magnitude of the work, it would have taken to accomplish such a feat, he said, "Peter and Gayle couldn't have done all this themselves."

"No. They had a handyman with a map and plan. He installed the cabinet and little fridge in the office and hung all the drapes in the right rooms according to the map outlines. He put up the wallpaper in the bathroom and the shelves. The movers had their maps too and they placed the furniture as outlined. Of course, the movers were busy hauling out the old stuff into the back yard. That's where we came in and were told we could help ourselves. We put our old stuff out back and came up to see what was happening when Peter and Gideon were placing the area rugs. Gayle and Liv were setting up the bathroom. We helped make up the beds with pillows. The office was set up when we arrived. We went downstairs and noticed the movers had taken our old stuff away on their truck," Kandy shared, winded.

Sugar smiled with a secret. "You should take a look in your linen closet."

Hannah and Flick stared at each other in dismay and opened the linen closet. They gasped. It was filled to the brim with bedding, blankets, and towels. "I feel like we won the lottery," Hannah announced.

The girls were all smiles as well. "We didn't do too bad ourselves. We're still trying to finish getting set up." Off they went downstairs in a noisy chatter of excitement.

All Flick could think was. *And I was worried about coming home.* He found himself smiling.

***

Flick gravitated to the new office. He noticed the phone and picked up the receiver. There was a dial tone. He decided to make a call to Peter and Gayle to express his thanks.

"Hi, this is Flick," he said, trying to sound casual. "I was calling to say; you guys have been crazy busy."

Gayle was holding her breath with excitement. Peter was smiling on the other line, both in anticipation and waiting to hear the words of reward for their mischief.

"I don't know where to begin. I'm crying right now. I don't want Hannah to see me weeping like a little girl. But, you turned our lives right side up," he said, choking on his words.

"Came home worried how Hannah would feel ..." He paused as the words of appreciation failed him. "Hannah is beside herself and thrilled. I am in shock at what you have done for us." His heart pounding with emotion, he added, "You said we are family. God sakes people, you went over the top."

The Pattersons said in unison, "It's just our old stuff." Both were pleased with the reaction to their escapade. "Oh... just wanted you to know we could have not done this without Chuck and his friends' help," Peter informed Flick.

"Chuck?" Flick thought out loud.

"Yes sir. Did all the work," Peter announced.

Gayle piped up. "And we got to have all the fun staging the place."

In stereo Peter and Gayle said, "So glad to help."

Flick finally remembered why he'd called. "Thank you so much. It's unbelievable."

The call came to an end with Hannah standing at the door with a huge smile. "Want to try out the new bed?"

Flick smiled. No man could refuse an such an offer.

A few days passed with reasonable peace. Hannah was recovering as her bruises faded into shades of yellow. Flick was working long hours and looked forward to coming home where Hannah had dinner ready and was happy to see him. The evening would end with the couple talking and sharing. Flick couldn't have been happier. Hannah couldn't have been more content.

***

The next morning, the doorbell rang. Flick had left for work hours ago. It was the officers who had arrived on that bloody, violent day last week. They asked if they could come in. Hannah stepped back, opening the door and then sat herself at the dining room table.

The officers looked around with raised eyebrows. "It's quite a change around here," one of them noted.

Hannah smiled. "Our family surprised us with a re-do before I came home from the hospital."

"Nice," Both cops stated. They were still standing near the door. "We came by to ask you a few questions."

Hannah nodded her understanding.

Taking out a notebook, one cop said, "Want to know if you want to press charges against Salt N. Pepper with the assault and battery incident."

Hannah hadn't thought about charging Salt. Quietly, she thought about what Flick would think being that Salt was his brother and of simple mind. "Can I ask you a question first?" she said.

Both nodded yes.

"What would happen to Salt if I were to press charges?"

One cop grumbled and grunted with hesitation. The other cut to the chase. "He would be charged, and the prosecutor would likely want to proceed against him as an adult. Likely, he would do time in the pen."

Hannah nodded. "And if I don't ..."

"He would likely get help to have a productive life. Counseling likely put in a group home with opportunities to work and join activities – a chance for a stable life. Worse case, he'd have to do community time."

Hannah knew her answer. Flick would not want her to lay charges. He loved the boy and worried about him. He knew he needed direction so that he could manage his temper and not hurt someone else in the future. Hannah wanted a restraining order in place but feared this would cause grief in her household, so she trusted that Salt was never to come to the house. Hannah was banking on it. She needed that security. She didn't understand much about Salt and why he behaved as he had. But she didn't think she'd deserved his reaction to her logical requests. Hannah hoped Salt would get the help he needed. For Flick's sake she would not lay charges.

She nodded and answered, "I do not wish to lay charges," and then she said no more.

The officers were perplexed. This woman had suffered the loss of her child and been battered within an inch of her life. They would not have faulted her if she did lay charges.

Most people would. "Are you afraid to prosecute? Afraid Salt will come back and assault you again?" they asked while writing notes.

Hannah had never thought of that. Flick had promised her Salt would never come back. "No. I think Salt will get the help he needs and a chance to have a better life." She did not mention that she feared her husband would be disappointed.

The officers nodded. One kinked his neck as though he'd gotten the final word. The notes were written and then they were off wishing her a good day.

Hannah shut the door. Tears ran down her face, but she wasn't certain why. Flashes of the day crossed her mind. Touching her empty tummy gave way to intense heartache and pain. Hannah cried herself to sleep in their room. The music from downstairs had a beat so strong and equal to the pounding in her head.

Chapter 31
Fool's Paradise, 1983

Flick was busy with work at all hours and every free minute with Hannah, so the girls were on their own. Kandy and Sugar got along most of the time, but arguments happened about who was getting what. Sugar wanted the larger room with her baby coming. Kandy wasn't having anything to do with that conversation. She already had the larger room and was expecting as well. Kandy didn't care if Sugar's bananas were rotting over the matter – then make banana bread as far as she was concerned.

One day Sugar disappeared with her boyfriend and never showed up for office cleaning. Kandy was livid as she had to do all the work and didn't get home till midnight. Sugar didn't come home that night, but she showed up in the morning to change for school and expecting a ride in Kandy's jalopy. That wasn't going to happen. Being a part of the team meant doing one's part. The arrangement had been violated. Until the matter was resolved Sugar wasn't getting any privileges.

The fight was on. Sugar was upset because she would be late for class and it was a violation of the agreement. She did her best to guilt Kandy into getting a ride. The argument carried on outside when Kandy got in her car and drove away. Flick was up having coffee with Hannah and he came out to see what was happening.

Flick stood by her side and watched the car go down the street. "What happened?"

"She's mad at me. Now I'm going to be late. It's going to cost me big time. I'll have to pay back the course." Tears came down her face.

Flick wanted to know what had happened. So, he decided to give her a ride to school in hopes he would get some answers. In the car, he asked, "So, what happened? Why are you guys fighting?"

"You know, girl stuff. Sisters fight you know." Sugar knew she was at fault and didn't want Flick to know she had been out all night.

Knowing he wasn't going to get an answer, he let the matter go. They came up to the curb at the school. "You have a good day."

"I will. Thanks. You saved my bacon."

"This one time. K."

Sugar nodded.

Kandy avoided Sugar throughout the day at school. Everyone noticed the girls' distance and silence. Later that evening, they met up at the offices they cleaned. Kandy did her work and said nothing though Sugar wanted to talk. Kandy was in no mood and had a vindictive streak – she had the power to make Sugar's life a living hell.

Kandy was aware that peeing a lot was normal in the first trimester of pregnancy. When Sugar went to the bathroom before leaving the offices, Kandy was long gone when she came out. Sugar didn't have a dime to her name and couldn't make a phone call or take the bus. Anger rose till her face was flushed.

The girls finished their work at 9:00 p.m. and then Sugar walked the whole way home –twenty kilometers. It would have taken an average person over four hours. Sugar arrived home at half past midnight, collapsing and at the point of exhaustion. She had no fight left in her should she face Kandy when entering the suite.

Kandy heard Sugar come in and stayed in her bed. She wanted to make the point not to screw with her since their lives had been put together as a joint venture.

Next morning, Sugar was ready and waiting at the car. Kandy let her get seated. The silent treatment was the final test. Either Sugar would get the point and leave it at that by doing her part and not leaving Kandy holding the bag. Or, she would argue with her, which meant she was dumber than Kandy thought.

In fact, Kandy believed dumb could be a moment of silliness. You couldn't fix stupid. Stupid was permanent. Sugar sat in the car and sensed the air was cool. She decided to stay quiet. She wanted Kandy to understand that she wanted a life and to be able to see her boyfriend. Kandy knew that and felt it wasn't her problem. Kandy had a boyfriend as well and didn't see him till the weekend.

Back at home that night, Sugar asked Kandy how things were with her boyfriend.

Kandy snapped, "Fine."

Sugar had made a late dinner for them and Kandy cleaned up the dishes remaining occupied. Normally she would ask Sugar how things were with her boyfriend. But knowing where that would lead, she decided to not entertain the topic.

Sugar pursued. "Don't you miss him during the week?"

Kandy needed to put an end to this conversation. "I do. But I don't have the luxury of dating my boyfriend fulltime. Neither do you. I don't want to start this conversation. Please."

Sugar nodded. She went out the back door to the alley and was gone for the night.

That night around 10:00 p.m. Flick came downstairs to visit with the girls and ask a favor.

Kandy was at the table with her books.

Flick asked. "Sugar in bed already?"

"I don't know." She stared at her book.

Flick had expected a yes or no answer. "What do you mean, you don't know?"

Kandy wasn't a stool pigeon. But, she wasn't going cover for Sugar either. "Like I said, I don't know."

Flick went to her room, then Kandy's room, and then the bathroom – all empty. "Where is she?"

Kandy answered, "I'm not my sister's keeper. I don't know."

Flick realized he hadn't been keeping tabs on the girls at all these days. With work flooding his time with inspectors and deadlines and Hannah being so needy these days, time was not on his side. He hadn't even touched base with Salt, who was on his mind. Now he needed a favor from the girls and one of them was off somewhere.

"Tell Sugar I want to talk with her and to call me on my cell." About to leave, he remembered why he'd come downstairs. "I was wondering if you could check in on Hannah when you get home. See how she is doing?"

Kandy looked up. "What's wrong?"

Flick said with concern, "She hasn't left the bedroom for two days. The officers came back and asked if she wanted to press charges." He headed outside for a smoke. "She hasn't been the same since."

Kandy followed him outside. She wanted to share a bit of what she'd learned at school. "I learned that people grieve differently. I think she's grieving about the baby."

Flick was impressed with her input. "Maybe. It's just that I have to motivate her to take a shower and then run out the door every day to get to work. She cries all day till I get home."

Being pregnant, Kandy wasn't sure it was a good idea for her to be around Hannah. No one had yet told Hannah the girls' news. Kandy wasn't going to make things worse.

Flick butted out his cigarette. "I wouldn't ask if I wasn't desperate."

Kandy nodded. "Sure. O.k. Is Hannah going to press charges?"

Flick shook his head no. "I think she's not laying charges because of me. I sense she wants to and feels powerless. All I know is that Hannah is really down these days."

Kandy said, "It looked really good when the place was redone. She was so happy. It's a shame. Really."

Flick nodded, said good night, and went back upstairs.

***

Child's Love

The next morning Flick was out the door. But this time Hannah had only pretended to be taking a shower and she was on his heels in her housecoat crying for him not to leave. She ran to his side and pulled on his jean jacket making a scene. Flick was proud of living in a nice neighborhood and wanted to blend in. This behavior from his wife had him angry and embarrassed.

In Montreal, Verdun, or the Pointe, this was a normal situation – spouses hollering at each other. He remembered his mother upset with one of her lovers leaving his underwear on the bathroom floor. They were dirty with tracks. She took them and hung them on the line with all his clothes. The only way the dude was going to leave was to retrieve his items in the nude. The neighbours were watching and laughing. Let's just say the guy never left his clothes hanging around again. He knew where they were always.

This was a different place and time. Flick's blood was boiling, and his temper was verging on explosive. He warned Hannah, "I am going to work. I am not entertaining this child-like behavior anymore. Now get back inside. We'll talk when I get home."

Then Flick was in his car, not looking back, and he drove into the morning sunrise that was blinding, squinting and struggling to see. He had to look at the grooves of dirt on the road to make sure he was nowhere near a car bumper or a parked car. He was relieved when he made it to the next street, which had taller buildings so his vision cleared.

Flick appreciated his life. He loved his work and loved his family. His nerves were getting the best of him. But he concluded he would take a nagging wife over a silent, needy wife any day. In fact, it brought a smile to his face thinking about dishing out the crap like a word contest. But, that was not his life. He knew he did not have the skills to cope with a needy, wanty person. He would have to do his best. He wanted so badly to have coffee with Liv.

His cell phone rang. It was Hannah crying and wanting him back home. "You call again, and I will hang up each time. I need this phone for business. It's what feeds us for Christ sakes." He hung up to make his point.

The cell phone rang. "I told you not to call me."

It was Chuck on the line. "Whoa buddy, it's me."

Flick was trying to get his agitation under control. "Sorry, thought it was Hannah."

Chuck wanted to ask what was going on, but he had more pressing issues at hand. "Inspector is here at the site. Said if you're not here in five minutes he's gone."

Flick ordered, "Tell him I'm three minutes away. Stall him. I should be there in five." He hung up.

The cell phone rang again. "Yeah?"

This time it was Sugar. "Kandy told me you wanted to talk to me." She was at a phone booth at the college and class was starting in a few minutes. She didn't want to piss off Flick. She had done a good job of pissing off Kandy.

Flick was dishing out the commands. "Be home after work." He hung up.

Sugar stood with the receiver in her hand and thought, *Yes sir.*

The damn cell phone rang again, and Flick wondered who it could be. He was on edge, on fire, on a roll. "Yeah?"

It was Hannah, crying and saying nothing on the other end. Flick hung up. The phone rang again and upon hearing the crying, he said. "If you call again. I will never come home. Got it?" Then he hung up again.

Shaking his head, he thought, *there is only so much a man can handle in a matter of ten minutes.* When he arrived at the site, the inspector was opening his car door.

Flick ran to stop the man from going. "Hey, I'm here. Can we get this done?" Pulled out a five. "I'll buy you coffee. You'll keep me on schedule. I'd appreciate it." He smiled.

The inspector liked Flick because he was a no-nonsense guy. Jokingly, he said, "Next time I'll expect a twenty." He took the five. The job passed inspection and Flick was on his game. He ignored his phone all day. All personal business had been was dealt with up to now and Chuck was at his side.

***

Liv had been trying to get a hold of Flick all day. Peter had a stroke and kept asking for Chuck. Gayle was at her husband's side. Left-side paralysis meant right-sided brain damage. Peter was having trouble trying to communicate and he was left handed. Speaking was a challenge. Even worse, he was in denial that he'd even had a stroke. Gayle realized that over the months Peter had come to consider Chuck his best friend. The family was desperate to reach Chuck.

Kandy arrived home at 9:30 p.m. and checked on Hannah. She found her in the bedroom with her wrists slit. Blood was everywhere. Kandy called the police. She tried to contact Flick but there was no answer. Flick arrived home at 10:00 p.m. as the ambulance was taking Hannah to the hospital. She was barely alive. Kandy was bouncing with energy trying to explain what she had seen when checking on Hannah. "I tried calling you. You didn't pick up."

Flick felt bad all round. "I'm sorry. I've had a bad day."

The police were waiting for Flick at the door. Their expressions implied he had something to do with what Hannah had just done. He shook his head and realized he couldn't win with these two. He was guilty before he could prove his innocence.

One officer asked, "So, what do you think caused Hannah to do such a drastic thing?"

Flick was losing his patience. "I wasn't home. I couldn't tell ya."

The officer said, "Well, something must have triggered her."

Flick did not have a crystal ball. "I'm not a mind reader. I can answer for my actions. I've been working like a dog. As for Hannah, I just don't know."

The first officer said, "Hannah should have laid charges. It helps to do something constructive after a traumatic event."

The other officer said, "I guess you talked her out of laying charges?"

Flick snapped, "I didn't do anything. Hannah informed me of her decision."

The first officer asked, "Did you ask her to go for counselling?" In an accusatory tone.

Flick had had enough. "I'm her husband trying to keep a roof over our heads and our bellies full. I'm not her dictator, psychologist, or doctor for that matter." He realized he wanted to get to the hospital. "Is there anything else? I need to be at the hospital."

Just then, at 10:30 p.m., the cell phone rang. "Flick here."

Liv was on the phone. "Been trying to get a hold of you. Dad had a stroke. He wants to talk with Chuck. It's a little late now. Do you have Chuck's number?"

Flick gave Liv the number and said, "I'm on my way to the hospital now."

Liv stated, "They don't allow visitors this late at night."

Flick ran out to the car, leaving the officers at the door. "I know that. Hannah slit her wrists. She went by ambulance."

Liv was stunned. "Oh my God, I should have gotten her into counseling or something. I feel so bad. We are so busy with our lives. So sorry, buddy."

Flick answered, "Me too. Got to go. Call you in the morning. K? In fact, I need to have coffee with you. Talk with someone who is sane." He was kind of laughing.

Liv offered. "I'm off tomorrow. I'll have the coffee pot on."

"See ya then." He turned the phone off.

***

The girls were up and talking and Sugar said, "I guess Flick forgot he wanted to talk with me."

Kandy, still stressed from her discovery, said, "Ya think?"

Sugar gave her a filthy look. "I'm going to bed. I'll be at the offices to clean tomorrow. I won't be home tomorrow night."

Kandy reminded her, "You know Flick has a good memory. He'll be back to talk with you, you know?"

Sugar answered, "Yeah, I know. I'm moving out and living with Butch."

Kandy asked, "Is he the father?"

"Yeah." Sugar went off to bed.

***

Flick was at their door that night and discovered Sugar had all of her things gone. Kandy was no snitch, but Flick was no fool and wanted answers. Kandy felt he deserved to know since he had done so much for them. "She moved in with her boyfriend. The father of her baby. Said she won't be back."

Flick went back upstairs. "And I thought you would be the difficult one," he grunted.

Chapter 32
Conditions, 1983

The night was long for Flick. Hannah was in surgery and had lost a lot of blood. She had a blood transfusion. At four in the morning, the same doctor approached Flick. "It looks like she'll make it."

Flick nodded.

The doctor frowned. "I distinctly remember something. Hannah was to come to my office to talk and book an appointment with a counsellor."

Flick remembered. "I know. I thought Hannah would have the time to book it since she was staying home. I didn't realize how lethargic she had become. I'm sorry. Now more than ever."

The doctor nodded. "She will be admitted to the psych ward. She is a danger to herself." He walked away.

Flick went to the nurses' desk to ask if he could see his wife. "I'm afraid she is not to see anyone without a doctor's consent. She is a form 1. This means she must stay in the hospital for thirty days, for observation and help."

Flick looked stunned. He didn't know what to say and didn't move.

The nurse stated, "I'm sorry Mr. Bick. Nothing I can do. Have a nice day."

Flick stood and asked, "Can I ask who her doctor is?"

"Dr. Punachi. I can give you his office number if you like,"

"Yes please." He took the piece of paper and walked to the elevator.

Upon leaving, Flick remembered Peter was in the hospital. It wasn't even 5:30 a.m. He went to the information desk and asked for Peter Patterson's room. He was given the number but was informed that visiting hours started at 8:00 a.m. Flick nodded and left.

It was that time of morning where fatigue was at a peak. Sleep was pleading in Flick's body. He usually started his day by 5:00 a.m. and he was wondering if he should get a few hours of sleep or just get a head start on his day. Then he remembered he was going have coffee with Liv sometime this morning. He got into his car and kept nodding off and snapping awake. The morning sunrise was in his eyes and he had to squint to see the road. In an instant, he heard crashing and banging till the car abruptly stopped into an electrical pole. Flick was knocked unconscious.

He woke with the sounds of a saw cutting him out of his car. His left leg was throbbing and when he put his hand down on his thigh he got a handful of blood. Flick shook his head. He had places to go and people to see.

He grabbed his cell phone. It was 6:00 a.m. A paramedic was attending to his bleeding. Another was taking his blood pressure. It was drastically low. Flick needed to get to the hospital and get the bleeding under control. He dialed Chuck's number, and Chuck answered in a groggy haze. "Morning."

"Chuck. I'm in an accident. I need you to install all the fixtures. You know the building that the inspector approved… the one with the preliminary installation." The pain was getting the best of him and he passed out from blood loss. The line was open.

Chuck's ear was glued to the phone trying to figure out what was happening. All he could surmise was that Flick was unconscious and they were doing CPR.

He hung up in tears. Forget work. Chuck had to get to the hospital. He arrived at 6:30 a.m. and informed the information desk he was Flick's father. They told him that Flick was in Emergency and he was escorted to Flick's bedside. Flick was on an IV and oxygen. A nurse asked Chuck to leave as they had to prepare him for surgery.

As Chuck waited outside the surgical suites, a doctor came out at around 10:00 a.m. It was explained that Flick was stable and that his leg had been shattered and repaired. The femur was damaged and concerned with blood clots, the doctor had put him Heparin. By 11:00 a.m. Flick was out of the surgery unit and settled in his room. Either from fatigue or drugs, he was hardly making sense. Chuck left the hospital not knowing what to do.

He decided to go see Liv and arrived around 11:30 a.m. He knocked, Liv answered, and Chuck asked if he could come in. Liv said, "Of course, come in." Walking to the family room she asked, "Can I get you a cup of coffee?" Pouring out a rich brew, she handed one to Chuck. "What brings you by?"

Chuck felt uncomfortable as his relationship with Liv was as more of a spectator than a participant. "Flick called me this morning around 6:00 a.m.…He was in a car accident." He tried to explain what he'd heard on the phone and then how he'd left Flick and come to Liv's home.

Chuck couldn't understand what Flick had been doing on the road so early in the morning and Liv realized he was not aware that Hannah had attempted suicide the night before. Liv had been waiting to have coffee with Flick this very morning. The night before, she had called Chuck to ask if he could stop by the hospital to chat with her dad, Peter.

Both remembered the call, but Chuck was embarrassed and said, "When I got the call from Flick, I didn't even think about Peter. I could have stopped by to see him. I'm sorry Liv." No one had to say that Peter and Chuck were friends. It was something that Liv didn't completely understand, knowing Peter. He was protective of his girls.

Liv never showed affection to Chuck for fear of hurting Peter. Chuck seemed to understand, and Liv appreciated that he stood on the sidelines and made no demands. He made no demands on her parents and no demands on her.

Liv admired Chuck. In some ways, he deserved more from her. Yet, he looked at her with kind eyes. His love was so great, and Liv knew he did not want to cause her grief or pain. She was certain he'd had his share, but he never burdened her with his losses. His presence showed he was grateful to just have the privilege of seeing her within the family dynamics. They had not developed a personal relationship.

The visit seemed awkward, to say the least. After finishing their coffee, Liv suggested that they go to the hospital to see both Peter and Flick. She called Milly to see if she would mind watching Liam. Milly said she would be over in a few minutes and confirmed that Gayle was already at the hospital.

By noon, Chuck and Liv were on their way to the Rocky Mountain Hospital. They decided to see Peter first. Gayle had gotten lunch from the cafeteria and was eating with Peter. They were both happy to see Liv and Chuck. Liv was shocked to see Gayle feeding her father. She wasn't prepared to see her father lose his independence. Gayle was helping her husband as though it was normal, and it was accomplished with great love.

Liv went towards her parents and hugged and kissed them. Chuck came on the other side and took Peter's hand. He wanted to say, *Nice to see ya,* but he bit his lower lip as words would not formulate in his mind or mouth. Gayle noticed the lower lip being bitten. It was the same gesture Liv had in awkward or uncomfortable situations. Chuck then stepped back.

Peter could not speak clearly, and Gayle did her best to interpret. Pen and paper helped. Writing with his right hand created a scribble. Gayle explained that he was left handed and the stroke had paralysed that side. Peter's face had the left-side droop. Liv wanted to cry. Her father was her rock and he was changing. He was getting older, but she wanted him a part of her life forever. As if Peter could read Liv's mind, he smiled, and his eyes were shining with love. It was love that would stay in his heart and stay in her heart, forever. Liv smiled, understanding her father's message. She touched his right hand. Peter raised her fingers and kissed them with the right side of his mouth.

Chuck could see the love of this family and felt blessed that his daughter had these wonderful people as parents. He couldn't have picked better himself. Then he came forward. "Is there anything I can do for you?"

Peter had struggled to explain what he wanted to Gayle over the course of the day and had succeeded. Gayle then said, "Peter loves you like a son. He's worried that he'll fail his girls because of his new condition. He cherishes his friendship with you and wants to know if you would be there for his girls."

Liv was flabbergasted. Her father was surrendering his title? Gayle smiled, knowing the heart of her man. His love for his girls was greater than his love of himself. He needed Gayle to be looked after. He wanted her to have her independence and would need Chuck around. He wanted his daughter to still have a father and he wanted Chuck to take the baton. He wasn't giving up being her father. That would never happen. But, when he should be gone, it was Chuck who he wanted to continue fathering his daughter.

Liv got the message and realized that she had Peter's blessing to build a relationship with Chuck. Both visited for a while but didn't tell Gayle and Peter that Flick had been in an accident because she didn't want to stress them. So, they didn't tell them they would be off to see how Flick was doing.

***

Flick was awake and sitting up in bed. He'd had a little lunch, but most was still on the tray. As soon as Flick saw Liv and Chuck he propped himself up in bed.

Liv smiled. "I thought we were supposed to have coffee?" she said, trying to tease Flick.

Flick grinned and handed her his cold cup of coffee. "Here you go."

Liv smiled and declined.

"It's terrible anyway," he said as if revealing a secret.

Chuck spoke up. "What the hell happened to ya?"

Flick moaned. "I don't even know where to begin." He looked rough, unshaved, almost homeless in appearance. "Last night I came home and found the ambulance taking Hannah to the hospital."

Chuck and Liv looked from one to the other.

Chuck asked. "What happened?"

Flick said with no emotion, "She tried to commit suicide."

Liv already knew from Flick's call the night before, but Chuck's eyes grew wide though he said nothing.

Flick continued. "I was at the hospital all night. I left in the morning debating whether to go to work or go home and get a few zzzs. The morning sun was straight in my eyes. I remember squinting and then seeing nothing. Before you know it, I was brought to a dead stop. I banged up a few cars on the street and hit a pole. I damaged my left leg really good." The cast was shown when Flick pulled back the sheets.

Chuck wanted to sign the cast. He found a pen and wrote, "Good luck doesn't mean you have to break a leg." Everyone laughed.

Liv asked. "How's Hannah?"

Flick answered, "She survived. They're keeping her here for thirty days. Something about a form and that she was a danger to herself."

Liv understood. Chuck didn't really know the legalities. But, he understood Hannah wasn't going anywhere soon.

Flick asked, "How's Peter?"

Liv answered, "He survived. But, he doesn't look the same. Mom was feeding him when we dropped by." Tears were in her eyes.

Chuck noticed and came over to touch her elbow to show he was there for her. Liv gave a small smile and nodded while dabbing her eyes with a Kleenex.

Flick noticed the subtle change in their relationship. "So, if things keep up the whole family is going to be here. Like a family reunion."

The joke had Liv giggling and then laughing at the thought. "I sure hope not." She was sorting out the situation. Three people in the hospital. She would see Peter every chance she could and see Flick if he was still admitted. Hannah, on the other hand, would depend on her visitor's list.

Liv had a similar thought process as her mother. "Chuck, I'm going to delegate some tasks. You make sure Mom is able to see Peter." She watched his reaction.

Chuck was thrilled he was needed by his daughter. "Sure thing. Anything to help." He cared for Gayle, had grown to love Peter, and had always loved Liv.

Liv frowned at Flick. "Who's to take care of you? I'll get the girls on board." She was a natural delegator.

Flick wasn't sure the girls would be able to help at all. With school, cleaning offices, their pregnancies, and now him. "They can barely take care of themselves."

Liv thought. "That's too bad," she said. "We are going to take turns cooking meals for you. The girls are in training to bathe and care for disabled people."

Flick had an opinion. "I won't refuse the meals. I will refuse the bath. I'll hire a stranger before that happens." Flick didn't bother to update Liv that Sugar was gone and out of the suite.

Liv disagreed with him. "I can't think of a better way for the girls to show their appreciation and be there for you." Then she thought about Hannah. "Who's got Hannah's back?"

Flick had called Hannah's parents and explained everything that had transpired. They were with their daughter and didn't know he was in the hospital and that he'd had an accident. Flick was concerned about Salt. He knew nothing as to what was happening with him or how he was doing. He worried that Salt would feel he wasn't there for him.

"I'll be there for Hannah with the help of her parents." He moaned as he moved to reposition in bed. "I am worried about Salt. I know nothing about his situation and I think he'd be scared. I'm afraid I haven't been there for him." He pulled out his cell phone. "Problem is, my cell phone has gone dead. I need to get it charged. I was trying to make calls to find out about Salt."

Chuck said, "I'll go by the house and put it on the charger for you. Bring it back to you later."

Flick whispered, smiling with mischief, "Not allowed cell phones in the hospital. I had to hide the damn thing."

Chuck then offered, "Maybe I should take the calls for business. I just finished my first-year plumbing, thanks to you. I can install all the fixtures. Can keep the business going."

Flick thought. "That might not be a bad idea. I'm such a control freak. I can't imagine not having my phone." Thinking out loud, he said, "You better come by two to three times a day to keep me posted."

Chuck reassured him, "You bet."

Flick then asked, "While you're putting the phone on the charger, would you check up on the girls and let them know what happened?" It had slipped his mind that Sugar had moved.

Liv interjected. "I think I could go over with Chuck and do that. I'd like to see how the girls are doing. I now have a reason – to tell them about you."

Flick informed them, "Kandy knows about Hannah. She found her with her wrists slit in the bedroom."

Liv nodded. "Got it."

Chuck's head was swirling. He hadn't known about that. He felt bad for Kandy and felt awful for Hannah. But he felt worse for Flick.

Chuck said, smiling, "We are family."

Liv grinned. "Yes, we are family. We are here for you."

Flick was feeling nauseous and hit the call bell. "I'm going to throw up."

The nurses asked for Chuck and Liv to leave. Flick was going to get something for the pain and have a good sleep.

***

The front door was locked so Chuck went around the back and entered. It seemed no one was home. He found the charger on the kitchen counter and placed the phone on the cradle. It was 3:00 p.m. The girls should still be at school, but he and Liv weren't sure since Kandy had found Hannah unconscious from her suicide attempt. They decided to look downstairs.

The suite was dark and quiet. Liv opened each door with Chuck behind her. When they opened Sugar's door, they found Salt standing in the dark looking at them. When they turned on the light, Salt's eyes showed fear. He was visibly shaking. He should have been at his new place of work or at the shared home for boys. He didn't belong there, but he wanted to be with family. He'd come in the back and stood in the room that was under his old one upstairs.

Liv offered her hand. "Come out and let's talk. O.k?" she said, backing away from the door.

Salt hesitated then came out. They sat in the living room. Salt had his hands together with his right knee shaking uncontrollably. His eyes were focused on the carpet.

Liv decided to ask. "You o.k?" No response. "Are you hungry? I can get you something to eat."

Salt nodded. Liv got up and went to the fridge. There was a bowl with spaghetti and sauce along with fresh bread and salad. She warmed up the meal in the microwave and toasted and buttered the bread. She put the salad and a salad dressing on the table. Salt inhaled the food saying nothing. Liv and Chuck waited for him to finish. Neither knew what to do next. It gave them a few minutes to think quietly.

Liv was much like her mother. She cared about people and made no judgements. "Salt, you want to stay here?"

Salt nodded and whispered, "Be with family."

Liv understood. "I have to go and take care of Liam. I need to go home too…

I'm going to get Kandy and Sugar and let them know you're here. O.k?"

Salt nodded.

"You'll be all right?"

Salt nodded again.

"I can stay awhile," said Chuck. "I'm waiting for the cell phone to charge. Then I was going to see Flick." Both knew he would let Flick know they found Salt.

***

Liv found Kandy and Sugar and explained what had happened to Flick and that Salt was at their place. The girls did not inform Liv that Sugar had moved out. They went to the hospital to see Flick, who was waking up from his drug-induced sleep. The girls were close to tears. They stood over him and couldn't even say hello.

They filled each other in on what had been going on. Just then Chuck showed up with his cell phone. Another family reunion. Flick was tickled. The girls needed to talk with Flick but weren't sure he could do anything to help. Sugar shared that she had moved out and was living with her boyfriend, Butch. The look in Flick's eyes showed great disappointment. For all he had done to help her, you'd think she'd be grateful. But she said nothing.

Kandy then explained that Liv had told them she and Chuck had found Salt in Sugar's old room.

Flick nodded. "Well, I now know where Salt is." He thought about what he'd been told. "Maybe that could work well. Salt can stay with Kandy. She knows him and understands him. We could set him up in Sugar's room." That would buy him time since Hannah was under doctor's care for at least four weeks.

Kandy continued, "Liv told us she would have to find out who is looking for Salt and if he can stay. You should find out what's happening with Hannah. She won't be able to handle Salt at the house."

Flick was normally sharp, but he felt a little dull this day. "Been thinking the same as you were talking. I'm going must depend on you, Kandy. I know there are so many questions that need answers. Can you take care of Salt for the time being?"

Kandy nodded. "Yup, but we have to get to the offices and clean them. I'll be home as soon as I can. But, yes I will look out for Salt."

Flick was now on business. "Chuck, did you get any of the fixtures installed yet?"

Chuck shook his head no.

"I'll need you to get on that right of way. Check back with me anytime, any hour. Ring once and I'll call you back as soon as I can. Got it?"

Chuck nodded. He liked how Flick thought. He could follow his organized mind. "I'll grab a bite and work all night," he promised. "See ya in the morning."

Flick corrected his thinking. "You need to get some sleep. Don't do what I did. Get a few hours of sleep. You can work all you want after that."

Chuck understood and gave Flick a smile. "Like I said, I'll see ya in the morning."

The group left the hospital with their tasks in hand. Sugar felt left out. Flick had made sure she knew he felt he could not count on her and he'd intentionally left her out. She got the message.

Chapter 33
Hannah's Hell, 1983

The next couple of weeks proved to be challenging for the Bick's'. Flick was discharged from the hospital with a full leg cast, crutches, pain killers, and labs for INR to determine whether his blood was thin enough from anti-coagulants to prevent clots. Flick was not a laid back, relaxed kind of man. The hospital was more a prison for him than a forced vacation.

A meeting was set up between Flick and Hannah's doctors. Flick believed the meeting was to inform him of Hannah's condition and what their plan was for her care. He hoped to see his wife and do whatever he could to have his woman back, at least the one he married.

Flick was escorted into a conference room and asked to take a seat. The chair was close to the door and at the end of the table, which allowed his cast leg room. Doctors and psych nurses entered with polite greetings and introductions.

Dr. Punachi conducted the meeting. He began with Hannah's history of events that had led her to her condition. These professionals had interviewed and counselled Hannah during her stay. Each expressed what Hannah would need and an undetermined time table based on her progress. Then Dr. Punachi held his hands together with his elbows resting on the table. Frowning in silence he took a thoughtful stance. "Flick. We would like to ask you a few personal questions if you don't mind."

Flick had not been expecting to be interviewed. He shrugged and then nodded, thinking if he could help Hannah, he would answer their questions.

Dr. Punachi began, "Hannah has expressed concern about the household. She does not feel safe." He waited to see Flick's reaction. "She believes you did not protect her."

Flick felt he was on trial. He said nothing as he did not trust his fury building up inside.

The presentation continued with no questions yet. "Your brother, a young man with disabilities, assaulted and battered Hannah."

Flick nodded. "Yes, it's in the police report. Your question is?"

"Well, Hannah believes you could have prevented the traumatic event."

On active alert, Flick said, "I'm waiting for you to get to the point. You made a statement. I didn't hear a question."

Dr. Punachi responded, "Fine. With Hannah feeling insecure, she's made it clear she would not feel safe in your home – her home, she is looking at other options upon discharge."

Flick couldn't help thinking, *who is in whose head?* "I believe this is a discussion between myself and my wife."

Dr. Gordosal said, "You may be right. But, Hannah's instability happened in the home where you reside."

Flick did not understand these people's thinking. "Let me get this straight, if you don't mind."

Dr. Gordosal said, "Sure."

"A man gets into an accident with his car. Who is to blame?"

Dr. Punachi said, "It depends on the variables."

Flick clarified. "Nothing more than the driver, the vehicle, and lost control."

The doctors sensed where Flick was going with his rationale. Both looked at each other and didn't answer.

Flick smiled. "I figured. Each person is the operator of their life, their vehicle. Everyone responds differently to stress and situations." Now flushed in the face, he knew better than to get defensive. "In other words, I am willing to answer for my actions. Protecting my family and my wife is my concern. Hannah was reassured that the man who assaulted and battered her would not be permitted in our home. This promise has been honored. How Hannah ended up in such a situation that reduced her to attempting to kill herself, is beyond me." Tears seeped from the ducts. "I was hoping you would have the answers since you guys are the professionals." The meeting was not as productive as Flick had hoped. He felt like he was on trial much like he had with the officers who'd responded during the incident.

Shaking his head, he said, "Hannah has lost a child. I lost a child." Feeling helpless, he went on, "I hoped Hannah would have time to take care of herself. I am a hardworking stiff who will do everything possible to provide for my family. I am a man who works with my hands. I am not a fancy man. I do not have the skills and training to get my wife though this horrible nightmare. It's like Hannah getting the measles. It happened in my house, so I must have caused it. Does this make sense to you?" He was no longer interested in what these people had to say. "What I will share with you is this: That tragic night, I lost the girl I fell in love with. I would do anything to have her back."

Eyes in the room softened.

Flick concluded, "Our marriage is based on talking, sharing, and working through whatever life dishes out. Hannah is emotionally reserved by nature. Now she's closed off because of the trauma … And I don't have the answers on how to make everything better … or at least back to the way it was." Sniffling he managed, "I love Hannah more than I love myself. Do you understand that?"

Struggling with his crutches, he rose from the chair. "Unless I can see my wife … I see no point staying and visiting any further … I wish you all a good day."

Everyone present in the room was silent as he walked out. They may have had their own opinions prior to the meeting, but what they'd witnessed showed a man committed to his wife, not a bully, even though he walked with a manly exterior. He himself had been hurt and was moving on by being absorbed with his work. What came out loud and clear was that Flick was a man with a heart that loved Hannah. It was sad to realize that Hannah could not see past her pain. Instead of believing in the man she married, she now saw Flick as the villain in her version of events. Flick had been Hannah's hero. But apparently, her hero had disappointed her to the point she had lost faith in him

Flick left wondering what choices Hannah had been considering. This was her home ... or so Flick thought.

***

The meeting left the professionals with concerns for this couple. Hannah had shared her disappointments. They knew that Flick was more outgoing, and she was a lot more of a calmer person. When Hannah had found out they were expecting, she wasn't sure how Flick would react. Turned out Flick was hardworking and a family man. Hannah believed she had married her knight in shining armor; a great provider and loving husband. A man with a big heart who cared for so many people.

The assault would have been difficult had the violence been inflicted by a stranger. As it happened, it was a family member of Flick's. Someone who would be a part of the family one way or another; a constant reminder that would never erase the traumatic event. Flick being busy with the growing business had Hannah feeling unsure, unsafe, and lonely. Living in her mind, the tragic event that ultimately caused the loss of their child, lost in time and encased with loneliness, proved too much.

It was like living in an ocean that promised drowning and no safety net. Flick was the lifeguard for the family. Problem was he was seldom on duty. The bottom line – Hannah had lost faith in her husband. Were her expectations unrealistic? Flick did not realize that Hannah had requested to not see her husband until she figured out her feelings. She felt safe with her parents visiting and promising to take care of her.

Hannah's parents were drenched in fear of ever losing their daughter to death. The attempted suicide was more than their hearts could handle. They were determined to make sure all variables contributing to their daughter wanting to die, would be circumvented. As far as they were concerned, the tragedy had happened on Flick's watch.

What the professionals did not know, or Flick either, was that Hannah's parents had initiated a divorce. Hannah acknowledged this option and didn't realize her nodding had given her parents the ok to pursue the divorce.

What Flick did not realize was the professionals were laying the blueprint of their situation, seeking solutions that would require all factors and elements that were the backdrop to the violent attack. Flick was not being accused of anything. He was quick of mind and felt a sense of judge and jury in the meeting. He was desperate to try and set the record straight. The circumstances that caused the horrible event could not have been prevented. To date Flick had never been given insight to what had provoked the situation to begin with. He felt the professionals had been keeping him from visiting his wife. But it was his wife, Hannah, who had not wanted to see Flick.

***

The months of October and November proved to be an emotional war zone for Flick. Hannah had moved in with her parents. Flick went to their home to find the house empty with a "For Sale" sign. He went to the realtor, who had his orders to keep all information private. They owned a little old house in Bridgeland area. Flick thought, if only someone could purchase the house he might find out where Hannah had relocated.

Bick arrived home late on a day in mid-November when a knock on the door startled the silence. He answered to a man who asked, "Are you Flick Bick?"

Flick responded. "Yes," with a frown.

The man handed Flick an envelope and said, "Consider yourself served." He walked away.

There were papers for divorce. Flick had sensed this was coming since his wife had technically disappeared. How does a man secure the heart of a beautiful woman? He loved their time together, the life they shared, and the dreams in the making. Flick would have given anything to keep the warmth he felt in his heart – to keep the peace and serenity he cherished above all material possessions. He had gained so much so fast and lost everything in a moment. Salvaging his marriage was obviously too late. He couldn't fault her parents for protecting Hannah. He suspected he could fault them for being instrumental and interfering with his marriage, though.

Flick was in no mood to be social. He felt so alone and needed a friend. He had his dad, Chuck, who was quiet. When it came to advice Chuck said very little. Liv was his best friend, other than Hannah, and he showed up at her house.

Gayle was home with Peter these days. Milly answered the door and said Liv would be there any minute and to come in. Flick wanted to run, his patience was being stretched. His mind went from nothing to fast forward with just the thought of the divorce.

Liv entered her home through the garage and found Flick standing at the hallway door. He was in anticipation of her arrival and presented himself anxiously. She gave her brother a quick hug and kiss on the cheek. "What a nice surprise to see you in the middle of the week," she said, knowing full well something was up.

Flick gave a faint smile. "I need to talk with you. Is that o.k?"

Liv answered, "Of course. Let me check on Liam and then we can sit down to talk."

Flick's nerves were unravelling within him. The pressure to contain himself was harder than holding on to a ball of fire. Milly had the coffee pot brewing, knowing a meeting of sorts would happen. Liv came to the family room with two cups and sat down, waiting for Flick to sit. His nerves had him standing and unable to coordinate his body to relax.

Liv motioned to Flick to have a seat.

He tood in front of one of the chairs, paused and said, "I've been served divorce papers." His eyes were red and holding back tears.

Liv felt sick to her stomach for Flick. "I think you should try to talk with Hannah. Or at least get mediation."

Flick nodded. "I agree. The problem is, Hannah and her parents moved away. Her parents' house is up for sale. The realtor is tight lipped." Flick finally sat down once he had blurted out the words that had been causing him so much pain. He collapsed from emotional exhaustion.

Liv nodded. "I suggest you get a lawyer. Get some advice."

Flick was irritated. "No, I should ignore this. Hannah wants the divorce. I don't want it."

Liv understood. "I'm afraid that's not how this process works. If you ignore the matter, it can only get worse."

Flick said nothing and sat in deep thought.

Liv came over and hugged her brother. "I wish I could take these pasts few months away. You deserve so much more and a better life." Sitting on the ottoman and facing Flick, she said, "Know you have a family that loves you and supports you."

Flick knew that – it was why he'd showed up at Liv's door. He grinned; a fake grin. "I guess I have to face up and accept the divorce." Shrugging as though not knowing any other options, he added, "I guess I'll have to get me a lawyer. What else can I do?"

Liv nodded. There were no words that could console the heartache and pain that was so visible.

***

At the lawyer's office, Flick was asked to take a seat and he found himself fidgeting with a magazine. A man came to the waiting room and introduced himself. "Hi, I'm Todd Jones. Come."

Flick followed Todd to a conference room, sat down, and put the envelope on the table.

Todd asked, "How can I help you?"

Flick was choking up with his words. He pushed the envelope over. "My wife wants a divorce."

Todd looked the papers over and stated the demands. "it seems your wife wants alimony since she is not working and is accustomed to a good life. She's asking for you to pay all legal bills and discloses you have a prosperous business."

Flick hadn't read the papers through completely and he raised his eyebrows. This information sparked a fierce reaction. "I get to respond to their requests, right?"

Todd asked. "Their?"

Flick nodded. "Hannah and her parents."

Todd said, "Yes, you can respond. I suggest you guys get mediation first."

Flick explained, "I doubt that will happen. Hannah's parents took her and disappeared. Hannah attempted suicide after losing our child. Things went upside down from there."

Todd understood. "Let's talk about the alimony. What would you consider reasonable monthly payments?"

Flick laughed. "Nothing. Hannah was working when I met her last December. We hit it off and we became pregnant. We married. She worked till last September."

Todd stated, "The papers state that you caused the trauma and Hannah won't be able to work for some time."

Flick felt defensive. "My brother, Salt, who has disabilities, assaulted Hannah. I found out she called him a 'stupid idiot,' which our mother used to call him, and he had lashed out at her too, years ago." Thinking for a minute, he said, "I'm not saying Salt did the right thing. I'm not saying Hannah had it coming or deserved the attack. I have been denied seeing my wife at the hospital to try and be there for her. I feel like I've been cut at the knees and expected to still jump and run."

Todd continued, "We'll go back to the alimony matter later. She wants her portion of the value of the house and assets."

Flick nodded. "We just bought the house in September. What's the equity worth in two months divided by two people? Really?"

Todd continued, "We will go back to the assets matter later. She wants you to pay all the legal costs."

Flick laughed. "That's where I draw the line. I am not the one who wants a divorce. If Hannah wants a divorce she will have to pay for her own legal costs…In fact, I am requesting she pay for my legal costs. I haven't been given the chance to make our marriage work. If she wants the divorce, I'll sign the papers. Nothing more. Oh, I'm sure her parents will eventually agree since they want me out of her life."

Todd continued, "I will write that up. Hannah wants a settlement of $100,000.00."

Flick busted into laughter and tears. "In her dreams."

Todd put his pen down. "Doesn't Hannah deserve something from this marriage?"

Flick said in all seriousness. "Yes, she deserves me. If she married a bank, I'd understand all the money matters. I'm not an ATM."

Todd grinned. "Can I suggest something?"

Flick shrugged. "Sure."

"You haven't been married long. You have a new business and it's not considered profitable yet. A new house with no equity. Hannah has a history of working in a drug store. Presently, she's not able to work and has no income."

Flick bobbed his head as though following Todd's line of thinking and waiting for the punchline.

Todd smiled. "What do you think of paying for Hannah to go to school? Enable her independence. Pay for school, books, tuition for two years with an allowance of $500.00 a month. She must prove her attendance and marks, otherwise the agreement is void. No extensions, no further negotiations."

Flick thought about it and figured he could afford this suggestion. He did want the best for Hannah and she did deserve a chance. "I'll agree to that. Once Hannah is registered for a program and in attendance, I'll make the payments."

Todd stated, "With no money she won't be able to pay the legal fees. I would suggest you take care of that."

Flick grinned. "I don't think so. I believe this whole matter is inspired by her parents. They want the divorce they can pay for it. Including my legal fees." He stood up.

Todd stood up and shook Flick's hand. "I'll have it drawn up and served this week."

Chapter 34
A New Year, 1984

Christmas was tolerable at best for Flick. The festive season came and went with the usual gifts and rituals surrounding the holidays. Gifts were mailed out to Gunner and Gavin with and a little something for Ruby. The new year was about to begin.

The girls, Kandy and Sugar, were happy with their course and doing well. Both girls were showing blossoming bellies with pride. Kandy remained in the mother-in-law suite with Salt. Kandy no longer had a boyfriend – Garth was back in Germany with the army. They kept in touch, but both was going their own way with their lives. Kandy was spirited and had the drive to be a single mother and provider.

Sugar was living with Butch, who was a derrick hand out in Fort MacMurray. Sugar applied for social services as a single person with an expected child. She pretended Butch was not in her life. Butch was not aware of the application and paid all the bills. He worked hard and never was home. Just the way Sugar liked her life. The social service check was her spending money. As far as she was concerned, life was grand. Sugar continued with the PCA program only because she didn't want to pay any money back to Liv.

Salt was given community service and remained under the care of Kandy and Flick. Gayle helped get him back into bowling and soft ball for extracurricular activities. With school and work, though, Kandy found it impossible to take Salt to his events. Gayle and Peter enjoyed the outings and supported Salt with his activities. Once the community service hours had been completed, Salt worked at a recycling station. He was smiling more and liked his routine.

Everyone was doing their thing and life had a peaceful pace till spring.

Flick had become quieter and worked harder than ever. Chuck was the only person who would see him on most days. Flick hardly talked, and Chuck missed his spirited anecdotes. From what Chuck understood about the divorce, Hannah was starting nursing, fast tracking on a two-year program. Flick was expected to pay all the books, fees, and tuition in August and start the monthly payments of $500.00 in September. Flick concluded that if this was life it was a dull normalcy.

Liv and Chuck talked about their concerns with Flick. He wasn't the same man once the divorce was final. Something in Flick had died. Liv suggested that Chuck move into the house to keep Flick company. Chuck felt that they spent their working days together and each needed a bit of space at the end of the day. Liv understood and pondered more options.

Chuck thought it might be good for Flick to rent out a couple of the rooms. He had been sleeping in the guest room. That left the master bedroom and the little room with the day bed. Kandy had mentioned there were a few girls looking for a place. They were classmates and secured PCA jobs once they finished their internships at long-term care facilities nearby.

Liv, Chuck, and Kandy were waiting at the house when Flick arrived home. Alarmed, but with his first smile of the year, Flick said, "Another surprise family get together?"

Kandy broached the subject. "We were thinking it might be good to rent out the extra rooms since you have extra expenses."

Flick shot out, "My financial business is none of your concern."

The room went quiet. No one had another plan. Flick sensed they were concerned about him and were there because they cared for and loved him. "O.k. It would be good to come home and there might be people around. I want to say that I'm not interested in inviting more trouble into my life. Having a boarder or two won't solve my heartache."

Liv was impressed that Flick had them figured out. "We know that. It's just that you are not yourself. We love the Flick that has his fingers in everyone's pie."

Flick laughed. "I thought everyone would be happy I'm not in their business."

Chuck added, "We miss the old you. Even at work your tone is almost a whisper. I guess I'm used to you hollering out the orders. Not used to you asking."

Flick looked around the room and finally let his heart feel. Tears came with the unexpected feelings of love. He ran out the back door and lit a cigarette. Everyone followed. Chuck lit a smoke as well.

"I miss me too," Flick said, laughing. He realized he was lonely and thought having people around might help get him out of his shell. "O.k. So what do you have in mind with boarders?"

Kandy smiled. "Well there are a couple of girls who need a place close to here to start work next week. Just thought if they had a room it could work for them and maybe for you."

Flick nodded. "The only room available would be the small one with the day bed."

Kandy stated, "I cleaned up the master bedroom and Liv purchased new bedding. Go see. It looks great."

Flick blinked. He hadn't been in that room since the incident. In fact, he'd purchased all new clothing to avoid going in the room.

Liv snickered. "Haven't you noticed the closet in the guest room is packed and tight with clothes? We put your things in your room."

Flick hadn't noticed much these days. He realized he had to snap out of this daze and get on with living. "You are right, I haven't been myself. I usually never miss a thing." Laughing, he said, "O.k. have the girls over for coffee on Saturday. I'll think about it and let them know. I'm not letting just anyone in my home. I don't want to be someone's emotional garbage can."

***

Friday night, Kandy and Sugar graduated from their PCA course. Liv organized a family dinner at her house.

No chocolate fondue fountain. No alcohol for the pregnant girls. Gideon was out back barbequing chicken and ribs. The spring weather was chilly, and the food was set up on the counter for self serve. Liv had learned that casual dinners were more relaxing with her siblings and that the formal affairs made them uncomfortable. Peter and Gayle joined in the festivities. Salt was comfortable and loved watching his siblings teasing each other. Sugar brought Butch, who was a quiet man. He'd join the boys outside for a cigarette and have a beer or two. Things were back to normal and the family was enjoying each other's company.

Liam was the center of attention, running about and engaging them to participate in his games. Gayle and Peter loved the family event and thought it was better than Christmas this past year. The joy was back, and the peace filled the air.

Flick was smiling, joking, teasing, and visiting with everyone. Chuck visited with Peter in the sitting room. Gideon joined the men and shared cognac and conversation. Gayle was focused on her grandson. Liv was enjoying her time with the girls. Kandy shared her stories about clients that had them laughing the night away. Salt sat back listening and cracking a grin with the girls.

Usually Milly catered the family events for extra money, but she was at the hospital attending to her husband who had injured himself. He had been changing the oil in their old car and the jack let go on his chest. He had survived with many broken ribs.

Everyone settled in and relaxed, feeling happy and content. They enjoyed the blessings of food, family, and interaction.

Saturday, Kandy brought the two girls up to Flick's to make introductions. One girl, named Beth, was quiet and shy. The other girl, Julian, was talkative and outgoing. Flick had coffee and chatted casually about the prospects of renting out the rooms. He was uncomfortable with Beth as she reminded him of Hannah. But he realized that if he didn't get involved in a relationship that the quiet girl might be a suitable roommate. As for Julian, who was spunky, alive, and bit crazy – she was interesting. As a roommate, though, Flick worried they could be at odds. Again, if he didn't get involved with either of the girls the house would have activity.

Flick decided to give the girls each a chance with the understanding that he would have the option to evict within the laws of the land. He was not providing for the girls – they were renters. He would have to give them a thirty-day notice. They would have to give thirty-day notice as well. Any damages would be fixed as presented or worst case, upon termination of tenancy. The large room was $500.00 a month. The smaller room was $350.00. Utilities, cable and basic phone were included. Food, personal items and long-distance calls were at the girls' own expense.

Beth decided to have the smaller room. Julian wanted the master bedroom with the ensuite bathroom. The girls moved in throughout the weekend.

Kandy wanted to talk with Flick about the office cleaning jobs. She explained that Sugar was no longer working or doing the job. Kandy had been covering for her the past three months. Sugar had been taking her portion of salary without informing Flick that she'd walked out.

Flick then said Kandy was to stop working and take care of herself. He told her to enjoy the next month and get ready for the baby. He cut her a check for missed wages for the past three months she'd spent covering for Sugar. He would deal with Sugar later. Kandy was thrilled and said she needed to get a crib. Flick then remembered there was a crib in the closet of the small room and he brought it downstairs. He set it up in her room and brought the dresser. All Kandy had to do was get a high chair, play pen, stroller, and baby items. Kandy was thrilled to have the extra money as she was having the nesting feeling.

Liv invited Kandy over on Sunday afternoon to have girl time. What Kandy didn't know was the whole family was invited to have a baby shower. Everyone was impressed with Kandy's hard work, her commitment to help Salt, and her devotion to help Flick. She never complained, and she succeeded with her own goals. Sugar was invited and informed of the baby shower. She declined, offended, assuming she was not having a baby shower as well. Sadly, the shower was for both the girls. Kandy asked where Sugar was, and Liv tried to explain. "We told her we were having a baby shower for you. We wanted to surprise Sugar as well. Sugar decided not to come. I think she's offended, and we feel bad that she assumed we would not think of her as well. I'm sorry for the way I handled the invite with Sugar. I hope you can forgive me."

Kandy laughed. "I wouldn't worry about Sugar. She's always the victim. If Sugar was happy for me, she would have been here whether there was something in it for her.

Now she has victimized herself. I quit feeling sorry for her a long time ago."

Liv was impressed. "I'll keep that in mind." She smiled at Kandy's stance and understanding of the situation.

The baby shower started, and the gifts were amazing. It felt like Christmas. Flick had purchased the most expensive baby stroller on the market. Chuck bought her a highchair. With Gayle's help, Salt had bought a few baby bibs, blankets, and outfits. Liv and Gideon purchased a playpen and Jolly Jumper. Gayle and Peter handed Kandy a set of car keys. It was their old car, six years old: a BMW. Kandy gasped in shock. Peter smiled and said, "You have been a great family member. We are proud of you."

Gayle joined in. "You need a more reliable car to get around if you are going to work and transport our grandbaby's cousin."

Kandy was a tough nut on most days, but today, tears had her jumping for joy as though she had won the lottery. Kandy's nesting needs had been met far beyond her greatest wishes.

Outside, some of the boys were having a smoke. Kandy went outside to get some air. She felt hot these days like an incubator while making her baby. Flick then informed Kandy in private, "I want you to know that you will not be expected to pay rent while living downstairs. You will have enough expenses raising my niece or nephew. You have insurance, gas, food, baby and babysitting expenses."

Kandy hugged her brother. "I love you so much. I love this family. Thank you for everything." Hiding her tears, she said. "I may not have the picket fence but, I have a home with so much love. This is the closest to it that I could ever dream of bringing my baby home to."

Flick smiled seeing Kandy's eyes with so much joy. Such moments reminded him that hopping on a bus was the best thing he had ever done. Yes, his younger siblings had followed on their own and he had been able to help them get settled...now established.

After the shower, Chuck and Flick loaded up Kandy's items and delivered and set them up. Then they went to Sugar's and delivered the same gifts, minus a car, to her home. Sugar refused to answer the door and was peeking behind the drapes. Flick noticed, and his face was flushed with irritation. He hated the games of emotional manipulation that reminded him of his mother, Ruby. Normally, he would have put the items in the back and called to say there were gifts waiting for Sugar. Instead, he left the items on the front doorstep and made enough noise to make sure Sugar knew he was there. He left and didn't expect to hear any thanks.

If Sugar was feeling ostracised by the family, she was doing a good job of it herself. No one was feeling sorry for her. Poor Sugar didn't get a baby shower. No, poor Sugar didn't bother to attend because she thought her sister's baby shower did not benefit her. Everyone wanted to tell Sugar to wake up...to grow up. The world didn't evolve around poor Sugar. Since Flick was the patriarch of this group of young ones, it was his job to set the girl straight.

Sugar didn't appreciate the gifts because she thought the attention had gone to Kandy. She acted like the presents were bribes to say "sorry." Sugar took the gifts and had no intentions of saying thank you. She felt the family should have had a separate baby shower just for her and was mad that Kandy got all the attention. She didn't have the capacity to realize she had brought all this grief upon herself. Acting like their mother, Ruby, did not pay off. But Sugar thought she was doing just fine without them.

***

Kandy had a healthy baby boy she named Champ. The attention from all the girls in the house and his uncles Salt and Flick created a nurturing environment. Champ loved his Aunty Liv and Uncle Gideon, Grandma Gayle, Grandpa Peter, and Grandpa Chuck. Salt was his best friend. Liam was enthralled with baby Champ. He wanted to give the baby all his favorite toys.

Sugar had a healthy baby girl she named Deidra. However, Sugar did not include herself or her family very much. Deidra was spoilt with tons of clothes and matching shoes with every outfit. Sugar did not find work. She played Nintendo all day, though she did cook and clean. She spent very little time with Deidra. When Deidra was tired and crying, Sugar would smack her and tell her to stop crying. The child grew up demanding everything she wanted. Sugar would spend tons of money on expensive toys to keep the kid occupied. She believed she was a superior mother and it never occurred to her she would be considered negligent.

***

Liv became closer to Kandy throughout the summer. They enjoyed each other's friendship and talking about motherhood. Their bond was getting stronger. Gayle was always included, and her wisdom often sought.

Sugar was often invited but always declined, saying that she was busy shopping, baking, or doing something else. Sugar had no friends and was isolated by choice. She was getting disgruntled with Butch for not being home enough. But she was upset when he was home and in the way. Butch had two weeks on and one week off. On his week off he would hang around and try to blend in. He found it impossible and resorted to starting the day on a pleasant note; a beer by 10:00 a.m. It wasn't his normal habit, but it soon was the pattern. Of course, Sugar found fault with Butch being an alcoholic. So, the man took to a bit of weed too. It did dull the woman's nagging for the most part.

***

Chuck had always spent Sundays at the Pattersons, either shovelling snow or doing the landscaping. He played poker every Monday night. The friendship was a blessing to both men. Peter often referred to Liv as "our daughter" meaning himself and Chuck. Gayle enjoyed Chuck's company during lunch between the chores.

Tuesday, Chuck received a summons to be in court within thirty days of the letter, to testify as a witness in the case of the fire back in Montreal. Chuck had to let Flick know he'd purchased a plane ticket and would be away for a week.

Flick decided he was going to fly to Montreal the same week. He hadn't taken any time off for himself. Well, he'd been off work a bit after he shredded his left leg. That had been months ago, though. He wanted to check up on Gunner and Gavin to see how they were doing, and to say "hi" to Aunty Jewels. He'd end up seeing his mother, Ruby, by default of seeing the boys.

The last barbeque of the year was Labour Day weekend at Liv's. The family wished Chuck and Flick a safe journey and gave pictures for the younger boys to see their growing family. Sugar did attend for an hour without her man. Deidra was crawling and snatching up all the toys. The boys didn't know how to play with her. Deidra did not acknowledge baby Champ and glared at Liam, who would be two this Christmas. Liam backed off from Deidra looking at the adults with questions in his eyes. He went back to playing with Champ.

Deidra cried when Champ took a toy out of her hands and Sugar snapped at Kandy for not teaching her son not to steal. Sugar was looking for any excuse to leave and did. She liked leaving the family events as though people had done something wrong and personal to intentionally aggravate her. Kandy muttered, "Victim syndrome again." No one said anything. Sugar always left without say thanks or good bye.

Outside, the boys were talking. Flick informed Chuck that he'd had a run in with Bob about the business. He wanted Chuck to come by the house before Tuesday to talk about the matter. The next week they would be off to Montreal.

CHILD'S LOVE

***

Monday morning, the boys went to Denny's for breakfast. Flick explained the situation –that Bob was upset that the two of them were going to be gone for a week. Even though during the past year Bob had not obtained any business for them, Flick had still been giving Bob thirty percent of the profits. All of the materials for start up had been paid off a year ago. Chuck was getting the contracts and making the business grow. Bob just kept tabs on the boys to make sure he was getting his cut. Flick needed to buy the guy out. He was dead weight and Flick had had enough. Chuck agreed but was afraid of the legal ramifications and costs. Flick said sometimes it was worth the amputation.

On Tuesday, Chuck was served with papers. Chuck and Flick were being sued by Bob. He wanted a million dollars. Flick came by to see Chuck installing a few sinks and Chuck handed him the papers. Flick almost choked on his cigarette. "The bastard wants what?" Flick gagged.

Chuck was nervous of legal matters. He didn't trust lawyers any more than detectives. "What are we going to do?"

Flick said without hesitation. "We sue him for a million dollars. He hasn't honored his end of the contract by getting us jobs. We have been doing it all ourselves and have still been cutting the bastard a check." Putting out his butt, he said, "Time to see Todd." He put in a call for an appointment.

Todd's office said he was in court all day. Flick informed the secretary, "Ask Todd if he wants a million-dollar case to give me a call today. Tomorrow we will be looking for another lawyer." He hung up. By 3:00 p.m. Todd called Flick and said to come in to the office at 4:30.

Flick and Chuck showed up and Todd was waiting for them. Flick pulled out the original contract and showed that it was exclusive for two years. At the end of December, the contract would end. He explained the situation and that they were being sued. He felt it was a tactic to get more out of the contract. Todd agreed, but explained that this was not his area of expertise and that he would recommend a colleague from his office.

Flick said, "Listen, you are the only lawyer who has been straight with me." Then, pulling out the papers they'd been served, he said, "If you will not take this on, then I have no reason to stay with this office." Eyebrows up, he asked, "Are you in?"

Todd smiled. "O.k. But I advised you – you will need to sign a document, so my butt is covered."

Flick agreed with a nod.

Todd continued. "If I need to seek further legal advice on your behalf, I will bill accordingly."

Flick again agreed. "Please use discretion. I don't mind paying you for research that helps our case."

Todd understood. "Because this is a business situation I will need $5,000 down."

Flick had the money. He was starting to pay for Hannah's monthly upkeep and had just paid for her schooling fees, tuition, and books. The boarders took care of most of that. He explained to Todd he would be out of town next week for a week. "We want to countersue for a million dollars. I know we won't get it, but I want to put the pressure on and see where this will go."

Writing notes for the new file, Todd recommended, "I suggest that you should finish out the contract till December. I believe by honoring your end completely you will have the right to refuse their demands. Especially since Bob has been receiving money for jobs he had nothing to do with."

Flick then stated, "I am a fair man. I would be willing to give something for the training given to Chuck to make bids. The bidding thing was thrown in to get Chuck employment. Bob gets nothing for Chuck now in his second year of plumbing as this was Chuck's personal achievement. He can't sue Chuck because the contract was strictly between Bob and myself."

Todd smiled. "That might be a nice token gesture when the Bob guy realizes he's getting nothing."

Flick liked the guy. "I see you have got this figured out. A plan?"

Todd laughed. "I'd hate to be Bob. Yes, I have a plan. Going to run it by the business department. But, I have a grip on this. If anything changes, can I call you?"

Flick shook the man's hand. "Sure thing. Taking my cell with me. Call anytime."

Todd returned the handshake and then shook Chuck's hand. "Hope to see you soon with good news."

Todd got on the case immediately and did a bit of research on this Bob guy. He learned Bob was into illegal gambling. One bit of information had the guy accused of selling girls in the sex trade. Todd knew he could put on the pressure. It sounded like Bob did everything except rooster fights.

Todd and his team requested a discovery meeting with Bob. One partner and five secretaries who looked like lawyers sat present in the conference room. Each was prepared to throw out a question with a cue. When Todd touched his ear, Jean would talk. Tap his nose, scratch his right cheek, and so on.

Bob sat with his one lawyer, shifting in his seat. Bob's lawyer, Jim, had a wrinkled suit and was unkempt. He appeared frazzled and not prepared. Todd found himself smiling. He enjoyed this kind of pressure more than court. The game was on.

Chapter 35
Montreal, 1984

The boys took a hotel downtown and arrived around 7:00 p.m. They settled in and went walking along St. Catherine Street where they stopped at a bar for a beer before calling it a night.

Being downtown would have Chuck to court within minutes. Flick could access anywhere in Montreal via Metro or the bus.

Chuck was anxious about the fire case. He hadn't been given any information about the findings or about what kinds of questions would be asked. He had hoped to meet with the prosecutor before testifying.

Flick was in his old element and was as excited as a kid to see Gunner and Gavin. He had no intentions of calling Ruby prior to showing up. He knew the boys should be in school, so he would show up around 3:00 p.m. If they were home, it meant they did not go to school. If they weren't home, it would be likely they would be home soon. Flick called Aunty Jewels in the morning and she came into town to have lunch with him. Chuck called the prosecutor's office and they wanted him in immediately.

Flick met Aunty Jewels at the Bar B Barn to have ribs. Aunty looked great, just a little older. He loved her energy and great personality. Her voice was filled with excitement and came across as sexy. Flick shuddered thinking this thought when it came to his Aunty, but the fact was it was true.

Aunty Jewels spotted Flick and squealed with delight. "Hi sweetie. So glad you called me. Can't wait to hear all the news." She took a seat across from Flick.

Flick knew his auntie's heart was about Liv. She felt more like a mother to his sister than Ruby and she was entitled as she had provided for, loved, and cared for Liv for three years. She wanted all the news. Flick was sipping his beer. "You remember Liv?"

Aunty laughed. "Do I remember Liv? Of course." Grinning, and sipping her coffee, she said, "Tell me everything. O.k?"

Flick shared about what a beautiful a person Liv was and how she helped him and their siblings. She was a professor at the University of Calgary now, and was working on her PhD. "She is very intelligent. You wouldn't know, though, because Liv is so humble. Heart of gold."

"Aw. That is amazing. I'm so glad to hear she is doing well." Tears seeped, and Aunty Jewel's mascara was running a little.

Flick handed her a Kleenex. "She is married to an engineer named Gideon and has a little guy named Liam."

Aunty was listening.

Flick continued, "An amazing family." He decided to share his good fortune about her parents and all they had done for them. Then he shared about Kandy's situation; her little boy Champ, and her good fortune with the BMW.

Aunty said, "I'm so happy for Kandy. How is Sugar?"

Flick explained she had been given the same opportunity of schooling and had finished but chose to not work. "Has a little girl named Deirdra. Her boyfriend is a derrick hand in the oilfields. Doing well." He didn't elaborate about Sugar acting like her mother, Ruby.

Aunty asked, "How is Salt?"

Flick did not share anything about the assault and battery on Hannah. In fact, he never mentioned his marriage or divorce. "Salt is good. He likes living downstairs with Kandy and the baby. Works in recycling. Bowls and plays soft ball. He really looks happy."

Aunty was pleased. "Salt is a good boy. Just don't call him 'a stupid idiot.'" Then she had some news of her own. Her daughter had married years ago and had two children. Two of her three boys had married; one last spring and one this summer. The oldest boy had married and was going through a divorce. Uncle Jerry wasn't doing well. He was over-weight and had heart trouble. Lately, he had a terrible temper. Flick wondered if the very rosy makeup was covering up something. He didn't ask.

Aunty remembered something. "Oh, your mother is getting married to some George guy at the end of the month." She looked up to see Flick's expression.

Flick looked up and frowned. Then he smiled. "For love or for money?" He was half being cheeky and half being serious.

Aunty Jewels was a lady. "A woman should marry for love. I hope so, because the guy is on disability."

Flick laughed. "Well, he's still bringing in the money." He shook his head. What was to change?

Aunty explained that this George guy was raising his twelve-year-old daughter. "His wife died years ago from cancer. Ironically, both of George's parents died of cancer as well. A meek and mild tempered man."

Flick didn't believe Ruby would care about the little girl, but he tried to be positive. "Sounds like a nice family guy."

Aunty bobbed her head side to side. "I think so. Time will tell, I guess."

They finished their lunch and Flick gave his aunty his number. They parted and hugged. It was good to see Aunty Jewels. She really was a jewel, a good lady.

It was time to take the Metro and head down to The Pointe. Ruby had been living there the past year with the boys. He'd heard she had been partying hardy with her friend, Sheena Aspens. Flick didn't have much faith in this George guy. Likely he was a partier as well. How else would she find this guy? He'd soon find out.

Flick showed up at the door on Ash Avenue. He heard a commotion and Ruby yelling, "What do you think was going to happen? You pull out your pecker here at the door and expect a performance? Get the fuck out of here. The next time I'll bite the damn thing off. You hear me?"

A guy was running out the doorway and zipping up his fly. He looked at Flick and ran off.

Ruby was still standing at the inside door. "Well, look what the cat dragged in." She walked into the flat.

Flick entered and shut the doors. "What was that about?"

"Ah, an old friend that wanted benefits. Thinks a woman can't clean up her act."

Flick stated, "I hear you're getting married."

Ruby looked exhausted. "I scrubbed the house. I'm trying really hard. George should be here soon. I'd like you to meet him. He has a little girl named Lina."

Flick wanted to know how the boys felt about the news. "How is George with the boys?"

Ruby had gotten used to running her own show and Flick was no longer the man of the house. She remembered he had tried to run a tight ship. "I guess they don't mind. He brings them gifts and candy."

Flick thought the boys were not little anymore. Candy? Really? He didn't say anything because he knew what he had to say would make no difference. "Well I wish you the best." What else could he say?

Flick looked at his watch. "Should be expecting the boys soon, eh?"

Ruby shook her head. "No, they like to go to the Boys and Girls Club down the street."

Flick walked out and went down the street to the club. Ruby suddenly hollered down the street. "You're not taking them to Calgary. Got it?"

Flick hollered back. "Yeah, Got it."

It took a half hour to find both boys. They were so excited to see Flick. Gunner hung on to Flick's sleeve even though he was taller. Gavin called him on his promise to come back and visit a year ago last summer. Flick felt bad. He started to realize how Liv must have felt when she got caught up with her new life. He was beginning to understand it didn't mean he'd forgotten the boys or that he didn't love them anymore.

"I know. I'm sorry. It took a lot to get set up. A home and a job. Helping Kandy, Sugar, and Salt." He was trying to explain when Gavin high-jacked the conversation.

"Oh my God. How are they? I miss them all." He danced about as they walked. "I need to know. Tell me. Tell me."

Flick was laughing. "They're all good. Why don't we go for supper and I'll tell ya everything?"

Gavin was all smiles. "Yeah. O.k."

The three walked up the few steps to Ruby's. Standing in the doorway was Ruby with a guy. "This is George," she said. "George, this is one of my other kids, Flick." Both men nodded.

Flick never called Ruby, Ma, or Mother. "I'm going to take the boys out for supper." Then he looked up. He'd forgotten he wasn't the man of the house. The look on Ruby's face indicated she was expecting him to ask permission. Fine. "Can I take them for a bit?"

Ruby hesitated. "Have them back by 8:00 p.m. If you don't, I'll have Kane come after ya."

Flick pretended to tremble. "Got it." The three ran off down the street towards Wellington Street.

Smiling about the prospect of a good meal and fun with the boys, Flick went to Connie's Pizza. He hadn't had a good pizza in a long time and he couldn't wait to have steamed hot dogs as well. Flick was on Memory Lane. He walked past Hibernia Street where Hogan's Bath was located remembering spending most of his summers swimming there. Then he remembered the auditorium where he'd gone skating in the winter. He'd watched boxing and wrestling when he could afford the five-dollar ticket. Walking past Marguerite Bourgeoys Park, he wondered if there hadn't been a stage with a huge shell-shape thing for performances? Many talents would sing, dance, and entertain the public with tricks. The place was so much fun in the summer. Where the hell had the stage gone? How odd considering it was a concrete fixture.

The boys didn't care about their surroundings; they lived every day in these streets. Going to Connie's was a treat. Poor people seldom ate out or ordered in.

They settled at one of the two tables at Connie's. The place was mostly a take-out or delivery establishment. They ordered a Hawaiian pizza and cokes. The young boys ate like they hadn't had food in days. Flick ate like he hadn't tasted anything so incredible in a lifetime.

Once the pizza vanished the boys started asking their questions about their siblings. Flick started with the girls and then Salt. Then he told a story about a lost girl, a princess so wonderful and intelligent with a heart of gold. The girl was Liv. The king and queen were Peter and Gayle. They too were so kind and generous. The boys were enthralled. It was hard for them to believe a magical world like that even existed. They held their heads in their hands, elbows propped on the table, and eyes focused on every word coming from Flick.

Flick loved these guys and was enjoying the time he was having with Gunner and Gavin. It made him realize how precious time was. Distance made the moments more special. If only he could bring the boys back to Calgary and the family could be complete. But he sensed he would be charged with kidnapping as Ruby's income would be altered. However, the boys never complained about their mother. Flick was not about to try to change their thinking. He needed to leave knowing they were fine and happy. Gunner had a flat look much like Salt's. Gavin had the spark that Flick, and Liv had. These gaffers were a great part of Flick's heart, just as much as his siblings back in Calgary. He only hoped they would one day be with him or nearby. Time would tell.

They went on the bus to Verdun and shopped at Canadian Tire. There was an end-of-season sale on bikes. Flick purchased both boys a bike of their choosing. The bikes were off the rack and already assembled. Now they would have to walk back to the Pointe, or Flick would have to run, and the boys would ride their new bikes. Flick had plans for ice cream, but time had run out. The boys were beside themselves with their bikes. He'd save the ice cream for another day.

Ruby heard the boys' excitement from down the street and was at the door watching the parade of two boys on bikes and a guy jogging behind. "What's this all about? You should have asked me. What if they were grounded or something?" Ruby was fabricating.

Flick snapped back, "You would have told me beforehand and they would not have been allowed to go to dinner." Laughing back, he knew he was right.

"It would have been nice if you had brought back some dinner for us," said Ruby the victim. Poor Ruby being left out.

Flick handed her a fifty-dollar bill. "Order yourself some Chinese. My apologies. Thanks for letting me take the boys. Can I come by tomorrow?"

The boys pleaded, "Ma, please, please," and pulled at her till she gave up.

"Yes." Then she shut the door. Flick thought it was odd. He'd expected to get invited in. Strange. He headed for the Metro thinking about Ruby's oddness. He was her son, not the boys' father. Yet, he felt more like a father with access. Oh well, he was looking forward to tomorrow.

***

Flick arrived back at the hotel around 9:00 p.m. Chuck was watching the news and sat up when he heard the door open. "Hey. How was the visit?"

Flick smiled. "Good." He threw his jacket in the closet and it landed on the floor. "What did you learn today?"

Chuck grinned. "I learned I'm in Quebec."

Flick blinked. As if Chuck didn't know. "Oh?"

Chuck laughed. "It seems court is going to be in French."

Flick laughed as well. "That could be a problem."

"Yup. My French is as good as my Spanish. I only understand cervasa and vino, vino tinto. Anything requested at the bar, I might comprehend." He shook his head. "They're going to arrange a translator. That would be a good thing."

"You think they might be trying to blame you for the fire?"

Chuck replied, "I wondered the same thing. Then they shared the evidence. They knew the owners, Serge and Jocelyn, were trying to place the blame on me. They would have detained me in Quebec if I was suspected. The fact that I came back of my volition indicates that I have nothing to hide."

Flick asked, "Anything interesting happen?"

"Not really. We went through a series of mock questions. In English of course. I have no intention of withholding information or adding anything I knew. In other words, I'll simply tell the truth."

Flick headed for the shower. "That's a good plan." Then he turned around. "When is court?"

"Court is all week, but I'm not allowed to attend to listen in. I'm expected the day after tomorrow."

"I could go with you, if you want."

"If you have the time that would be great."

The two went for a beer in the hotel and then called it a night.

***

The next day Flick asked Chuck if he wanted to hang out with him and the boys. Chuck thought it might be a good idea. The two took a leisurely day to shop around 20/20 and Alexis Neon Plaza. They took the Metro to The Pointe and showed up at 3:15 p.m. when the boys came running down the street. Flick had half-thought the boys would be coming on their bikes, but he didn't think about it much after they came and hugged him tightly.

Then Gavin informed Flick that their bikes had been sold and that Lina, George's daughter, had gotten a new bike today. Just then Ruby was at the door.

Flick blew a gasket. "What the hell happened? I heard the bikes I bought were sold. Is that true?"

Ruby muttered, "George sold them. To teach the boys that they should have mentioned their new sister, Lina."

Flick lost his cool. "No, YOU should have told me so that I could have bought one for Lina today." Chuck was watching the altercation. "Get that asshole out here. I'm going to teach him a lesson."

Ruby was about to blow Flick off when George showed up with Lina on her bike.

Flick was in his face. "What the hell do you think you're doing selling the boys' bikes?" He didn't want the girl to feel bad, so he didn't finish the thought about buying Lina a bike.

George looked shocked. "I didn't sell the bikes."

Flick didn't understand. "How did she get a new bike?"

"I bought it for her. Out of my own money." He looked at Flick from the corner of his eye wondering what his problem was.

Then Flick was in Ruby's face. "You lied. Didn't you? You sold the bikes and blamed your husband to be."

Ruby had her arms crossed and a stance that said, *what you going do about it?*

Chuck whispered to Flick, "You still have the receipts?"

Flick nodded.

"Well you have the serial numbers," Chuck said smiling.

Flick was on it, grinning with mischief. "Well, I have my cell here and I'm going to call the police and report the bikes stolen."

Ruby unfolded her arms and gasped. "You wouldn't?"

"Oh, I would. I might mention that I suspect that you stole your own kids' bikes and then sold them. I am willing to lay charges. I think it's about time you grew up and cared about your kids instead of yourself." Flick wanted to keep on but instead, he started dialing.

Ruby was afraid of social services and having her resources compromised. "O.k. I'll get the bikes back. It's just that I'm short twenty dollars."

Flick almost handed her the twenty and then decided against it. "It's up to you. Your call." The police answered. "I'd like to report two bikes stolen."

Ruby grabbed the phone. She'd never seen a cell phone and didn't know how to hang up. "Hang up. Hang up. I'll get the bikes back. O.k." The police were familiar with Ruby and thought it was her voice. They sent dispatch to her door to follow up.

George handed Ruby twenty dollars and Ruby ran into the house and made the call. "Listen, those bikes I sold you. I need them back. My bastard of a son, Flick, is threatening to report them stolen. You'll end up losing the bikes. I'll give you your money back. Sorry about this."

Ten minutes later, the bikes were back on the balcony. Flick came with locks and chains and secured them to the rail. The boys worshipped their big brother. Everything was made right when he was around. The kids stayed quiet, smiling.

Flick and Chuck had a great night with the boys and Flick explained that he would be sending gifts for Christmas much like last year. The boy explained they'd never gotten any gifts from him.

Flick confronted Ruby once again and made it clear he would be sending Christmas gifts for the boys and Lina, if Ruby was married to George as planned. He told her he would be calling the boys and if they didn't get their gifts he would be on it like flies on shit. Ruby knew he meant business and realized the boys had told him they'd never gotten his gifts last Christmas.

Flick hugged the boys and promised he would stay in touch the best he could. He turned to Ruby glaring and almost spitting with fury. "If the boys weren't standing here right now, I'd tell you exactly what I have been thinking about you. What a selfish, horrible mother." He walked away and joined Chuck, who was smoking a cigarette at the corner.

***

The next day the guys went to court and waited in the lobby until the prosecutor was ready to bring Chuck to the stand. Everything went as rehearsed and the defendant's side asked incriminating questions. The prosecutor had prepared Chuck for the inquisition but needed to know that Chuck had nothing to do with the fire that had taken so many lives. Realizing that the questions from the defense would be designed to try and implicate him, Chuck answered honestly. When the question had nothing to do with what he had seen, he simply said, "I can't say I witnessed that. I can't answer for … I wouldn't know, I wasn't in the back where the fire originated." The prosecutor was satisfied, and Chuck was told he would not be called back to the stand – that they had gotten all that was needed and he could go back to Calgary.

On the flight back … another case was waiting for Chuck and Flick.

Chapter 36
Calgary, 1984

The trip back to Calgary had Chuck and Flick happy to be home. It had felt odd to visit Montreal, which had once been their only form of existence. The consistency of their lives proved to be in Calgary. They liked their work, their routines, their family, and their life.

Flick was relieved of the chaos and dysfunction that plagued Ruby's household. He would miss Gunner and Gavin, but he believed the young boys would never forget him or his siblings out west. He'd been pleased to have had some time with them and to be there for them – especially when their bikes had been sold. And he was tickled at how he'd handled Ruby and set her straight about his Christmas gifts coming for the boys. He was so over her stupidity and her manipulative ways and thrilled that Ruby had no hold on him anymore.

Chuck was pleased to have been back to Montreal and to realize that his life was now in Calgary. He'd called all his siblings to let them know he was in town. None had responded. Chuck had visited his parents' gravesites, had a chat, and said a prayer. He was glad that the court issues were over, though he hadn't learned the final decisions of the court before he and Flick left Montreal. It saddened him that so many lives had been ruined by the greed of the bar owners. This time leaving Montreal, he was truly leaving chaos and messes created by others completely behind. He came off the plane feeling refreshed, rejuvenated, and glad to be home.

The weekend was awaiting them with time for family and sharing their experiences back east. Liv loved to hear about the boys and she enjoyed hearing how Flick had taken care of business when Ruby had stolen the boys' valued possessions; their bikes. She was pleased he'd set the record straight and the young ones would likely get their Christmas presents this year. Flick mentioned he'd given the boys pictures of them all, including Gayle and Peter, who they referred to as the queen and king. Everyone one wanted to hear the young boys' reactions to their pictures.

Kandy felt much the same way as Liv. Between the two it was more like a cheering committee. Both Flick and Chuck enjoyed entertaining the family about the visit. Kandy moaned when she heard they'd eaten at Connie's Pizza and had steamed hot dogs. She'd forgotten some of the simplest joys that can be had in Montreal. Even smoked meat sandwiches and potato lattices were something to salivate over. Kandy occasionally craved these foods, but she would never trade them for the life she had come to cherish living in Calgary.

Salt sat back, listened to the anecdotes and grinned. He sipped his ginger ale like the other men sipped the cognac Flick had brought out. Salt liked being like the big boys. Everyone noticed and loved how he had found his way to fit in with the family.

Sugar did visit and listen a bit, but it annoyed her to hear how her mother had been treated. Sugar felt her mother was a liberated woman who had found ways to make ends meet and enjoyed life the best way she could. So, what if there are givers in the world and takers? It's what makes the world go around. What crime was committed if Ruby was clever and creative? Sugar was disgusted that her siblings found it amusing to make fun of Ruby and put her in her place. She couldn't help her feelings. She believed she'd become the woman she was because of the scrapper/survivor her mother was. What pissed Sugar off the most was her mother wasn't there to defend herself. She left feeling like the odd man out.

The worlds of East and West were shared that night. Gayle and Peter enjoyed the story telling and went home content that their lives had helped so many people that they loved. They reflected on how the East had met West when Liv came into their lives. That had been the start of their life and the beginning of their hearts feeling full. Who would have guessed that Liv's family from out east would bring them so much joy? The family they wanted, craved, received, cherished, and loved had been a huge blessing.

Gayle thought about the thousand prayers that once had felt as though they had not been answered. That night snuggling with Peter, she thanked God for answering every single prayer. Though God had done so on His own timetable, He had done them till they were just right. She fell asleep with no regrets.

Sunday morning came and the Pattersons slept in. The sound of Chuck working on the property awoke Gayle. "Honey, it's time to get up," she said. But when she turned around she noticed that Peter did not move. Gayle's heart lunged into her throat and stopped for a moment. Tears came down her face as she knew she had lost the love of her life in the night.

She took a few minutes to say a prayer and talk to her husband. She wanted to reflect on the beautiful life they'd shared. "I appreciate how you loved me. Loved Liv. Gave of yourself and made sacrifices out of love. How your heart dictated the pace and environment of our great life. You are the anchor, the stronghold, the heartbeat of my life. How will I ever go on without you? I only ask God to keep you close and safe till I'm at your side once again, my love." Her tears of joy and love soaked Peter's pillow.

Gayle felt weak and sick to her stomach. Her emotions had her in an abyss of flashing memories of their life together. Forcing her mind to think, she looked out the window and saw Chuck working on the lawns. She opened the window, called, "Chuck," and waited a moment.

Chuck looked up to see Gayle saying something. He took off the headset that protected his ears from the lawnmower and smiled at her.

"Can you come up here for a minute?" Gayle asked.

Chuck nodded and was in the house and up the stairs within a minute. He stood in the doorway of the master bedroom and saw Peter asleep and Gayle with tears in her eyes. Then he realized what his mind refused to accept. Peter had passed on. In a whisper he said, "Oh, my God."

Gayle stood by Peter. "I have to call 911. Can you call Liv and ask her to come over? Don't tell her what happened … just not yet. I want to hold her when she gets the news."

Gayle made the 911 call. Liv seemed to be over by the time Gayle put the receiver on the cradle. Liv entered the room, looked at her parents and realized that Peter was asleep ... forever. She put her hand over her mouth and tears poured out uncontrollably. Gayle was at Liv's side and hugging their daughter. No words had been spoken.

Chuck answered the door to the police. The sound of footsteps upstairs led them to the bedroom. An ambulance arrived right behind the officers. Within the hour, Peter had departed their home that late September day.

The girls talked about deciding. Gayle and Liv would have to go to the morgue. It was Monday morning. Liv did not want Gayle alone in the house now that Peter was not present, and she asked Chuck to stay at the house to watch over her mother and make coffee in the mornings. Milly came to the house to work and found herself busy with food preparations for expected visitors. Liv called the funeral home and explained the situation. The funeral home said they would take care of everything from the morgue. Anything the family needed they would be there for them. A consultant would be over in the afternoon to help with preferences and preparations. Liv was on the phone all morning with family. She called Peter's old office and spoke with a secretary, who said she would inform all the partners and staff. She just wanted Liv to call back with the of times and dates.

Flick was over in a flash supporting Gayle and Liv and keeping Liam occupied with food, toys, and games. Milly had lunch served with finger sandwiches, a vegetable tray, a fruit tray, juice with 7-up, and coffee on the go always.

The consultant showed up at 1:30 p.m. and most decisions had been made by 2:30. The announcement in the paper was written carefully and with great love for a man who was a giver. By 3:00, they were putting together pictures of his life: When he was in the arms of his parents. Activities as a young boy such as hiking and fishing. School pictures. Wedding pictures. Pictures of achievement throughout his career. Pictures of their vacations and weekend getaways. Pictures with young Liv and the stages of her growing up. Pictures of the whole clan up until yesterday.

The consultant had everything in hand and promised all would be handled with efficiency and great care. Tuesday, the funeral home would prepare the body. Wednesday was the viewing. Thursday was Mass. Friday would be the service and then the graveside burial with only family. A family plot was purchased along with a casket in solid oak with white satin lining. Flowers arrived, more than triple than was normal. The church would look like a floral shop by the time Gayle was finished. There was catered foods for all days. The day of the funeral, there would be a hot buffet for the family before going to the graveside to say goodbye, or to see Peter laid to rest.

Kandy showed up after work at 4:00, asking if there was anything she could do. Liv and Gayle smiled and said everything had been taken care of right down to the guest book and signing pen.

Liv and Kandy cornered Chuck and insisted that he stay in the guest room this week. He promised to leave the door open should Gayle need anything and to have coffee on in the morning. Anything Gayle needed Chuck would do.

Chuck had already made a promise to Peter he would look out for his girls. Liv was worried that Gayle would become lonely and miss Peter. Though his death had been expected, she did not want her mother to suffer. But Liv could not stop the grieving process. It was a part of life.

Gayle and Liv did a wonderful job with all the arrangements. They wanted family, friends, and peers to have the opportunity to say goodbye. There was an incredible slide presentation celebrating Peter's life and lots of tears and many smiles throughout the days. Kandy set up a jar with pieces of paper and asked the guests to write down what they felt about Peter. There were students, staff, and strangers who wrote notes on how Peter had blessed them and refused anything in return. Even Gayle was overwhelmed by the notes of appreciation, which were well over a hundred. Peter was honored and then settled in his final resting place. He had journeyed ahead and left behind all those who loved him.

Gayle now walked alone …

***

What two people had created together was now in the hands of one. Gayle was the matriarch of the family. She spent her nights reliving her treasured moments of a life embraced by her husband. Gayle's dreams brought her comfort as each one she recalled had Peter with her. Sleeping was an oasis where Gayle never felt alone. Her days were long as she wished for her solace of peace, having conversations about the past with her companion.

Each morning began with the smell of coffee brewing. Gayle would wake to a trance of habit filling her cup. Sitting quietly in the kitchen nook in a daze, she'd look out the window. Chuck was not present by then because he'd be off to work with Flick. The days were long as the family Gayle cherished were occupied with their lives, occupations, obligations, and duties. Gayle was living on automatic with no goals, no ambitions, and not a single focus. Existing became a habit. Was this state of mind and heart a form of grieving or a new reality?

Gayle realized Peter's death had caused a paralysis. She also realized she would die a slow death if she continued her monotonous life into an oblivion of nonexistence. She decided to get dressed and go over to Liv's to see her grandchild. Liam was the engine that would spark life in her dead battery, so to speak.

When Liv arrived home, she was pleased to see her mother engaged with Liam and his antics. The love these two people shared was like watching a painter take on a colorful story. Liam knew how to touch Gayle's heart and draw her into his world. Liam was much like Peter – skilled at knowing how to find Gayle's smile.

Liv watched with hope that her mother was returning to the land of the living. But she herself had trouble mending her broken heart and she missed her father. The comfort of her husband and the necessity of normalcy for Liam forced Liv to move on. Her peace with her father had been the love he'd showered on her all her life. There was a note in the jar that said, "May your grief be short. May your memories of love last forever." That is exactly what Liv planned.

She showed Gayle the note with a smile. Gayle froze and went into deep thought. "Yes, my memories of love will last forever. Unfortunately, my heart cannot seem to understand and is in pain. I don't know how to get rid of the grief. I do pray it will be short." She gave a fake smile.

Liv smiled and nodded. "Me too. But we don't have to let go of a great man. He would be sad that we're hurting because of him. He would want us to live and be happy because he blessed us so greatly."

Gayle had her eyes on Liam. "I know you're right. I have to start living again. I just don't know how."

Liv smiled watching Liam entertain his grandmother. "I think you're at the right time, the right place, to begin. Because of you and Dad, I am here. Because of both of you, Liam is here. Mom, because of you and Dad, this great big family is here. You taught us to love, to share, and to sacrifice because we are family." She was trying hard not to cry. "We all need you, Mom. You are a great woman with so much more to teach and share."

Gayle was listening. "Well, there is Chuck who's like a son, and Flick as well. Not to mention sweet Salt…and Kandy who has a lot more to learn." No one ever mentioned Sugar these days. Though she was invited to all family functions and gatherings, she had failed to show up to support Gayle in the loss of Peter.

***

Chuck and Flick finally met with Todd, their lawyer. The negotiations were intense. Though Bob believed he had a good case, his lawyer wasn't that convincing. He acted like he was doing his job to get paid and the outcome of the case didn't matter. Todd, on the other hand, liked to win for the sake of the principle. Sure, he was going to get paid, but he liked to sleep with a good conscience at night.

Todd explained how his plan had played out. Bob had pulled every last hope in an effort to sue for anything, but each issue or matter had been flattened with hard facts and disclosed consequences. The vein in Bob's right temple had throbbed with stress when he heard Flick had countersued for a million. Todd had thought the man was going to have an aneurism when he learned there was a viable case. "I didn't even have to throw the man a bone. I didn't have to suggest giving him money for training Chuck. The only thing Bob wanted was the last of the projected money that would be paid up to the end of December as per the contract, within fifteen days."

Flick smiled. "What did you tell him?"

Todd grinned. "I told him you were adhering to the contract and the contract only. In other words, he could hold his breath."

Flick and Chuck laughed. "I think we will get the matter over with and send him a check this week. Put other ten percent on it to seal the deal. There must be a waiver to never come after us again," Flick instructed.

Todd then said, "Now for the matter of our bill. I did a fair amount of research, involved staff to create a huge legal team, and promised them a bonus for their excellent acting. I am not a manipulative man. But my bill will be $20,000.00"

Flick nodded and frowned with a knowing smile, thinking of Peter and his powers of negotiation. "Does that include my $5,000 retainer? Don't answer that. Keep it and I'm going to cut you a check for $25,000."

Todd blinked in surprise.

Flick explained, "You saved me, us, at least a couple hundred thousand dollars. The least I can do is show our appreciation. Thank you for a great job. You saved our business." The three men shook hands, smiling.

Flick had Peter on his mind when it came to business. He had learned so much by example. The man had been admired and justly so. Flick liked the look he got from Todd for engaging in fair business. If doing a man right felt this good, it was great being a good man to begin with. Flick concluded that he liked the man he was becoming. It was all because of Peter, the father, or grandfather he'd never had.

Flick thought of Chuck as his father as well, but it was a different relationship. It was a family bond that tied them together for a purpose. It was Liv. Now their purpose would be to always be the men in the family for both Gayle and Liv, not forgetting Gideon. To walk in loving memory of Peter.

Chapter 37
Playing the Game, 1984-1985

The fall had set the stage for cooler weather. Winter followed, and Christmas had come. Gayle and Liv decided to make the holidays special. They felt it was important to keep the family bonds strong. Peter had expressed his wish for Chuck to look out for Gayle should he die, and so Chuck moved into the guest room. This move had everyone's blessing. Chuck was not isolated and stayed more involved with family. Gayle was not alone and had a man in the house making sure she was safe. Gayle didn't mind the company as Chuck was a quiet man and unobtrusive.

Gayle planned activities each evening called, "The Twelve Days of Christmas." The family would meet after dinner around 7:00 to 8:30 each night till Christmas Day. There were treasure hunts, games, stories, and various activities filled with fun. Evening snacks and hot chocolate were arranged in the kitchen with Milly's help.

Liv had a dinner on Christmas Eve and had members of the family read the notes from the jar and share how they felt. It was her way of including Peter because she wished to never forget this incredible man. The family was a little uncomfortable at first, but once the notes had been read and the stories shared, the memories came with smiles. Everyone's heart felt the strong connection to each other and the love that kept them together. The love of Peter.

Sadly, Sugar declined to have anything to do with the family and did not attend any of the festivities.

On Christmas Day at Liv's, the family came together for a breakfast brunch and gift exchange. The children, Champ and Liam, played together. It was a wonderful day to share some news...

Gideon and Liv announced, "We are expecting another child. The baby is due in July." They delivered the news with smiles as if it was the greatest gift they could reveal to those they loved.

Kandy and Gayle jumped up with excitement and hugged Liv. Gideon smiled and said, "I knew you would think Liv did this creation all by herself."

The three girls teased him, hugging him as well.

The guys looked from one to the other, and then Flick announced, laughing, "I think us guys need to knock up a girl. We'd like to get a hug too." The girls ran and gave each of them a hug and teased them for being jealous.

Kandy announced she was entering a one-year LPN program, clarifying that it was a Licensed Practical Nurse. The government would finance the schooling. Kandy would have to finance uniforms, shoes, and books. Because she had a child she would get funding for daycare and enough to cover her expenses each month if she handled her budget wisely.

Flick was impressed and hugged Kandy saying, "I'm so proud of you."

Liv expressed her pleasure and told Kandy if she needed help not to hesitate to ask.

Gayle was pleased as well and congratulated Kandy. She asked how the car was holding up.

Teasingly with a smile, Kandy said, "It's great. I don't need another one."

Gayle smiled too.

Gideon announced he had been promoted to a senior engineer. In a few years, he hoped to be a partner in the firm.

The boys teased, and Flick said, "We have too many jobs these days. Anyone willing to become a plumber?"

Everyone laughed.

The sharing of information had the family cheering each other about their news. They all were reaching out, bettering themselves, and growing.

The new year would be welcomed with a new set of goals, new dreams, and hopefully no tragedies. Everyone knew they had each other's backs. They were a strong family and the bonds could not be broken.

Flick went outside with Chuck lighting a cigarette. Both of them had been thinking about the young boys in Montreal. Chuck mentioned, "I hope they got their gifts from all of us."

Gayle had even sent Bay cards for new clothes. Kandy sent games for Nintendo even though she couldn't afford a new gaming system. Salt bought the boys baseball caps and balls. Chuck and Flick sent Ruby $600.00 with a complete list of instructions: $100.00 for Christmas dinner and

$100.00 for each of them; Ruby, George, Gunner, Gavin, and Lina. They suggested Ruby go shopping on Boxing Day to get whatever anyone needed or wanted. Flick stated he would be calling in the evening on Boxing Day to inquire about the boys' purchases.

Flick confirmed, "I'll be calling tomorrow night. I don't think Ruby will mess with me. I'd be tempted to send the police and charge her with theft if she didn't follow my instructions."

Chuck grinned. He knew Flick would do exactly that to prove a point.

Flick shared with Chuck a private secret. "I don't want the family to know this, but I'm getting along with the Julian girl staying at the house. She's sassy, fun to visit with." He didn't explain that they deliberately provoked one another in fun. He liked the spunky gal and knew he would enjoy a good argument with her any time, day or night.

Chuck asked, "How do you think Kandy would react if you were to pursue a deeper relationship?"

Flick wanted to say, *it would be none of her business*, but he decided to say, "If it did get serious I would talk with Kandy and hope she would be supportive." Thinking for a minute, he crushed the butt under his shoe. "Besides, I don't think Julian and Kandy are real friends. Not close, for that matter."

Chuck then had a thought. "Well, if I didn't know better, I would say Kandy set you up with the girls in hopes of you having a relationship." He grinned. "I can't say for sure."

"You might be right," Flick said with a smile, knowing he was. "What about you?"

Chuck glared and frowned. "What about me?"

Flick didn't think he was being nosey. They were family. "You know. Having a lady. A girlfriend."

Chuck shook his head and laughed. "You have me too busy."

Flick walked back into the house. "Oh, so that's how it is?"

Chuck laughed. "Yeah. That's how it is."

***

The new year proved to be busy for everyone. The boys had enough business for five more people. They worked around the clock keeping up with the demands. Liv was working hard to wrap up her thesis before the new baby was born. Also, she was an instructor at the university and busy with assignments and papers. Making time for Liam and Gideon had its challenges. Gayle was busy with Milly, taking care of Liam. Gideon was putting in longer hours now that he was a senior engineer. Kandy was in the LPN program, doing assignments, and being a good mother to Champ. No one heard anything from Sugar.

By spring, everyone was screaming for a break. Liv and Gideon always found a way to cuddle every night even if for ten minutes. They reflected, focused, and readjusted their schedules as needed and talked about getting away or having a family function.

Liv thought the family function would be best for now. She quickly called and left messages for everyone to come to their home and share a meal on the coming Saturday. Then she hired Milly to put a catered meal together. Liv thought about the Friday afternoon lunches they used to share, and she wanted to do her best to make Sugar feel welcome, so she decided to go and visit her on Friday.

Liv showed up at noon and knocked on Sugar's door. No one answered the door, but Liv noticed the drapes move and realized she had been ignored. What was it going to take to have a simple conversation with this girl? Her gut told her Sugar was much like their mother. Money talked, though she hated herself for even thinking of bribing Sugar to answer the door. Liv was a patient person, but time was never on her side. A half hour of talking through the door ensued, with no success. Finally, she gave into to a bribe. Walking away, she hollered, "Give me a call if twenty bucks works for you – make it fifty." Then she heard the door open.

Sugar stood with her hands on her hips. "Make it a hundred."

Liv ran back to the stair's half in anger and half in relief for finally reaching this girl. "Hi, can we talk?"

Sugar was in a mood for being in control. She already had her big sister dangling at the door and pleading. "You can talk. Who says I'll listen?"

Liv had her spunk and said, "A hundred dollars tells me you'll listen." Then she touched the door to indicate she was entering the home.

Sugar wanted to stop Liv from entering. But she suspected Liv was not going to talk unless it was in private, and otherwise she would not get the hundred bucks. She stepped back, and the girls sat in the living room. Sugar thought of offering a pop and then decided Liv might stay too long. Besides, if you're hospitable to people, they will think you are generous and get more from you. No one was going to take advantage of Sugar. As Liv put her purse to her side, Sugar said, "Don't make yourself too comfortable. This should take no longer than pulling money out of an ATM. Understand?"

Liv's stubbornness was coming out and she said, "This is going to take as long as I want. A hundred dollars is a lot of money. At least worth a few hours. Got it?" Liv believed that bullies were scared people. They needed to be stronger for their own good.

Sugar hadn't seen this reaction from Liv coming. She thought of talking back and then bit her tongue. Not out of respect for Liv – out of respect for the money. Sugar also wasn't prepared for Liv to have a backbone and thought it might be fun to push her buttons. This might be a fun afternoon after all…with getting paid. A win/win situation.

Liv decided to focus on how she used to enjoy their lunches. "I miss having lunch with you and Kandy. It was the highlight of my week."

Sugar didn't care. She knew Liv wanted something. "Yeah, so what? What do you want? You didn't come here to kick my door in, now did ya?"

Liv almost said, *No, to kick your head in and smarten you up.* "No, I came to knock some sense into you. To let you know you are so loved, appreciated, cared for, and embraced by a wonderful family." She waited for an answer.

Sugar had her head down. There was no reply.

Liv decided to pour her heart out. "I loved you from the first day you were born, and I felt so fortunate to have you close by and get to know you all over again. Don't you see the opportunity?"

Sugar had her hackles up. "What I see is YOU running away and never looking back. You didn't care for us until we were in your face. We're an embarrassment to ya. You come here pretending to care. Like you're my mother. Some mother you are. You think your money can buy my love?"

Liv was sharp. "No, but it bought me time with you. Time to get all your frustrations out. Time to let you know that you're an important member of the family. Your beautiful girl, Deidra, deserves to have family and enjoy her cousins." Being pregnant, the hormones of emotions were at play in her. In tears she said, "Don't you know you are loved?"

Sugar was tough. "Don't you know life has nothing to do with love? It has everything to do with making it happen. Making your life work." She laughed. "Ever hear the song 'What's Love Got to Do With it?'"

Liv was on it. "You're right about 'life is about making your life work.'" She almost wanted to get up as her back ached from the stress. "You have an amazing family as a resource for support, encouragement, affection, and love." She wanted to say, *not to be used or abused* but realized that would come across as an accusation.

Sugar said nothing and was juggling her own thoughts.

Liv was on her game. "So how is life treating you these days? Going back to school? Working? New friends? Tell me about the makings of your life." She stood up to enter the kitchen for a glass of water.

Sugar had nothing to say. "My life is fine. Busy with Deidra. I don't need anything else or anyone else." Sugar had her welfare check and all her bills were paid by Butch. She figured she was doing better than anyone else including her mother. Sugar only had to mess around with one man to get all of this. Liv, Flick, and Kandy were all working stiffs. Slaves to society. On the other hand, Sugar was free as a bird and living a comfortable life. She loved to get a good deal and chase the sales.

Liv felt cramped in the small place. It wasn't so much the size of the room but the number of things in every inch of the place: Bulky furniture that needed a larger room. All of Deidra's things; large castle, doll house, rocking horse, carriage, and a volume of toys cluttered the place and left little room to maneuver. The kitchen had a highchair and a playpen that blocked the back door, and the counters were covered with every small appliance. Liv could see too much was not a good thing, especially when it came to safety.

She did not know what to say when Sugar said, "I don't need anyone else."

"You seriously don't need people in your life? You don't need the love of your family?"

Sugar shrugged. "It keeps my life simple."

Liv had to hold back her laughter about living a simple life. "Well, the way I see it you could stand to handle a bit of extra love in your life. I'll call it 'the clutter of love.' What do you say you come over tomorrow and enjoy a wonderful meal with the whole family? We really miss you and would love to get to know Deidra." Liv wondered where Deidra was. Then she thought of her plan and wanted no excuses. "What if I send a limousine to pick you up? It would be a fun experience. What do you say?"

Sugar answered, "Give me my hundred dollars and I'll give you my answer."

Liv smiled. Two could play this game. "Why don't you show up and I'll give you your hundred dollars then? I don't carry that much money on me anyway." Liv had a few hundred on her but had decided to play the game.

Sugar was pissed. "Fine, I'll be there. What time?"

Liv had gotten what she wanted. "I'll have a limo pick you up at 11:00 a.m."

Sugar didn't want to spend the whole day there. "It's too early for me."

Liv smiled. "That's the time. Take it or leave it." She smiled knowing Sugar wanted the money.

As Liv was leaving, someone knocked on the door. Sugar peeked through the drapes. "Be quiet. It's social services."

Liv whispered, "Did they take Deidra away?"

Sugar shushed her. "No, Deidra went down for a nap." She kept an eye on the door.

Liv wanted to go. "I have to go now. I'm expected back at the university to talk with one of my students." She was about to touch the door knob when Sugar pounced forward to stop her from leaving. It was too late. The door was open. Liv spoke to the woman at the door. "Hi, can I help you?"

Mary Bertall introduced herself. "I'd like to talk with Sugar."

Sugar came to the door and gave Liv a filthy look, but she allowed the woman inside. "What can I do you for?"

Liv stayed at the door.

Mary stated, "We've had a complaint …"

Sugar barked back. "From who?"

Mary continued, "That you are living with a man believed to be the father of your child and also collecting welfare." Mary looked around with eyes wide open, seeing all the new purchases most people could not afford. "How can you afford all of this, then?"

Sugar was quick. "My sister here, Liv, and my family spoil Deidra and me when they can. Mostly Christmas and birthdays. Is that a crime?"

Liv said nothing. It was true they were generous when the need arose, though never with massive indulgence to the point of spoiling.

Mary stayed focused. "So, you are saying that you are a single mother and are not being provided for by anyone else?"

Sugar answered, "That's what I'm saying." She had set up the bills in her name and had her man give her cash to pay them. There was no way to track that information. Being on welfare and paying cash was no surprise.

Mary politely prepared to depart. "We will be keeping an eye on things." She was doing her masters at the university and recognized Liv as one of the instructors. "It was nice to see you, Liv."

Liv nodded.

The door closed, and Liv stood saying nothing. Sugar collapsed.

Liv smiled. "Your wonderful family that spoils you will see you tomorrow, right?" She grinned as she left, shutting the door behind her.

Sugar didn't even get up or look at Liv.

***

Liv was back in her office at the university where she grabbed a sandwich, juice, and water. After her interlude with Sugar she felt dehydrated. A student named Annie was expected. Liv had finished her meal when the sound of knocking occupied her ear. "Come in." Looking up, she saw a girl who seemed familiar and realized it was Hannah.

Liv stood up. "Please come in. How can I help you?"

Hannah had known the instructor was her ex-husband's sister. "I wanted to say 'hi' and let you know that I'm fast tracking in the nursing program. I'm going to take your course on abnormal behavior as one of my electives. It was one of the few courses that fit into my schedule or I wouldn't have taken it."

Liv smiled. "How are you doing?"

Hannah smiled back. "I'm doing better. Doing good." Her nerves had settled down a bit. She wasn't sure, though, if she should let out her secret.

Liv noticed a subtle change in Hannah's demeanour. "Is there something else you want to tell me?"

Hannah felt Liv's kindness and decided to share. "You know I was in bad shape when I left Flick."

Liv nodded.

Hannah continued. "Well as it turned out I was pregnant. I had a little boy – his name is Jonathan Sport. I wanted our child, if a boy, to be called Jonathan. Flick had wanted our boy to be called Sport."

Liv nodded. "Does Flick know about Sport?"

Hannah shook her head. "No, my parents won't allow it. They take care of Jonathan while I'm at school." Looking a bit scared, she said, "I took a risk telling you. Flick was kind to help me get through school. It gave me a focus, something to accomplish, something to do. I'm grateful. I'm not interested in taking anything from Flick."

Liv appreciated what Hannah was saying. "I can't see Flick worried about you taking anything when it comes to his child. I believe he would be thrilled and would love to see his baby."

Hannah nodded. "I know he deserves to see his child. I'll never hear the end of it with my parents, though."

Liv had an idea. "Listen, we're having a family dinner tomorrow night at my place. Why don't you arrive around 4:00 p.m. and bring Jonathan Sport?"

"I can't do that." She was shaking.

Liv reassured Hannah. "I think the news would be best from you. I will hold off till Sunday. Is that fair?"

Hannah got the message quite clearly. "Yes." She got up in a daze. Why had she told Liv about the baby? What had she been thinking? Now look at the mess she was in.

Chapter 38
The Family Reunion, 1985

On her way home, Liv realized that Hannah's reluctance to attend might have something to do with Salt. She decided to talk with her mother when she arrived home.

At home, Liam was at the door asking to be picked up. Liv loved her son and lavished a few kisses on him. In a minute Liam was in a hurry to play with Grandma. Liv asked if Gayle would mind staying a bit as she wanted to take a quick shower. Gayle was never in a hurry to run home to be alone. "Sure."

Liv was back from her shower in a short while, toweling her hair and sporting a new maternity outfit. Gayle handed her a cup of tea. They sat down watching Liam exploring his world. Liv shared with her mother what she had done… that she'd visited Sugar and how she had made her promise to come to the family dinner tomorrow.

Gayle was grinning.

Liv asked, "What?"

Gayle smiled and said, "You're becoming more like your father than you know."

Liv blinked. "What do you mean?"

"Well, Peter always managed to offer a nice gesture and then accomplish what he wanted." Gayle was referring to the limo.

Liv caught on and smiled. "It worked. I'm sure it did. We'll see tomorrow, won't we?" She sipped her tea and then thought about her meeting with Hannah. "Oh, I had a surprise visit from one of my students."

Gayle knew this was the beginning of their "chat dance." Smiling and on cue, she said, "Oh?"

Liv was grinning. "A girl named Annie came by." She paused for effect. "It turned out to be Hannah."

Gayle gasped. "You're kidding." Now she was all ears.

Liv nodded. "I'm not kidding. The news is she had a little boy. It's Flick's and his name is Jonathan Sport."

Gayle was blinking at the questions running in her mind. "I take it Flick doesn't know."

"No. I invited Hannah to the family dinner tomorrow night. I'm not sure she'll be here."

Gayle teased her daughter. "You didn't bribe her with a limo?"

Liv stated, "I gave her the option of coming; to bring Jonathan Sport and tell Flick herself, or that I would let Flick know by Sunday. It was her choice."

Gayle thought for a minute. "I don't think she'll come anyway. You are telling Flick would be letting him know without seeing him...and without seeing Salt."

Liv had thought about Hannah running into Salt. Hannah had changed since the incident and Salt had changed a lot too. But Gayle was right, feelings don't often change. "I was thinking of finding a way to have Salt occupied should Hannah show up."

Gayle announced, "Salt has a bowling tournament Saturday night. He's doing so good and looks like he's going to the Special Olympics. Chuck and I were thinking of attending if you wouldn't object."

Liv was thrilled. "That's great. I told Hannah to come around 4:00 p.m. It could work. You guys would miss out on dinner, but I could have a great lunch as well."

Gayle said, smiling, "Don't worry about dinner. We can take Salt out on our way to the game and keep him overnight as he is expected in a soft ball tournament on Sunday morning. Oh, and he is doing well in that category as well."

Liv was pleased. "I have Hannah's number with me from the office. I'll give her a call."

Gayle was in a mischievous mood. "Maybe you should bribe her with a limo ride as well."

Liv laughed. "Not a bad idea." She got the Yellow Pages out and circled a limo number before dialing Hannah's number. "Hi Hannah. This is Liv."

Hannah answered, "Yes?"

Liv looked at her mother for support. "Ah, just wanted you to know that Salt will not be at the family dinner. We wanted you to feel welcome." She held her breath.

Hannah hesitated and then said, "O.k. I'll be there with Junior. Thanks for the call." She hung up.

Liv said to Gayle, "She said she would be here. That's a good thing."

Liv quickly called the limo company and made a arrangements for a round trip. The car would pick Sugar up at 11:00 a.m. and the return trip was at 9:30 p.m." This way Sugar would likely stay and visit the whole time.

Gayle smiled and was proud of her daughter for being the glue of the family. She was working so hard to have them all together for a dinner to interact and create memories. Gayle was a little naïve, believing memories created with good intentions got good results. Liv knew better, though, and wondered if the memories would end up being landmarks or scars. She reminded herself that she had to think positive like Gayle.

Gayle stayed for dinner. Gideon was home around 6:00 p.m. in time to visit with her. He heard about the day's events and the plans for the family dinner tomorrow. Then he left the ladies to visit and went off to play with Liam. Gayle left around 8:00 p.m. as Liam was getting fussy and it was time for his bath and bed. Liv didn't have time for herself till after 9:00 p.m. Gideon was in the hot tub and she decided to join her husband in the tub to snuggle. The night permitted some quality time exclusive only to the couple.

***

Saturday morning arrived with Chuck doing the lawn care at Liv's. Gayle had ordered the man to go and help Gideon to get the yard in tip top shape. Liv was busy with Liam and his morning rituals. Milly and her assistant were busy cleaning the house and with the food preparation for the lunch, snacks, and evening dinner.

It was early June with summer trying to find its way to warmer weather. The sun peeked through the clouds. The forecast was for a few showers. This would not deter Liv and she continued to place lawn games out in the yard. Bending over was becoming a challenge these days as her baby was due the first week of July.

It was already 10:00 a.m. and Liv need to have something to eat. Milly had a plate of soft poached eggs, toast, and tea ready as Liv entered the kitchen. Gideon came in looking whipped with blades of grass on his shoes. He hugged his wife and poured himself and Chuck a cup of coffee. Milly asked if they would like some breakfast. The boys ate quickly and then ran off to get ready for the family day.

Kandy arrived at 11:00 a.m. with Champ and Salt. Gayle was right behind with Chuck. Sugar arrived around 11:30 with Deidra. Flick wandered in around noon with a girl. He introduced the spunky gal as Julian. Liv and Gayle looked from one to the other and knew what the other was thinking. Mother and daughter knew about Hannah coming later. Gideon was in on the secret and glanced their way.

Liam took charge of his guests, Champ and Deidra, handing out the toys and offering to play. The adults were getting plates ready for the children. Liam brought his cousins to the kids' table and handed them each a napkin. The adults thought Liam's service was impeccable if not hospitable. Sugar sneered. Gayle, Liv, and Kandy giggled and commented on how cute it was. The guys were talking business with Gideon.

The boys talked about their strengths; how Gideon, being an engineer, could design homes. The boys could do all the plumbing, gas, and Hvac. They decided they needed some framers, dry wallers, and electricians, and joked that they had a great lawyer. Salt shared that he was in the recycle business. Kandy, who was soon to be a nurse, laughed and decided there weren't enough family members to create the perfect building company. Flick thought himself a good contractor and figured he could hire these trades. The possibility was not all that far-fetched in his heart. Chuck liked watching Flick, the risk-taker, trying to convince the caution-taker, Gideon, as they discussed the pros and cons. Liv enjoyed watching Gideon moving from one foot to the other, wiggling out of possible commitments.

The girls chatted about the children and their obligations. Kandy was entertaining as she described a window-washing escapade. She had been hell-bent on getting her spring cleaning done but realized she did not have a squeegee to make the windows sparkling clean. So, she went out and took the wiper off her car. When she'd finished the job, she was pleased at how creative she had been. The ladies sat back enjoying the story and visualizing Kandy returning the wiper back to her car.

Sugar sat back frowning and trying to find a better, cleverer story to out-do her sister. She resented the attention Kandy was getting and thought Kandy was stupid to stoop so hard to fit in. Sadly, she couldn't think of anything and sat sulking, curled up in the chair.

The afternoon went reasonably well and then Gayle noticed the time and glanced at Chuck. Chuck looked at the microwave to check the time. It was 3:30 – time to leave and take Salt to the house to get ready for the dinner out and bowling. The three departed at 3:45 with hugs, kisses, and thanks for a great time. In the whirl of activity, Liv realized it was soon time for Hannah to arrive.

Hannah arrived at 4:30 p.m. with her newborn baby in her arms. Liv had not said anything to Flick. She'd decided to let people respond as they chose. Julian was an entertaining gal and was out back with Flick having a smoke.

The two entered the kitchen when Flick recognized a voice from a life of long ago, looked around, and saw Hannah. His heart stopped pounding like a lump in his chest. Julian noticed Flick's face flush and turn beet red. She wondered what was going on. Flick whispered in Julian's ear, "She's my ex." All eyes turned towards Hannah. Then Julian noticed the baby in the basket and glared at Flick.

Flick noticed the baby and stood in shock. Finally, he found his voice. "What's this all about?"

Hannah just looked up toward the familiar masculine voice of a man she once loved. She was realizing she still had feelings for Flick when she noticed a woman at Flick's side. She wondered why Liv had set her up and never told her Flick had a woman.

Liv recognized the question in Hannah's eyes and whispered in her ear, "I didn't know he was seeing anyone. I'm sorry Hannah."

Hannah nodded and believed Liv. "I didn't have the courage to say anything about the baby for a long time. I'm sorry. This is your son, Jonathan Sport."

Flick walked back outside to get his composure and Julian followed. Both lit up cigarettes. Flick kept his eyes to the ground thinking and feeling awkward. Julian wasn't mad, as she realized this news had not been known till this moment. She wanted to be supportive and in truth wanted to know where she stood. Their relationship was fun and had possibilities with practically no history.

Flick looked up at Julian even with his head down. "I honestly don't know how I feel. I'm divorced and want to be content with that. The baby, Sport, is a mind blower. K? I feel like I've been hit in the head with a hockey puck. The sting is all I feel right now."

Julian nodded. "I agree this is a shocker. I think I should go. Let's talk when you're ready. K? That's what good friends do. Catch up with you later. Bye for now." She went back into the house and thanked Liv for everything.

Flick remained outside wishing Chuck was around. Gideon was still in the house as he was not inclined to chat outside when the boys were smoking. It gave Flick a bit of time to shake off the shock. Thinking was his strong suit, but just this moment he had his mind on pause and couldn't think or feel. At last, his mind came alive and he wondered what Hannah wanted. How come she had waited so long to let him know he was a father of a little boy, Sport? It was time to face the questions and see about the answers.

The Hannah who was sitting in the living room was the girl Flick had married long ago. The pain between then and now was numbing. Flick did not want to feel. His heart gravitated to seeing his boy, but he was afraid to open his heart. Loving the boy would remind him of the time he'd loved Hannah and when she was with child. He remembered loving them both. If his heart loved the boy, would it instinctively love the mother? He could not afford to love Hannah again. The losses, the pain had been so great. Flick now understood he had been living a catatonic life for months. He never wanted to be on that plane of life ever again.

Liv went to Flick when she saw him hesitating to come in. She hoped he was not upset with her. "I'm sorry Flick. I didn't realize you had a girlfriend. I am so sorry. I just thought you should know about your son."

Flick had tears and nodded. "Yeah. I get it." He couldn't say anything else.

Liv led Flick to come in and sit at the kitchen table while Hannah remained in the family room. She realized her presence and news was too much for Flick. Her heart felt bad for him.

Sugar got up and announced, "Could have told ya marriage doesn't work. You two divorced and now look at the pain." She walked towards the bathroom.

Kandy got up and pushed Sugar faster to the bathroom. "What the hell do you think you're doing?"

Sugar shrugged. "Not my fault they're all stupid idiots." She tried to shut the door on Kandy.

Kandy hollered through the door, "What do you care? There's a kid involved. Look who's the fucking stupid idiot." She was mad as hell.

Sugar wasn't coming out anytime soon. Kandy knew the antics and wasn't going to waste her time on "stupid."

Hannah sat on the sofa holding her baby. No one was talking with her. The family had looked divided once she arrived. "I think I should go. I realize this was a surprise and I'm sorry. I didn't mean any harm."

Normally Liv would have objected. Instead, she stayed quiet. Gideon was with Liam and the little ones playing on the floor.

Flick sprang out of his chair and went to the family room. "I'd like to see my boy." He went over, and Hannah handed Sport into his arms.

Tears came down and a grin showed that Flick's heart was coming out. "Sport, you say."

Hannah smiled back. "Yes, Sport."

Flick held his son for the longest time. Everyone was quiet including the children. Sugar was out of the bathroom now, but she too stayed quiet as Kandy kept an eye on her sister. One false move and the girl was going lose a few hairs.

Flick handed the baby back to Hannah. "Let me know what you need for Sport...even if it means going through my lawyer." He walked outside to get another cigarette.

Milly began serving out supper and trying to encourage everyone to take a plate. Liv handed Hannah a plate and Hannah took the food and sat at the table. She was hungry as she was breastfeeding the baby. She finished her meal in ten minutes and then got up and decided it was time for her to leave.

Liv understood and thanked her for coming. "Hannah, the news would have shocked Flick no matter what, no matter when. Know that he needed to know. O.k?"

Hannah nodded while she was packing up her things and picking up the baby. "Thank you for letting me take care of this. I didn't mean to spoil the family dinner."

Liv smiled. "It's all o.k." You have a good night. I want you to stay in touch. We don't know how to turn our hearts off, we never stopped loving you. Please let us love you and your little guy. O.k.? Please?"

Hannah smiled. "You're the best, Liv."

Liv walked Hannah to the sidewalk and helped carry the diaper bag while Hannah settled Sport in his car seat. "You take care. See you in class," they said to each other.

Liv walked up the stairs with the echo of Hannah's car disappearing in the night. Entering the house, she could hear a huge ruckus in the back yard. Flick was trying to tear the girls apart from each other. Each had a handful of hair. The screaming was nerve wrenching. Liv hollered over the noise, "What on earth is going on around here?"

When Sugar lunged herself away from Kandy and landed on Liv, Liv landed backwards with her back bent and her head in the pool. Gideon and Flick did all they could to get Sugar off Liv. Liv was not moving when they pulled the top portion of her body out of the water. She began spitting out water and breathing irregularly, and it put Gideon into a panic. Flick called 911 and Liv was on her way to the hospital within ten minutes. Kandy stayed with Liam and settled the boys to bed.

Sugar's limo arrived, and she went home with her daughter.

Flick and Gideon drove to the hospital right behind the ambulance and Kandy called Gayle's with no answer for the next hour.

Then the phone opened with, "Hello."

Kandy said, "Gayle. I have something terrible to tell you. Are you sitting down?"

Gayle answered. "Yes. What is it?"

"There's been a terrible accident. Liv fell backwards in the yard, near the pool. The ambulance has taken her to the hospital. Gideon and Flick are at the hospital now. They haven't called back. I don't know anything yet. I thought you'd want to know."

Gayle wanted to ask what had happened, but she decided to head out to the hospital. She would get her answers from Gideon, if not Flick. "Thank you. I'm on my way now."

Chuck drove Gayle to the hospital. Then he dropped Salt at Liv's and asked Kandy to settle him to bed. Kandy nodded.

Chuck asked, "What happened?"

Kandy said, "Sugar picked a fight with me. I had enough and had her by the hair of her head." She felt sick to her stomach. "Liv came out to see what was going on and Sugar thrust herself away from me and fell on top of Liv. Liv fell backwards over the edge of the pool. Her head was in the water. The guys pulled her out."

"Was she conscious?" Chuck wanted to know.

"She spoke. Didn't move." Kandy said with tears. "I'm so sorry I started all of this. You should have been here to see how bad Sugar was behaving. But I handled things wrong. Badly."

Chapter 39
Family Bonds, Severed Ties, 1985

Gideon had been in the waiting room for over an hour when Gayle came walking towards him. He got up and greeted her with a long hug. Chuck came into the waiting room after he'd dropped Salt off. Gideon explained what had happened at the house. Now he was waiting to find out how Liv was…and the baby. It was well after midnight when a doctor came to talk with Gideon.

"How is my wife?" he asked but he wanted to say *and child*. He saw that the doctor was uncomfortable and decided to listen to what needed to be said. "Your wife was brought in to surgery for an emergency C section. The baby was under stress."

Gayle was holding on to Gideon. "How are they?" Gideon asked.

"The baby is stable, doing well. You have a girl, her weight is 5 lbs 6 oz. You will be able to see her in a few minutes."

Both Gayle and Gideon asked, "How's Liv?"

The doctor explained he was only attending to the baby. "Another doctor will come and update you on her condition."

Both Gayle and Gideon said, "Can we see the baby?"

The doctor motioned for them to follow and brought them to the nursery. A nurse approached and brought them to the baby. Gideon was not allowed to pick her up. The baby was in an incubator. Gayle and Gideon watched the little girl as she lay on her back with tubes attached. She was yellow in color, but her head was adorned with a knitted pink hat. Gideon whispered her name, "Emily."

Gayle remembered this was the name Liv had wanted. "Emily," it meant Em with the acronym I = I, L = Love, Y = You. For Liv it was a symbol of I Love you in her little girl's name Em ily.

Gayle and Gideon were then escorted to the waiting room where Chuck was waiting. They chatted about the baby's condition, hoping Emily would be fine. Now it was just waiting to find out how Liv was doing. Some believe that no news is good news. Others believe the longer the wait the more serious the situation.

At 3:30 a.m., a doctor came out to talk with Gideon. Gayle hovered nearby to listen without being obtrusive. "Liv's condition looked serious when she first came to the hospital. Our main concern was to maintain vitals, meaning take all measures to keep her alive and get the baby out safely, out of harm's way. This has been accomplished with success." The doctor paused. "We were not certain if Liv would be paralyzed since she fell hard on her back. There are discs cracked and fractured. But there's no nerve damage. We believe this is a miracle. Liv will have to wear a brace to support the thoracic bones in her back, and there's to be no lifting for some time. I understand the baby is one month premature being over five pounds and jaundiced. Both mother and baby will remain here at the hospital for a few weeks. But both are stable and out of danger. You may go see your wife for just a few minutes – she needs rest." The doctor departed.

It was 4:00 a.m. when Gayle and Chuck went home and 4:15 when Gideon arrived home and found Kandy asleep on the sofa with the phone in her hand. He realized her dedication meant she deserved to know what had happened. He nudged her shoulder and awoke her as she tried to focus. Then she sat up abruptly, ready to listen to what Gideon had found out. He explained the situation with Liv and the baby and said that the baby's name was Emily Gayle Genevieve Harly. Gideon knew the initials spelled 'EGG H.'

Kandy was worried about Liv. Gideon explained that her back was injured, and she'd need to wear a brace. For how long he did not know. He expressed how pleased he was to find out that Liv was not paralysed.

Kandy hugged Gideon and said she had prayed all night till she had fallen asleep. She asked if she could go back to sleep till the children woke. She said she would stay with Liam till Gideon woke after a bit of sleep.

Gideon thanked Kandy and headed for bed.

The family function would be one going down in their history because of its infamous fight.

The next morning, Liam woke up asking for his mommy. For some reason with all the trauma, Kandy hadn't prepared herself for this simple question or request. Thinking on her feet she said, "Mommy is at the hospital having her baby."

Liam smiled. "Mommy is going to bring the baby home today?"

Kandy answered. "Not today. It's up to the doctor."

Liam and Champ sat at the kid table waiting for breakfast. Kandy made French toast with berries. The boys ate well, but Kandy only nibbled at her food. She nursed her coffee as her first choice.

At 8:00 a.m. Flick came by to find out how things were going with Liv. Kandy handed him a cup of coffee and offered French toast. She updated him on baby Emily and Liv's condition. They talked about how all this could have been preventable. Flick was going to set Sugar straight. He felt her behavior had been deliberate and that she seemed to enjoy the soap opera style of amusement. When an event is boring, stir things up. Flick wondered if his mother and Sugar had been born with consciences. His face flared up with anger. "That girl needs a whooping. I am going to get her to apologize to everyone. What happened last night almost killed our niece and almost killed our sister. This kind of behavior cannot be tolerated...ever."

Kandy agreed.

Gideon entered the kitchen and overheard Kandy's comment about Sugar and Flick's plan to address the behavior. "Morning," he greeted them as he was getting his morning cup of motivation.

Liam came up to his father tugging at his pajama bottoms. "Dada." He put his arms in the air asking to be picked up. Gideon put his cup of coffee down on the counter and hugged his son.

Kandy and Flick watched Gideon, wanting to get his feelings on the matter. Flick said, "We want to know how you feel with everything that happened last night."

Gideon was not much of a talker, especially if his mind was occupied. But this time it was more so that his heart was hurting. His love for Liv was great. When she was hurting, he was hurting. He had missed their few minutes of snuggle time last night and even with his exhaustion had trouble settling to sleep. The bed felt cold and empty without Liv in their nest. Gideon knew he was deeply attached to the love of his life. He was a homebody kind of man, but he'd never realized he would suffer so much alongside his wife's trauma. "I'm at a loss for words this morning. I'm worried about Liv. Worried about Emily. Scared of the pain they must have gone through and still might."

Flick shook his head in disgust for what his sister had done. The action had seemed directed at Liv and appeared to be intentional. The spirit of Sugar's actions was disturbing to everyone, though this was not said. "I have to get a grip on that girl. This cannot continue to happen." Frustrated, he went outside with his cup of coffee to have a cigarette.

Kandy approached Gideon and asked, "Is there anything we can do for you?"

To Kandy's surprise, Gideon said, "I'd like you to keep Sugar away from my family." It was said in a stoic tone that indicated finality. Gideon couldn't have said how he felt any more plainly.

Gayle and Chuck showed up looking just as tired as the group present. "Any news?" Chuck asked Gideon.

Gideon just shook his head. "I'm going to head out to the hospital." He looked over to the family and asked, "Can anyone stay with Liam while I go?" Everyone nodded yes. Gideon excused himself, went upstairs to take a shower, and was out the door in fifteen minutes after giving Liam a hug and kiss.

Flick announced he was going to pay Sugar a visit.

Just then the doorbell rang. It was Milly asking if there was anything she could do. Gayle asked if she would watch the two little ones as the family wanted to get to the hospital. "That would be just fine." She helped herself to a cup of coffee. "Does anyone mind?"

Kandy and Gayle stated, "Of course not. Help yourself to breakfast."

Gideon was at Liv's side while she was holding their baby, Emily. Breastfeeding was unbearable for her as it involved slouching forward to get the baby to latch onto her nipple. The circumstances required bottle feeding to allow Liv's back to heal. The baby had been changed and fed and had fallen asleep. It would have been a perfect picture if no one had known the events that transpired the night prior.

The clan showed up and the room was crowded with smiles. Everyone was happy to see Liv propped in bed and looking content. Gideon didn't look as stressed either.

Gayle was given the leeway and right of passage to embrace her daughter and granddaughter. But the concern on Gayle's face could not be masked even with her gentle smile. "How are you doing?"

Liv smiled and reassured her, "I'm fine. What matters the most is that Emily is fine."

Everyone nodded in agreement, smiling and relieved that their worst fears had not transpired. Liv looked o.k. and the baby was alive and breathing.

Liv noticed Flick was not present. "Where's Flick?" She thought he might be sorting out his business from the night before. Was he over to see Hannah? She wondered how serious he was with Julian.

Kandy answered in a matter-of-fact tone, "He's gone over to talk with Sugar. Wants some answers and plans on straightening her sporting attitude."

Liv nodded and watched her daughter snuggle. She felt the event was a miracle and knew they could have lost her, much like Hannah had ... Her heart gave way with tears and she said, "I'm just glad Emily made it."

Gideon hugged her and nodded in agreement. The family visited till a nurse asked them to give her patient some time to rest. Everyone hugged and kissed Liv good bye.

Gideon remained at his wife's side and whispered in Liv's ear, "I missed us snuggling last night. Couldn't fall asleep."

Liv smiled back at him. "I missed you too, sweetheart."

Gideon then asked, "Can I bring Liam in to meet his little sister?"

Liv wanted that so badly, but she was worried. "I'm not sure how to physically manage Liam with my back injury."

Gideon understood and offered, "I would work with him and you. I could get him to sit beside you on the bed. Then you could cuddle him. He missed you this morning."

Liv nodded. "I know Liam would love to meet his sister, Emily."

"I'll bring him by after supper for a short visit," Gideon promised.

Gideon left to go back home where he hoped to get a few hours of sleep. He thought of how closely his family had been put into jeopardy. How blessed he felt knowing they were doing all right. The wounds of the past evening would heal with time. But to Gideon, the near miss was too close, and he had his own thoughts on the matter. Gideon recognized he was angry with what had happened. He felt his rage engulf his kind spirit.

Gideon entered his home and found Kandy talking with Sugar with Flick standing guard. Deidra must have been spending time with her daddy as she was not present. Kandy was coaching Sugar on how to approach Gideon to say something. Gideon did not have the patience to listen. Flick watched the situation.

Sugar looked down as her sister pushed her from behind.

Gideon was about to pop a fuse. "Don't even come near me. In fact, I'm going to ask you to leave my house. Know that you are never welcome back here. Do you understand me?" He tried hard to bite his tongue and not finish what was on his mind. In his heart, she had been accused and convicted of her malicious act towards his family and was never to be tolerated again. He must at all costs protect those he loved. Now was the time to stand up and make his claim to protect them.

Sugar looked up and glared at Gideon with intense hatred. "You are judging me, Mr. Fancy Pants?"

Kandy was to stun to move.

Flick was up and between Sugar and Gideon in an instant.

Gideon simply said in a low growl, "It is my job to protect my family. You are a danger." Then he raised his voice. "Now get out!" He moved towards Liam as he had the urge to protect his son.

Kandy and Flick escorted Sugar out of the house. Flick now understood that Sugar had gone too far this time and that it was too late to make amends. Flick left, taking Sugar back home. Kandy came back to the family room and sat on the edge of the sofa.

Gideon said, "I believe that family bonds are important. I also believe when treated like family we do the same. When someone acts like a dangerous villain then one must be treated as such." Gideon seldom felt the need to defend his position. He loved his family and loved Liv's family too, as long as they showed love as well. "I'm sorry if the family will be angry with me. I must protect my family. It came too close last night. I could have lost our little girl. I could have lost my wife who I love so much."

Kandy reflected and said, "Sugar has made her choices. People have the right to respond."

Gideon concluded, "I believe you are right. Sugar's actions are her own. Sadly, the family ties with her are now broken. The ties are severed. I'm sorry this had to happen."

"Don't be sorry. Sugar had it coming," Kandy confirmed.

Chuck came by and explained that Gayle was staying at the hospital. Kandy wondered where Salt had been this morning.

Chuck explained that there had been a breakfast prior to the soft ball game. "We dropped Salt off at the restaurant and explained there was a family emergency, so the coach offered to take Salt to the game and bring him home afterwards."

Chuck hadn't seen Flick since last night. "Anyone see Flick this morning?"

Gideon simply said, 'Yeah, he was here an hour ago with Sugar. He took her home."

Kandy gave Chuck a funny look and walked towards the back door. Knowing something had happened, Chuck was soon out the door and lighting a cigarette. His ears were up like an antenna. Kandy informed him of what Gideon had decreed.

Chuck agreed with Gideon. "That girl, Sugar, is more like her mother every day." He took a puff. "I've never known Gideon to lay down the law. She must have hit his limit of tolerance."

Kandy nodded in agreement. "She had it coming. I can't blame Gideon. Honestly, he has to think of his family."

Chuck put out his butt and went inside to where Gideon was sitting on the floor playing with Liam and telling him he now had a baby sister. They were going to visit the baby and Mommy at the hospital. Gideon got up when Liam was busy with his building blocks.

Chuck brought him a fresh cup of coffee and said, "I don't blame you for drawing the line with Sugar. Just wanted you to know."

Gideon responded, "I appreciate that."

Kandy was right behind and said, "That goes for me too." She felt Sugar had done it this time and that no one was going to put up with her shenanigans any longer.

The look on Gideon's face told the two that the ties of family with Sugar were severed – severed forever. He called one of his partners to let them know he'd had a family emergency and to announce the news of their baby girl. He was told to take at least a week off and to take care. Gideon expressed gratitude and the call ended. In the morning, he would have to call the university and explain the situation. He'd also have to ask Liv about her thesis and when the deadline was.

Kandy interrupted Gideon's thoughts and asked, "Is it all right if I head home? I need to get ready for the week and there's so much to do."

Gideon gave Kandy a hug and thanked her for all her help. "I can't thank you enough. I really appreciate all that you've done helping us through this weekend."

Kandy smiled, "I love you guys. I could never do enough. It was a pleasure."

Gideon smiled for the first time in days. "Thanks again." He helped her load up her things and get Champ in his car seat.

Chuck had already left to see if Gayle needed anything.

Chapter 40
Healing and Mending, 1985

Mother and child came home a week after Emily's birth and the back injury to Liv. Gideon was happy his family was home safe and sound. He never shared with Liv that he had barred Sugar from the house. But Gayle heard about Gideon laying down the law and protecting his family. Her heart was delighted that Gideon was the man she and Peter had believed him to be.

Liv was given the remainder of the semester off. Her thesis was extended though the extra time was not really needed. Liv never left her deadlines to the very end. She got on her research for her papers immediately and formulated a plan based on the evidence. She had written her thesis statement and her conclusion first. Then she'd worked her paper to its obvious conclusion. This thesis was the largest project that Liv had ever taken on. It was her best work to date. But she wasn't ready to hand it in before proofreading and critiquing the material. With so much time off, she could easily accomplish the task.

Gideon would get up with the baby twice in the night. Liv miraculously managed to breastfeed little Emily after all. Gideon would bring the baby into their bed and nod off till the baby was satisfied, then he'd change her diaper and put her back in her bed. This arrangement was working well for Liv.

Gideon was a driven man who no longer cared if he had his hot tub time in the evening. He was a parent as much as Liv and he was a partner just as much as his wife was a partner in their marriage. They pulled together no matter the challenge. They found joy conquering and accomplishing as a unified family.

Milly and Gayle would arrive at around 7:00 a.m. when Gideon was off to work. Liam would hear Grandma and skoosh his bottom down each step till he was hugging Gayle's legs. Milly would get breakfast on the go for all of them. Then she'd go upstairs to see if Liv needed help with a shower and getting dressed. Applying the brace was worse than putting on a girdle. Gayle would dress Liam and do what she could for Emily till Milly was free.

Gideon appreciated how the family came together to help his family heal and get on the road to recovery. Kandy would cook each night and bring what she made to the house. It helped the aging women with one less task. They were able to go home and take care of themselves for the rest of the evening.

One would think that tragedy might weaken the resolve of endurance. However, this group of people stepped up to the plate and created a bond that tied the challenges of life to their passion of love for each other.

Liv and Gideon's relationship were much like Gayle and Peter's. Gideon had her back, literally, and she had his. It seemed the tougher life became, the greater and stronger their bond would become.

The family respected Gideon as a pillar of strength; a person one did not want to reckon with. Especially when it came to his family. They all suspected Gideon was a man who would have their backs as well should the circumstances be reversed.

Gayle often visited Peter's grave and talked to him as though he were present. The latest revelation had been how Gideon was becoming the patriarch of the family. He had Peter's values and principles, and this thrilled Gayle. She loved to share her thoughts with Peter, letting him know that all was good on the Western front.

Chapter 41
New beginnings, 1985

During the week, each family unit had its routines. On the weekends, the boys would come together to help Gideon and Liv.

On Saturdays, Flick would bring the pizza and movies over while entertaining the little ones. Kandy would join in with hopes of interaction with the girls.

Sundays involved Salt helping Chuck and Gideon with the yard work, and then Gideon prepared a barbecue for the clan. Kandy often stayed home on Sunday to catch up with her week. Flick was often over with Sport. The boys chatted around the smell of grilled fish, chicken, ribs, or steak.

Gideon asked Flick, "How are things going in your world these days?"

Flick had a grin. "I can't complain. Really. Hannah has moved out on her own, and it makes things easier without her parents' involvement." He didn't share that he had given Hannah a substantial amount of money to set up a home; the first and last months' rent, security deposit for rent, deposits for utilities, and money to get furnishings for herself and Sport.

Gideon flipped burgers and hotdogs on the grill for the little ones. He nodded. "You still seeing Julian?"

Flick grinned. "We have an understanding." He took a sip of his one beer. "I'm not in a hurry to screw things up now that I have my son…and now that Hannah is working with me."

Gideon took the flipper and pointed to Sport. "Your little guy is crawling around quite well these days."

Flick glanced in his son's direction and bolted. "Shit, he's shredding my smokes. Got the lighter too." Picking up Sport, he said, "I don't know what I'm going do with you once you find your legs."

Gideon found himself laughing. "You'll be chasing your life from this day forward," he said, grinning with experience.

Hannah and Flick were becoming good co-parents. They were divorced but they did what was good for the sake of the child. They were developing a friendship that had Sport as the center of all their decisions. They were becoming a family except for habituating together.

Gideon began preparing the plates for the children present as Flick held onto his son to give his legs a rest.

Gideon asked, "How's business these days?"

"It's really busy. Had to hire three guys. One like smashing concrete for lines and finishing the pouring. It's going great. Chuck never stops finding bids and working in between to meet the deadlines. I don't know what I'd do without him."

Salt was sitting on the rock bench enjoying the sounds of the waterfall and eating up his share of hotdogs. "Where's Chuck? Where's Gayle?" he asked.

Gideon answered, reassuring Salt, "They should be here anytime soon."

***

Milly continued her morning routine taking care of the Harly family. Gayle joined her each morning with great concern for her daughter's lack of mobility. Once the morning found a calm moment, the girls would chat over a cup of coffee.

Gayle began talking with hopes of starting up their "chat dance." "Have you heard anything from Sugar this past month?"

Liv shared, "Kandy mentioned that Sugar no longer resides in Calgary. She found out that she was being investigated for collecting money from social services while being provided for by her man, Butch, I believe it is." Maneuvering herself to be comfortable on the sofa, she continued, "From what I understand, Sugar disappeared to Vancouver, B.C. and left Butch to answer the questions. I hope social services realizes Butch was an innocent victim."

Gayle responded, "It's too bad. Shame she up and left the man to pick up the pieces of that mess."

Liv nodded, sipping her coffee. "I only wish Sugar well. Hope Deidra will be all right."

Gayle agreed, thinking of all the members of the family. "Just thinking of Salt and how far he has come with the family supporting his life."

Liv smiled, thinking about the young man. "To think he had difficulties communicating and had a temper and a violent streak that was scary."

Gayle smiled. "He's made quite a change since the Hannah incident. I'm so proud of him. Two gold medals with the Special Olympics. Amazing. Really."

Liv smiled as well. "I don't think he would have accomplished so much without you. You are a wonderful woman, a great mother."

Gayle chided her, "You are too kind."

Liv grinned. "I don't think so."

"Last weekend he whooped the whole family at bowling. Salt was gloating, and everyone was playing it up. It was wonderful."

"Salt has found his way. I love it when he takes his ginger ale in a cognac glass, sipping it just like the boys." Liv smiled. "He loves to be a part of the family. He's so happy."

Gayle added, "I agree. He works so hard at the recycle depot. They appreciate Salt, and he does love his work. It's truly amazing."

Liv found herself reflecting and nodded in agreement. "Kandy has made huge strides when it comes to making changes." She took her cup once Gayle had refilled it with fresh coffee. "I honestly thought she was going to follow her mother's pattern of life."

Gayle had believed Kandy would be the most difficult to work with, considering her stubborn nature. "Kandy is headstrong. Glad that she took that drive and used it to create a better life for herself. She started out getting pregnant and having Champ and now …" Gayle was getting choked up with emotion realizing how much she loved the girl. "She took her challenges and made them work."

Liv responded, "I agree. She's a hard worker pursuing her education and now she's an LPN, on various committees, and a wonderful, responsible, loving mother to Champ. Honestly, I don't know how Kandy does it all be a single mother. It's amazing. I feel Kandy has become a positive family member and a great friend to me."

Gayle was pleased. "I'm so glad…I'm also glad that Flick made contact and came out west." She held back her thoughts that she was glad that Chuck had come out as well. "It pleases me that you have a good-sized family to love and that they love you too." Tears welled up in Gayle's eyes. "With your dad gone … Peter would be so pleased that you're not alone."

Liv refuted, "I have you. I have Gideon and the children. I have so much."

Gayle understood. "I know." She went deep into thought. "Your father wanted you to get to know Chuck better. They became friends and Peter grew to love Chuck. It might be time for you to open your heart and let Chuck be your father. Peter gave Chuck his blessing, and Chuck promised to look out for you till his dying day."

Liv had tears as her heart burst with loneliness for Peter. "I just loved Dad so much." She took a Kleenex to her nose. "I kept a wedge between Chuck and me, and I can't turn the clock back. I wouldn't know where to begin to create a stronger bond. I know deep down Chuck has always loved me and that in his heart I am his little girl."

Gayle listened and smiled. "I think you have your answer."

Liv nodded knowing her mother was insightful.

Gayle announced, "I would never want you to turn the clock back. I am so grateful you came into our lives. You found the courage to leave the life you knew and travelled all the way across Canada. How did you survive that life? How did you survive the journey alone? And you were so young."

Liv grinned. "I hated that life. I didn't know the dangers and could have died on the journey. All I wanted ...." Then she looked at her mother.

Gayle had tears. "All you wanted was a good mother." She smiled at her daughter. "I thank God every day for you."

Liv had tears of her own. "All I wanted was you as a mother. Thank God for that."

***

Liv remembered the day she'd left Montreal – the decision that had changed her life forever and had changed the lives of her adoptive parents. It had also changed the lives of her siblings who had pursued her across Canada. Had she stayed with Ruby, Liv would have never had the opportunities and quality of life her parents provided. She realized she would have never met Gideon in university, have her career, or have the children or family that were the anchor of her heart. The crazy move to crawl into the luggage compartment of that bus line and suffer the brutal ride across Canada was the smartest decision she had ever made. That strong, stubborn, driven, little girl was now a woman – a woman who had grown to be mature, wise, and of course wonderful. She loved her man and loved her two children; Liam and Emily. The little girl, Liv, who had followed her heart ... was now living her life in full of love. She had no regrets about chasing her dreams. She'd just found the courage and before she knew it, she'd found herself living her dreams.

About the Author

Frances Hanson was born in Montreal. Came to Calgary to start a new life. Had a number of careers including Legal Assistant, PCA, and LPN. Enjoyed her studies with Abnormal Psychology. Works as a nurse in a Geriatric Unit. Has a wonderful husband, Graham, and two grown children, Andrew and Sylina. Past time is travelling, painting and writing.

This book was inspired with the love of family.

CPSIA information can be obtained
at www.ICGtesting.com
Printed in the USA
LVHW022030071218
599694LV00001B/1